The subject of gold mining in Alaska is not just historical. Mining, big time mining, has been continuous since 1901 and some say it is the back-bone of the Alaskan economy. Gold is being mined by many methods in the state and is still one of biggest businesses.

Diamonds most likely do exist north of the Brooks Range to the west of the Colville River. A savvy miner with the bank-roll and the proper equipment might find them, but gold is right here, right now.

Angel's Alaska

Angel's Diamonds

Angel's Treasure

Angel's Odyssey

Piloting the Alaskan Bush

ANGEL'S

TREASURE

Wayne Pinger

Angel's Alaska: The Series

Angelsalaska media Publications

Cover: **Minto Flats**, by **Page Hall** of **Alaskarain Arts,** Wasilla, Alaska.
alaskarainarts@aol.com

First Edition July 2018

Kindle -------- ISBN: 978-1-7325206-2-2

Paper-back-- ISBN: 978-1-7325206-3-9

This book, Angel's Treasure, is a publication of **Angelsalaska Media**. This writing is the original writings: the first edition.

This book is fiction. The story line is not to be confused with real events or happening's in the time period of the writings. The characters are totally fictional however the personalities of some of the fictional characters have been assumed from several of my friends and acquaintances from my years in Alaska: with their permission.

Special Thanks to my wife Jeanette for putting up with the many rereads and rewrites and editing out my time-line mistakes. Her compassion shows when ignoring my lack of attention to her needs when word-smithing left me totally preoccupied and unappreciative of the companionship she offered. Also special thanks to **Barb Flavin** for the seemingly endless task of editing the very first text of this writing.

Thanks to **Page Hall** at **Alaskarain Arts**, for the cover photo and thanks to **Ray Ballantyne** for his help with proper radio communications protocol and other things relating to the FAA.

PROLOG

The quest for gold brought American adventure seekers north to Alaska to settle and develop the territory that eventually became the 49th state.

An American miner prospecting in Canada made the first major gold find in the far north: The Klondike gold discovery. George Carmack and his Brother-in-law, Skookum Jim Keish, discovered gold on the Bonanza Creek drainage which is a tributary to the Klondike River, in the late 1890s. This discovery started the Klondike gold rush and in just two years the sparsely settled Klondike River area was bursting with a rush of miners and others infected by the Gold Fever Virus

The Canadian Government found it nearly impossible to control and police the area. The Royal Canadian Mounted Police was hard pressed to find qualified Troopers because the Mounties, more than half in their first year of employment, traded-in their uniforms and steady pay for the chance of striking it rich in the gold fields; they joined the miners in their pursuit of riches. From the Klondike discovery, the gold fields rapidly expanded further north and west past Dawson and into Alaska. Here new and larger gold deposits were discovered: in just a few short years, the upper Fortymile River and many of its tributaries, proved to be among the richest and best gold producers in the world.

But the quest for gold has not just been written about in the history books. The search for gold continues, and as before, when new discoveries are made they quickly develop into producing mining operations. There are many hundreds, maybe a thousand, active gold mines in the state; the search for gold is big business in Alaska.

And along with these adventurers, the hard-working miners, come the support services that supply their needs. Miners must be fed, housed, clothed, and even entertained, after a hard week of work. Towns spring-up close-in to most mining operations to supply these needs. And very soon come the bandits, the con-men, the charlatans, and the quick buck artists. These scavengers always seem to follow the boom times and boom towns, to steal from or otherwise take advantage of the hard work of others.

Fairbanks is a small city that was founded by mistake, by a man of mystery, that was bound for another place. Captain Barnette's leased river-boat was stranded miles short of his destination by low water in the Tanana River. He had planned to build a trading post at Tanacross, where the Valdez-Eagle trail crosses the Tanana River. Barnette and his company of men were nearly two hundred miles short of their destination when grounded in the fall of 1901. On learning of a new gold strike, from a couple of local miners, Barnette built the trading post where he was grounded; and founded the town of Fairbanks.

INTRODUCTION

Fairbanks is the small frontier city in the golden center of this very large state of Alaska; the city is said to be a mile wide and about a foot in depth. Goods and services are available in Fairbanks that might only be found in a city of half a million in the lower forty-eight, though Fairbanks has only about thirty-five thousand people. The city supports a large trading area from Tetlin Junction to the east, north as far as Point Barrow, and west as far as Nome and the Bering strait.

The University of Alaska is just a few miles to the west of Fairbanks and beyond that campus Just 10-miles further north-west and over a few low rolling hills lays the Goldstream Valley. The Valley is a bedroom community of the College and University area and its population is as varied and diverse as any place on earth. Almost all the Goldstream Valley folks are from somewhere else and nearly all come in search of a better life though a few come simply seeking refuge. Folks on the frontier are mostly an assortment of both winners and losers; very few might be considered normal.

The Golden Valley General store and The Ivory Exchange Restaurant sit side by side on Goldstream Road; this defines the valley center. The Ivory Exchange is one of the better eateries in the Fairbanks area and the General Store serves the local population with gas, groceries and more.

Chapter (1)

The Golden Valley Store   Nov. 1984

Claire Jamison was an unemployed State Licensed and registered Geologist with little more than a framed diploma, a half duffle of clothing, and a loyal German Shepherd named Angel when she met Josh Browning in Yakutat, five years ago. At 29 years old, 5'9" and 140 pounds, Claire was hardly dainty. But she had curves in the right places and Josh being 6'2"and nearly 225 pounds was not the least intimidated by her size and her: "I can damn-well take care of myself persona".

Claire rescued Angel, a rather large 75-pound female German Sheppard, when she was retired early from the Seattle Police Department for misbehaving after she had a litter of pups. It sometimes happens that a new mother will forget her training. Regardless of the reasons, Claire was happy to have a new friendly companion. Angel bonded with her from the start and was thrilled to be let out of her kennel or what she considered to be a stinky prison. After completing Graduate School in Washington State, and rescuing Angel, she wandered north and found herself in the coastal town of Yakutat, Alaska. Here she was teaching school part time, waiting breakfast tables at an airport café when she could, and not so patiently waiting for a Geologist position to open with the State of Alaska.

Yakutat was where she met Josh Browning. He was an infrequent customer at the airport café until first seeing her; after that he was a regular. Josh was a pilot that had been flying helicopters for a local charter company. It was easy safe work but he was not really enjoying the wide-eyed tourists on the almost daily photo outings. The favorite destination was flying north-east low over Disenchantment Bay to the Russel fiord. There he would land his helicopter on the lower moraine of the Variegated Glacier. On a clear day it was a spectacular view and his tourist passengers would see and photograph the Hubbard Glacier that was just across the narrow bay. As often as he would fly there he never tired of visiting

13

the Wrangell-Saint Elias National Park, but he did tire of the tourists. Though Josh is no diplomat, he is friendly to most folks. But he is not everyone's instant buddy, as some of the tourists desired. He once complained: "If I have to stand and smile like some sort of instant Fly-Boy-Hero to have my picture snapped once again, I think I will puke".

Angel liked Josh almost immediately and this intrigued Claire because Angel had very much been a one-person dog until then. Angel was very protective of her but seemed willing to let Josh get close. She never tried to interfere with the hand holding and such.

Claire is highly organized and a planner but willing to adapt to a changing situation. Josh is rigid to the point of obstinance. He typically thinks immediate problems through and then commits to them 100%. Though being different in character their personalities seemed to complement one another and they dated a little, a very little, before getting married: neither has ever looked back.

Their journey to Fairbanks was convoluted. In the early 1980s the state budget was being cut back and Geology positions were being eliminated rather than added at the Department of Natural Resources (DNR). Both Claire and Josh tired of the coastal rain and fog in Yakutat and made the decision to relocate. They knew Fairbanks was cold, but it was typically as clear as any other place in the state and they decided to try it, at least for a while.

It started with Claire taking a chemistry teaching position at Lathrop High while trying to start a geology consulting business that even after a year's time, barely made expenses. Josh flew a Piper Seneca almost daily, toting oil company executives around the state for a now-failed Air Taxi service. After that business folded and flying gigs became scarce, he took a short-term job as a metal and wood-shop teacher: also, at Lathrop High School.

On one of his last trips before the air taxi went out of business, Josh was in the Seneca overflying the north fork of the Chandalar River carrying a charter. It was a Deadhorse to Fairbanks flight that he had diverted west to avoid some rain. His passengers were two oil company executives that were having a good time and were busy snapping photos for their family albums. Flying fairly low josh spotted a stacked-up tail-high, nearly vertical Super-Cub that had apparently crashed; it was on a quarter-mile long sand-bar. A highly disguised and mostly buried willow root system had argued with the Super-Cub on take-off and the Cub lost the contest. There was a lone pilot waving and Josh decided to land the Piper twin and rescue the stranded traveler. It seemed un-wise to land a twin engine retractable, with very small tires, in an off-airport situation. And it was totally crazy to try it on a river-bar. Just the same, and over the vocal and repeated objections of his passengers, Josh landed and picked up the lonesome stranded traveler.

The stranded pilot was Skip Davis, a Fairbanks businessman and now retired bush pilot. Skip at one time, owned two businesses in the Goldstream Valley and now owned and operated The Gold Bar and Lounge in the City. Josh and Skip became friends and drinking buddies and after the air taxi service folded Skip offered Josh some week-end work tending bar.

It was on advice from Skip that Claire changed her business plan just a little; with Josh in reluctant agreement, they bought the Golden Valley General Store. It took their entire saving plus Josh had to sell four of his favorite antique and very pricy Greener shotguns, just to make the down payment. They bought the general store, and a well-used black on gold Cessna 185. In addition to being new Store Keepers they also started Goldstream Aviation Services, or: 'Goldstream Air'. It's a typical general store that sells groceries, liquor and tobacco, Native crafts, has two gas pumps, and includes an eight-machine laundromat in a separate but close outbuilding: Soapies. But the main reason for buying the store was that behind it there was a 2200-foot dirt and gravel airstrip; Claire planned to have the new company deliver groceries, dry goods, and whatever else was needed to the bush villages and small mining operations that dotted the map north and east of Fairbanks. Josh agreed with Claire's business plan but insisted they should not pursue an air taxi license: he hated hauling passengers and though it would be less profitable, Claire halfheartedly agreed.

Her business plan now included a bush air delivery service that she thought would make some small amount of money, but equally important, the plane was to satisfy her travel needs for her consulting business that she very much intended to pursue big-time. Claire looked at the store as being a stepping stone in her quest to develop a successful Geology Consulting business: C&J Consulting Services.

Gold nugget jewelry and carved ivory are by far the biggest dollar sellers in the many gift shops in the Fairbanks area. With the recent increase in the price of gold, winter tourists have bought heavily into the supply of locally mined jewelry-quality gold nuggets. The very largest jewelry nuggets, quarter-ounce and larger were retailing for more, sometimes twice their melt value. The local buyers for the refiners were hi-grading the larger nuggets and selling directly into the jewelry trade; they were taking large profits. As the nugget, or two-tier pricing information became public knowledge, the miners were feeling cheated and started demanding higher prices for their larger nuggets. Most of the miners who had a ration of common sense simply held back their larger nuggets from the refiners and sold directly into the jewelry market themselves.

Then finally, as if to prove they do have a lick of sense, some of the miners started to melt raw gold dust and began making their own larger nuggets. They would melt and pour the gold into odd shaped plaster molds with a few bits of quartz and fractured river gravel and then tumble them for a few days. These results are hardly distinguishable from natural nuggets and though the supply of jewelry-quality nuggets started increasing, the higher prices for these premium nuggets have been holding. The more sophisticated miners are mixing in a little extra base metal; a few silver coins and copper pennies and even a few lead pellets to increase the profit margins a little.

The Golden Valley Store has been a retailer of gold nugget jewelry that is usually bought from wholesale sellers. From time to time Claire has bought a few nuggets from miners who are also store customers but usually the transaction is a trade for store credit: gas, groceries, or liquor. This has helped the bottom line and the bottom line needed the help, because when first starting operations the store's profits and bush air deliveries barely made the mortgage payments. As Claire tells the story: "It was tight for a while, but finally because of some of Goldstream Air's high-margin liquor deliveries to the North Slope, and also profits from the State of Alaska Firefighter's food box contract, we had some success". Claire's business plan worked well, and with long hours and hard-work, she was able to pay off the mortgage on the store in just four short years. With the mortgage paid off Josh started to think about a plane that was meant to carry cargo. The store's Cessna 185 is a great plane for flying the Bush but hardly perfect for the store's demands; the business of delivering groceries and dry-goods to the many villages and mines that dot the state's interior demands a different type of plane. Josh needed a plane that would carry more; one that was designed to haul cargo. He needed a Cessna 206 with an easy to load cargo door and when one became available he was able to trade for it.

Claire has always managed the business end of the store and aviation business. The profits have allowed them to recently purchase a small home with a big hangar a short way down the airstrip. Josh thinks it's a perfect situation and wonders how they could possibly have been so lucky. Claire insists that luck has nothing to do with it.

Jean Lathrop is the head clerk and other than Claire and Josh she is the only full-time employee of the store. Jean will soon be named Manager because Claire's Geology consulting business is starting to take more of her time and she can no longer effectively manage the store and do the work called for in her contracts: she is licensed by the State of Alaska and considers herself a Professional Geologist, not a Store keeper.

Casey Smith, another employee, was a Graduate Student at the University, that until recently worked at the store about 22 hours a week. It turns out that Claire is a pretty good writer and she offered to help Casey write and edit her thesis about the chemistry and dissociation of chlorine based refrigerant gasses in the upper troposphere. While helping Casey she was introduced to some of the very newest remote satellite sensing techniques used by the scientists at the Geophysical Institute, University of Alaska. Here

17

Claire had access to a mountain of data from a Synthetic Aperture Radar (SAR) operated by NASA but downloaded to computers at the Institute. The SAR, among other things, precisely maps the earth's surface, and in some cases, can map permafrost boundaries and other sub-surface irregularities.

Claire thought she might be able to apply this new tool to solving old problems. After Casey claimed her PHD, Claire wrote several proposals relating to geology exploration and two of them were funded. The Director at the Institute agreed she could have an office there and could keep it as long as she continues to get funding, publishes her findings, and pays her share of the overhead. Presently Claire is contracted to do location studies for two proposed roadway construction projects north of the Yukon River.

When she works in the field she contracts with Josh for transportation and usually she takes Angel with for company and protection. As hard as she tries Claire has yet to figure out how to get Angel on the payroll. Still she has had some limited success and is able to bill her contract for both her and Angel's lunch when in the field.

Also, through her work at the Geophysical Institute she has the use of a Scanning Microprobe which is the business end of an Electron Microscope. This instrument can determine the ratios of gold to other base metals in any gold nuggets without melting or disfiguring them in any way. One day after her normal hours she checked a few gold nugget pieces from the jewelry display case at the store. Claire was not surprised to find that the ratio of gold to silver to copper varied greatly in most of the nugget jewelry. But Claire was very surprised when she found the alloy was very much standardized in the nuggets from one or two sources. One nugget source from a major producer in the Forty-mile Mining District had nuggets that were very standardized. The alloy amounting to twenty-eight troy ounces of gold to a little less than two ounces of silver and about ten copper pennies' worth of copper and zinc alloy. Claire smelled a rat, a big fat gold-plated rat.

Chapter (2)

A trip to the north   Nov. 1984

As Josh was crossing over Eagle Summit, clear air turbulence bounced the Cessna around showing as much as 800 feet per minute changes in vertical acceleration. Full aileron movement was sometimes needed to keep the plane just reasonably upright and pointed in the right direction. Vertical shear winds were as bad as he had ever experienced and his seat belt harness was not only a safety issue in the event of a mishap; it was now a necessity to just keep him in the seat. The duffle of survival gear was no longer neatly stowed in the far-back luggage area but was now in the passenger seat after having first bounced off his shoulder during the last real bad bout of turbulence. The 206 was being tossed around like a child's kite and Josh had to slow to maneuvering speed to avoid overstressing the airframe.

After crossing north over the summit, turbulence slowly abated and quieted to nearly zero as the plane descended into the Yukon River Valley. As the turbulence moderated, air temperature dropped and quickly went to minus fifty-five degrees; it was still getting colder as the 206 flew over the resort's A-frame covered hot springs pool. Josh exercised the prop to announce his arrival and then, heading north toward Medicine Lake, he overflew the resort airstrip and lost the last 500 feet of altitude before starting a left 180 for a straight-in landing on the Hot Springs airstrip. He tuned in the radio to 122.8 and pushed the transmit button.

Josh: "Hot Springs traffic, as unlikely as this sounds Cessna 734 Mike Kilo is one mile east, turning final inbound landing runway 27, Hot Springs traffic."

This trip had not been planned; Goldstream Air got the call early Monday from Jackovich Tractor Supply in Fairbanks. They reported that the Circle Hot Springs Resort was having a serious problem; the second and last generator had failed. Their source of heat was down to wood stoves and a diesel-fired Herman Nelson forced air heater driven by a gasoline engine that should most definitely not be used as source of indoor heat. The staff of five and a half dozen regulars were huddled in the bar feeding firewood to the stove and feeding firewater to themselves. To them it was not life threatening, they knew how to cope with the Yukon Valley cold but if the lodge froze up the plumbing-heating system, and other temperature sensitive things, would be a disaster to repair or replace.

The Steese Highway begins in Fairbanks and runs northeast ending in Circle City which is on the Yukon River at milepost 162. The eight-mile-long turnoff road to the Circle Hot Springs Resort begins at the town of Central at milepost 127. Though the hot springs are only about 95 miles from Fairbanks as the crow flies, it is nearly 140 miles by way of the road system and the roadway is not maintained in the winter. It is usually closed by heavy snow fall in late October just south of Eagle Summit and likely opens in April or May, the next year.

People travel from Fairbanks to Circle, or Central, or to the Hot Springs, by air during the winter months though there is one stalwart snow machine club from Fairbanks that makes the trip nearly every winter over the roadway. It's a wild two or three-day party of food, booze, and often some Skinny-dipping in the pool. This annual snow-go outing has also been the reason for multiple divorce proceedings in past years and most likely a few more to come.

When the last generator failed the resort's short-wave radio was useless, so the news of the failure and description of the parts needed were delivered to "Jackovich Industrial & Construction Supply" by a private pilot and his wife who had been in the pool for a short-extended weekend soak. Fortunately, Jackovich had the parts in stock and after calling two other flying services Goldstream Air agreed to make the delivery. Josh accepted the job to make the delivery before he got the weather briefing, or he would not have agreed to make the flight. It was just too damn cold to be flying in the Yukon River Valley but the folks at the Hot Springs desperately needed their generators on-line and he had said he would do the delivery.

On final approach Josh came in slow with 30 degrees of flaps and he would have hit the numbers had there been numbers to hit. He managed to slow enough to make the mid-field turnoff. He then turned slightly farther left taxiing uphill to the visitor tie-down area where his was the only plane there. An old Ford pickup from the Lodge was parked and idling, waiting for the needed parts. Josh shut down his engine and walked the parts for the generator repair over to the pickup driver who didn't even have the wherewithal to get out of the truck. The driver said they should head back to the Lodge and do the invoice for the delivery and have some coffee. Josh thanked him, said their parent company in Fairbanks would be billed by month's end; he wanted to get back into the air as quickly as possible. A simple hand-shake ended the male bonding effort and as the driver quickly drove away back to the lodge Josh was wishing for a hand turning the plane around; he was cold as hell and wondered who was supposed to be helping the intrepid Bush Pilot that was risking life and limb flying a mercy--; Aw, bullshit! Let's just get this flying machine back into the air.

He put some of his 225 lbs. on the aircraft tail feathers and managed to get the plane pointed back toward the runway. The engine fired instantly, glancing at the outside temperature gauge he saw it was minus 68 degrees; far too cold to be flying for any reason. Taxiing back to the airstrip he wanted to turn hard left toward the run-up area for 09. But the plane did not want to turn and when he looked out the side window to see if the tire was skidding or something, what Josh saw was the bright red brake fluid spilling out of the brake cylinder and onto the taxiway; frozen O ring seals will do that. Even from midfield he had nearly 1600 feet of runway to the right which was overkill, so he turned right for a mid-field takeoff and put the balls to the wall. But the engine stumbled a little and seemed to drop a cylinder; then it seemed to pick it back up, lost it, and then it was good again. In a few seconds he started the takeoff again but now from much less than mid-field. The windshield had slowly frosted opaque on the inside from his moist breath which was also growing a fine pair of snottcicles hanging from his manly mustache; and his fingers were starting to lose their feeling. He put his one

21

finger and thumb gloves back on his left hand, but it seemed no help at all. The high flotation tires extending past the ski bottoms were not even close to round and seemed to be beating the hell out of the floorboards despite the skis being pumped at least halfway down.

As most pilots know, the three least important criteria involving safe flight are: length of runway behind you, altitude above you, and gas in the airport fuel tanks. In this case it was the runway behind that could have been used but was not, that might have been critical.

The engine still didn't seem to be developing anything near full power and the end of the runway and the wall of stunted spruce trees behind it, was approaching quickly. As the speed picked up some and with the tires starting to round out, optimism or blind hope, take your pick, reigned supreme. Josh noticed the airspeed indicator was jumping around, not working quite properly, so he reached over to the right and thumped it. In his experience thumping has been known to fix most cockpit instruments. As he tapped the gauge he noticed the magneto key just below the airspeed dial was mistakenly turned to left magneto only.

With still nearly five hundred feet to go he turned the key two notches to the right with his gloved hand and with that the engine quickly picked up the sixth cylinder, and much added power. Josh gave the plane 10 degrees of flaps and the 206 lazily stumbled into the cold dense air in a tail low attitude. The plane seemed to hang there in ground effect trying to decide if it would fly or not. Then, almost flying; almost not, and with five, maybe ten feet to spare, the plane crested the forest of stunted Black Spruce trees that defined the east end of the airstrip property. He very carefully peeled off slightly to the left and just a bit downhill toward the lake. Fearing a stall Josh kept the wings nearly level and turned the plane slowly, using little more than the rudder. The stall horn had been warning, but by now, and in the very slightest nose down attitude, the 206 was starting to claw out some added airspeed and escaping the very low end and dangerous portion of the power curve.

The cabin heat defroster mostly cleaned the windshield by the time they were over Medicine Lake. Finally, when achieving decent airspeed, Josh started the lazy climb to warmer altitudes. Nearly ten minutes later, still over the Resort airstrip, and having climbed to a toasty nine thousand feet Josh was enjoying almost warm plus ten degrees. His gloved fingers warmed to the point that he got some feeling back and no longer had to hold the yoke with hooked thumbs.

Life was good in the clean Arctic air at nine thousand feet. Josh looked southerly and could see the sunlight reflecting off the hangars at Eielson Air Force Base 20 miles East of Fairbanks almost one hundred miles southeast of the Hot Springs. It turned out to be a pretty nice day for Sir Josh Browning and his flying warhorse; his Pegasus.

In less than an hour, and after covering the distance it would take a man more than a week to walk, Josh put the 206 down on the small airstrip behind the Golden Valley General Store. Arriving back from his Circle Hot Springs adventure Claire met him with the bi-fold door open and helped push the plane into the hangar. She generally tries to greet him and to give him a special hug. In addition, and as usual Angel, their German Shepherd, also greeted him. She usually jumps up, puts her feet on his shoulders and gives him a nose lick, only one, just to say Hi.

Claire: "How did the flight go, how was it?" "It was bumpy over the summit but worked out Ok; and it was a little brisk at the springs, so I didn't stick around. I think we'll need to spend some extra bucks and have Jonny change out the O ring seals in the brake cylinders to some of those special low temperature ones he's been bugging me about." "Oh boy, look at that." Said Claire.

She had spotted a bungee on the nose wheel ski that was almost shredded in half. Claire: "What caused that?" "It was really cold there and the tires got flat spots really quick, I'm not sure those bungees should be used at sixty-five below; they have natural rubber in them and I think that's just too damn cold for bungees."

Claire: "The hundred-hour inspection is due soon so let's let Jonny Beard make a few bucks from Goldstream Air and do it right for a change." "That's fine by me; you're in charge of the checkbook." "Next week on Wednesday you are scheduled to take a load of soft drinks and several hundred pounds of produce to Allakaket. Let's see if Jonny can get the inspection done by then, Ok?"

Josh agreed: "Yes for sure; remind me after lunch and I can call and make an appointment." They looked off to the south and saw the sun just fifteen, maybe twenty degrees high in the blue sky over the Alaska Range to the south. The air was brisk but not nearly as brisk as the Yukon River Valley. Claire flipped the switch and the bi-fold door silently closed as they walked up the runway to the store.

Josh makes the flight to Allakaket about once a month; this month along with the normal delivery of groceries he will take along a crate of two dozen military surplus Bunny Boots. The Bunny Boots are very popular in the villages, so Josh buys them surplus when available and trades for whatever Native crafts his friend Sterling Redhorse has managed to collect since the last trip. Sterling is the Manager of the Native Owned General Store in Allakaket and is also the town's main wholesale buyer of 'one of a kind' Native art. He buys or trades the art and craft pieces, off the store's books, as a secondary business of his own. Most of his sales go to Josh and Claire at the Golden Valley General store.

The air delivery business is formally named Goldstream Aviation Services, or Goldstream Air, but Josh calls it "Fly by Knight"; he claims to be a founding member of "The Brotherhood of Intrepid Bush Pilots and Adventurers", and sometimes refers to himself as "Sir Josh Browning, Chief Pilot."

"Fly by Knight" as Josh calls it, or Goldstream Aviation Services, as it is on the income tax forms, was first operated out of the general store, but recently grew in scope and is now managed out of their new home and three-plane hangar that is just a couple hundred yards from the store down a dirt road. There is a small dirt and gravel airstrip assessable from both the hangar and from the rear loading dock of the General Store.

Snow is the main topic of conversation lately because of record-breaking snow storms and many feet of total snowfall. Josh tried to draw snow shoes on the Winged Pegasus depicted on his "Fly

24

by Knight" business cards. His hope was to have them reprinted but the drawings kept looking like just big webbed feet; Pegasus does not look good with duck feet.

Claire reminds him that he is not the renaissance man, the "Knight in Shining Airplane" of his wannabe persona but is really the Owner-Operator of Goldstream Air. She tells him he should make some effort, at least a small effort, to act the part. She thinks being a professional bush pilot should be enough adventure for anyone, even Josh. He promised Claire he would try to be more professional, but then after uncrossing his fingers, he promised himself that he would continue his Fly by Knight fantasy; if only in his mind.

Claire does not recognize and probably will never understand the need to fantasize about anything. She is one of the most pragmatic and exact people Josh has ever met. Claire just shakes her head in wonderment and unwillingly accepts the fact that he is a legend in his own mind; she wonders if maybe Josh was born a thousand years too late. There are times that Claire could almost imagine Josh standing at King Arthur's round table with a sword in one hand and a severed dragon's head in the other; that is, if she could fantasize.

The Golden Valley Store faces Goldstream Road and is right next door to one of the finest dining restaurants in the Fairbanks area; strange that it is so popular being 10 miles out of town. The Exchange, as it is known, is short for "The Ivory Exchange Restaurant and Lounge". This is indeed an excellent restaurant and its bar and lounge area makes it a general meeting place for a lot of the Valley residents. The Exchange has a two-table pool lounge and dart competition area plus a satellite dish and receiver with a 50-inch rear projection TV. This is of importance to the fans of Monday Night Football. The circular bar is unique, and the second-floor dining area is highlighted with many shadowboxes filled with displays of carved Ivory and soapstone figures. These displays in the bar and restaurant are legendary; they have been photographed by many professionals and the photos have been distributed worldwide.

The Ivory Exchange is owned by Don Peters and Tommy Wilson which are the Valley's first openly gay couple. Tommy is a paradox; he is a business man that once owned a gay bar in San Francisco and he may well be the best pool player in Alaska. Tommy certainly is one of the kindest and gentlest people one would ever meet, and no one expects such a genuine and nice person to be a pool shark, but he is. According to Don, Tommy is a cross between a Great White Shark and a Bengal Tiger when he has a pool cue in his hand. Tommy takes on all challengers and these players come from as far away as Seattle, Chicago, and even Baltimore to try him out. Tommy seldom loses a game of pool.

Don is almost totally different; he is a retired Seattle Lawyer and a very creative Chef. He constantly tries to improve the menu at the Exchange and spends most of his spare time in the kitchen concocting new and different food creations.

Don and Tommy retired to Alaska at fairly-early ages to relax and spend some time enjoying their lives instead of just chasing the California bucks. Don is a big quiet guy and runs a spotlessly clean kitchen. He sets the rules and insists on gentlemanly conduct in the bar and restaurant and takes no backtalk from anyone, no one! Tommy manages the bar, Don manages the restaurant; they share custody of a Golden Labrador Retriever pup by the name of Spider who is a good friend of Angel, the retired drug sniffing guard dog at the Golden Valley Store.

There are several other homes and one other aviation business on their little airstrip. The store's affiliated bush flying business, Goldstream Air, is about two hundred yards or so from the store and sits next to another house and hangar; home of Grizzly Air Taxi. Grizzly Air does not haul cargo and Goldstream Air does not carry passengers, so they get along just fine and share the expense of maintaining the twenty-two-hundred-foot dirt runway.

Normal deliveries to the Golden Valley store are not possible because the loading dock is blocked by a gross amount of snow. The deliveries are instead made to the garage and hangar down the road so on most mornings before the store opens Josh must move the store's needed inventory into their van, drive to the store, and then bring everything up the stairs and through the front door.

Josh: "I am a bush pilot, not a Teamster Warehouse worker. I think we should hire a kid to tote the groceries up the stairs; what do you say?"

Claire speaking to Jean: "He knows very well that in a few months the snow will melt and deliveries to the loading dock will return to normal." Claire said to Josh: "If the truth be known I'm just seeing that you get enough exercise that you are able to keep your muscles in shape for your other duties." "Ok, now I understand, I got it; just the same, moving inventory twice runs up our costs and it's killing my back, did you think about the back problem regarding your other uses for this trim manly body?"

While Claire begged out of the conversation to answer the ringing phone Jean took her place as the chief antagonist of our hero.

Jean: "When my Uncle Cap (Austin Lathrop) first came to Fairbanks there were wooden sidewalks and dirt, not even gravel roads. Folks heated their mostly windowless cabins with wood and it wasn't easy. They took a warm toilet seat with them to the outhouse if they could afford one and thought toilet paper was something to dream about and long for; it was a hard life. Quit whining and start toting the goods boss man; you've never had it so easy." "Jean, have you ever thought of helping, maybe just a little?"

Jean thought a little and responded: "The store manager does not carry in the goods; though I might stock the shelves. My efforts are to increase this store's profit margin. Appreciate my management skills Mr. Fly by Knight; and close the door behind you, it's starting to cool down in here."

She is neither the store manager nor does she oversee the operation, but Jean soon will be offered that job. Jean is very smart with a quick wit and she has a sarcastic sense of humor that Josh wishes he could equal; and he also likes her very much, as does Claire.

An airplane needs skis to do any serious flying to the bush and needs wheels at the better maintained airports like FAI; though there is a ski strip for small planes in the winter. Late in September Jonny Beard at Northwinds Aviation, installed a set of retractable wheel skis on the store's Cessna 206. These skis were very expensive but during the worst snow days of winter they remain a necessary item because these skis are the one thing that allows Josh to make most deliveries to the bush villages. The 206 is fast and it regularly carries over a thousand pounds of cargo. Even during the very short winter days Josh can make a decent living flying groceries and most everything else he can stuff into the Cessna to the outlying Native villages.

Weather is the one variable that bush pilots ponder on every single flight they make. They get fuel, a chart and destination, and then they get a weather briefing, and of course, the forecast. Some pilots file a flight plan with the FAA and some do not, but all that want to live beyond tomorrow make someone aware of their route and destination; if only to ensure that someone might find the pieces and debris of an unlucky flight.

Josh has been fired once in his flying career and that was for weather-related issues; for refusing to fly and keep a schedule according to the wishes of his employers. Sadly, Josh has known a few pilots who have pushed weather and distance one too many times, some of those friends are now just memories. The old stories published in books about flying bravely in the Alaskan bush are typically about successful flights. The many flights that ended in tragedy or mystery are largely unpublished and by now mostly forgotten.

One infamous flight that has not been forgotten started in Juneau and ended up somewhere in the fog and rain, possibly sleet, while approaching the Chugach Mountains in Southeastern Alaska bound for Anchorage.

In mid-October of 1972 Alaskan Congressman, Nick Begich, went missing along with Hale Boggs, a Congressman and House Majority leader, a Congressional aide of Boggs', and Charter Pilot; Don Jonz. They were in a Cessna 310, a good solid four place twin engine airplane that probably should never have started the flight due to weather issues.

Nick Begich, the one and only Alaskan Congressman, was a "GO-GO" guy. Nick was young, full of energy and optimism, and like most of us when young, probably felt he would live forever. These were some of the things that made him so very popular. It may have been this optimism that contributed to the incident; or maybe not.

While the plane's disappearance may have been due to a mechanical failure, the demise of the 310 and its occupants was more than likely caused by weather related issues. It was suggested at the time that charter pilot, Don Jonz, was possibly intimidated by the Washington Legislator's strong desire to get to Anchorage and maybe the pilot's desire to please led him to take an unnecessary chance: maybe.

Most Alaskan Pilots will agree that if you don't run out of fuel and if you avoid bad weather, flying small planes, even in the bush, is a safe pastime; it's the weather or the fuel that will get you every time.

From the very start of his commercial flying Josh flew by his own set of weather minimums and tried never to vary from them. He has never had a weather-related incident and only a few other close calls with mechanical difficulties of which one was proven to be sabotage.

The placer mines and the few hunting camps that Josh supplies in the summer are mostly closed for the winter, but the rural villages are "open all year round" and usually have cleared, maintained air fields. Most villagers no longer live the subsistence lifestyle of years gone by and now mostly purchase goods from grocery or general stores just like the city folks do. Filling these needs by air is the backbone of the Goldstream Air business plan.

Josh flies bush deliveries usually twice but at least once a week; one flight a week seems to be enough to pay the overhead. During the summer when the rivers are running, and placer mines are operating, more flights are needed so Claire on occasion pays Matt Smith to fly for them. Matt is a young bush pilot and a friend; he is dependable, owns his own airplane, and best of all; Matt is a pretty good pilot. He has been under contract with "Thomas Security and Consulting", a pipeline security company, for nearly a year. The work involves making weekly photography flights along the pipeline corridor; north one week and south the next. Flying the pipeline corridor is safe and very easy on his airplane, a Cessna 185. For almost a year it has been a round-robin to Deadhorse and back flying as far as The Mapco Refinery in North Pole, just south of Fairbanks. It is also a mundane boring job, but it provides Matt with a good steady paycheck to pay the bills and a livable schedule. For a young Bush Pilot this gig is like manna from heaven. Matt is always happy for any extra work that Claire has for him when he can fit it in between his pipeline surveillance flights. They are considering another pilot and plane in the future and will probably offer the job to Matt if and when they make the big move to a second plane.

Claire has finally set up a "Sinking Fund" to pay for maintenance and repairs and eventual replacement of the 206. Josh insists it should be called a floating fund because it's increasing, going up, and because he likes to remind her that life should be a pleasant journey and not everything has to be pre-planned and fit into a tightly organized schedule. Claire just rolls her eyes when he says things like that and wonders about the virtues of urine testing.

Angel is the store's security team. She is a highly trained German shepherd that was once a Police Canine patrol animal for the Seattle PD where she was a Drug Sniffing Cop; she is now retired or at least they think she is. Now, since being rescued by Claire four years ago at the tender age of seven she is a one dog Security Officer. Angel is not concerned about the number of planes and hardly notices the change of seasons. Winter might bring snow but for Angel it's just a time for a little more sleep; though now it's inside the store and very near the wood stove. She is totally recovered from a big fight she had with a Pit-Bull over a year ago; she knows she would have taken that bull easily if Claire had not put him down first. Angel thought that bull was big and tough, but stupid.

Angel's friendship with Spider, the Golden Lab from the Exchange next door, is as close as ever. Spider is really growing and is a good companion except when Angel is working or when she goes to see and check on her special treasures. Angel's favorite treasure is her diamonds, her small leather satchel of stones. They have been hidden away and secure for a long time. She took the small satchel of stones right out from under the noses of some bad guys that were yelling at Claire and Josh and she pretended to have lost them. But Angel knows where they are and keeps her diamonds safe and dry with her other treasures: her stash of pancakes and curly fries and also a stupid hat that Josh gave her. She doesn't want to eat her stash now but is saving it for tougher times.

Since Claire and Josh moved to their home down the road, Angel has more places to patrol and it's sometimes confusing to her where she should be and what she should be guarding. The store was supposed to be the number one place, but Claire and Josh are not always there anymore. The "Dream Team" now lives in their house down the runway a bit so that's where Angel sleeps and eats too. But she still does her patrol work for the store and also the apartment.

Jean now lives in the apartment above the store where Josh and Claire were last year and sometimes Casey sleeps there too, but according to Angel it's not like it used to be. Jean's stuff smells different from Claire's; besides, her door is not always open as it was when Claire and Josh lived there.

Also, there is the Exchange; Tommy and Don at the Exchange give Spider and Angel bones, and she can almost always get an ear rub from Tommy. Don is strict with Spider, but Angel still likes him a lot. And then there's the hangar where the big 206 is parked. Angel guards the hangar and the 206 as well as any other place and makes the rounds at least three times a day.

Another in Angel's family is Casey. She is special and gives the best ear-rubs, but Casey doesn't come every day and Angel misses her a lot. She now comes in and works in the evenings three days a week and usually sleeps on the sofa in the apartment, and she also works the late shift on weekends to help Claire. Still more than that there are the two other new folks: Tony and Rita. Angel is not yet sure about them but just the same she tries to be nice and polite. Casey is the very special one and except for Josh and Claire and Jean, Casey is her favorite. But it's tough seeing the changes at the store. Angel likes things to be like they were last year; this changing stuff is for the birds.

Chapter (3)

The friendly NTSB   Dec. 1984

Toward the middle of December around the shortest day of the year Maury Fitzgerald stopped by the store in the morning to visit; at least that's what Josh thought. Maury is a National Transportation Board Investigator (NTSB) who was working on the investigation of several old Alaskan air crashes. He is presently just finishing his involvement with an accident at Anchorage International Airport.

The accident happened in the fog on Runway 24 in December of 1983, about a year ago. The flight crew was disoriented; the KAL DC 10 ran over a Piper twin that was parked near the threshold waiting for takeoff. Several people were hurt but none died. It looked like pilot error because the DC 10 attempted to take off from mid-field. Josh thought it might have also been a bit of Controller error; maybe. This investigation is still in process; slowly albeit, but still working. Josh thought this was yet another fine example of federal tax dollars at work.

On this visit Maury was asking questions about the sabotage of the Cessna 185 when Josh and Claire owned it. Maury noted how similar it was to the condition of the cables on a Piper Super Cub that killed a mine operator's son, David Littlejohn, in Bettles, nearly a year and a few months ago.

Josh: "I never saw the wreckage of the Cub, but I was of course interested in any similar accident. As you may know we had a major problem, an incident with Jim Littlejohn and some hired thugs, regarding a previous mining misadventure. I thought that Jim Littlejohn was the one that sabotaged our 185 at the Hot Springs. But I changed my mind and lost interest when his son died in the takeoff crash in Bettles."

Maury: So why have you lost your interest?" "Because similar damage probably meant the same perpetrators, I don't think Littlejohn would kill his own kid: do you? So, I thought it probably was not him that screwed with our control cables after all." "So, you just gave up?" questioned Maury. "I really don't give a damn anymore; why should I? I'm surprised that the investigation is now just starting because at the time you seemed to take no interest in looking into any aspect of the damage. I have no clue about how you people do business. Your indifference frustrated us to the point that Claire contacted Senator Ted Stevens and tried to get an investigation started. Ted told us he got some promises that an investigation would happen in the future. Is that what's starting to happen now?" Maury: "Well, what about the cables, the missing cables and other damage in the 185?" Josh answered: "What about them? I can only guess that whoever removed the sabotaged cables was trying to remove evidence of the damage altogether. As a reminder, you personally inspected the corroded cables, I did not."

Maury then accused Josh of taking the corroded cables out of the plane and getting rid of them. Josh nearly went ballistic and considered throwing him out until he realized that was what Maury wanted. It seemed that Maury was trying to start trouble and Josh wondered why? He noticed a small recorder in his shirt pocket and guessed it was recording their conversation. Josh walked into the front part of the store where Jean was watching a morning talk show on a small TV while checking out an occasional customer. Maury followed obviously irritated that Josh had walked away. Josh wanted the TV sound track to wash out their conversation and to make any recording useless. He needed to talk to Claire and his friend Skip Davis before he continued with Maury and didn't want him to know he suspected he was recording his words. Maury might be an expert plane crash investigator, but he was way over his head when it came to investigating people. Josh told Jean she could take her 10-minute break now, as if they really took breaks at the store. "I'll watch the register for you while you and CJ have a cup of coffee."

"CJ" was a signal that only a few people knew about; the signal meant something was wrong. Whenever any of their close-knit group of friends referred to the others by their initials, there might be, there probably was a threat.

"Thanks, I've been going strong since we opened. I need to check the plug-in on the Ford; it's near 30 below out there and I want

33

to make sure my pickup will start a little later; I have a date with Skip." Angel was laying down very close to the wood stove that was putting out a friendly amount of heat but seemed to understand that all was not right. Though laying down her ears were up, and her eyes were open. She had just made the rounds all the way down to the hangar and back and that included a short visit with Spider, the retriever pup next door at the Ivory Exchange Restaurant, where she had just gotten a treat. Not much ever seemed to happen in the winter but Josh seemed up-tight about something. she was a Guard Dog of habit and decided to pay attention.

Jean checked the plug-in to her circulating heater on her pickup and found it was working Ok. She also found Claire in Soapies, the laundromat. Claire was collecting the tokens from the machines and making sure the hot water boiler was running. There had been a small problem with the boiler's pilot light going out and not restarting but it was supposed to have been fixed and it seems like it was.

Jean didn't have to say anything except "J.J. is talking to Maury and wants to see you in the store" Claire just nodded her head and walked toward the store but when she entered the back door she first visited her desk in the little office area next to the beer and wine cooler. She pulled out her Colt 38 snub nose revolver that was in a lock box in a bottom drawer and stuffed it under her belt in the back covering it with her shirt-tails. In this case it wasn't necessary, but she didn't know what the problem was. Claire walked out into the front of the store and said Hi to Maury. "I think you must be Maury, I'm Claire, I saw you at the airport about a year ago, but we have never been introduced; it's nice to meet you."

Maury said hello and continued talking to Josh about the cables in the 185. Josh pointed out again that Maury and Jonny Beard were the only ones that saw the parted cables in the plane. Josh: "I have a bunch of Polaroid pictures and you are welcome to as many copies as you want. I only saw the corroded ones thru a under wing inspection port and never really saw the plastic straws and electrician's tape. I'm not really sure how the whole thing was put together." Still, Maury was asking about the damage and wanted to know where Josh was when the Super Cub that David Littlejohn was flying went down in Bettles. Josh said he had no memory of when that was and other than hearing about the crash second hand he had no knowledge of the event.

Josh: "Why the questions, do you think I was somehow involved?" "Yes, of course I think you were involved, who else would do it?" "And they pay you for this crap? If I wanted him dead I would have shot him when he was here robbing the place. That might make more sense, would it not: Well?" Maury thought for a few seconds: "Maybe, but I think you're responsible for the Littlejohn crash and I'll do my best to prove it."

The conversation was getting louder, and Claire thought she should intervene before Sir Josh got his temper out of control and decked him or something and got arrested. Claire walked between Maury and Josh and said: "Maury; you will leave this store now. You are trespassing; I am the Store Manager and directing you to leave these premises." "You can't throw me out like this, I'm with the NTSB. You try to throw me out and you'll be in really big trouble." "Angel: hold!" Angel was up and standing in the short distance between Claire and Maury; her hackles were up, her teeth were showing, and her warning growl could be heard out to the parking lot. Maury was backing up fast and just about ran into a couple of Goldstream regulars who were just coming into the store. Without missing a step, they turned quickly and retreated to the store's front porch. From there they were able to rubber-neck the scene and gather some really great information to gossip about in the coming weeks; there are damn few secrets in the Goldstream Valley.

Then Maury backed out of the store onto the front porch and when he was totally out of the store Claire said: "Angel: Cut".

Angel relaxed but was paying very close attention. Claire walked past Angel and once out on the front porch got up close; to with-in eight inches of Maury and his now very red face. "Get out now fat boy and don't come back unless you have a warrant; you are on notice that you're not welcome here, not at all."

Maury started to speak but seeing an audience of Goldstream regulars, he said nothing; he turned and walked down the steps and across the parking lot. Instead of leaving he walked into the Ivory Exchange, probably for an early expense account lunch. The folks that had been coming into the store were now unsure whether to enter the store at all. Claire just smiled and said: "Maury is with the government and has a stomach ache but will most likely get over it: probably".

Claire was fuming as she came back into the store: "If I were king I wouldn't allow that dork to breed." "If you were king you wouldn't allow Dorks. Ok, so now what? I can't believe that jerk really thinks I sabotaged Littlejohn's Super Cub. Did you see the small tape recorder in his shirt pocket?" "I damn near grabbed and stomped it; It was so obvious: I think he wanted us to see it, at least that's my guess"

As far as the Littlejohn plane crash was concerned, both Josh and Claire had guessed that the syndicate from Reno was probably responsible for it though Josh wondered how they managed to do it in Bettles. It's hard to sneak into that place without being noticed.

The Reno Cartel was the group that eventually ended up with the sub-surface oil and mineral leases on the Coleville river property. They took over the mining operations there when they kicked out Hector Redhorse and his silent partner investors who were supposed to have discovered a new source of real diamonds. Jim Littlejohn, an ambitious wanna-be Wise-Guy, had been running the operation for the Fargo Group and was allowed to continue the day-to-day management after the Reno Cartel screwed the mostly inapt folks from Fargo, out of the operation.

Littlejohn had grandiose ideas and a great sales pitch. He had been the one that proposed the plan to steal the diamond mining operation out from under the folks from Fargo, even though he was just one of their low-level managers at the time. Unlike the Fargo Group the Reno Cartel was not just a bunch of wanna-be players; they were a real crime family with juice as far as the Nevada Attorney General and the Governor's offices; they were big time Players and anyone with a brain knew they were to be left to themselves.

The Fargo Group, or what was left of them were thought to be a bunch of clowns. It was rumored, according to Skip, that the

36

Reno Cartel told Littlejohn to have his kids stay out of the drug trafficking business; or else. After the warning was ignored they probably ordered the hit on Jim Littlejohn but got his son instead.

A customer at Skip's bar said absolutely that his sons, David and Justin, had been dealing drugs, despite the warning. This customer was a frequent buyer, seller, and also a user of drugs. It might or might not be true, but Skip thought it was probably close to what had happened.

Despite David's death there was still a constant and rather large supply of drugs coming into the Fairbanks area, and from there by extension up to the North Slope, making it fairly certain that Justin and a few other associates were the ones driving the local drug distribution business.

Claire: "Maury is sniffing around gathering recordings, per diem, and expensing his meals; when he gets tired of living out of a suitcase he'll go back to DC and write a report. Big God-damn deal; he's a bureaucratic punk with a badge; no more, and I don't think he has a clue what the hell is really going on." Josh offered: "Drugs are a source of money for a few and real misery for many, what do you think; do you think Justin is on a short list also? More than that I wonder if maybe the brothers had been running the drug network from the start and that their dad maybe knew little about it?" Claire: "He knew, he damn well knew. Jim Littlejohn may have been spending 100% of his time managing the mining operation. Ok, I'll give you that; he had no time to be dealing drugs anyway, but he damn well knew about it: how could he not?" Josh said: "According to Skip neither of his sons worked at the Coleville site. David had been around Fairbanks and also managing the Deadhorse network, Justin was supposedly spending some time in Victoria on Vancouver Island greasing the suppliers and then also some time in the mid-west making sure his little operation on the north slope got proper notice; and their fair share of drugs to distribute. Between the two of them they had plenty of time to pipeline and distribute multiple drugs." Josh said: "Justin is a little younger but a whole lot smarter while David was a cry baby and acting the part of a weak little sociopath. David was said to have any number of venereal diseases and very willing to distribute them locally. Skip's druggie friend said before he died he was unwelcome at many of the shadier places in Fairbanks including Ruthie's. Notwithstanding the STDs, what kind of man are you when you have a lot of money and are still unwelcome at a running 24-7 poker game at a whorehouse?"

Claire: "One down and two to go; they are a family of low-lives and they can all buy the farm as far as I'm concerned." "Stop holding back Claire; and tell me how you really feel." "Go soak your head Fly-boy."

With that said Claire leaned over and kissed his forehead; he smiled and after some other discussion they agreed to retain a lawyer just in case Maury didn't go away. Claire said she thought Don, from the Exchange, might know of one or at least know how to find one.

Josh: "I'll walk over in a little while and see what Don might know about the NTSB and whether or not they even have a roll in criminal investigations. I don't think they can legally investigate criminal acts. I am pretty sure that's the purview of the FBI; what the hell is Maury doing anyway?" "Maury is eating high on the hog right now, he's on a big fat expense account and pretending to be important, that's what".

Don had a few ideas that did not involve retaining a lawyer. He said he would find out which government office would be doing the investigation; he was sure it would be the NTSB for the crash of the Super Cub but was almost positive the NTSB would not investigate the criminal act of sabotage. Don said he would find out for sure; as sure as could be if no one changed the rules.

Claire called Skip Davis to see if he might have some insight or other advice and Skip, sensing a new adventure and a chance to be around Jean for a while, decided to drive out to the Valley in the afternoon. There was also that Christmas thing. Skip had a very small box of jewelry for Jean and he asked Claire. "May I put it under the tree in the store?"

Claire: "Yes of course you may, and remember that we're planning on you for dinner?" "I remember".

He had forgotten about the invitation but was a little too embarrassed to admit it.

Claire: "I'll have a turkey in the oven in about half an hour, come as you are, sober I hope." "When have I not been sober?" "Really, do you really want an answer to that?" "I guess not; at what time shall I plan my arrival?" "Are you trying to be formal; you are far from a formal person? Just the same try to be here no later than 5:00, if you can, Ok? See you then."

Jean and Casey had been invited for Christmas Eve Dinner and accepted. Tommy and Don were also invited but could not make dinner because they had to feed a few of the more unfortunate Valley residents at the Exchange. Don said to Claire earlier in the day: "But we will come to welcome Christmas and partake of the Wassail Bowl a little later, maybe around 7:00, if that's Ok?"

Claire: "Yes that sounds great, bring Spider of course." "Will do."

The store closed at 6:00 on Christmas Eve and would not open till noon Christmas day. Casey and Josh closed-up, Claire and Jean left much earlier and had already walked down the road to their house, prepared the turkey for the oven, and started the rest of the kitchen stuff.

It was starting to snow hard and the traffic on Goldstream Road diminished to near zero. Josh brought the van into the hangar and pushed a pallet of paper towels against the wall to make room for Skip's Travel-All. Just as he made room for the car Skip arrived and drove right into the rear car door of the hanger. Josh flipped the switch and the door closed tight and they walked into the house for a toast and reflection of the past year. Skip did not plug in the circulating block heater because there was more than enough waste heat from the house to keep the inside temperature of the hangar well above zero.

Angel was usually not a fan of anything coming out of the oven except beef. She knew from experience there would be no bones, but she thought the turkey smelled Ok and would be happy and willing to partake when invited. She found out long ago that the time to be especially friendly was when folks were eating. She would slowly walk under the table nuzzling random knees finding that there was usually a small treat available form a stealthy and friendly hand. This little trick worked with almost everyone except with Don from the Exchange; but Angel still liked him; though a little less than she liked Tommy.

She had just come back from her rounds and knew that Claire and Jean were at the house but was still surprised that the store was closed-up so early; that had not happened for a long time.

Life at the store had been going along well this last warm season. Since the snow started falling many weeks ago, there were a lot more people coming and going at the store and she, of course, had to keep track of all of them. The local people she pretty much knew and had learned long ago to ignore their smell of weed or whatever it was she had been trained to detect years ago in the big city. Around the Goldstream Valley weed seemed to be of little importance. When Angel would point out the weed smokers to either Claire or Josh they would just ignore her. Jean would at least acknowledge her diligence and detection skills, but she would only say, "Not now Angel." Moreover, there were almost never any treats or even an ear-rub as a thank you for her efforts.

The most single important thing Angel did was to guard the brown leather satchel with the stones in it, the one that the big argument had been all about when she ran off with it when that big jerk was yelling at Claire.

Angel *"That was the day that the bad guys got away with the other stuff but not the little brown satchel. Claire got so mad she spoke harshly to Josh and that was a real big problem; but at least Claire didn't give him swats, and then they finally made up. The next time that big guy showed up he was not so lucky. Tommy bonked him with a big stick and Claire put down that Pit-Bull that I was fighting with. We kicked the bad people out that day but not before they hurt Spider very bad. If they ever come back I'll protect Spider a lot better, just like I will Claire and Josh"*.

Angel was quite pleased with herself and Claire would sometimes wonder what she was doing: acting so proud and important. Angel would be strutting around holding her tail so high and Claire could only wonder what she was so proud of; she never guessed it was because of Angel's Diamonds.

Pete had also been a problem because sometimes he was good people and sometimes bad; Angel never really knew for sure. She hadn't seen him for a while but when he had been around she really kept an eye on him whenever he got close to either Josh or Claire. Angel knew she would never tell Pete, or anyone besides Josh, where the treasure was, even though Pete's scent was all over the satchel. Angel had it hidden away and would keep it safe until Josh asked her for it: only Josh. The satchel was in her special place that only she knew about and only she knew how to get.

Skip had arrived earlier for dinner and at about 6:30 Tommy and Don knocked and walked in followed by Spider. They planned on closing the bar, but a bunch of Valley folks showed up and needed the warmth of the Ivory Exchange and a little fellowship to put their souls at ease. Don made the decision and left the bartender, Molly Sherman, in charge of the restaurant for the rest of the day. Don told her the drinks were to be ample and half price, he told her to get the car keys of anyone that overindulged, and he would personally drive them home if necessary after closing, whenever that would be.

Skip owns a bar and restaurant, so does Don and Tommy, and Josh and Claire own a store that sells groceries and liquor, so there was no lack of food and drink. When they took the Christmas photographs after dinner there were four couples: Josh and Claire, Don and Tommy, Skip and Jean, and Casey and Angel, along with Spider.

After dinner and drinks and more drinks and even a few more drinks, the conversation wandered from the condition of the Goldstream Valley Road to the government of the State. Skip is a dyed-in-the-wool Republican and Claire, it turns out is a libertarian or maybe even a Democrat. As the rest of the folks listened to the arguments for one or the other parties Don really surprised everyone by also declaring himself a libertarian. Tommy claimed to be a free-

41

thinking Independent and then asked if that was all right to be Independent; Don just said: "Whatever".

Josh said he was a Pilot of small aircraft and wanted less expensive fuel, clear skies, and more customers. He said he would vote for any party that offered better weather and longer days. Skip recalled that when he was actively flying he wanted 25 hours of sunlight every day because he disliked flying at night. He said the last time he landed a 206 at night the runway unexpectedly jumped up in front of him and he stubbed the nose wheel and nearly stacked it up.

Josh: "When were you flying a 206?" Claire looked over at him and said: "You don't want to know; Let's all have another round of good cheer?"

Skip excused himself to the bathroom and Jean asked if Casey would work on New Year's Eve. The conversation turned to Maury FitzGerald and suddenly everyone that had just produced plans to heal every ill on earth had not a clue what was going on with him and the NTSB investigation. Josh promised to start the search tomorrow or January one at the latest.

Chapter (4)

A new source of gold   Dec. 1984

Sales of liquor at the store over the holidays were better than they had ever been. The store had to buy another display rack just for the increased required inventory. Claire, Jean, and the two newest clerks were more than busy just keeping the shelves stocked and the beer cooler filled. Jean was delighted to finally be named Store Manager and even happier with a small pay raise. She had long ago considered herself the Store's Manager so there was little outward celebrating but deep inside she was thrilled. Jean did the grocery ordering and scheduled the staff's working hours. Josh still handled the liquor department and the store's infrastructure needs such as the maintenance of the gas pumps or the boiler, water softener, and washing machine and dryer maintenance at Soapies.

Josh is staying so busy in the aviation business that he is about ready to hand his liquor store responsibilities over to Jean. He knows she would probably do a better job than he has been doing but feels if he did turn it over he might be distancing himself from the day-to-day store business and relegating himself to the role of a handyman; that does not appeal to him.

Claire is the store's Business Manager and she handles the finances, the Fire Box bidding, and she writes most of the checks. Claire also does the buying, markup, and pricing of Native Crafts and any local Art that comes into the store. She is stretched pretty-thin being in the store really about half time or less, usually before noon on most workdays. To say she is busy is an understatement because she also works about thirty hours a week as a Geology Consultant for some of Alyeska's biggest civil construction contractors. Presently she is working two roadway contracts for the oil companies, one for exploration and the other regarding access and development of two smaller fields.

This work is mainly performed on the fourth floor at the Geophysical Institute, University of Alaska, in the Remote Sensing

Lab. Claire's office is there and the very specialized equipment she needs for her consulting work.

At some time or another Claire's work takes her out to do field work using simple solid earth valid geology techniques such as a traverse, chipping rocks, and collecting samples for later laboratory analysis. This is a part of Ground Truthing and is an important factor of every final report she writes to satisfy her contracts. Goldstream Air (Josh) usually provides the transportation needs for her field work and receives pay checks from the Business Office at the Institute just as Claire does.

When she is working alone in the field she seldom has human assistance. If she was considered University Staff she could take a grad-student, but she is not so Claire takes Angel as a companion. Angel likes the fieldwork because she can run around and chase rabbits or squirrels and not get spoken to harshly; it is free in the field. But it's not all fun because Angel knows she is there to take care of Claire. Last Fall Angel had to back down a smelly obnoxious Black Bear. She was not all that sure she could have taken that bear in a fair fight and on that day, it had been scary. Angel knows that Claire always has her noise banger that will chase most bad things away. That noise banger is pretty neat, and Angel likes it and the noise it makes, except it did hurt her ears a little.

Angel is not sure if she is a member of the extended family or the center of it. She really likes all the people in her family and would never ever bite any of the group, but she has some very special attachments that make some of her family members a little more special than others. It might be complicated for people, but Angel understands it perfectly because canines have strict pecking orders in their families and these also apply to her family of people.

Two days after Christmas Don completed a list of lawyers he considered to be qualified Defense Attorneys and brought the list over to the store in the morning before the Ivory Exchange opened. Two recommended attorneys were in Fairbanks and three practiced law in Anchorage; the rest were in Washington State and these were all members of the Alaskan Bar licensed to practice law in Alaska. Of the Washington Attorneys all are in Seattle except Harry Strubee

Esq. who now lives in and practices law in Spokane. Don thinks Harry Strubee is the best of the group because of his experience with the FAA, and most other "too big to be effective government agencies." Don knows him personally and says of all the lawyers he had ever met Harry was the one he would want to represent him in most any legal action.

Claire considered Don's opinion for a full three seconds before deciding on Harry Strubee, if he would agree to represent them. Don said he would contact Harry if Claire wanted him to and then Josh spoke up and said he might also have an opinion on a lawyer; but unfortunately, Jean was part of the conversation and asked: "What the hell does Josh know about Attorneys anyway?" Josh admitted: "Nothing, I just wanted to be included in the decision". "Go polish your propeller or whatever mostly unemployed pilots do in their spare time." "That's cold Jean, real cold" "Sorry Fly-Boy, I haven't seen Skip in two days and I have to be nasty to someone, it just builds up in me". "So, find someone else to vent on Shorty, and don't call me Fly-Boy!" "Shorty? Really, you call me Shorty? I'm hurt Josh, really hurt."

Josh left quickly before Jean could recover from her loss and strike back. He walked down the road to the hangar and after measuring twice and crimping once he put a new bungee on the nose wheel ski on the 206. He also cleaned and polished the windshield and tried both new headsets that Claire gave him for Christmas; they worked just fine, and he longed for the phone to ring with a grocery order from the bush.

The guys from Grizzly Air in the next hangar down the strip had the snow plowed earlier and were now running a snow machine up and down the strip to pack the last two unplowed inches of snow. In the winter they only use their Cessna 180 and the Super Cub for bush flying since they both have wheel skis; their 206 does not have skis and is for taxi service on paved and plowed runways only during the winter. They left huge snow berms between the end of the airstrip and the back end of both the Ivory Exchange and the Golden Valley Store. There are no brakes on skis and planes equipped with skis pretty much stop when they feel like it. A fresh headwind is nice for landing in the summer and extra nice in the winter.

Grizzly's Cessna 206 is in for its 100-hour maintenance inspection by the crew at Northwinds Aviation. It probably will need an overhaul of its engine and a rebuild of the propeller. The plane lost oil pressure to the prop on the last trip and maybe hurt the engine because of over-speeding it. Jonny Beard at Northwinds will look at it closely before signing it off. He's a great engine mechanic and will be missed because he is going to retire as soon as he can find a buyer for the business. Josh is hoping Kevin Ferguson from Bettles would put in a bid for the business; at least he hopes. He wonders if Kevin's wife Molly would like Fairbanks, he wondered if she would like to live here. She does like to visit, and they are great people to be around. Josh is very comfortable around Kevin because like Josh, Kevin is a no bullshit square shooter, but he can still tell a good story.

Just about the time Josh was getting ready to quit for the day, the hangar phone rang. It was a satellite relayed call from the North Palmer Mine that is one of the most productive of the year round working mines in the Forty-mile District. North Palmer is on a tractor trail about 18 miles off the Taylor highway fairly near the town of Chicken. They need a small amount of groceries and a major propane delivery. He was promised a plowed and packed a 950 foot 2 or 3-degree uphill runway. This would be the first time Josh has delivered propane, for that matter anything, to the mine and he is wondering what the heck they need six hundred pounds of propane for. Usually the miners cook and heat a little water with propane but mainly heat their cabins with wood. Still, he can put six one hundred-pound cylinders in his 206 and haul a couple hundred pounds of groceries. Josh has built a rack for propane cylinders that is pinned to the rear seat rails of the plane, so he can stack three tanks on the bottom row and two on top of those, and then one of the hundred pounders on top; then he straps them down with his trucker's ratchet hand winch: like any good Loadmaster would.

Matt Smith allows the propane cylinders to be delivered to his hangar on the west side of International and has a battery

46

operated mini fork lift available for Josh to use to load his plane. Josh can load 6 tanks right through the cargo door of the 206 without getting even the slightest backache.

Matt and Josh slowly became friends after they traded planes almost two years ago and a year later Josh recommended him for a pipe line surveillance photography job when he tired of his job as an Assistant Guide. The surveillance-photography flights are for Thomas Security Consultants, a Alyeska Sub-contractor. Matt flies one day a week; it is an easy flight and pays reasonably well.

Matt rents a hangar on the west ramp at FAI and gives Josh a few hundred square feet of space for storing mining equipment and other cargo that comes to Fairbanks by air that he will be delivering to the mining operations that he supports. They also sometimes help each other out with odd flying jobs; Josh has been a bit of a mentor to Matt and after some varied flying experiences Matt has developed a basic and nearly complete set of flying skills; no one is ever complete because there is a lot more to bush flying than just landing short and dodging bad weather. Common sense is a very necessary addition to the mix and that can't be learned. But If you do have a dollop of common sense, and only a moderately sized ego, you can live a long and happy life flying the bush; that is if you don't run out of airplanes before acquiring the rest of the proper flying skills.

Another very important thing about Matt is that he is dating Casey. He would have been with her at the store's Christmas party, but Matt's father is very sick and wanted Matt and his sister around for what he thinks might be his last Christmas. Matt's sister is an RN at The Swedish, a high-tech Seattle Hospital. She came to Fairbanks for the Holidays for a bittersweet family get together. Matt was both happy to see his small family this Christmas and very sad thinking it was probably his last holiday season with his Dad. Though Matt had been flying for a while it was his Dad who put up the cash for his first good airplane, the Cessna 206 that Josh now owns.

The phone call was for more than the propane and grocery delivery. The caller asked if Josh might have any interest in and would consider becoming a Bonded Transportation Agent. Would Josh collect and transport gold from the producing mines at the

Forty-mile to the vaults at Bank of the North? A group of miners in the Forty-mile Mining District had a meeting, they proposed to pay the bonding and insurance premiums for Goldstream Air, if they would transport gold from the mines to the vaults at the bank.

Josh: "You mean kind of like Brinks?" "Yes, just like Brinks. If you will consider the work we can have our security consultant deliver a proposal and contract for you to read over, complete with what services we require and the compensation rates we will pay; that and a few other contingencies." "Are the shipments that often that you need a contract?" said Josh. "This is the problem; we have been doing it mainly in-house and have been robbed and ripped off on three separate occasions. We want number three to be the last time. Our group will pay fairly for a bonded pickup and delivery service and we've heard you to be dependable and capable of the services we require. If you have an interest in taking on such a job, we can have our security agent deliver a contract proposal to you to look over with your attorney. Would you be so inclined?"

Josh: "I would certainly be interested and yes, I will have my attorney look over the deal. When can I expect to see the proposal and how soon do you want this to happen?" "An agent will call on you at your place of business. Would this be the hangar where your office is, or shall we deliver it to the Golden Valley Store?"

Just how in hell do they know about my office in the hangar?

Josh: "Delivery to the store would be my preference" "We hope to deliver it soon; can we hear from you within a week after you get the contract, is that possible?" "If you include all pertinent contact information and a fairly complete history of the people I will be performing services for then I think yes, one week's time should be adequate for either a counter offer or a final decision".

Josh said goodbye, hung up the phone, and turned off the tape recorder. He pulled a blank tape out of his top drawer and exchanged it with the newly recorded tape that he put in his pocket. It might be a new line of business or just a dead end, he would see. Josh locked the door and whistled a happy tune as he strolled back to the store in a gentle snowfall to tell Claire about the conversation and to talk to Don about looking over the proposal, if and when it was delivered. The tape recording was for Skip's sage council.

After a talk with Claire about the proposed gold transport business he called the propane distributer and arranged for a delivery of six one hundred-pound tanks to Matt's hangar before noon tomorrow. Then Josh called the hangar and Matt answered. "Matt, I am having six full propane tanks delivered tomorrow some time before noon. Will you be there in the morning to open the doors for the truck?"

Matt: "Yes, all morning. I will be loading the cameras for a photo trip on Thursday with not a darn thing to do till then. Got any work for a great pilot and loyal friend?" "Ok, how would you like to do a little delivery for me?" "What do you need me to do?" "I need you to fly the 206 down to the North Palmer Creek mining operation 20 or so miles north-west of the Pedro Dredge on the Taylor Highway near Chicken. It has a short 950 foot uphill and packed runway at about 4,300 feet elevation. It probably sounds harder than it really is, but I don't know for sure because I've never been there. Deliver six tanks and a couple hundred pounds of groceries and pick up six empties. Claire will pay fifty bucks an hour for your flight time and twenty for ground time both rounded up, plus fifty for taking the job. Beats checkers, what do you say?"

Matt: "Give me a chart with a big X on it and consider it done. I'll be there in half an hour or so for the chart."

Chapter (5)

Safer than Brinks   mid-Jan. 1985

January 15 of 1985 was a Tuesday, a red-letter day for the crew at the Golden Valley Store. Bonuses were paid, and smiles were beamed as broad as the Northern Lights after a solar storm. Bonuses are computed on the amount of time a person is employed during the year and the hourly pay multiplied up by a very small amount of the store's net profit. Josh gets a headache just listening to the formula, but he is as eager to get his bonus as are the other employees.

Josh and Claire, Jean, and the store, split the profits on an equal basis; one third for each. This seems right since Jean is the only real full-time employee of the business and also the Manager. Everyone still receives an hourly pay, but the profits of the store are another thing to consider. The end of the year bonuses comes out of the store's net profit and they amount to a bunch of bucks.

Claire had asked Jean once if she might like to buy part of the business and Jean said she was not sure but wanted to think about it. What Jean didn't say was that she wanted to see if her relationship with Skip was going anywhere before she made a commitment of partnership in the business.

Josh and Claire got small checks compared to Jean, but the Goldstream Air and Native art and crafts profits were not included in the mix; only the store's net profit was computed, and Claire thought fairly.

It's a time of no complaints except Angel gets nothing except ear-rub and jerky; from everyone. Angel knows now for sure that she is not just a member of the group, but she is really the center of it. Being the Alpha, the lead dog is great; because if not the lead dog the scenery is always the same. After a little more beef jerky and probably more than she should have eaten, Angel strutted over to the Exchange to share a strip with Spider; just a small share, but a share just the same.

Around noon an Avis rental car from the airport arrived and parked off to the side of the newly plowed lot between the store and the Exchange. The car was driven by Pete, just Pete; he seemed to have no last name and had been one of the fringe characters involved with the diamond mining misadventure of last year. Carter Thomas was his passenger and, as usual, was dressed in a perfectly pressed, three-piece suit. He had an attaché case in hand and a rather large friendly smile. The attaché case proved to contain the proposal and contract provisions from the Forty-mile Mining Association (FMA) that Josh had been patiently waiting for.

Pete just said: "Hi" and no more. He stood off to the side, observed the surroundings, and listened to the conversation. He was obviously Carter's body-guard but that seemed odd for a man of such small stature. On a tall day in boots Pete might just exceed 5' 6" be no more than 125 pounds. Carter was maybe 5' 11" and 180. Of the two It seemed Carter might be the body-guard instead of the other way around.

Josh neither liked nor disliked Pete, but to Josh, he just seemed to be sneaky and likely untrustworthy. Pete was a person of interest for a short time after an attempted robbery at the store two years ago and was last known to be living in Hawaii; Pete's olive complexion well hid the expected South Seas tan.

FMA, as the association wants to be called, is a rather large consortium of mine owners. Carter's security firm is under contract to provide the FMA with a full range of his services that includes secure transportation of gold from the producing mines to the vaults of Bank of the North. Gold prices are down a little now to about $375.00 a troy ounce, but still high enough to be looked on as a target for theft. FMA represents the mines on or near the Taylor Highway, north of the Alcan Highway near the Canadian border. The area is The Forty-mile Mining District because of the Fortymile River that runs right through the middle of the gold fields. It was probably forty miles from somewhere when gold was first discovered in the Klondike River area in the late 1800s.

The Fortymile River runs easterly out of Alaska into Yukon Territory, Canada. It then joins the Yukon River at Dawson City and from there the Yukon runs northwest and then west and eventually flows into Alaska. After crossing the breath of Alaska, on its way to the Bering Sea, the mighty Yukon flows into Norton Sound near the village of; well there really is no village because the Yukon splits and flows in the Sound across a huge delta area in three main places near the villages of Emmonok, Kotlik, and Numan-Iqua. So much for geography.

Carter walked into the store like it was yesterday but in fact he has not visited for well over a year's time. Jean greeted him as he entered the store. She is not a big fan of his nor is she much of a critic; but Jean does feel a subtle common bond with Carter. She can plainly see that at some distant time he likely was "rode hard and put away wet". Jean thinks there must have been some tragedy in his personal life, some haunting and forever lasting hurt that probably will never leave him. Jean reads this in his eyes and mannerisms; she can see the fringe of the hurt, just the fringe. The rest of it he has likely managed to neatly store away behind a facade of a pleasant and seemingly meek persona. Jean suspects Carter is not very meek at all but might in fact be a very dangerous and unpredictable man; under the right circumstances.

When Carter arrived, Pete followed him into the store and did a fast walk thru seeing that it was empty of customers. Pete then stood between the door way and where Carter was standing and while saying nothing kept his beady little eyes constantly searching for something, anything out of the ordinary.

Jean knew as much about Carter's little "diamond mining scam" as anyone at the store. It was a classical sting; well thought out and played even better. Arrogance, greed, and selfishness are some of the key personal characteristics needed to get caught up and snagged in the sting. Jim Littlejohn had these in spades and though being a mere lieutenant in the Fargo Group, he still managed to drag the whole Cartel into it. Those thugs got what they deserved. Jean still smiles when she thinks about her involvement and the final outcome. She got a broken nose to show for her experience but won the respect and love of both Josh and Claire and more importantly, Skip. Jean had proven herself to be a loyal friend and fierce fighter; far more than her nearly 5'3" 122 lb. body would have predicted.

On reflection, Jean is now fairly positive that the diamond scam was not just randomly looking for a mark but was indeed set up to specifically attract Jim Littlejohn. She wonders what the history had been for Carter to bait Jim Littlejohn the way he did. Jean wonders what the bad deed had been, what the Fargo Group had done to Carter Thomas that might make him go after them the way he did. She is sure it's more than just money and thinks it was for sure personal. Jean wonders if the vendetta has been satisfied or if Jim Littlejohn and the Fargoettes, now as before, is still a target; time would tell.

More than a hand shake Carter gave Jean a little hug and then exchanged the required pleasantries necessary when meeting a friend after a long absence. Carter asked about Josh and Claire, the store, and he wondered how Angel was, if she is completely healed from her injuries from the fight. The one thing Carter truly has in common with the folks at the store is his total appreciation of Angel: Michael's Angel of Jordon. Angel heard her name as she was coming back inside from a visit with Spider at the Exchange. She recognized Carter and bumped his knee with her nose. For Angel that is a pleasant greeting and she sat down waiting for an expected ear rub; it was immediate.

Josh heard Carter's voice as he was carrying in yet another armload of logs from the stack on the loading dock for the wood stove in the front of the store. It's about -20 degrees outside and the stove is busy doing its job. Angel has two favorite places to rest depending on the season; under the swing on the front porch in summer and next to the antique wood stove in the winter.

Josh: "Carter, how nice to see you, how have you been? How is the security business treating you?" "Just fine on both accounts Josh, in fact I am here to see you on a security matter that you may have some interest in, where can we talk?" Jean had been listening and said: "Josh, I can handle the store for a while by myself if you guys need to cogitate over business. The special at the Exchange is bacon double cheese burger, I think Carter is buying." Carter winked at Jean, nodded toward Josh, and the two of them turned to walk over to the Exchange. "Jean, will you please tell Claire that Carter is here; tell her where we are and ask if she might like to join us when she returns from her bank run".

With that said Carter and Josh followed by Pete and Angel walked over to the Exchange for lunch. Pete was wondering if he was also going to have a bacon double cheese burger. Angel is hoping to see Don for a steak bone. Tommy was sweeping up from the day before and pointed out that they are the first customers of the day but that there is no prize despite that august distinction.

Tommy said: "Welcome to the best food and service in the Goldstream Valley." "I have been here before and this may be just the best in the whole of Fairbanks". Tommy was thrilled to hear that from a man so well dressed that obviously possessed the very best manners and said: "Drinks with lunch are with our compliments; please enjoy."

After placing their lunch orders the conversation turned to the business of security consulting. Carter's new and updated business plan includes more than just consulting services; he now has a business plan that includes supplying complete security services. Three of his supervisors are deputized and can make legal official arrests; and they are required to enforce Alaskan law. During the winter months when ground transportation is next to impossible they even have a small helicopter available for both law enforcement and medical emergencies.

Carter: "The Chopper allows us to respond quickly to situations that need policing. The FMA employs Thomas Security to oversee the security issues and privacy of many of the producing gold mines in the Forty-mile Mining District. We keep track of the Taylor Highway traffic and have people available to respond to any security matters at any of the operations that we are responsible for within one-half hour of a security intrusion. So far, we have earned our keep by arresting some smalltime Canadian thieves that were sneaking into the operations at night and doing some unscheduled and unauthorized sluice box cleaning at one of the seasonal placer mining operations. This was before freeze-up of course. A lot of our work involves vetting and policing employees of the mining business. A lot of the thefts so far have involved insiders already working the mines and some embezzlement from payroll and purchasing department employees at the bigger operations. Most folks don't know hard rock and shaft mining efforts go on all year round in the Forty-mile District." "I didn't know it; I thought it was a lot of drinking and a little dry panning in the winter. When do these poor miners get any time off?"

Carter continued with the presentation: "Back to my reason for this visit. There are several fairly short airstrips in our area that we patrol and otherwise provide security services for. We are looking for transportation of gold dust and nuggets and some gold-bearing quartz from these airstrips to the bank vaults in Fairbanks and in addition the transportation of payroll dollars into these airstrips for the workers." "What's this about payrolls; is this green-backs one way and gold the other?" "Pretty much as you just said; but it is proposed that you will be paid by the delivery so a payroll trip to the mines and a gold transport back to Fairbanks, can be billed twice. And one other thing, almost all the payroll deliveries will be to a single place; from there we will sort out the money and deliver it to the individual mining operations ourselves with our helicopter. Before you ask, I can tell you the same folks that fly in the groceries and other supplies to the twenty-odd mines in the FMA cannot all be bonded and insured. We need one single flying service and one or two pilots that my security officers can recognize on sight."

Josh:" You are saying that a payroll trip to the Forty-mile and a gold transport will be separate billable items?" "Yes, that's what we propose. So, Josh, do you have any interest in being the 'Brinks of the Air'? Also, and do not forget this; the mine operators will see you delivering payrolls and will get to know you. You will probably pick up a bunch of their ordinary business during the winter maybe flying in groceries and possibly even fuel. If you want that kind of extra work this could be very good for your business plan."

"I will be happy to look at the details of the contract. You said one or two pilots; if this were to work out I have a person in mind for the second position that I would recommend to you". "If this works out the second pilot would be your choice, not mine; were you going to say by chance, Matt Smith?" "Yes, and why did you not consider him for the contract instead of my operation, Goldstream Air?" Carter thought for a minute and responded: "Matt's dependable and smart but has almost no formal education beyond high school. He does not have the military background that you have and there is a small chance that that sort of skill set might be required someday. I will not send Daniel into the lion's den."

For some reason Josh glanced at Pete who was standing next to the bar about twenty feet from their table. Carter noticed the glance and added; "Don't make the mistake of underestimating him." "And just how did you learn of my military experience?" "I vetted you before you flew the liquor deliveries on the Coleville. I know a bit about you and Claire, but that changes the subject from Matt. He flew the pipeline surveillance contract for us and did a Cracker Jack job; very careful and more dependable than we thought he might be. Are his flying skills up to snuff on short runways and mountain flying?"

Josh responded: "Short runways are no problem for a good pilot and I can help him if he has fewer mountain flying skills than needed. It would not be a problem, but I think before I sign him up I should see if he wants the job. On another note, I have been thinking of getting a high-performance tail dragger for some of my bush deliveries into less than pristine landing areas. This might get the Boss Lady over the hump on whether or not we can afford a second plane. Some places need less cargo capacity and more performance from the delivery vehicle."

The food arrived, and they ate without saying even one word of the past events involving the diamond mine and the final disposition of David Littlejohn. Josh told Carter about the new contract work Claire was doing and how she was able to perform a lot of preliminary Geology investigation using remote sensing techniques. He talked about them separating off the aviation business from the store's business and how they both were so far successful.

Carter said he started his new security business also separate from his existing consulting business and that he was stretched thin watching over both of them. Carter indicated he might need some help soon managing the new business but for now he thought he could handle it. There was still a question about if it was profitable or even possible to do what he wanted to and to see if the business plans were feasible. He did not get investors for the new business but put up all the money himself. Also, Hector was still working for him now in the Forty-mile and if Josh took the contract he would be interfacing with him in the future.

Claire arrived just then and ordered a Chef Salad and a Coke. She not so much ordered it but rather shouted it into the kitchen as she walked by the swinging doors.

Don responded back: "My ears are working very well, thanks for asking. My Christmas wish is for a quiet and tranquil beginning in this New Year." Claire backed up a few steps, opened the left-hand swinging door and whispered her apologies; she wished Don only the very best for the future. Don: "Whatever."

Claire sat down in the booth and said her not-so-pleasantries to Carter. Claire was still a little miffed at him and did not understand why the others that had been involved with the diamond deal were not. She saw him as the root cause of the incidents involving the phony diamonds and though having made a lot of money from the liquor sales she still thought of the store, and its proprietors, as innocent victims that were barely able to escape with their skins intact. Still for some reason, she did sort of like him in a strange way and like Jean, wondered what had turned this quiet, intelligent and seemingly gentle person, into a con-man with an irresistible sting capable of taking on multiple professional criminals and beating them badly at their own game.

Claire said with a wink: "So what scheme are you planning to involve my innocent fly boy husband in, and by extension, also myself? I hope to God it's not another diamond deal, we barely survived the last one. What is it this time, a gold mine?" "Claire must be short for clairvoyant; how did you know?"

57

Chapter (6)

Carters proposal, Claire's concern   Jan. 1985

Neither Claire nor Josh had talked to Carter or anyone about finding what was most likely evidence of two Kimberlite Pipes nearly a-hundred miles apart that Claire had discovered on the North Slope. She spotted and identified the remnants of the pipes using returns from the SAR (Synthetic Aperture Radar). Claire found these pipes while looking at the SAR data that was filtered thru a sophisticated FORTRAN computer program that she and Casey had written. Claire had been looking for gravel deposits from ancient waterways either for a roadway bed or as a material source for new roadway construction needed for travel to some oil field development sites. They had originally written the program to validate Casey's thesis on upper atmosphere chemistry to complete her graduate studies to win her PHD. Claire was then able to modify the code somewhat and needed to make only minor changes to adopt the program for her solid earth uses. When Claire copyrighted the software code, she included Casey's name as a co-author.

One of the pipes was barely visible and very near the Coleville River, fairly close to the mining operation that had been the heart of the Diamond scam. This was a discovery that was almost not believable. It was not only a really big coincidence, but it involved a part of their history that neither Josh nor Claire cared to relive. Also, it might be digging up evidence about a motive for the store's involvement in the sting. The truth is they had no knowledge of the sting at that time but probably no one would believe that story?

So, Clair's discovery of the two Kimberlite pipes was not presented to anyone and went unpublished. Both were happy to just let "sleeping diamonds lie". Maybe someday in the future they would become diamond miners, maybe in their old age or maybe in another life; but sure as hell not now.

The FMA proposal to Goldstream Air seemed legal and straightforward. Don read and reread the contract terms and was positive that it limited responsibility for losses only to the not yet identified insurance company. If Josh insured his airplane he had nothing to lose financially in the agreement. He also liked the guarantees of a small monthly retainer for the business even if no flying services were required and that the pilot had the final say regarding the go/no-go of the flight if it were a safety issue because of weather or most anything. Also, and a really big also, the monthly retainer would guarantee that the Aviation Services business could make payments on a high performance short landing and takeoff (STOL) airplane.

On Don's advice that the contract was legal and not financially risky Josh and Claire both signed the contract on the dotted line; that was not dotted at all. Claire thought that was funny. Josh thought he achieved another goal in his flying career but was unsure of what it was except it probably had to do with a second aircraft. After signing the contract Josh was deep into thought about how to portray multiple flying steeds; mythical horses, on his business cards. He wondered what the plural of Pegasus was. English has never been his long suit or forte and rather than admit he didn't know the answer to question of multiple Pegasus he decided to someday find an expert on old English, or was it Olde English?

Claire was very supportive of the contract and since there was a monthly retainer, almost a guarantee, she felt it was now time to get that Maule airplane that Josh had wanted. The hangar was big, big enough for three planes so there was plenty of room for two and space to warehouse supplies going to the bush. Claire had planned on two planes when they bought the house and hangar. She wanted Josh to get a smaller bush plane that was easier for him to get in and out of smaller fields. He was constantly flying the 206 into places he should not be going, and she did worry about him though she seldom told him of her concern. Claire thought her worry might be interpreted as a sign of less than complete support for Josh and his competence as a pilot. This was not true, and she wanted no such misunderstanding.

Claire knew a little bit about bush aircraft and she had seen several copies of a Maule; it was a smaller plane with a passenger side door and an easy loading cargo door on the right. It was a four-place high wing plane with a metal wing, but a fabric covered tubular steel body. It was smaller than the 185 that Josh traded to Matt Smith when he got the 206, a lot smaller, and the plane was light enough that a single person could easily push it around on the ground; a man could pull the tail around with one arm. The performance specifications of the plane were spectacular, and it had a handsome stance on the ground. The plane that Josh had an interest in was a Maule M-5-235, very popular with bush pilots second only to the Cessna 180 and 185s.

Josh is sometimes accused of being naive but is never thought to be stupid; he is a dreamer and has zero fear of the unknown. His business talent, if he has any at all, is for seeing through the muck and unimportant details and although he is sometimes thought to be slow making decisions he was really just thinking through problems completely. There were damn few decisions in his life that had gone wrong; even Jean Lathrop, their Store Manager could see this but of course would never admit it.

Two weeks after first reading the Security Contract Claire and Josh signed it; they also made a handshake agreement with Matt Smith for employment with a promise of a very limited partnership in the agreement with the FMA.

Just one-week later Josh took his contract signing bonus and boarded an Alaskan Airlines flight to Anchorage for a look-see at a Maule M-5-235. Kevin, a friend in Bettles, had heard about it and it seemed to fit his needs. Jonny Beard from Northwinds Aviation at FAI had completed a search of reported (Airworthy Directives) A-Ds on that exact plane type, the M-5-235. Jonny listed out the A-Ds, the necessary ones that were either important or costly. When Josh was going thru the log books these A-Ds appeared to all have been completed. It was a fairly low time plane, less than 400 hours, on engine and airframe with some custom wing tips and flap seals. These modifications gave the plane a slightly better performance than the factory specs. But these modifications showed Josh a little about the owner and how he may have treated and maintained the airplane.

The plane also had newly installed retractable wheel skis that had been used only once. It happened that the owner of the plane landed it once, only once on skis, and wanted no more to do with it. Something that Josh absolutely positively needed for his bush work scared the crap out of the plane's owner and made him decide to sell it and give up winter flying. Josh made an executive decision to buy it as-is where-is, with no pre-sales inspection.

Josh had been approved for a business loan at Bank of the North and had only to sign the loan papers when he returned to Fairbanks. He wrote the seller a check from his Aviation Air checkbook for the slightly reduced negotiated price and for about 30 seconds felt like a big shot negotiator. Quickly returning to reality he realized that in less than 4 hours after first seeing the plane at Merrill Field he and Claire were the owners of a blue and white Maule M-5-235. A great high-performance bush airplane.

Early February in the afternoon is hardly the best time to ferry a plane from Anchorage to Fairbanks. Josh called Claire at the store and said he would spend the night and see her by noon the following day. She asked if he had purchased the plane and he said, "I guess I forgot to tell you that, yes, we did. Sorry." Claire asked: "Does it seem Ok? is it pretty easy to fly? Will it be a good plane for me to learn to fly in?" "I really don't know because I haven't flown it. You really want to fly? Hot damn!" "See you tomorrow Fly-Boy. Stay safe."

In the morning Josh did a preflight and checked that the long-range tanks were nearly three quarters full. He cycled the wheel skis on the ground and they worked just fine. Also, he paid to have the engine preheated and prepared a list of likely airports along the way with radio frequencies and runway descriptions. Unlike most of the professional pilots in Fairbanks Josh had only made the Anchorage flight a few times. Most all his charter work was to the northern or north-western villages and mines. Even the Forty-mile to the east was relatively new to him.

The flight would be just a little over 230 nautical miles and he had a choice to make of whether to fly above the clouds or to fly under them. Although Josh was rated for Instrument Flight Rules

(IFR) the plane was not. It did have proper instrumentation for the task, but the transponder was not legal because of an A-D on the antenna that had not been updated. It worked just fine but there was an A-D on it that should be put to rest before flying under instrument rules.

Josh could also fly under Visual Flight Rules (VFR) above the weather but was hesitant to do that in an unknown flying machine. He would have faith in the plane after 20 or so hours of flight but didn't care to risk his butt in an unknown vehicle just yet. Also, the cloud tops were reported to be marginally higher than was legal for VFR flight, and besides that, he had no oxygen available.

All this considered, he decided to just fly under the cloud cover and just land and wait out bad visibility if it showed up. Josh was very much a bush pilot and the low and slow choice made sense to him. He would fly home VFR and he would be very careful. It was only 233 nautical miles straight like a crow and about 260 the way he planned. The flight would take maybe an hour and three quarters, how hard could it be?

The weather was crisp and cold in the morning, a very nice bright February day for a trip to Fairbanks. According to the FAA temperatures were 5 degrees. in Anchorage and about -15 degrees in Fairbanks. Light snow was forecast from Eagle River north, but it would clear up after passing Cantwell, near Denali Park and remain clear the rest of the way to Fairbanks, at least that was what the forecast said. Josh left Merrill field at 10:00 am.

An icy light fog hung low over the Knik Arm of the Cook Inlet and fog continued up the Knik river most of the way to Palmer. Still, visibility was 5 miles or so with broken clouds at around 3000 feet. Farther, going west toward Wasilla, the weather cleared a little until approaching Big Lake, and then north again. After that it started to fog up and cool down and past Willow it was just plain skuzzy and getting worse when nearing Talkeetna. After Talkeetna the Susitna River separates from the Parks Highway but the Alaska Railroad follows the river, and the low icy river fog continued. Josh followed the Parks highway, the fog decreased, and he started feeling pretty relaxed about the trip.

Josh had been flying slow and low; what some pilots referred to as 50/50 IFR. This was 50 miles an hour, 50 feet altitude, and "I follow railroad". He was, of course, faster and higher than that but flying barely 500 feet above the ground (AGL) and around 90 miles per hour, he knew the trip would take more than the two hours predicted. When very closely following the railroad tracks the elevation tends to change very slowly. Now however, above the Parks Highway Josh found the roadway elevation increasing. While the roadway elevation was increasing the bottoms of the clouds were not and the wedge of visibility between the clouds and the ground was rapidly going to zero.

Josh finally decided to land and wait for the clouds to lift when the roadway again joined the railroad at a crossing. He felt the railroad tracks were the better path to follow but really had no choice because he was already committed and then he found himself in a canyon that was too narrow to turn around in without some stunt flying and he was smarter than that. The Maule was very low and barely over a safe cruise when the rail tracks and the roadway converged again.

Josh was remembering an old story that Skip had once told him about Ben Eielson who was a local icon and a very revered bush pilot in years past. The story goes that Ben Eielson was the first pilot to successfully fly a scheduled mail delivery from Anchorage to Fairbanks. The story went on to say that on one of his very first trips Eielson was in skuzzy weather for about the whole trip up through Nenana. When he landed at Fairbanks the now semi-famous Eielson was interviewed by a reporter from the local weekly paper, The News Miner.

The reporter asked: "How did you ever make the trip; how do you fly in such bad visibility." Ben responded: "Mostly I just fly low over the railroad tracks and it is not all that hard to make the trek. I lost track of the rails several times but then managed to find them again without too much trouble." Reporter: "That sounds good enough but what did you do when the train tracks went into and through the Moody Tunnel?" Ben: "What is the Moody tunnel?"

63

Josh thought he remembered the Moody Tunnel was in a narrow canyon maybe near the McKinley Lodge just off the Parks Highway.

Chapter (7)

A flight in the clouds   mid-Feb. 1985

Josh pushed the prop, mixture, and throttle controls to the wall and as though answering a command to Attention, the Maule rose rapidly above the river fog and into the clouds. He trimmed the Maule up in a 700 foot per minute (FPM) climb and switched the Pitot tube heat on and the radar transponder off. Totally blind in the clouds he just held his course magnetic north and kept the wings level; it was smooth, and he just applied as much right rudder as needed to center the ball on the turn and bank indicator. He could only hope for no or little icing. Josh flew this course for what seemed like 15 minutes, but it was really much less than that. The new plane was really performing well but he had no idea how high the cloud tops were. Based on a pilot report he got before leaving Merrill field he was thinking the tops would be 6,500 to 7,000 feet but the official forecast predicted higher than that. The Maule has an advertised service ceiling of almost 19,000 feet and he was sure the plane could outfly the cloud tops. Josh thought sarcastically he might die of hypoxia at a very high altitude, but he would at least depart this life in the sunshine.

At 4,500 feet MSL the Maule started to pick up a little ice and at 5,500 he picked up enough rime ice to feel it in the controls. Josh started to get concerned and began wondering where the cloud tops were. Still climbing past 7,000 ft. the controls were getting heavy and he had to trim the nose down just a little to keep the speed up to 85 knots. By now the climb rate had fallen to 400 FPM and the windshield was almost solid ice; nearly totally opaque with only a small thawed oval just above the heater vent outlets. Not really important though, there was nothing to see out front anyway. Thru the side windows he had some visibility and he could see the thick ice starting to buildup on the struts and the leading underwing edges. The Maule was starting to tote a bunch of non-paying cargo.

Very much alone in the icy clouds Josh was beginning to wonder if they, whoever they were, would ever find the wreckage;

He had no intention of calling on the radio because there was absolutely no one besides himself that could do anything about his situation. Turning back was not really an option because according to the weather briefing and pilot reports, the clouds should be clearing, and the weather would be improving toward his destination, it should be; it very definitely should have been clearing!

Josh had always decided to fly, or not, by his own personal set of weather minimums. This time as always, he had followed these standards but just the same, he decided to revisit and possibly even modify his personal guidelines in the future, if there was a future; Josh wanted to be home.

The forecast for the pass had been better than was the case. But weather forecasts are in fact just best guesses about the future. They're usually fairly accurate but not always so. Better than trying to climb thru the icy clouds maybe Josh should still be in Anchorage at Merrill Field drinking a friendly cup of coffee waiting for clearer, far better weather in the pass. He was instead in the soup with a load of ice trying to climb above an unknown ceiling in a strange unknown airplane: what a jerk!

He thought of Claire, and the crew at the store, but especially about Claire and Jean. He wondered if they would continue to run the store, or maybe sell out and go their separate ways. Josh was sure Claire could make it just fine without him, but he was wondering how he would ever make it in this world if she were gone and he was the one left to continue. He kept busy pumping the glycol deicer fluid out onto the propeller: sadly, he was having little results deicing the prop and it was slowly and steadily, losing its bite. He trimmed the climb down a little more; the rate of climb was now barely 300 FPM at 75 knots. Still taking on more ice Josh again trimmed the nose down just a little and noticed he needed more and more right rudder to center the ball on the turn and bank indicator.

He reflected back to when his instructor, Horace Black, referred to it as a slip/skid indicator instead of turn and bank. When Horace flew the ball was always centered; he had twenty thousand hours of bush flying in his log book and Josh wished he had just half of his flying skills. Josh really liked him and wondered if Horace had any good feelings for him. He wondered if Horace would join the searchers. Probably not, there was a pilot in the Civil Air Patrol that reportedly could find a Ptarmigan in a snow storm and Horace was a firm believer in not wasting the resources.

The Maule was running at full power making almost 60 knots in a climb of barely 200 feet per minute and Josh was needing major, nearly full aileron movements, to keep the plane level and on course. In reality Josh had little idea how well he was flying; he was on instruments doing slow-flight maneuvers and maintaining a course and a rate-of climb in a grossly overloaded aircraft that he had less than two hours of flight time in. Slow flight had always been exhausting to him but never boring; it was the one thing that he constantly practiced. Rather than making many cycles of touch and go landings and beating the crap out of an otherwise fine aircraft, Josh would practice slower and slower flight on the far back end of the power curve flying only on the primary instruments, flying on the brink of a full power stall; but this time it wasn't practice. Josh wondered if the clouds would ever top-out.

He needed a cigarette and though he quit smoking over 10 years ago Josh really wanted a smoke. He realized his left hand was cramping and felt as though his glove was nearly leaving finger indents on the yoke; Josh had to concentrate his thoughts to relax his grip, just a little.

He wondered if Angel would miss him and pondered if someday she would find someone to replace him. Of all the crazy things to think about he wondered if she still had that little satchel of diamonds, if she was guarding them, or if maybe they had just been lost on the day of the robbery two years ago.

The controls were very heavy and as the plane approached stall it shook heavily. As it did looking out the side window Josh saw some ice cracking and falling from the under wing. He thought maybe the necessary full aileron movements might somehow be flexing the wings just a little. Whatever the reason was he noticed a little more rime ice occasionally cracking and falling from the leading edges and the underside of the wings. The engine would shake and then smooth out and then shake again as the three-bladed prop would lose ice unevenly and unbalance and then rebalance. He wondered if the engine shaking so violently was quaking the plane enough to crack and break away some ice. Josh had been out of propeller deicer now for several minutes, yet the plane still seemed to be holding on to a very slow climb; he was still slowly, in spite of the icing, very slowly gaining altitude.

The Maule M-5's fuel injected 235 hp engine had been at full power for over twenty-five minutes at just over 2,700 RPM; the blue and white Maule was making barely 45 knots indicated with little more than a 100 foot per minute climb when it crested the clouds at 11,500 feet. Josh spoke to his new airplane that was now one of his closest friends: "Good job, you only lose when you quit trying".

The sun was out and sitting very low in the southern sky. The sun is always out above the clouds and on this really beautiful day Josh could hardly believe it was so calm and clear on top and so dingy and skuzzy a mile and three quarters below. Denali was shining and reflecting warm rays on his left and Mt. Debra to his right in the distance was equally beautiful, though not quite as majestic or as high. He was still more or less on course and on his way, albeit slowly, to his Goldstream Valley home.

Wing and elevator rime ice slowly sublimed away and as it did airspeed increased, finally to a lively 85 knot indicated cruise. He was soon able to pull back engine RPM to where it belonged at 2,350 with manifold pressure at 11,500 feet at 20" almost 21" of HG. The windshield cleared up almost immediately and under cruise power at altitude the cylinder head temperatures soon returned to the green arc on the gauge.

Josh needed a shower but would have settled for a dry tee shirt and underwear and a beer. He decided on maybe two beers five minutes after the wheels skis touched the runway behind the Golden Valley Store.

Ten minutes later above Cantwell, which is considered the gateway to Denali, the cloud cover began to thin out a little. Slowly decreasing in altitude, the clouds became a little broken and soon he found some holes in the cover that he could get down through. Through some of these small holes he could occasionally see the

Parks Highway and decided to get down thru the clouds before they closed up again.

He really wanted nothing to do with the underside of the cloud bank but made the decision to get back down to earth while there was still the chance. Josh side slipped the Maule thru a moderate hole in the clouds and found he was over the Healy River in the clear at 3,500 feet above the ground in just a few minutes.

He turned the transponder back on and called Flight Services announcing his intention to land at Cantwell on runway 4. Flight Services asked for a pilot's briefing on the weather in the pass and Josh said he barely made it through underneath the cloud cover and was sure it was now well below minimums and pretty much closed for VFR flights. They said he went black 35 minutes ago and they wondered why. Josh said his transponder antenna may have had a problem though it seemed Ok now. He said it would be replaced in Fairbanks in a day or so even though it was now working properly. Josh pumped the skis down and did a full stall landing with full flaps on the short 2000-foot runway in Cantwell. The touchdown speed was less than 35 knots; he was pretty good with slow flight.

Takeoff power for 25, almost 30 minutes running up through the icings conditions had burned a bunch of fuel. Josh checked his fuel supply and determined he had more than enough to complete the trip and still have a very healthy reserve of maybe 15 gallons. But he didn't land to check his fuel, he landed because he needed to land. He no longer needed a cigarette; he needed to pee and strangely he needed to check on his little Red Pegasus flying horse stick-on that he applied to the rear window just before leaving Merrill field. The "Fly by Knight" Pegasus was alive and well and it seemed now to be maybe just a little brighter.

The plane had long range tanks which held around 63 gallons. The engine was fuel-injected instead of being carbureted which meant the air intake on it would never ice up as it might on a carbureted engine. It would probably be hard to start when the engine was hot but Josh thought this was a worthwhile trade-off; and fuel injection also meant better fuel efficiency over a long run. Josh wondered: what if he had a carbureted engine; what if applying

69

carburetor heat to avoid carburetor icing would have cut the plane's performance enough that it was unable to outclimb the clouds and icing conditions. He just wondered.

It took less time to calm down than he imagined, and his thoughts turned quickly and were no longer about his personal survival but were rather back to the reality of life; making a buck for himself and his pal Claire, and maybe a biscuit or two for Angel. Josh was philosophical about his flying, his life's work, and expected this kind of excitement from time to time. He made a point of never publicly reflecting or even admitting to these incidents. He learned from them in spades but usually remained less than public about the few close calls he had experienced in the past.

After nearly five minutes on the ground at -15 degrees the heated cockpit of the Maule was a desired place to be. Josh took off from Cantwell and headed homeward. He still had about 90 nautical miles to the store; he would go directly home and fuel up at International tomorrow afternoon. Maybe Claire would want to ride in the new plane or maybe he just wanted to be home.

Josh followed the Parks highway east and as the clouds started to clear he gained some altitude to lessen any turbulence. After crossing over the Nenana hills, he again dropped the nose and was doing nearly 160 as he over flew "Skinny Dick's Halfway Inn"; which is not surprisingly halfway between the river city of Nenana and Fairbanks, the gateway to the gold and oil fields north.

Losing the last thousand feet of altitude, Josh flew low over the Goldstream Creek drainage and was turning long final approach less than 3 hours after leaving Merrill field, just north of Downtown Anchorage.

Josh was not able to stop the Maule short enough to make the turn into their hangar and had to turn around behind the Ivory Exchange and taxi back to the hangar. Claire had heard him coming and drove her jeep quickly to the hangar. She raised the Bi-fold door just as he made the turn and taxied nearly into the hangar, home at last.

Claire always had a warm hug for her returning husband and after the hug it was customary for Angel to greet Josh by standing on her back feet with her paws on his shoulders and give him a nose lick, just one. It was always the same and Angel never tried to go first; she just knew he needed a welcome and was always ready. Somehow these greetings today seemed to be important to him, a bit more important than usual.

Claire: "How was the trip?" "It was Ok, and it is a damn fine plane. We got into a few clouds over the pass and had a little icing, but it went just fine; how about here?" "Casey and I decided, we both want to take flying lessons. What do you think, Is the Maule a good plane to learn in?" "Hey, I just got back and want to relax a little, but I think it's a great idea. I think the Arctic Flying Club has a Cessna 152 that's a perfect trainer. Horace isn't teaching anymore but I bet he has a good recommendation for an instructor. And you say Casey wants to do it too? What am I doing; dreaming?" "It's almost 20 below and you must be starved, let's go to the Exchange, and warm up, and have a nice lunch." "Food sounded good to him and maybe the beer that he promised himself an hour ago." "Ok, let me get my log book and I'll be ready for a burger. How is business? It seems like I've been gone a week, did anything interesting happen?"

The conversation continued at the Exchange but instead of Claire asking the questions it was Tommy that wondered about the flight home. Don had a chili size special for the day, so they blew off the burger and tried the chili; and it was indeed special.

Chapter (8)

Plans for the new plane   Feb. 1985

IRS laws are such that taxes to be paid on mined gold are due when the gold is sold into the market place and not when it is blasted, clawed, panned, or otherwise taken out of the gravel. Because of these tax laws and because gold prices are expected to rise (ask any miner), they typically hold onto their gold until their need for spending money exceeds their desire to hoard. Typically, instead of selling their findings and putting the cash money in the bank the miners take gold gleaned from several thousand cubic yards of pay dirt, put it in a small gold poke and bury it right back into the ground. Or so the story goes.

Many of the miners who haven't had a new shirt in five years have tens of thousands, or more, in gold dust and nuggets stashed away in their pokes, under rocks, in hollow trees, or in many other likely or unlikely places. A lot of the miners are reluctant to leave their mining operations because they have their fortune stashed close and want to protect it.

And the miners do protect their finds. The bones of outlaws, con-men, and claim jumpers lay under the tailing piles of many Alaskan mining operations. In mining country, thieves of the night often disappear at night; quickly, completely, and quietly. As a group, gold miners are very hard working and they have a strict honor code. They are among the most generous and friendly of folks. A total stranger can almost always get a handshake and a meal at a gold camp for just showing up; but that same stranger can get stone cold dead for trying to steal a miner's poke.

This is part of the world that Josh and Claire bought into when they signed on the bottom line of the agreement to become a bonded and insured gold transport contractor. Goldstream Air was now officially or rather unofficially, a mini Brinks Armored.

As part of the bonding process Josh was deputized as a Reserve Alaskan State Trooper. Because of his military service and honorable discharge, along with a firearms safety instructor rating, the vetting process to be deputized as a Trooper took less than two weeks. Claire was impressed, and they had received and spent a signing bonus and the first monthly guarantee pay check before he ever made a payroll delivery or gold pickup and transport.

It was decided that Goldstream Air would share the monthly leasing fees of Matt Smith's hangar on the west ramp at Fairbanks International. Josh would run the security business out of there rather than his hangar in the valley. Claire agreed to do the books until the business could afford a real accountant. After all, she had nothing scheduled to do Sunday evening between 7:30 and 8:45. *That might have been a small demonstration of sarcasm.*

FMA agreed to buy and have installed, a large combination safe in the hangar for times that deliveries would arrive at the airport when the banks would be normally closed and also for the cash payrolls going to the mines that Josh or Matt would be delivering. Matt was also to be bonded and insured; his vetting was just taking a little longer. Until his vetting was completed Matt would act as an assistant to Josh. After he was bonded he would be a limited (junior) partner in the security operation. Airport Security was happy to include the west side hangar in their regular patrols, they always did anyway. Although Josh had less than full confidence in their professionalism he said little. Any added security would help, even if it was from Rent-a-Cops.

Deliveries had to be coordinated; in particular the payroll deliveries. Miners want to be paid once a week, on Friday, and they do not want or need a check. The miners work long hard hours and want hard pay in dollars. Matt was less concerned with security than Josh. Josh saw a highwayman behind every closed door, hiding in every shadow and in every other possible hiding place so he simply steered clear of such places. A little paranoid he was more of a realist that knew thieves were made, not born; except he thought maybe in the case of the Littlejohns it might have been genetic.

The first payroll was to be delivered to the North Palmer Creek Mine, a six-man tunnel and shaft mine 20 miles or so off the Taylor highway, very near the town of Chicken. From there the payroll would be distributed to other operations by Carter's security company. Josh was to pick up the payroll at Bank of the North on Thursday evening just before closing and fly the money to the mining operation on Friday morning not later than lunch time. From that same mining operation, he was to pick up 350 troy ounces of dust and nuggets for transport back to the bank but stopping first along the way at Birch Creek Mine, a smaller shaft mine for a few hundred ounces more, also bound for Bank of the North. Both of the mines had prepared landing strips that were Ok for a wheeled airplane if it could land in less than 950 feet. The forecast was for clear and cold weather; maybe -15 to -20 degrees.

Josh decided he would take the Maule and deliver the mine's payroll and make the 350-ounce gold pickup. But instead of stopping at the Birch Creek mine, he would continue back to Fairbanks and deliver the gold to the Bank of the North. The 350 ounces of gold was the take from the time period of November till now. The partners were reluctant to ship the gold until the new bonded transporters; Goldstream Air was licensed and fully insured. Future shipments would be less. It seems strange that a mining operation would be producing in the middle of winter but all summer long the mine had been slicing farther into the hillside and sinking shafts down to the pay gravel just above the bedrock. This produced some great pay dirt and it was now being separated and dry-panned by the mine manager indoors and apparently producing some real nice nuggets and a bunch of gold dust.

Most of the miners were off for the season and this one payroll was for five separate but cooperating mining operations. Still it was nearly $96,000 and a very nice target for a thief.

A little later in the day Matt was to fly his 185 to the Birch Creek operation that is on the same drainage as the North Palmer. Birch Creek had a 1,200-foot airstrip. Josh decided on using two planes because he did not want to land anywhere with 350 ounces of gold on board other than at Fairbanks International. At FIA he could taxi directly to the security post where his transport van would be parked. Skip Davis would be in the van and they would drive to the bank and not leave the satchels until they were verified; until the gold was weighed and signed for, and secure in the vault. The value of the gold would be nearly two hundred thousand bucks and Josh was concerned and very nervous about the trip.

It was planned that Matt's pickup and delivery was to start a little later. After making the trip Matt was to wait at the security post. He would not leave until Josh and Skip returned from the first bank run. Josh and Skip would pick up the satchel for the second trip to the bank and again they would not leave until the gold was in the vault.

Claire was also involved with the operation as a bookkeeper. She wanted the players to keep track of their hours and wanted a complete flight log of both trips for billing purposes and for insurance contingencies. Claire also wanted information about any communications with anyone and what those communications were all about.

Matt: "This is an overreaction to self-induced paranoia." Josh: "If you say that to Claire you're on your own." "Ya, well Ok, just forget I said anything."

Skip agreed to make this one trip and said Josh should hire an off-duty Trooper for his next trips. Skip had been a deputized Reserve Trooper for several years; he liked wearing and showing off the badge and had gotten the appointment because of his long-time friendship with Governor Jay Hammond back in 1979.

Skip: "I'm too old to be playing Cops and Robbers but I will fill in from time to time if I can log the flight hours as PIC (Pilot in Command). But you will have to ask nicely; basically, if you really beg, cry, and grovel I will be there to help out in the emergencies you are sure to have." "So, you are now also a Psychic?" said Josh. "You will see my friend, you will see."

Thursday in the afternoon, Josh and Matt showed up at Bank of the North to pick up the payroll cash. They were expected; the bank officers knew Josh by sight but still checked his ID and took his thumb print. The cash was in a leather and canvas satchel a little bit bigger but very much like Angel's. They opened it and counted out $95,500 in cash. Josh and the bank's officer signed a receipt, and both kept a copy of it with a third copy placed in the satchel. It was locked and sealed with a wired lead slug.

The satchel was given to Matt to carry. Josh and Matt walked to the van and drove straight down Cushman to Airport Way and turning right, straight to the airport, thru the security gate, and into the west ramp hangar. Josh opened the newly installed safe and put the satchel in it, closed the door, and spun the combination dial. They agreed to meet in the morning at 9:30 at the store and preflight the plane. Tonight, Josh was to leave the van in the hangar with Matt's 185 and fly the Maule back to the valley for dinner. That was the plan.

At the very last-minute Josh opened the safe and took out the satchel and then relocked the safe. Matt asked what was going on and Josh said he just felt like he shouldn't leave the payroll in the hangar; didn't know why, just felt he shouldn't.

The phone rang, and Matt turned to answer it; it was Claire wondering if Matt would join Casey and them for dinner at the Exchange and he said he would. While he was on the phone Josh found a few grains of black sand on the floor and pressed a couple grains in between the dial on the safe and the body of the lock. Josh was spooky nervous as he did a fast preflight on the plane. Then he put the satchel in the Maule and flew back to the valley while Matt locked up the hangar.

Josh overflew the store and exercised the prop to let Claire know he had arrived. Whenever anyone overflew the store Claire pretty much knew by the sound whether it was Josh or not. Just the same he always did, and she nearly always met him at the hangar and had the bi-fold door ready to open when he taxied up the strip. It was just her special way of saying welcome home and Josh came to like and respect it. It was fairly dark by now and about 15 below; it promised to get a little colder as it was a clear cloudless sky. He left a small electric heater going under a tent that was covering the engine.

Josh locked the payroll in his gun safe, the big one, the one that was bolted from the inside into a concrete-filled interior wall in his bedroom. The front of the gun safe was hidden behind a chest of drawers that hinged upward and was only released by someone who knew the location of the latch. He felt pretty clever since he had a smaller gun safe in the office that would be obvious to any thief. He thought burglars would stop looking when they found the small safe and it would probably distract any further search effort, he hoped. Everyone knew he had a safe in the office but no one except Claire knew about the bigger one. Josh kept a field grade Browning Superposed over and under and an Ithaca pump shotgun in the office safe. Also, he had an old Damascus barreled Dan Lefever side-by-side double in the safe that would probably blow up the first time it was fired, but it looked pretty. This smaller safe had a keyed lock and Claire kept her Ruger mini 14 and also her handguns in it. Josh kept his very rare collection of shotguns locked away in the big safe.

Claire asked him about the change of plans and he said, "Not sure, I just have a feeling something is not quite right; not a clue why, just a feeling.

Skip and Jean were also at dinner and Skip managed to put his foot in his mouth by pointing out that if Casey and Matt got married, since her last name was already Smith she would not even have to change it. Jean kicked him under the table hard enough that he involuntarily said, "ouch".

Skip looked around the table wondering if someone farted and he was getting the blame: "What?" And then he received another kick, this time from Claire. Casey was blushing, and Matt was trying to apologize for Skip and didn't have a clue how to or why he should. Tommy saved the day by arriving with the drinks and wondered if he had said something to make everyone so uncomfortably quiet. Then he realized he had said nothing and thought maybe he was being too quiet and maybe that was the problem. It just seemed to be in Tommy Wilson's DNA to think if something was wrong it must be his fault; he would do just about anything to make folks happy.

Tommy asked: "Who's minding the store?" Jean replied: "Tony and Rita, our newest underpaid and overworked clerks have the late shift tonight; they should be closing as usual around 9:00."

"Do they already know how to close up the store, they have only worked a few weeks?" "You ring out the register and lock up the cash in the floor-safe next to the gas pump controller. How hard can it be? Oh, and you have to lock the doors." Tommy: "That's all there is to it? Maybe I could do it sometime." "Whatever it takes to get the job done; it's no big deal." "Was that a sarcasm?" And then Tommy thought maybe he was too abrupt and was embarrassed by his question. Tommy was not a big person standing just 5' 7" and never in danger of stretching the springs on a scale. Blond hair and a quiet and kind personality makes him appear non-threatening which is exactly what he is; except around a pool table.

Tommy had done everything he could to solve the nonexistent problem and with semi hurt feelings he finally retreated to the safety of his bartending duties. He had done his best, what else was there? The other folks at the table glared at Jean and she pretended not to notice but she did notice. Finally, she left the table and walked into the bar area and told Tommy she was sorry. This further embarrassed him, so Jean finally kissed him on the forehead, smiled, and went back to the table.

Don took their menu requests because Tommy by now was pretending to be busy at the bar and the waiter was either on break or hiding in the bathroom. Skip won back the confidence of everyone at the table except Jean by buying a large bottle of very inexpensive White Zinfandel. Don was ready to compliment them with a better bottle until he considered the food they ordered and thought, "cheap wine for cheap people with cheap palates."

By this time the usual Thursday night dinner crowd had arrived, all three tables of them; it was a Thursday after all. There were a few regular folks at the bar and dinner was a quiet affair. During the winter months the restaurant is just able to squeak out enough business to cover the overhead. Tommy was always worried about the business failing and Don spent hours trying to sooth his concerns, constantly telling him the bar was the main profit center during the winter months and things would be just fine in the summer. This bit of wisdom seemed to compound Tommy's agony because now he felt the burden was really on him. Don wondered if clothing with brighter colors would cheer him up a little; how Midwestern!

About ten minutes after the store was to close Rita came into the Exchange and talked to Jean. Rita said that two really shady characters had been hanging around the liquor department in the store and at closing when Tony went to lock up Soapies, these guys started to get real spooky.

Rita: "One just stood by the door, maybe as a lookout, and the other one came sneaking behind the counter when I was about to ring out the register. Angel came up behind the guy and growled. He turned white and jumped completely over the liquor store checkout counter back into the general store area. Then the two of them ran out the door. The last one, the one that was behind the counter before Angel chased him ran into Tony as he returned from Soapies and knocked Tony down, and then they were gone. Tony said they were on snow machines and he did not recognize them as regulars."

Claire: "Is Tony Ok?" "I think so, he is just locking up now. Nothing seems to be missing and I think I can tell because I just faced the liquor and wine bottles, but it was spooky; do you think they were going to rob us?"

Skip and Josh were already out in the parking lot that the businesses shared but it was snowing, unlike the weather forecast, and hard to see even which direction the men had gone. It was also 10 degrees below zero, much warmer than predicted, but still no time to be standing around in short sleeves.

Chapter (9)

The first trip to the Fortymile   Feb. 1985

Friday morning was not clear and cold but warmer than the forecast and snowing lightly. Josh called Flight Services for a weather briefing for the Tok or Tetlin area and was rewarded with no information. He asked about Chicken on the Taylor Highway and again received no current information, no pilot reports; not even a Canadian forecast.

Chicken Creek was the center of the gold discovery in the 1890s on the Fortymile River. From there the gold field was explored and it expanded both up and down the river and spread up the many tributaries. The town was to be named "Ptarmigan" for the Grouse-like bird that lives in the North Country; the one that turns white in the winter and matches the color of the tundra in the summer. But it seems not one of the town planners could spell Ptarmigan, so they named the town Chicken instead, or maybe it was Chicken Creek, no one knows for sure. Whether calling it Chicken or Ptarmigan there was still no weather information from the FAA about this area.

Without a weather report or substantial forecast Josh was hesitant to go but he felt pressured to since it was his very first trip to the now snowed-in Taylor highway mines. He decided they would fly if and when the snow stopped, and not until. Then as if by divine providence, the light snow stopped and almost immediately the sun came out. The temperature was about -5 degrees; just balmy. Not usual for February and kind of tempting for a flight to the Forty-mile area.

Josh decided he would fly as long as it made sense and the visibility permitted and would turn around if the weather got skuzzy. He had more faith in the Maule M-5 than when he first flew it. It is a very easy to fly little airship and handles more like a very muscular version of a J3 Cub and less like the over-powered hot rod as he has been told.

It's about 160 nautical miles at 107 degrees to the town of Tok Junction where Josh would decide whether or not to continue to the North Palmer Mine. Tok has a nice airstrip where, if he got weathered-in he would have food and shelter available. From Tok he would fly further east along the Alcan Highway to Tetlin Junction. There he would turn north and follow the now snowed in and closed Taylor highway to the old FE Pedro Dredge which was another 60 miles or so.

The Fairbanks Exploration Company (FE) built the dredge and a few others like it in the early golden days of mining in the Forty-mile District. The Pedro Dredge is named after Felix Pedro who is credited with one of the very first gold strikes very near Pedro Dome which is 25 miles or so north of Fairbanks. Several dredges are still in the Fairbanks area. They are now mainly tourist points of interest and get photographed more than Miss America. They are huge and haven't moved or otherwise operated in 80 years' time. The Pedro Dredge is a great landmark that is within 15 miles of the North Palmer Creek Mine.

Josh opened the safe and grabbed his 44 and his Crown Royal sack with a couple dozen extra rounds. He pulled the payroll satchel out, closed the door and spun the dial. His cold weather survival gear which had about anything he might need if forced down was already in the plane and he included an over and under 20-gauge shotgun-222 Remington center fire survival rifle. He and Claire both did the preflight, a very complete preflight that seemed to include everything short of an overhaul. As Claire opened the bi-fold hangar door Josh pushed the Maule out and turned it south down the runway.

Claire said: "Be safe fly-boy, see you tonight."

Josh: "Show some respect for the Deputy Trooper; a proper salute would be nice."

The Maule fired instantly and in less than two minutes Josh started his takeoff run and was on his way east toward Tok. The limited sun was not yet up to the south but twilight, moonlight and starlight off the snow, made for a fair amount of visibility. Five minutes into the flight Josh was over the town of North Pole flying the Richardson Highway. At Delta Junction the "Rich" turns south toward Valdez and the Alcan Highway continues east to the bustling metropolis of Tok: population 1,100 or so. The sky was clear, and the air was still, absolutely still. The Maule was making 135 knots as Josh radioed Fairbanks Departure on 126.5 and then Eielson Tower on 127.2 when passing Eielson Air Force Base which is just a few hundred yards to the northeast of the highway.

At Tok, Josh continued to follow the Alcan Highway a few miles further to Tetlin Junction before making the turn north to follow the Taylor Highway to Chicken. The Taylor Highway is not plowed and so it's closed to traffic during the winter, but it's a good roadmap to follow to the Chicken general store. From the store it's just 12 miles to the North Palmer Mine's 950 ft. mining strip which is about 20 miles south of Mt. Warbelow on a fairly well-used tractor trail. Snow machines and other all-terrain tracked vehicles use the trail in winter.

Communications with the Palmer Mining strip will be on Unicom at 122.8 and the strip was promised to be snow packed and have a few Spruce boughs next to the touch-down area for landing definition. There is also supposed to be a wind sock.

Josh: "North Palmer Mine, this is Blue Maule 4 miles south inbound landing on ski strip."

After calling twice he heard:" Blue Maule, this is North Palmer Mine; wind is generally south at 5 knots, advise runway 02, snow is hard pack and uphill about 2 degrees. Josh thought about it for a minute or so and finally figured out he was being kidded. There is no runway 02 and what there is resembles a straight packed strip of snow and if he was lucky maybe a few spruce boughs for contrast from the white strip.

Josh: "Roger Palmer, will make a turn and be landing in about 3 minutes, are the runway lights on and which hangar shall I park in?"

Josh wanted to show he also had a sense of humor and he thought maybe he recognized the voice.

Palmer: "See you in a few; temperature is minus 10, coffee is hot."

Josh touched down at a full stall 35 knots and ran out the slight uphill strip turning back south and stopping near the cabin with the most smoke coming out of the stove pipe high above the roof. The smoke had been the promised windsock. He got out of the plane and poured some water from a plastic bottle toward the back on both skis to freeze them in and anchor the plane. He reached back into the plane for the payroll satchel and walked to the cabin for a cup of coffee.

There were three men in the cabin but two left when he arrived. The one that stayed was his friend Hector Redhorse. Hector worked for Carter at the supposed diamond mine two years ago, now Josh guessed he was in the business of mine security. He did not appear to be a miner; his clothes were way too clean. They shook hands and sat down for the counting of the payroll. While Josh sipped some coffee, he was greeted by Charlie, Hector's Border Collie who really liked ear-rub. Charlie was a handsome black and white large dog for a collie with shorter hair than normal. Though not a purebred, he was obviously a border collie, maybe upwards to 45 pounds.

The payroll was complete, and Hector opened a small gun safe and put the money in it and took out two canvas satchels. They hit the table top with a thud.

Hector said with a smile but with a very official sounding voice: "There is about 38 pounds of gold here in these two satchels. They are locked and sealed and will be accepted without question at Bank of the North by the Branch Manager, Allen Balla, if they are still sealed with this stamped and coded lead ball that is crimped around the braided copper wires you see here. There will be no counting or weighing if the satchels are delivered unopened. If either of the satchels have been opened or damaged in any way, you and your bonding agents will be responsible for any shortages. Hector handed Josh a folder with a bill of lading and a weight certificate.

Josh: "When you get to Fairbanks next time please come out to Goldstream and visit; you can meet my wife Claire and the rest of the crew and we will buy you dinner. We have a home now and a guest room if you ever get the urge to visit for more than a day."

"That is very nice of you and I might someday; how is Angel doing? I still would want a pup if she ever has a litter." "Angel had one litter years ago and I think it was her last. She is fairly old you know, she is going on ten and that's pretty old for a big dog. I could try to find the contact information of the folks that might know about her prodigy. Shall I?"

Hector: "Yes, please do, let me know."

Josh said he would and told him about the run-in with Jim Littlejohn, how Claire had shot him and how Angel took out the guy that was attempting to shoot Claire. Josh told him about the arrest and that it stood an investigation, and about the guilty pleas instead of a trial. He told Hector that there had been limited jail time for all three of them, but Littlejohn had somehow gotten his sentence reduced to probation.

Hector said he had heard that Mike, the PI with the unfortunate knee, was back in Alaska but was no longer involved with the mine on the Coleville. Curiously, that operation is now somehow producing gold. He said that Mike's partner, Noel, disappeared and no one knows where he is or if Littlejohn has done him in. A few of his friends thought he might be in Hawaii.

Josh: "There is no gold there, you know that, right?"

Hector: "We found a smidgen of dust, maybe five ounces altogether but somehow there are some really nice nuggets being shipped to an Anchorage jewelry buyer from that operation. Something funny is going on there. Remember, I ran the diamond operation and if there were any nuggets I would have them. We ran almost nine thousand yards of gravel through a damn fine sluice box; I know there is no appreciable amount of gold there."

Getting back to immediate business Hector said the gold pickup at the Birch Creek Mine was still a go. Josh had not planned to tell him he was flying straight back to Fairbanks and Matt would be making the Birch Creek pickup just a bit later. At first Josh did not know what Hector's involvement was with the mining association but on second thought, that since he was working for Carter, Josh knew he was trustworthy.

Josh: "Hector, we have had a small change of plans that involve the Birch Creek gold pickup. My friend Matt Smith who is also a bonded gold transport specialist will be making the pick up at the Birch Creek Mine. He has the proper ID and credentials and should be picking up the satchel in about one hour. The change of plans should be obvious; I only want to make one landing with that much gold in the plane and I want it to be at FAI."

Hector nodded his head and said: "I would do the same thing myself. I was surprised when I heard you were putting all the eggs in the same basket; well thought out Josh. And Josh, good luck and give Angel a few ear scratches for me." "I will do that, see you later and stay alert because something is not right with that Coleville operation; maybe around here also; and who knows how far it spreads."

With that said Josh shook hands with Hector and did a pre-flight on the plane that involved checking the fuel supply and kicking the frozen skis free of the snow. He fired the engine and was off; next stop Fairbanks.

Josh flew the Taylor highway back to Tetlin Junction and turned toward Fairbanks over the Alcan. He radioed in the blind to see if Matt was anywhere near and Matt came up on the radio and said he was cutting the corner from Tok to Chicken since the visibility was so good. He thought he might be at the Birch Creek Mine within twenty minutes and would not waste time on the ground.

Matt "I will see you for a late lunch in about three hours' time."

Chapter (10)

Now where did Matt go?　　　mid-Feb. 1985

When Josh landed at Fairbanks International he was cleared and taxied directly to the East ramp where he parked right next to the Security Post. The folks at Security were not expecting him. They had no idea who he was or what he wanted. Josh asked about Skip Davis and was told he was in the pilot's lounge and that he had been there for over an hour. Skip had heard the Maule's arrival and came out to meet Josh; he was in a foul mood that would make a funeral seem like a family outing. He was, to say the least, not pleased and he pointedly and openly informed the shift supervisor that their security procedures redefined the term: "Typical Alaska Operation." A few heated words not found in Webster's were exchanged between the supervisor and Skip who was ready to belt someone: Josh stepped in and tried to moderate the situation. After calming down a bit the supervisor said he would talk to his guards, but better information should be given before the next gold transport if they wanted any cooperation at their end. Josh said he would ensure that would happen and hoped there were no hard feelings; the supervisor insisted there were none. Then as they turned to leave on their delivery trip to the bank the Supervisor told Josh to move his plane; Josh went ballistic!

Josh: "I am a Deputy State of Alaska Trooper on official business and that is my vehicle. It will move when I say it will move and not sooner. If you have any questions regarding that just call Chris, your airport Manager"

Seeing that the shift supervisor showed at least some respect Skip then displayed his badge and blustered, "We're on an undercover assignment to break up a hijacking ring. That blue Maule out there on the tarmac is part of the bait for the sting. We will be back in less than one hour and when the black and gold Cessna 185 lands it will be best to show the pilot more respect than you have shown me. You would do well to drop your Barney Fife imitation and act just a little professional." To say the least Skip was pissed. "This isn't fucking Mayberry for Christ sake! You do have a uniform and maybe you should try to act the part of a real law enforcement official."

Before the supervisor got a chance to reply they turned and walked out the door. Skip's Travel-All was parked in the unsecured parking lot but Josh was not worried about getting held up at the airport. Just the same he did check the back seats for visitors before Skip burned rubber driving away. Skip smiled and said: "345 horsepower, did you feel it?" Josh was not impressed with Skip's ability to spin his wheels on an icy tarmac but did ask: "Where the hell did you get a Trooper's badge that doesn't say Reserve?" "Thought I told you that I'm a friend of Bill Sheffield's, you know; the Governor: the guy in Juneau; the guy that runs the place? I first got sworn in way back in 79 by Jay Hammond's Deputy Commissioner of Public Safety. I got this new badge two weeks ago; I knew you would never pull off this gold transport crap without me."

It was 11:30 when they got to the Bank and, as promised Allen Balla, the manager, was available and ready for them. At least it seemed the bank was running well. Two signatures and a couple of receipts later, and Josh had officially completed his first delivery as a licensed Security Officer; well, one out of the two at least.

After the bank run they drove slowly back to the airport thinking they would wait for Matt in the pilot's lounge at Airport Security. In view of Skip's blowout with the security post supervisor Josh needed no extra time there. There are times when Skip can be a royal pain in the ass and today was certainly one of those times. It was just noon when they arrived, so the office was empty except for one security secretary.

Matt had not yet arrived but would be there soon, Josh hoped. After another half hour Josh was getting concerned. Then finally at 1:30 he was ready to go looking for Matt.

Josh planned to fly down the highway toward Tok and Tetlin Junction and see if he could find Matt. Skip would call around to Eielson Center and see if they had any information on Matt. Josh called the FAI tower on the aircraft radio and found they had no information on any aircraft in trouble. The snow had started falling again and visibility was just at or maybe a little under minimums.

Skip called on the land line from the Airport Security Office and got Fairbanks Approach at Eielson Center. Although loaded with seemingly unlimited regulations the controllers at the Center do give a damn and are very cooperative when it comes to air traffic. They had logged the Maule going east and also coming back west. They had also logged Matt's 185 going east but had no information on him coming back west. Josh surmised Matt was still east of Eielson Air Force base.

Josh decided to fly east and call in the blind and try to find Matt before the 4 hours of daylight were gone. Skip insisted on joining him saying more eyes were always better in a search. Josh called Claire at the store and got Jean on the phone, Claire had gone to the Geophysical Institute for a few hours and Jean promised to deliver the message that they were going to search for Matt.

The Maule was airborne in less than 5 minutes. Josh decided to fly the Richardson Highway east. He was flying on the far-right side of the road because head on collisions with aircraft are un-good. Just barely above minimums the snow was a little more now and they flew at a little less than 500 feet above the road.

Josh: "Fairbanks Approach: this is Maule 430 Sierra-Whiskey."

Center: "30 Sierra-Whiskey: go ahead."

Josh: "30 Sierra-Whiskey is 14 miles east 500 feet over the Rich headed east at 85 knots in a search for 9240Alpha, a Cessna 185 that is not yet missing but late to arrive at FIA."

Center: "Center logged 9240Alpha going east at around 08:33 local."

Josh: "Roger Center, 30 Sierra-Whiskey will continue east and fly the highway to Tetlin Junction."

Skip suggested a slower search speed. The snow got thicker, and visibility was getting critical. They were coming up on the Salcha River boat launch and picnic area. Josh was now 300 feet above the highway and just barely able to make out the pipeline corridor north of the roadway. As they made a little right-hand turn, Skip spotted the 185 in the parking lot of the Salcha Park Road House. Matt had landed on the road and probably was having lunch waiting for the snowfall to end or at least let up a little; good for him.

Josh pumped up the skis as he overflew the Road House and made a very low 180 to land North West; wheels would be just fine for the highway and as he turned to land Skip radioed Eielson Center and explained that the search was over. Josh turned on his landing lights and aligned with the right-hand lane hoping for no traffic. They touched down at 45 knots and after slowing down a little he made a right turn into the parking area and taxied up next to the 185 before shutting down the engine. There were two vehicles in the lot, about what might be expected on a Thursday in the middle of a snow storm. Salcha Park was obviously not having a great lunch crowd today.

Skip was hungry for lunch, but Josh first wanted to see that the gold shipment was safe and secure. After that he would order and pay for whatever his friend wanted; or rather, Claire would pay.

Entering the doorway Josh saw Matt backed into a corner with what looked like three miners in his face. He was holding the satchel with both hands but was losing a "tug-of-war" with the biggest one of his inquisitors. Matt is not a big guy and he looked hopelessly inadequate for the task of protecting the precious and valuable cargo. Maybe the odds will change now; just a little.

Josh: "Ted my friend, how goes it and what kind of party game is this; can I play?"

Skip: "Ted, what the hell went on here; are you Ok?"

Ted Ferrara is a transplant from Hawaii that both Josh and Skip have known for a few years. Ted and his wife have operated the Salcha Park Road House ever since his Aunt passed away eight years ago. Ted and Helen had come to Alaska to settle his Aunt's estate. By the time the estate was settled they refused to leave, finding all kinds of excuses to stay including buying a dog and arguing that there was a six months quarantine time to get the animal into the islands and that the dog would get lonesome during that extended time.

Ted answered Skip's question; his voice picked up and the look on his face went from despair to excitement because he knew what was about to happen. "Not so pretty good right now Brah; seems to have got me a bit of headache."

Ted was sitting in a chair next to the food ordering counter by the door to the kitchen with a cut lip and what looked like was going to be a very black eye. His tee shirt was torn, and his face was scratched and swollen. The shirt was ripped nearly in half and hanging to the side. Ted is just a little guy, 5'4" at the most and kind of skinny. The guy standing next to him in a torn red shirt was 6'1" at least. He also had some facial damage but obviously had been the victor in the altercation.

Josh had his 44 in a shoulder holster that was not obvious under his vest. He had no idea if Skip was armed or not because Skip had left his shotgun in the Travel-All back at FAI. A fifth guy, armed with a shotgun, was standing off to the side and seemed to be the leader of the bandits. When he turned Josh recognized Mike Thompson, the PI, one of the hoods who had tried to tear up the Golden Valley store with Jim Littlejohn almost two years ago. Josh had broken Mike's knee and smashed in his face with the butt end of a shotgun. Mike, along with Bob Adams and Jim Littlejohn, had gotten a six-month jail sentence because of the assault. Josh always thought he might see Mike again but was not happy to see him now.

Skip: "What the hell is going on here?" Mike: "Shut up fat man and sit down over there or bleed out where you are." He pointed with the shotgun toward a booth near the kitchen door. Skip gave Josh a look and shrugged as he walked toward the booth. What was that all about? I guess he's armed after all.

Josh: "Matt, are you Ok?" "It's a long story; sorry, but I really screwed up, I am so very sorry!"

Mike said; almost boasting: "Don't be sorry Matt, it's not your fault. I had a good plan and it worked out. Now my friends and I own the loot, and by the way Josh, your security business plan has a few little holes in it. Fix them or I will be seeing you again." " This is nuts; no way in hell will you ever get away with this. What the hell Mike; you're a known felon. Short of murdering everyone in this place you are identified; you will be arrested, prosecuted and you'll be in jail in

90

less than a week. For Christ-sake, you are still on probation for your last fuck-up at the store. Are you stupid or something?"

Mike: "Don't call me stupid, you sound like my mother, and you aren't my mother. And don't be so concerned about me. Your bosses will never let me be arrested, they won't even file, because I know where they got the gold." "Just what the hell are you talking about?" said Skip.

Just then there was a small crash as Helen, Ted's wife, came out of the kitchen backwards with a tray of burgers. She had been in the kitchen preparing the food while listening to a soap opera on TV with the dishwasher going. She was totally unaware of the attempted robbery. Helen backed right into the guy who apparently had punched out her husband.

Helen: "Dumb lolo Haole. Don't stand behind a kitchen door in a diner Dammit! Everyone knows you don't do dat; everyone, you dumb lolo! Who guna pay for da grinds?" Which was a fair question. The tray with the dishes had gone flying; burgers, coleslaw, and fries covered the floor. Mike looked away toward the distraction and was almost immediately hit in the upper thigh area by a 9mm slug fired from Skips Glock.

It was like a tennis match with heads following the action. Everyone then looked toward Skip when the shot was fired; everyone except Matt. He grabbed the satchel back from the surprised guy that was holding it and took his hand-gun. Two seconds ago, Mr. Surprised had a pistol in one hand and the satchel in the other; he lost them both to Matt with one well timed grab.

When Mike was hit he yelped and jumped sideways dropping his shotgun. Josh caught the shotgun on the first bounce but not before it went off and blew a saucer sized hole in one of the ceiling tiles, and dislodging several others surrounding it. Mike caromed off the wall and tried unsuccessfully to catch himself before hitting the floor and being covered with shattered ceiling tiles and pink fiberglass insulation. It was the second time in two years that during a robbery Josh had literally been handed a loaded shotgun. The last time it was Bob Adams that had handed Josh the gun; it brought back an instant recall of a dangerous but also funny incident at the Golden Valley store. Josh thought; old habits are hard to break.

Josh to Skip: "Why did you shoot him in the leg?" "I was aiming for his head; I don't have my glasses."

Mike: "You shot me, I'm bleeding dammit, and you shot me!" Skip, glaring at Mike: "Fat man; you maybe don't want to say that again. I ought to bust your fucking chops right now!" Josh, still speaking to Skip though being mostly ignored: "Well get some damn glasses then and start carrying them, you do have pockets you know." "They frost up in the cold weather, I tried plastic lenses but they're almost as bad with the cold." "Have you considered contacts?" "They hurt my eyes, I'm very sensitive." Josh; "Well have you thought about Lasik surgery, they use lasers and"—; "Hey; I'm bleeding over here, and it hurts like hell!" Moaned Mike.

Josh had his revolver out and directed the other four bandits to sit in one of the booths after Skip looked for weapons: he found hand-guns, four of them. Josh looked the guys over as he helped Mike up and onto a barstool. It was obvious that Mike's four fellow bandits were not professionals at all. Except for the fact that there were four of them, probably to intimidate Matt, these guys were harmless and in to this adventure way over their heads. Mike was tying up his thigh with a bandana and brushing the tile residue and pink insulation out of his hair. He had a mustard stain on his left sleeve and a ketchup stain on the right sleeve with also some on his chest; he looked like a Jackson Pollock painted mannequin.

Matt quickly and silently claimed ownership of the new pistol and aimed it at the other would-be hoods who just sat there and looked at one another.

Josh: "That was really ignorant Mike; even you aren't usually this dumb, what the hell is going on?"

Mike countered: "I want a lawyer."

Skip: "You'll need one along with a shoe horn to pry my boot out of your ass."

Josh: "Matt, are you Ok? Did they open the satchel? Now tell me what happened."

Matt told the story: "That guy over there, the one with the ketchup stains on his shirt- not Mike, the other one. He was at the Birch Creek Mining strip and he asked me for a ride to FAI. It seemed like if he worked at the mine it would be Ok, he just needed a lift to the airport. He said he was done for the late season and just wanted a ride to the Alaska Airlines gate. He had one small suitcase; it seemed Ok to me."

Josh: "So?" Matt continues: "So I say Ok and we find ourselves at 500 feet in a little snow doing 110 knots coming up on the Road House and he says he will buy me lunch and I say he can eat at the airport. Then he puts this pistol in my face and says for me to land. So, Ok, I agree to land. We're still a mile from the Road House flying along and I say, 'Oh shit' and look past him out his side window and so he looks too and when he does that, I changed the transponder code to 7700. Is that why you're here? Did you get a call about a hijack code?"

Josh: "No, we just came looking when you failed to show up." "Yeah, I thought we were probably too low for the transponder to relay the code. Anyway, in a thousand yards more we land on the highway, and after pulling in we are met by these three guys in the parking-lot, and a few minutes later that dolt over there, the one with the bloody thigh, drives in."

Mike: "Don't call me a dolt, it's not respectful and I'm not a dolt!" Skip countered: "Shut the hell up Mike or I swear I will bust your pathetic ass." "Mike, which is his name right? Mike takes the satchel from me and is about to leave in one of the pickups when this mental giant", he points to Mike again," decides that he wants a cheeseburger with bacon." He says he's buying, says he is sorry he has to disable my plane, and will do it after lunch."

Skip: "This is unbelievable."

Josh: "Then what?" "So, we go into the Road House and find that booth over there, the big horseshoe one, and order. They have me sitting in a booth surrounded by those two creeps and Mike says he is going to the men's room to "Tinkle"; he really said tinkle. And he takes the satchel with him, walks over into the Men's room and in a few minutes, he comes back to the booth without the satchel. I can't believe it, he went in to pee and forgot the damn satchel in the bathroom, and he doesn't realize it. So, I say I have to pee too and Mike says Ok but the Ketchup guy, the guy with the ketchup on the front of his shirt has to go with me."

Ketchup guy: "Stop calling me Ketchup Guy, I have a name you know, it's Marvin, got it? Marvin!"

Josh: "Ok Marvin; calm down a little, I got it, it's Marvin." Skip: "God dammit Marvin, shut the hell up or you're going to be next, I do have two boots."

Matt continues: "So the satchel is not by the urinal and I think it must be in the stall. And I tell him I have to take a dump and he says, Marvin says: go for it. Then he walks over to the window, opens it a crack, and then turns on the fan. When I find the satchel on the back of the stool I grab it and decide to make a run for it but he catches me before I can even get out of the bathroom. He's a big guy but he still moves pretty fast."

Marvin: "I'm pretty fast, I played football in High School and was a star."

Skip: "And I guess that was about the best six years of your life." "Comments like that are just plain mean." said Marvin. Matt continues: "So I kind of pretend to give up and we march back to the booth and just as he's about to sit down I trip him and shove him down against those other assholes and grab the satchel to make a run for the door. The other guys had trouble getting out of the booth and I might have made that strategic exit if Ted over there hadn't thought I was trying to run out without paying the bill. He tackles me hard, kind of grabs me so I can't leave, and I have to push him away and keep hold of the pouch. So, I punch him, and he grabs me again and his shirt gets ripped and I punch him again, this time pretty hard. Hell, we hadn't even been served yet. Why was he so worried about the damn bill?"

Josh and Skip turn and look at Ted and Ted looks at the floor.

Josh: "Ted, it's not your fault Ted, don't look so glum, it's not your fault."

Ted: "I know who's fault: God damn Haoles from da Taylor mines. My face be flatter then Mama's Pancakes. Look my shirt Josh; it be clean last yesterday."

Matt: "So then I hear you taxiing into the parking lot and I kind of decide to distract them; that's so you can come in without being shot or something. About then that other jerk grabs me, not the ketchup guy, but the one in the red shirt over there. So, I know I'm about to get rescued and I belt him, this time for real, this time I mean it. Then he takes a round-house at me from the right and I duck, and then I hit him hard, real hard. I got him with a good combination, a really good one two, and he falls backward, and ends up on the floor. I might have run for the door, but I went for the far corner where no one can get behind me and you guys could make a safe entrance from behind them. True, I was kind of cornered, and it's five and a half to one, but I thought the odds would be changing soon; and I still had the satchel. How come it took you guys so long to walk in? I was beginning to wonder if it was really you."

Josh: "We had no idea you were in trouble, Skip and I were covering the windshield with an old raincoat, you know, so it wouldn't ice up. It's a little windy and we had trouble tying it down. Skip wanted to have lunch here; I swear he must have a tapeworm or something."

Ted: "I am sorry Brah, really I am". And Ted sticks out an apologetic hand to shake with Matt as he introduces himself. "When I finally figure out who da bad guys it was little too late; sorry Brah, really sorry, guess I give da Stink Eye to the wrong Haole." I'm sorry too Ted, sorry for the punch out; are you Eskimo?"

Ted: "No Brah, Pacific Sea Islander; I from da big one, da big island, Hawaii. It's a nice place to visit but boring living dat place." Ted's wife was sitting next to him not saying a word; she was looking at her broken dishes and wiping some blood from Ted's face with a dishcloth. It looked like Ted's face would be messed up for a while.

Skip: "I'm so very happy you guys are now friends. You can bond a little later; maybe plan a picnic or something when it warms up.

Helen: "You be asshole Skip; real Haole asshole." "Sorry Helen, but this is serious shit." "Ya, so's my dishes, dat china don't grow out the sand Ya know." "Helen, I said I'm sorry! Mike, it looks like your leg was shot thru and thru; no bones hit, can you walk?"

Mike: "My leg? It's got a bad spasm, but it's wrapped with my bandana; the bleeding has almost stopped"

Skip looks around the roadhouse diner as if trying to make a decision: "So Ok now, this is what's going to happen. You four guys are going to get in one of your trucks out there and drive off; don't even think about coming back. Skip points toward the door and they just about ran for the door and were gone. Josh went to the door to see the planes were not disturbed: they weren't.

Skip: "Mike, you are to pay the food bill double and give Ted $50.00 for a new shirt and you give Helen another $50.00 for the broken dishes, and $100.00 for the ceiling, got it? Then you will apologize to these fine folks and never darken their door way again."

Mike: "Yes but" "No yes buts, you will do that, or I will beat the crap out of you right here, right now; got it? And if you ever refer to me as 'fat man' again you'll be breathing out of your asshole."

He is almost in tears, but Mike realized he has been beaten and it's a question whether he is just sorry he got caught or if he is sorry his plan went south. He may not be the brightest bulb on the Christmas tree, but Mike has feelings and they had just been crushed.

Mike turns toward Ted and his wife: "Ted, I'm sorry I tried to use your Road House for a robbery. Here's $100.00 for the broken dishes and burgers."

Mike gave Ted two fifty dollar bills out of a large roll of bills; even Skip was impressed.

Skip: "Are you listening at all Mike? I said pay the food bill double, then $100.00 for the ceiling, then $50.00 and $50.00" "What's the second fifty for?" "It's for the shirt, are you stupid or something?"

Mike: "Don't call me stupid, you sound like my mother." "Damnit Mike; Just do it and stop asking questions." "This did not turn out as it should have; you guys sure know how to screw up a good plan". With that Mike paid Ted another hundred and fifty and he grabbed a jacket and went out the door. Then he came back in, put the first jacket back and picked up his own jacket and left again. Skip watched as he drove out in the remaining pickup, he turned left, back toward Tetlin Junction, and Skip was willing to bet he would be in a bar in Tok within an hour, bragging about how he outsmarted Josh and Skip and kept from being arrested. The snow was almost stopped, and it had warmed up a little; it was almost 2:00 and they still had not eaten lunch.

Matt wasn't sure why they didn't just call the Troopers, but Skip told him the Troopers were already here: he and Josh. Then Matt said they should have been arrested for assault at least, and Josh explained that he was the one that punched out Ted and he was also the one that punched out Marvin's lights. Those injuries would have been the only solid evidence of a crime and he wasn't even scratched; the rest was "he said, she said." Matt nodded like he understood but he really didn't totally get it. Skip: "You are one tough S-O-B Matt, I think I'll show you a bit more respect in the future."

Josh: "Nobody really got seriously hurt except Mike. Skip was right shooting him but the paperwork for a Trooper shooting a civilian is unbelievable and we really don't want to open that can of worms; besides, it would be argued that we weren't in mortal danger. It was not only a bad shot; get some glasses Skip, but also might be argued, a "bad shoot". Hell; Skip would be lucky not to get sued." Skip: "Cut this post mortem crap; it's only about 5 below outside; we can have a quick burger and the planes will still start just fine. What do you say? Who wants a burger?"

Josh: "Do you remember what we are here for? Let's get this delivery over with and then we can consider lunch, Ok?" "So, I have to be a delivery boy and be on a diet to boot? This is total bull-shit, I want a damn pay raise." "You get twice minimum wage plus $2.00 per hour for your time on the ground. You get $50.00 for any flight under one hour; and $50.00 an hour for your flight time. You want anything more you can talk to Claire about it; and good luck with that."

Skip: "How long did it take you to memorize that little spiel?"
"I think it was the part of our wedding vows that she wrote; I was younger then".

Chapter (11)

Let's make some nuggets   mid-Feb. 1985

Josh decided to have Matt fly the gold shipment in the sealed and locked satchel to FAI in the 185, as planned, and go through the ordeal of logging in, and doing the Airport Security routine. Skip would go along riding shotgun and promised to say little, or in case of a small miracle, nothing. After much pleading from Josh, he promised to be civil when they were at the Security Post and draw no blood unless provoked. The security workers didn't know anything about the incident at the Salcha Park Road House, nor would they ever, that little incident would be part of an unwritten history.

Matt and Skip landed but instead of going directly to the Airport Security Post they taxied to and parked in Matt's hangar on the West ramp. They caught a ride with a security patrol around to the East ramp and then logged in at the Security Post. Josh was there waiting for them. The three of them drove Skip's Travel-All into town to the Bank of the North. Josh and Skip stood back as Matt did the paperwork. The seal was intact, so no weighing was necessary and the Bank Manager, Allen Balla, certified the delivery.

After driving back to FAI, Skip took his vehicle and said he would meet them at the store. While Matt did the unnecessary preflight, Josh went in and talked to the Shift Supervisor. He apologized for Skip's yelling and foul language and explained that he would do his best to not let it happen again. That bit of diplomacy seemed to smooth any hard feelings and they shook hands as Josh was leaving.

Matt flew the Maule back to the Valley from the right-hand seat; only Josh knew that Matt was acquiring hours for his Certified Flight Instructor rating (CFI). He had to fly as well from the right as from the left; for him it was a no brainer. That was one of a very few secrets being kept among the friends, another was that Casey and Claire were both taking flight instruction at Phillips Field in a Cessna 152.

It was moonlight and fairly dark, nearly 4:30, before they had the Maule secured and parked in the hangar. Matt was eager to see Casey. Although she normally was not working on a Thursday, she would be at the store just the same to celebrate the first successful gold transport from the Forty-mile. Jean had been concerned when Josh and Skip were late and had called Claire saying they were late. When they finally did arrive, Jean called Claire again, but she was already on her way back to the store and did not get the message.

It had been their first delivery and Josh was not happy with the results. Sure, the payroll and packages did get delivered but it was not how it should have been. There would be a better plan next time and a bit more coordination between the main actors. Though he claims not, Skip had gotten his juices flowing at the road house and now wanted to be a more active player in the security business. We will see how well that works out.

Claire arrived in time to get the story and was really taken by surprise when she heard about the statement when Mike declared that the FMA would not allow an arrest or even admit to the theft. Claire needed to know the details about the misadventure because that comment made no sense at all. Both Skip and Josh were sure he meant what he said but that didn't mean it was correct, it only meant that Mike believed it totally. Of course, FMA cared about security; why else would the FMA hire a transport security business?

Claire offered: "Maybe it's not the FMA but someone a little closer that Mike was talking about. Maybe it's Carter. After all, you work for Carter and he is the one that sets the schedule and does the packaging, the weighing, and the paperwork. He's at both ends, the source and the destination, and may well be right in the middle of this mystery. He is certainly able to affect everything going on that really matters. Pete might also be part of this scheme. If he is involved with the planning, he might have sold the information to Mike or whoever Mike is working for."

Josh: "I don't trust Pete but neither do I think he's crooked; I just don't know about him."

Then Claire added: "There is also the question of the alloy in the gold nuggets from the Birch Creek mine; what about that?

100

Remember, I did some Micro Probe scans on a few of those nuggets. They were all the same alloy which is very strange; and I'm sure they weren't nature's nuggets. I think someone is making nuggets. That is not illegal, but it is very suspicious because of the fuss they are making trying to hide it. As I see it someone is buying dust and maybe even bullion, melting it and adding a little silver and copper and other base metals, and then reselling it as nuggets." Skip: "So what". Looking at Josh: "Your miner friend in Livengood, what's his name? Ralph Sims, he's your Wednesday night poker buddy, right? He's been doing that for a couple of years now: It's no big deal, a lot of the smaller miners are doing it."

Claire: "Ok, maybe Sims and a few others are also doing it but it's not just a matter of a little dilution of the gold because that spread would barely cover the cost of the fuel for the melt. It's the nuggets themselves; Jewelry quality nuggets have been selling for a lot more than the melt value but slowly, sooner or later that market is going to dry up. Besides that, the markup has largely been with the retailers, not with the hard rock miners or the placer producers. And one other thing; there are too many nuggets coming out of the shaft and hard rock mines; nuggets should be coming from the placer mines."

Josh: "It's like someone is trying to disguise the source; who would do that?" Skip was thinking out loud: "Someone trying to launder gold bullion, that's who, that's my guess." Josh questioned: "Can it really be just that simple? There are many ways to launder greenbacks but how the hell would you launder gold except either through the jewelry trade or the mining industry?" Claire had an idea and said: "I would like to test a few more nuggets from a few more mines before we go public with this. Can you arrange a few samples? The test results would be interesting."

Skip: "I think so; I can probably get some nuggets from a few different Forty-mile mines for you to test. I get a pretty wide trade of mine owners from the Forty-mile at the Gold Bar. I see a lot of them on a weekly basis, especially in the winter. Most folks don't know it, but I exchange a lot of nuggets for a lot of booze. I have several outlets for raw gold; I'll have no trouble pulling back a nugget or two. Heck yes, I can just buy a few nuggets. They resell quickly when I need the cash and besides that I've been thinking of adding to my gold and silver investments for a while anyway. I think the gold price will be going up pretty soon anyway; it's a good investment. I think in 20 years gold will be over a grand an ounce, it will most likely more than triple in price. Then I can sit back in my wheel chair, wet my diapers, and count my nuggets." Life will be great and one hell of a lot less complicated than it is now.

Josh: "A thousand bucks an ounce? Are you serious? That little prophesy makes you a candidate for a urine test." Skip argues:" Gold is going up; ask your banker friend Balla, he knows about inflation and hard assets, ask him," Josh was having nothing to do with thousand-dollar gold. "Anyone with a brain would wonder Just what the hell have you been smoking? Tell you what, gold will be less than a hundred bucks an ounce in the year 2000 or I will wash and wax your car every Sunday for a month, fix your dinner, and I will also join your church. A prophesy like that must be the product of nearly a Holy vision." Skip was having a great time with this. "I am going to write that down and hang that little epistle of your doubt, and my wisdom, on the refrigerator. You better get a damn good recipe because there will be a lot of crow to eat."

The two youngsters, Casey and Matt, came out of the back liquor and tobacco storage room and into the office. Matt wondered what they missed; both he and Casey were blushing.

Casey: "Matt told me about the cluster-fuck and the almost-robbery at the Road House, I hope you do better planning next time. He wants to keep the handgun he took from his passenger. Can he, is that legal?"

Jean said with some pretend shock in her voice: "Where did you learn language like that Casey?" "From you"

Josh back to Casey:" I guess so; I'm keeping the shotgun I took from Mike. It's the second Ithaca pump shotgun that someone in that gaggle has handed me. They either have to learn how to fight better or else buy less expensive weapons, because they are going to go broke at this rate, Ithaca's aren't cheap," he said that with a twinkle in his eye.

Just as they were going to go over to the Exchange, Tommy arrived with six burgers and fries that Skip had ordered "to go" just after he arrived from the airport. It was almost dinnertime and lunch had been missed. Tony was a little early for the late shift and Casey said she would cover for Jean if she wanted to be involved in planning the next "Circle-jerk."

Jean: "Now where did you hear that one? Never mind: where's my hamburger? Tommy, are there any rare ones?" Yes: "Skip special ordered a rare one with extra onions just for you Jean; I think he cares!" "He better care, I've given him the best rides he has had in his golden years."

Casey: "Now Ms. Garbage mouth, where the hell did you learn that?"

The friends went back to the Exchange to eat the "to go" burgers. Casey and Tony handled the store as Angel guarded the left side of the wood stove.

The method of picking up gold from the FMA mines would be changed. Josh and Claire wanted nothing to do with a system that put pilots at risk. It should be easy to develop a better system, so a few guidelines were developed that sounded workable.

Claire said a minimum of two folks should be on every trip and there would be zero stopping along the way, and no riders regardless of their plight. Also, the flights would not even start unless there were good solid positive reports on the weather. The last point; and a good one, was the time table. The destination and the route would be known only to the few people who really needed to know.

These things seemed simple enough and when looking at events after the fact, it seemed surprising that these few guidelines had not been adopted before the first flight. Claire thought the insurance and bonding companies were lax and should have demanded at least some of these requirements before starting coverage. Josh thought it was the fault of his optimism and he promised himself to be more pessimistic and negative in the future. "Did I really just say that?"

The burgers were good and got better after they were lubricated with several bottles of White Zinfandel. Back at the store Angel got at least half of Casey's burger. Angel does not like curly fries and will not eat them, but she doesn't turn them down either. She just takes them to her secret place and hides them along with her very special satchel.

The light snow continued through the night. When morning broke it was wind calm at 20 below zero and there was a 10-minute power outage that was not enough to raise the temperature in the coolers but just enough to time get the Coleman lanterns lit and, of course, making it necessary to reset every clock in the store. Around 10:00 a.m. the sun started to rise over the Alaska Range to the south.

Soapies had run so well for so long that Josh was actually surprised when the #2 dryer went berserk. This time it was only the main drive belt, but it was one of the most difficult things to replace on the whole thing because he could not move the dryer away from the wall.

In the late morning Josh got a call from Jonny Beard asking if he would recommend Kevin Ferguson as a good A&P mechanic. Josh explained he was a good friend of Kevin's, so he might be biased but he thought Kevin was a good guy and a very good mechanic; he said Kevin was also a good helicopter pilot. About noon as Josh had hoped Kevin arrived from Bettles and made an offer on Jonny's business. They negotiated a little and in less than thirty minutes his best and final offer was accepted. Since Kevin had a good leasing history in Bettles the Airport Leasing Office at FAI considered him qualified to accept a transfer of the lease on the hangar. He only needed to make the down payment to Jonny Beard and buy the small parts inventory plus seventeen hundred gallons of hundred octane low-lead aviation gas and nearly five thousand gallons of JP4. It was a pretty done deal and Kevin was pleased.

Jonny also said as he was digging through a stack of parts and going through a couple of barrels of used stuff, he came upon the missing corroded cables from his old 185. Jonny wanted to know if Josh wanted any or all of the stuff.

Josh: "Yes, please hold the corroded cables and connectors and if there are any plastic straws and plastic tape on the cables don't touch them because they may contain sulfuric or nitric acid. Also, I want to see how it was all put together. Please just put the cables aside and I will fly over tomorrow for a look-see. Thanks for calling. That jerk from the NTSB has been prowling around. If you see him I would appreciate it if you said nothing about this discovery." Jonny said that sounded good: "Will do, see you tomorrow."

As Josh hung up the phone the Mayor of Fairbanks, Bill Walley, came sauntering into the store. He had a few other folks with him and was showing them the ivory and Native craft display case. Bill was saying that the Golden Valley Store had the best and fairest prices on ivory and soapstone carvings in the interior and quite probably the whole state. Josh saw they were all tourists because they had identical parkas and over boots. The Mayor introduced himself to Josh and Claire and also to Jean, though not nearly with the same grace. He then continued his sales rhetoric. Jean gave Josh a look and rolled her eyes as if to say, 'what the hell is going on'?"

Josh "Welcome to the store, besides the items in these two display cases we also have a new supply of sheepskin hats and vests from New Zealand. They are on the far wall over there right next to the raw wolf hides. The vests and hats are new arrivals to the Fairbanks area and will sell out quickly, so now is the time to invest in cold weather clothing."

Bill said: "Skip at the Gold Bar Lounge recommended a visit; you do have some really nice ivory pieces. Are you the same Josh Browning that had "Fly by Knight" air taxi in Valdez six or eight years ago?" "Yes, I was in Valdez then and my part time business at the time was, and still is, "Fly by Knight." But I never had an air taxi operation. I just worked there for an air taxi service and did a little contract cargo delivery on the side. I flew cargo when they had overflow work and they had too few aircraft.

105

Besides being Mayor, Bill Walley is the General Manager of a local radio station; he has a small news half hour in the evening and is a part time TV personality. Bill is well known around Fairbanks and although a conservative Republican, (what else would you be in Fairbanks?) He is popular with most all the political busybodies of both major parties. Bill's son has a radio slot that plays rock and roll music and does a fair amount of local advertising. Bill has no understanding of the music his son plays, none at all. Bill claims he can see good music and that the crap that his son puts out into the ether is just "an out of focus blur."

Bill: "Skip said he was thinking of selling the 'Gold Bar and Lounge.' If you are the prospective buyer he is talking about, I would recommend it as a first-class high-end business with a good future." Josh said: "I'll keep that in mind, thanks Bill." That was the first Josh had heard about Skip selling out. Why the secret he wondered? After Bill Walley and his guests left for dinner at the Exchange Instead of waiting for tomorrow Josh flew over to the airport to see the cables and connectors from his old 185. It took about ten minutes and he was on the ground talking to Jonny. After Josh looked at the cables he learned nothing, and suggested Jonny trash the stuff sooner than later. Jonny said he would put them in the dumpster right now; he had a bunch of other trash, 20 years accumulation of junk that he thought maybe he might someday use but never did. He filled two dumpsters and would be almost sad to see it go. It was Sunday, the 24th of February, and the last of the hangar trash would be hauled out on Monday morning. Kevin was supposed to take over the operation of Northwinds Aviation in one week's time, on the first Monday in March. Josh was sorry to see Jonny leaving the business but happy to find his friend Kevin taking over the operations.

On the flight home, light from the crescent shaped moon was slight but what there was reflected off the snow fields and made the trip to the valley a magical one; a flight into a beautiful blue tapestry of the imagination. Josh flew in silence and wondered how it would be to live in the trenches, on the ground, and never enjoy the complete feeling of freedom of flight, sad!

Chapter (12)

Skip's big change   late Feb. 1985

Josh was surprised about the news that Skip might be selling out of his bar and lounge business. He had not spoken of it and Josh wondered if Jean knew about it and if not, why not, how it might affect her. At first Josh had not been a big fan of Jeans, but after working around her for several years he had become used to her sarcasm and started to appreciate her harsh almost bitter sense of humor. He enjoyed her company and missed her zingers when she was not around, and he really liked her comments on life in general; Josh was concerned about her as he might be for a sister, albeit a very ornery and cantankerous sister.

When Josh finally caught up with Skip or rather when Skip came by the store two days later he got the real scoop on the bar. Skip was not selling out completely, but he had found a partner. This same guy also had the lease on the gift shop at the airport. Bill Walley had the wrong gift shop owner when he talked to Josh and Skip wondered if possibly Bill was not the right person to share his plans with. He thought that Bill Walley should keep confidential information to himself. It seemed Bill was only trying to help along the sale but that was the kind of help Skip did not need. Skip said: "I wanted to pick up a managing partner, so I can get away from the day-to-day routine at the bar."

He explained that the economy would be slowing down pretty soon and thinks business in Fairbanks, even running a bar, might not be fun anymore. He claims to have no debt at the Gold Bar and thinks his business can make money even if sales fall off by half; and more than likely they will.

Skip: "The story goes that bars are less apt to fail in a depression because the unemployed end up drinking in bars all day long. Let me tell you this; it's bullshit and it's totally not so. Bars are just as likely to go tits-up as any other business. Boom and bust, then boom again and now, soon, there will be a bust. This is Fairbanks, Alaska and I've seen this before. When I say its Déjà vu all over again,

I mean it. Have you ever seen a town when payrolls go to half of what they were? Well this will be a third, not a half, and this time it really won't be pretty. You're lucky that your business is out of town some ways. You never really were able to take advantage of the boom and your little store won't be hurt much by the bust. Just don't run up any big debt or credit card charges and you'll be Ok." Josh: "What are you going to do with your time?" "You'll see pretty quickly. I plan to lay back and cut my work load a bunch. I am going to enjoy myself for a change. I might even get another plane and fly around some and do some fishing." Josh thought: *Fat chance this guy will ever slow down and do some fishing; wonder what he's really planning?*

The phone rang, and it was a call from a satellite relay phone. The caller was a familiar voice that needed a gold pickup at the Birch Creek Mine. Carter wanted to schedule a pickup only, no payroll this time. Could Josh make a pickup on Wednesday, two days from now? "I also need six 100-pound propane cylinders and we will give you six empties to take back. I guess that means you have to bring the 206, is it running Ok now?" "Yes, it's just fine, it just had the hundred-hour inspection and its air worthy and ready to go." "If you can get back to me tonight with a yes or no answer, I would appreciate it." "As it stands right now I would say yes it will be a go, but I have to check the forecasts to be sure; I will confirm tonight by Satellite phone at about 6:00, Ok? By the way I now have direct satellite phone service, so the relay stuff is no longer necessary. I had it installed at the store because that's where it will be tended to most often. So just call my number at the store as you always have, and it will go through direct to here." "Sounds good, I will wait for the call. The air strip will be packed, and we will have some definition markers just as it was before."

Josh replied: "Good, especially in a snowfall I need the definition; whiteouts are poopy and flying the 206 I need all the runway definition I can get. Were you aware that we had some trouble with the last shipment? I called and talked to Hector about it and he said he would inform you." "Yes, I heard about it. That guy in question was a temporary, a cat skinner that was only pushing around snow, lots of snow. He should not have been given a ride back to FAI under any circumstances; that was a bad on you, let's make the next trip a good on you." "I agree but maybe you ought to do a little better job of vetting your folks; I think we can both accept a little blame for that one." "You are the guys that blew it, but I see your point. I will wait on your call tonight at six." "Oh, you were right when you said Mike would show up again. You do know it was Mike that was the brains in charge of the robbery attempt?" "If that's your definition of brains you might rethink your personal dictionary. Yes, I knew it was him: if that guy was any dumber he'd have to be watered twice a week. I remember the look on his face at your store two years ago when he was trying to be a player. The poor guy is really pained, and I'm not convinced he's a sociopath at all, I'm not so sure but I kind of think he hates what he's doing." Josh said almost sadly: "I don't know what it is about him, but I almost kind of like the poor dumb bastard. I'll call at six."

He hung up the phone and turned back to his second-best friend. Josh wondered what else Skip could say to shock him: and there it was.

Skip said he just had a checkup and was cleared for a FAA Class III Medical Certificate so the next time he flew it would be legal. He said that he might be looking for a Cessna 180 or maybe even a 182, a nice one; and then he really dropped a bomb shell. "I am going to ask Jean to marry me. Do you have any snide comments to make regarding my age or our age differences? If you do, let me hear them now or forever hold your unneeded and unwanted remarks." "Nothing bad comes to mind, in fact, if you just add your mental age to your physical age and divide by two you guys would be almost the same age; and my good buddy Skip, you should be prepared to be trained. Jean is very much like Claire and you better look out if you go astray. Marriage is defined as a partnership and if you do marry Jean you will be getting a full partner, not the quiet doting little womenfolk you have historically tried to ruin, so be prepared." "Screw you Josh and I hope your dog bites you." "Cold Skip, real cold." "So, what do you think, will she say yes?" "My guess is probably."

Propane tanks, twelve of them, were delivered to the west ramp hangar the very next day. Josh decided to maintain an inventory of six of them and if, by chance, they were not needed for a mining operation he would exchange them with his store customers. Matt was asked to fly the pipeline for an extra unscheduled photo trip and deliver the films to the MJA Photo Lab for rapid processing. Apparently, there had been some suspicious activity that needed clarification and documentation. Whatever the problem, Matt was not able to fly the propane delivery and gold pickup with Josh.

Skip reluctantly agreed to go but insisted on logging both legs of the trip as Pilot in Command (PIC) and Josh suspected he was looking for some FAA pilot rating other than Commercial pilot, single engine that he now has, or says he has. Josh wondered if he was even current, just wondered. The round trip went without a problem and since it took most of the daylight hours because of handling the tanks, the security service was required to buy lunch for the two pilots. Both Skip and Josh were thrilled. Claire was not and insisted on receipts and told the pilots ahead of time that she would pay for no more than a 15% tip.

Other small incidentals popped up now and then in the next few trips, but the gold transport security business made money from the start and proved to be a good earner.

Several weeks went by and Claire and Josh were still waiting for the big announcement from Skip. Maybe he changed his mind or maybe Jean said: "Take a hike." Then one Thursday afternoon Jean casually asked Claire if she could have Friday and the weekend off to go to Las Vegas with Skip to be married, and then two more weeks to honeymoon on Maui. She also casually mentioned that she would continue as the manager of the store. And further she would be moving her stuff out of the apartment, so Casey could have it all by herself, instead of sharing it. Claire guessed that when Jean moved out Matt would just move in; just a guess. They would worry the rent later, much later.

110

Jean had set a new schedule with Tony and Rita where Claire would only have to fill in on two or three days because she had hired, on probation of course, another new clerk.

Claire only said: "Fine, what took you so long?" "I would have said yes right away but the Big Man decided to share the proposal information with Mr. Fly by Knight even before he asked me. So, I thought he deserved a little training on couple's etiquette and I teased him a bit, do you blame me?" " Not one little bit, go for it girl."

Chapter (13)

New neighbors and a passenger north   Mar. 1985

Josh had been correct when he guessed that Skip was not about to slow down and take up fishing. Before his trip to Nevada to get married he finalized the process of selling off half ownership of The Gold Bar and Lounge. When he and Jean returned from their honeymoon on Maui they purchased both the Grizzly Air Taxi Service, just down the airstrip from the store, and the home and hangar that the taxi service had been using for their operation. Skip had been living in one of the apartments over the Gold Bar but it was just too small for the both of them and he really didn't like living in town anyway. He kept one of the Grizzly Air pilots on as an independent contractor. It was obvious that Jean's business sense had prompted that decision; it was that or hit the road. The pilot reluctantly agreed to work on a per flight basis plus the promise of a bonus at year's end. Skip agreed but really didn't like the bonus part of the agreement; but thought the guy would probably quit fairly soon anyway.

Things were changing quickly. Within a month's time Skip was the new owner of an Air Taxi license, three fairly worn out airplanes, a hangar, and a rather beat up house that was rumored to have last been painted by two Civil War veterans in the late 1800s: *at least that was the rumor.*

Jean and Claire had worked out a more complete definition of Jean's management role at the store. Jean Lathrop, she kept her name, would receive a 40% split of net profits on everything except the ivory and crafts sales which would remain totally with Claire and Josh. The store would ring the craft sales as a distinctly different class of merchandise. Josh would no longer have any responsibility for the liquor store or inventory. Jean would become the real General Manager and CEO while Claire would do all the books and be the CFO and write the checks. This should free up both Josh and Claire to pursue the work they truly wanted to do. The only one that it did not affect was Angel; she was still in charge of store security and would continue to guard and protect the store, the house, and very important, her treasure. Angel still visited her satchel of diamonds on a regular basis and became very nervous when someone would get close to her special hiding place.

Angel has been at the store better than three years now and despite the changes she still had the job down pat. Angel visited the hangar and the Exchange a few times each day whenever the store was open for business. This was 9:00 to 9:00 every day except the store closed at 6:00 on Sunday. She would still keep strangers off the store's porch until the store opened in the morning when she was there. It was a little confusing at first, but she finally figured out that although her home was with Josh and Claire she still had a much larger family; they just slept in different places. Life remained centered around her and the store; Angel was the queen and she knew it.

Then there was the Casey and Matt situation; Angel didn't know for sure, but she thought maybe Matt was also a family member. Only time would tell but Claire seemed to like him, so Angel did too.

Although Josh had recently been spending very little time on the liquor store management he felt relieved to be giving up the duties. He would do any emergency work necessary to keep the laundromat on line, but any non-emergency work would be done by paid contractors scheduled by Jean or Claire. Jean gave everyone at the store a pay raise of $2.00 per hour; the rate went to twice minimum wage plus $2.00 an hour for employees with more than six months experience. With the winding down of pipeline construction and many folks out of work this was considered a very good wage for non-skilled workers.

Skip was kept busy managing the air taxi service to many varied villages to the north and west. Grizzly Air had made a bunch of one-way trips to Umiat and he was puzzled by their frequency and the fact they were mostly one way. These flights involved well-dressed folks from the Midwest and he was pretty sure their business was not all oil related, and they sure as hell weren't all oil

113

company executives that were making these trips because most were packing heat and not trying to hide it.

The charters to Umiat were so curious to him that he decided he would fly a few of the trips himself. The 206 needed an overhaul on its engine but instead of wasting the shop time to overhaul it he bought a factory new engine and prop that Kevin at Northwinds would be installing as early as next week. Skip was sure the engine R&R would take at least a week or more. With the 206 getting a new engine, its 100-hour airframe inspection, and having the interior spruced up a little, it was like a rebuild of the entire aircraft.

Skip was planning on having the worn engine from the 206 rebuilt with smaller cylinders and then installed on his 180 when needed. That rebuild would be soon because the 180 had already passed its recommended time before overhauls (TBO) by a few hundred hours. Kevin, at Northwinds Aviation is happy to get the work because during the winter work-orders are fairly sparse. He made an agreement with both Josh and Skip that he would give them priority on any work needed if they would buy their fuel and repair work from him exclusively when they could.

On a calm Tuesday morning Grizzly Air was scheduled for a charter to Umiat. No return was scheduled so the plane would dead head back; a trip that would barely cover expenses. Skip decided to make the flight and was to find his passenger in the VIP lounge at main terminal at FIA at 9:00 am. He offered to pick up the traveler, Mr. Ralph Kelly, at the Northward building where he was staying but was told to fly only and not bother with other details of the trip. Screw you very much Mr. Kelly.

Grizzly Air insisted that passengers wear parkas and warm over boots when traveling during the winter months and supplied these items at no added expense if needed. Ralph was a little late arriving and it was nearly 10:00 by the time they were loaded up. As Ralph was putting on his parka and boots next to the plane Skip took his small pad-locked travel duffle and an overnight suitcase and secured them under a netted restraint in the rear baggage area. The duffle weighed about 18 pounds, about the same as bowling ball, and the weight was so unexpected Skip almost dropped it. He must have half a dozen Ruger Blackhawks in it.

The takeoff was normal, and it was a pretty nice day for mid-March. Crossing over the small town of Chatanika Skip pointed out the old FE dredge and the Poker Flat Rocket Range; the passenger was not impressed. After about a half hour into the trip Ralph asked: "How long will this flight take?"

Skip: "A little under three hours, we have nearly a 20-knot headwind today; it will be bumpy crossing the Brooks Range north-south divide but I will try to take it up a little to minimize the turbulence. If you are hungry we can stop at the Bettles Lodge for lunch; it's just a little out of our way.

Ralph; "Will it cost anymore to go there?" "No, this trip is billed by the distance as the crow flies, the cost will be the same, but you will have to buy my burger." "Really, I really have to buy?" "No, just kidding." "Ok then, let's go to this Bettles place; I brought my camera and will grab some photos if anything is there to photograph?"

Skip: "The lodge is a mid-1950s log building; it is beautiful and if you can get to your camera before we land you can get some really great pictures from the air. Like I said it is really a pretty building." So, Skip set in a heading of 305 degrees and Evansville (Bettles) was the lunch destination. The flight was textbook until they were just crossing the Yukon River Bridge over the Haul Road. Skip noticed the oil temperature a little above normal and it seemed to be climbing. The passenger was busy with photographs of the pipeline corridor and was unaware of the possible engine problem. The closest airstrip was Prospect Creek, but Skip made the decision to continue the flight into Bettles, which was only a few miles further. He had already decided to stop the flight of the 180: to go no further than Bettles. He thought he would call on the satellite phone and pay Josh to fly his 206 up to Bettles and continue the passenger's trip to Umiat. Also, there are repair facilities for the plane in Bettles, and food and lodging for his passenger; Skip figured out that there was likely trouble brewing under the hood. Now crossing over Bonanza Creek, the oil pressure was starting to fall, and he powered back just a little.

Twenty minutes later the oil temperature went into the red and oil pressure fell and was no longer in the green arc on the gauge.

The 180 was 21 nautical miles south of Bettles and Skip could begin to smell the hot engine in the heating vents. He had opened the cowl vents a while back and now went to full rich on the mixture; he further backed the power down just a little. They were down to 6,000 feet MSL and about 4500 feet above the ground. If the engine quit now they could glide about six or seven miles. Skip informed Ralph that there might be a small problem. They were now 16 miles out and Skip got on the radio to announce his engine problems. He was now on the 124-degree radial of the Bettles VOR at 119 knots inbound to runway 10. He tuned in Flight Services at 122.2 and keyed the mike.

Skip: "Bettles Radio: this is Cessna 82344 Sierra Charlie.

Flight Services: "82344 Sierra Charlie go ahead" "82344 Sierra Charlie is in bound to Bettles on the 124 radial at 6000 feet MSL making 115 knots 12 out. The engine is critical, and I expect a total failure soon. This aircraft has two souls on board; it is a red and white Cessna 180. We are now 10 miles from the runway with the cylinder head temperature off the gauge and oil pressure showing next to zero. I do not expect to make the Bettles Airport."

Skip tuned the other radio to 122.9 and keyed the mike: "Bettles traffic this is red and white Cessna 8 miles south east inbound landing on a right base to runway 10 with serious engine problems. Please clear the airspace: Bettles traffic." With that said he dropped the nose and further reduced power: the 180 was in a slightly powered glide. Switching back to 122.2 he announced. "Bettles Radio, 44 Sierra Charlie is on a 6-mile right base in bound to Bettles: will advise"

Bettles Radio: "Good luck Skip."

Skip just realized he was talking to Ray Ballantyne, the Flight Service Station Supervisor (FSS) in Fairbanks. At least he knew someone would be around to coordinate the search for him and pick up the pieces. Skip's mind turned away from the immediate as he thought about Jean and how he was so lucky to have found her and now, how unlucky to have so little time before he might be lost to her. At least she would have financial stability and be surrounded by their friends. Skip had zero optimism about his situation. They most likely would survive the crash into a stunted Black Spruce forest but would probably not survive the forty-below or lower night-time temperatures until the rescue effort tomorrow, at the earliest.

The Cessna was at 4500 feet 4 miles out when the Engine packed up completely. The whole airplane shuddered when the engine seized and totally, abruptly, stopped; the quiet was deafening. Skip turned off the fuel supply to the engine and radioed to the FSS.

Skip: "Red and white Cessna 44 Sierra Charlie is on right base 3 miles out landing Bettles runway 10. Engine unproductive at present, a Hemmingway quote I believe. We will not make the runway, 44 Sierra Charlie. My regards to Lisa, Ray"

Bettles Radio: "Regards hell, best glide speed must be around 70, airport road should be to your right half a mile, in front of you if you come up a little short, it's probably plowed and must be better than a spruce forest. See you in a few days"

For the last ten minutes or so they had been in and out of low scattered clouds and light snow. After clearing thru the clouds and some very low skuzzy foggy crap off the river Skip could see that Airport Road was indeed to the right and in front of the 180. It was now more than obvious they would not make the glide to the airstrip; though it might have been close. But the roadway was there just to his right and he could see no power lines and the road was as straight as an arrow.

Still while being too low to make the airstrip he was too high to get the Cessna down on the road. He got lined up well and added the full 40 degrees of flaps while side slipping to lose another hundred feet of altitude. Still they were too high as they came side slipping in over the road; too high, too fast. What little sun light there was came from behind him and the light was flat and there was little depth perception or definition; everything was just plain white. Skip brought the 180 down smooth but way too hot. Still the landing could have been Ok if the roadway had not taken a firm 90-degree right hand turn a quarter mile short of the airfield.

In spite of full flaps and ancillary promises to God concerning good behavior far into future, they were still doing about 45 knots when the roadway turned, and the red and white Cessna did not.

Fresh fallen snow is soft but when it has been plowed and sitting as berms for several months it is not quite rock hard, but almost. The road turned and as the skis hit the berms the 180 was way too slow to fly, but because of momentum and other fundamental laws of physics that Skip was ignorant of, the plane was launched upward in what could have been an arc but was in reality, not an arc at all. It was better defined as a total nose high stall from about 40 feet in the air. For the briefest moment the Cessna was nearly vertical, tail down, and totally silent. Though the plane was silent anyone listening might have heard one of the occupants utter;" Shit!"

Skip's old flight instructor and friend, Horace Black, had recently given him a Bi-Annual Commercial flight review and while he passed the review with flying colors Horace had mentioned Skip's flight planning and navigation skills were subjects to be worked on. Whether or not better planning could have saved the situation is a subject better argued on another day. But as Horace would say: "A nose high tail down stall from 40 feet of altitude is poor form." And it was that bit of aviation certitude that ensured 44 Sierra Charlie would never fly again.

The 180 hit the ground tail first at nearly a 90-degree angle. Nose down from that altitude would probably have killed both passengers but hitting the ground tail first let the aircraft's frame and seats absorb most of the energy and other than falling off to the left and having the passenger end up on top of the pilot, both occupants were more or less unhurt. The passenger rolled off skip and was out thru the passenger door quickly; he went scampering away from the plane into waist deep snow. For Skip it was more difficult because his seat did not break away from the rails and airframe and he was forced to cut his way clear of the harness and tumble into the back of the plane which was still at about a 60-degree angle to the ground.

The passenger's suit case and small duffle had escaped the restraint netting and the duffle had been speared thru and thru and ripped open by one of the passenger side seat-rails. The duffle looked like a shish kebab hanging on about the only thing in the plane that was neither bent or ripped. The seat-rail remained straight when the plane's fuselage had twisted. Skip had nearly been impaled but found instead he was lying on top of a small pile of eight gold ingots. That was what made the duffle so heavy, not some Ruger Blackhawk revolvers as he had imagined. Without missing a beat Skip slid one ingot down into his boot, managed to stand up and cut off the master switch, and just about head over heels he Jumped, kind of tumbled out of the cargo door on the passenger side of the plane in almost a somersault; but not quite. Instead he landed face first in three feet of snow.

There was no fire because the engine had been stone-cold minutes before the plane argued with the earth for a parking spot. As he recovered his senses Skip just stood back and said silent thanks for answered prayers. Ralph also seeing no fire climbed back into the plane to retrieve his luggage and duffle. Skip was wringing out a kidney on a Black Spruce tree when Ralph got back out of the plane with his belongings. About that time two pickup trucks came racing down Airport Road and stopped, or rather tried to stop. They ended up sideways in the middle of the roadway just about 50 feet from the crumpled Cessna. The drivers, one sober and one not, both had fire extinguishers, but they were not needed.

By then Skip was pulling out the emergency food kit and the extra gear he always took with him when flying in the winter. Summer survival was a little different, so the survival cargo changed with the seasons. Skip also got his over and under survival gun (20 gauge - 222 Remington) and his pouch of ammunition. Also, he grabbed charts and extra glasses plus bunny boots and the first aid kit; fortunately, it was not needed this time.

Skip had stacked-up only one airplane before; it was a Super Cub and he snagged the gear during take-off on a river bar. The accident was very much his fault and it could have been avoided if he had just been a little more diligent in his aviating and not been so cock-sure of himself. Horace, his friend and flight instructor, told him to always overfly an off- airport landing area and look closely: very closely. After landing walk the area, don't just look at it but walk it. Just because you landed doesn't mean there will be no trouble taking-off. And do it every time, every single time and scope it out thoroughly. So, Skip would go low and slow whenever he was putting his Cub down off-airport; each and every time he would go low and go slow and pay attention. But he didn't do the walk afterwards because It looked so smooth, it was nearly a quarter-mile long, and he was in a Super Cub: and besides that, he had been here before. If there was a moral or something to be learned it might have been: if you lower your boxing gloves, you most likely will get hit. It cost Skip a fine airplane and put a few dents in his ego, but he learned his lesson well.

This incident was his number two but already somehow, he didn't feel at fault. The first one with his Super Cub he freely admitted that he had "done dumb." This time he had cut no corners on maintenance, he was not hurried, he had not over stressed the engine, the propeller, or for that matter, any part of his airplane. He wasn't overloaded, the weather was good, and as his father said, longer ago than he wanted to admit; he slowed for the bumps.

Skip had no answers and felt almost foolish standing there surveying his crumpled airplane with not a clue what had gone wrong. A man like Skip who is used to being in command of most every situation is seldom lacking for words; he simply said: he never planned to do it again and summed it up with just one word. He said it was 'un-good'.

Men from the first pickup tried to help but there was little to do so they mainly stood around drinking brandy complaining about the cold weather. In a few minutes they lost interest and after taking a few photos drove off for a refill of their hip flasks. The two men from the second pickup were Paul and Chuck Mason, the brothers that had bought out Kevin and Molly's aviation business, home and hangar. Paul disconnected the battery from the plane and since it was going to be some time till they could pull the wreckage out of the snow and onto a trailer they decided to put it off till tomorrow.

Skip and Ralph were starting to cool-down; they were dressed well but not for the nearly 40 below that it was then. Skip asked if they could catch a lift to the lodge since his transportation unit, the 180, seemed in need of servicing. One of the brothers just looked at him with a blank stare while the other politely laughed.

Skip and Ralph were delivered to the Old Sourdough Lodge where they got rooms for the night. A message was relayed to the Goldstream store, to Jean Lathrop, that there had been an incident and Skip would need a plane to continue the charter tomorrow if possible.

They were settled in eating a late lunch when a Cessna 206 landed and taxied up to the old commercial hangar near the lodge. Josh Browning exited the plane and before doing anything else drained the engine oil into a large polypropylene container; he put a blanket over the engine cowling after tying the plane down and carried the oil container into the lodge along with a Coleman heater and fuel that he would warm the engine with tomorrow. The crash had been the subject of most of the radio traffic. Josh had seen the wreckage when he was approaching the airport and already knew from some radio traffic that Skip and his passenger were not broken and bleeding.

Skip could not believe Josh had gotten there so quickly but was happy to see him. Ray Ballantyne from the Flight Service Station had called Josh about Skip's problem and Josh had been in the air crossing over Clary Summit just as Skip made his less than perfect landing. Josh got the last available room for the night and made plans to deliver Skip's traveler to Umiat in the morning. Ralph said he had to go back to the wreck to find something he had lost but said he would probably be ready to fly in the morning after revisiting the wreck; said he lost some papers and his camera.

The Old Lodge at Bettles is really a fine place to visit and even despite the circumstances it was pleasant. Skip and Josh excused themselves and said they had to do some business. Ralph said he had to make a satellite call and would join them in the bar in an hour or so. He said he needed a shower and a change of underwear.

Josh: "Sounds about right to me, see you in an hour for drinks and dinner."

As soon as Ralph was gone Skip asked Josh if he had a camera. Josh said yes he did, but it was too dark to go back to the wreck today; Skip said he had something in his boot that required photography skills. When they got to the room that Josh had for the night Skip pulled the gold ingot from his boot. It was a one kilo bar of 99.99 gold that was issued and stamped by the Bank of Zurich. The top of the bar had been partially re-melted; enough so that the serial numbers were gone but Skip noticed that the mold numbers on the bottom were still visible in the ingot so the place where the ingot was cast was likely still traceable. Skip took a few pictures from all angles and then said they had to get the ingot back to the wreck plane, so Ralph could find it in the morning. Skip was sure that that was why he wanted to go back there. " I can put it back there now, I am pretty sure there's nothing out there that will bite but it is a bit of a walk."

But Skip thought maybe someone else would visit the wreckage tonight looking for "Light-finger Salvage" and it should best be put back in the morning.

Josh had maybe a better idea and said they should go see Ralph in his room and invite him for a dinner and afterwards a few too many drinks. Skip agreed, and they walked down the hallway a few doors and knocked. Ralph answered and accepted the complimentary dinner; since Grizzly Air had nearly killed him he felt he was entitled to a freebie or two. Skip ordered wine with dinner but before that they had a couple of drinks of 15-year-old scotch, three drinks. Two bottles of wine were consumed with the moose steaks and they had a couple after dinner Irish coffees followed by more Scotch on the rocks. Josh was fairly-well blasted, and Ralph was totally in the bag; amazingly Skip was just doing fine. They walked Ralph back to his room and when Josh was helping a very drunk Ralph Kelly on to the bed Skip found the damaged duffle and pushed the gold ingot into it thru the tear in the fabric caused by the seat rail that the duffle had been impaled on. He was sure Ralph would open it in the morning to make sure he had not been robbed during the night and Ralph would be happy to find the last ingot, and probably would say little because he had much too much to drink.

Skip put the duffle on the floor upside down making it look like it may have fallen from the chair next to the bed. That would ensure that he would open it first thing in the morning: with any luck. Skip wanted a night cap and Josh wanted to toss his cookies; they agreed to disagree and went their separate ways.

In the morning at about 9:30 Josh wandered into the restaurant and found a smiling Skip and a less than cordial Ralph Kelly. Ralph wanted to get to Umiat yesterday and if there was something to be complaining about he was already on his second rant. Skip pressed him on his trip to Umiat but Ralph was mute about it. He just claimed it was a routine business trip, but he did whine that there would be no extra pay for his lost day in Bettles. Skip reminded him there was also no added expenses, but Ralph insisted he should get extra pay because of the wreck. When pressed on it he insisted it scared the crap out of him: that's why! Josh predicted he would no longer need to go back to the site of the wrecked 180 and that proved true. Ralph had found or borrowed some duct tape and the small duffle was wound up tighter than a three-dollar watch. He was ready to go: right now, but first he needed a drink.

Josh had a cup of coffee and one slice of toast. Ralph almost puked when he saw food and insisted they open the bar at the lodge, so he could have some "hair of the dog". Though totally pissing off the Lodge Manager they did open the bar for him. Skip had a full three egg onion and mushroom omelet with a half inch thick slab of ham and hash browns on the side. He seemed happy to be alive and was humming a tune after talking to Jean on the Satellite phone. Jean had talked to Ray Ballantyne from the FSS yesterday afternoon and got the details of the incident. She already knew that Skip was Ok, and that Josh had arrived in Bettles, but Jean was happy to hear Skip's voice just the same. Josh had not seen him in such a good mood and wondered how after wrecking his plane he could be so serene. He said: "Piss on it; the God damn plane is history and I'm planning to enjoy the future, besides we're still on our honeymoon."

It was nearly 35 below zero when Josh filled the engine of the 206 with nice warm oil. He put the heater under the cowl blanket and warmed the 206 to slightly less than toasty. The plan was for Skip to complete the charter as the pilot and Josh would stay in Bettles and help pull the 180 out of the snow. He would rescue whatever was left in the plane and Skip would pick him up and anything that he salvaged on the trip back to Fairbanks. It was planned that Skip would not refer to the 206 by tail number over the radio and maybe, just maybe, no one would connect the plane to Josh. He was pretty sure that at least a few folks in Umiat were not his biggest fans.

Chapter (14)

The source   Mar. 1985

It took power winches on two pickups that were tree anchored to move what was left of the 180 to a trailer that would carry it to Kevin's old hangar. The 180 had been frozen in solid and did not want to move at all. The Cessna had a broken back, one twisted and one totally crumpled wing and the tail feathers were worth less than junk; almost all the sheet metal was twisted and even one of the landing gear struts was bent. The prop looked Ok but most everything else had been destroyed. The instrumentation was probably intact, and the radios and navigation gear were Ok also it seemed. The engine was most likely scrap, maybe the case could be saved but not many moving engine parts can usually be salvaged when an engine seizes in flight. Still there was value in the starter, the alternator, injectors and such.

A few hours later when Skip returned from his Umiat charter he sold what was left of the plane for twenty-two hundred bucks if he could get the Ok from his insurance carrier. The guys, Paul and Chuck Mason were brothers from Portland, Oregon, and they were on an Alaskan adventure that they hoped would never end; to the brothers it was just pure fun. They pulled the plane back to the hangar and wanted no payment and would take no compensation for their effort. They wanted fifty dollars a month storage if they could not have the plane for the agreed-on price; that was the same as the tie down fee for airworthy aircraft. Skip agreed to that and tried to pay them for a couple of months, but they refused and said the first month was gratis. Finally, they agreed to let Skip buy them lunch; paying the tie down might have been cheaper.

During lunch Josh and the two brothers were deep into stories of salmon fishing and moose hunting, each one trying to come up with bigger lies than the last one. Josh told the story of the 57-pound King Salmon that jumped into his boat while motoring upstream thru some rapids on the Gulkana River a few years ago but he was bettered by a story about an uncle of the brothers; their uncle killed two Bull Moose with only one shot. The moose had been standing side by side and both were killed by the same bullet. It was a shot to the lungs; the bullet didn't hit any ribs in the nearest moose and had enough energy left to penetrate the lung cavity of the farther moose; top that one my friend."

Skip was quiet during the contest of questionable and stretchable happenings; he was deep in thought. Now that the wreck was a thing of the past Skip had some time available to consider the present. The one kilo bars of gold that he discovered sprawled in the rear seat of the 180 stimulated his curiosity as never before. He absolutely-positively loved a puzzle and the more abstract and convoluted the better. He was not the least bit interested in taking the one kilo bar of gold he had hidden in his boot; he just wanted to identify the source. Ten Grand is well below his theft threshold, but he really wanted to know where it came from and even more curious why was it going to Umiat.

He thought the gold was likely being laundered, probably into jewelry grade nuggets but wondered why here, why not south Africa or Mexico, or anywhere but here. Transportation is an obvious problem in Alaska and he wondered if making jewelry quality nuggets was really necessary and why not just narrow the spread a little and sell it on one of the world wide black markets, why Alaska?

He had no answers to the puzzle until Josh said: "They must have a bunch of it to go to all this trouble." And after that statement of truth Skip was pretty sure he had it figured out.

Skip: "They must not have just a lot of gold; they must have a ton of it."

A while ago, nearly two years ago, there had been a gold bullion robbery in London that amounted to over five thousand pounds of gold and also a bunch of cut but mostly uncut diamonds. Some of the gold had been recovered but more than half of the ingots were still missing and thought to be unrecoverable and by now probably in the safe deposit vaults of the Swiss Bankers. Before returning the gold bar to the courier Skip had gotten a picture of it. Now he wondered how he could confirm that it came from the London robbery; to find out if his suspicions were correct. Josh was a bit more pragmatic and simply said:" maybe we should let Carter in on our suspicions and see if he could trace it somehow; maybe it was from the London gold heist, maybe not." "Or maybe we should just stay the hell away from this crap and not get involved at all." Said Skip. "The Reno Cartel is not the same folks as the Fargoettes. These guys are big time and would blow you away in a second; before you even knew they were after you. Let's not get them pissed off, let's do nice."

Josh:" If I wasn't flying gold from the Forty-mile I would stay away from this little mystery altogether but there might be an Coleville involvement there and I really don't want to be blindsided. Remember what Mike said at the Roadhouse about knowing where the gold came from? That contract Claire and I signed with the FMA was for one year only and this may convince me not to renew after the year is up. Skip questioned: "And what if Carter is in on whatever is happening?" "And what if he is? If you and I can find out about some laundering in a few months' time it's hardly a scheme worthy of Carter's time." Said Josh, and then continued: "No, I'm pretty sure that Carter's not aware of the ingots to nuggets if that is really what's going on. He may know the miners are making nuggets, but he most likely does not know they're melting bullion."

Skip: "Well at least we finally know how the phony mine on the Coleville River is involved." "Players from the Reno Cartel have an involvement, I am sure of it; how else could they be producing nuggets from a place where there has never been any significant gold found?" Skip said with a wide smile: "Crap, this is getting better than the God damn diamonds."

The trip back to the Valley took about an hour and a quarter. Skip flew under the hooded IFR Visor and though his hood time was rusty he did the entire flight holding both altitude and direction well. Josh tried to distract him with talk about the gold for nearly the entire trip. They finally did decide to talk to Carter about the gold but would wait until he came to the store; they would not talk over the phone about their suspicions.

After returning Skip spent about an hour telling his story to Claire and Jean. Jean was just happy to see him Ok and cared less

127

about the plane. She knew that just by flying in the winter Skip was doing something that was marginally unsafe, but she was cautious about calling it just bad luck. Jean wanted that engine torn down and inspected and wanted to find the root cause of its failure. It was more than just a gut feeling because she had read the log books of the 180 and knew it had been maintained by Jonny Beard at Northwinds according to Cessna and Lycoming recommendations. The plane might have looked a little worn, but it had passed its engine check during the last inspection with good compression numbers and she knew that the Continental O-470 engine was one of the best and most dependable six-cylinder power plants ever bolted to the front end of a plane. Jean suspected shenanigans: again.

Skip agreed to have Kevin either tear down the engine or go to Bettles and observe it being dismantled there. While arranging for the engine teardown he talked to Paul, one of the partners in Bettles on the satellite phone. Paul said they took off the oil filter and found it was really loaded with sand. Skip asked if they could pull one cylinder and hold it with the piston/wrist pin assembly for pickup tomorrow afternoon. Paul said he would do that, but it was a useless expense to make an extra trip up there to Bettles. The 180's engine had been loaded with sand and this was obviously done on purpose to destroy the plane; this was not an accident or caused by a marginal maintenance problem. This was positively absolutely vandalism, plain and simple. Paul said he was surprised the plane made it as far as Bettles.

Skip agreed: "I suspected it was something like that all along; I guess I don't need to see the engine parts after all."

He thanked Paul and said he was happy to pay whatever he thought was fair for a teardown. Paul said they had to do it anyway; it was gratis to him because the NTSB Anchorage office had asked for the teardown and promised a fat pay check for the effort. He said goodbye and hung up the phone.

Skip told his pilot not to fly their 206 or their Super Cub until the oil was drained and inspected. He was not to start either engine and would have a few days off until the issue was resolved. His pilot seemed angered with that news and threatened to quit if he did not get to fly the next charter, claiming he really needed the money. He said Skip took his last flight and implied if he had made the flight to Bettles it would have gone just fine. They finally came to an agreement where the pilot would calm down and Skip would not beat the crap out of him; also, that he was fired.

On Tuesday Kevin Ferguson drove out to the valley and inspected both of Skip's remaining aircraft. They were near the 25-hour oil change time anyway, so he did this work and both the Cub and the 206 checked out just fine. Josh also had his stable of airworthy steeds looked at and they proved to be Ok also but the 185 of Matt's that had been parked overnight behind the Exchange had raw sand dumped into the crankcase; in fact, some sand was spilled around the oil filler hole and was not all that hard to see. Matt will have to have the engine completely torn down, the case will even have to be split, and vapor degreased. The plane will be out of service for two weeks or more and Kevin will have to pull and then reinstall the engine right here in the Valley instead of at his shop at FAI; it will be a time consuming very expensive process.

Matt was unsure how he was going to photograph the pipeline on his weekly trip: one option was to borrow Skips Super Cub and handhold the motor drive camera; that might be a bit of a chore.

Skip suggested: "You might just slip in the photos from a previous trip in and hope no one would notice." "I am not even going to respond to that; I think I might just call Carter. I vaguely remember a missed photo trip clause in the contract but don't remember what it said.

The sabotage of the 185's cables when Josh owned it and the sand in the engine of Skip's 180 was curious; most non-aviation folks might not know the difference between the two planes and it made Josh wonder if putting the sand in the oil was meant for him. Skip's Cessna 180 was sometimes parked outside the Grizzly Air hangar and Matt's 185 had been a frequent visitor to the store, very close to

Grizzly Air: and both planes fueled up at the same pumps at FAI. The paint jobs were not similar but at night maybe not all that different.

Josh rightly or wrongly decided someone was trying to screw up his business and by extension himself. He also decided it probably wasn't a mental giant doing the mischief and he thought immediately of Mike Thompson; he would fit that bill to a tee.

He also decided this crap was going to stop and was going to stop right now. Josh needed a little help with this problem and told Kevin to do what was necessary; he walked up to the store to make a call to Carter Thomas. After two calls he found Carter's number thru his answering service in Houston. Josh called a local number that he did not recognize.

Carter: "Hello, this is Carter." "Carter, this is Josh and I need a little help, do you know anyway I might get a location on Mike Thompson?" "More mischief I guess? No, I don't know much about him, but I think Pete said he was back in Alaska. Maybe you could try Pete; he might know how to contact him". "Do you have a number for Pete?" "Yes, I do, I have several, do you have a pencil?"

Carter gave him two contact numbers for Pete. Josh also asked if he would meet with him, said he had some business to discuss that he did not want to do over the phone. They agreed to meet for lunch on Thursday at the Captain Bartlett lounge on Airport Way. Josh said he would try to get Skip to join them and Carter agreed to that. Josh tried Pete's first contact number; it turned out to be the Elbow Room's bar on Two Street. The Bartender gave Pete the phone.

Pete: "This is Pete." "This is Josh Browning, I need some help finding Mike Thompson; do you have any idea where I can find him." "You won't have much trouble with that. You would find him at Ruthie's down on 23rd if you were there right now. As I was leaving a while ago he was just coming in thru the door with a couple of other guys: Ya, just about half an hour ago." "Thanks, I owe you one."

Claire was just arriving and as she stepped out of the van next to the store Josh kissed her on the cheek, asked for the keys, and said he was on his way to Ruthie's.

She said: "What's going on?" "I am on my way to find the jerk that I think filled Skip's 180 engine with sand. I think I shall have a talk with that boy," Claire looked with curiosity but said only: "Be safe Fly-Boy and come home by dinner time or call. I see you have your Christmas present on, the driving gloves; how do you like them?" "They seem to fit well, I like them, and they are great for flying, and I will be home for dinner."

The trip into town took about 15 minutes but Josh did not hurry all that much because according to Skip, Ruthie usually lubricates her clients with vast amounts of liquor from her semi illegal bar before starting the negotiations. And besides, Josh would like to find Mike "half in the bag". He intended to get some information before extracting the repair costs for the plane. Mike could cover his own repair costs, or not, that would be his problem; but Mike or whoever did the deed, would likely pay more than just the repairs when Josh found him.

Finally, down on 23rd Avenue Josh found the building Skip had told him about many times. He drove into the rear and parked the van at the far end of the parking area. Josh took off his jacket in spite of the 15 below temperature, locked the van, and walked across the parking lot and up the back steps into Ruthies where he found a lounge and bar area. As Josh came slowly through the doorway he scanned the room and found maybe a dozen men that looked like pipeline construction workers drinking and getting friendly with five or six girls of varying age and ethnic groups. He quickly spotted his target on the far side of the room sitting on a deep red overstuffed sofa drinking something in a tall glass with an umbrella in it: a neat little red and yellow umbrella. Mike was with two other men and as he noticed Josh come in he had a look of question on his face.

As Josh approached the three of them Mike said: "With a hot wife like Claire I'm really surprised to see you here." He smiled apparently thinking Josh was at Ruthies for the girls. He almost certainly felt he was fairly safe and was likely only worried about losing his place in line. Josh walked toward the sofa and one of the men in Mike's group, the one with the heavy black beard that Josh recognized from the Road House incident started to get up off of the sofa.

Mike said: "Josh, meet my friend Todd; you might remember him from the Road House."

It's a law of physics and a fact of balance that to get up from a sitting position on a sofa a person must lean forward when rising. Todd did and without saying a word Josh gave this big guy a haymaker punch hitting him squarely, high in the nose and forehead. He hit him with such force that the crack could likely have been heard in every room of the house. The lounge and bar room went totally silent and only the rhythmical sounds of squeaky innerspring mattresses could be heard.

Stunned and half knocked out Todd fell back into the sitting position and was blinking his eyes and shaking his head slowly, trying to get his vision back after being hit. Josh grabbed Mike's jacket and walked back across the room toward the door; unfortunately for Mike he was still wearing his jacket and the two of them were headed out towards the parking lot; Josh forward on his feet and Mike backward on his butt dragging his heels. Mike's shoes were leaving black rubber drag marks on the well-polished hardwood floor of Ruthie's House of Pleasure; he decided he would apologize to Ruthie later. Josh opened the door, walked thru the doorway pulling Mike thru also, and then he slammed it closed.

The carved and decorated solid core door gave the entrance to Ruthies a look of class. During the summer the door kept out the mosquitoes and in the winter the door helped to keep in the heat. In this case the door was instrumental in changing the general shape of Sammy's face, Mike's other friend. Sammy had been trying to follow them out to the parking lot. As he fell back with a door smacked face and a bleeding nose he tripped up Todd, the first recipient of Josh's' anger. Todd had somewhat recovered his balance, and dignity and was trying again to join the argument.

As for Mike he didn't even try to feign ignorance. Even before he hit the rhythm of the bounce down the stairs he started shouting. "I didn't do it; It was Justin Littlejohn that did it. It was Justin that did it."

Mike's other friend Sammy, the one with the mark of Ruthie's highly decorated back door imprinted on his bloody face, made it back up to his feet and past the door this time. He ran down the stairs and came up behind them as Josh continued to drag Mike across the parking lot. He was about to Sunday punch Josh in the kidney but instead got an elbow in the teeth; Josh turned still holding Mike's jacket collar and smashed his right fist on Sammy's left cheek bone. Sammy was just an average sized man and Josh was surprised he did not fall. Josh let go of Mike's collar leaving him on his backside in the middle of the parking lot.   Sammy, now face to face took a roundhouse swing at Josh and was given a matching pair of cheeks; one bleeding badly and one just bruised. Then Josh hit him with a combination of punches to his stomach and ribs and this time he fell to the ground and stayed there. Mike partially cushioned his fall and it looked as though Josh was trying to build a stack. Mike then tried to stand up, but Josh wanted both men down and hurting and he hit Mike again, but with a less that full punch to the stomach, and Mike went down on top of Sammy. He struggled to get back up and was kneeling, trying to steady himself and beginning to stand up again but he still had a bad knee from an earlier incident. Josh pulled Mike back up by his now ripped jacket collar and sat him down on the hood of a car. Josh got in close, about six inches from his face and said: "Tell me the story and don't miss a name."

Mike: "Justin Littlejohn hired Todd to put sand in your Cessna's engine. He wanted me to do it and I said no. I really said no, so he hired Todd to do it." "So, Justin is in Fairbanks now?" "Yes" "And just how the hell did Todd do it?"

Mike: "He's coming down the steps right now, so you can ask him."

Josh left Mike sitting on the hood of the car and walked over in the direction of the back steps. Todd was coming down the steps with murder written all over his face. He was a pretty big guy and his black beard gave him the look of Bluto, Popeye's nemesis. The look on his face was rather frightening and Josh thought a little more blood might give his persona some added character. He had been hit less than two minutes ago and already he had two black eyes. Todd pulled a pretty large skinning knife from a sheath stashed under his belt and tried to take a sweeping slice out of our hero's face. The parking lot was slippery, and he nearly lost his balance as he took a big slice out of the frigid Fairbanks air. With his other hand he grabbed at Josh to gain his balance but instead lost both a canine and an incisor on the left-hand side of his now less than handsome face. Todd did not back down; he regained his footing and took one more well aimed thrust at Josh's stomach. As he lunged forward with the thrust Josh stepped aside and grabbing his wrist, yanked him even further forward. Todd dropped the knife as he had his left testicle inserted up into his groin an inch or two by a well-used size 12 Red Wing Field Boot with high traction rubber soles. He more than likely was not going to require the amorous skills of Ruthie's Ladies for some time. His eyes went crossed and he looked and seemingly felt pretty much abused; Todd needed medical repair to his manly parts but as he was moaning and falling slowly to the ground to compound his grief Josh hit him square with a right crossing punch that broke his nose in probably several places and opened a two-inch gash in his left cheek. He sat down hard on the packed snow in the parking lot and while bleeding out of his nose and cheek, he made the sound not unlike that of a horny goat. Josh stood over him and said: "Mr. Skip Davis sends his regards."

Josh turned back to Mike and his other assailant Sammy. Mike was still on the hood of the car straddling the hood ornament afraid to move; he kept saying he was not a bad guy and that Justin Littlejohn planned and paid for the sand in the oil of the planes.

He said: "I would have phoned to tell you what was going to happen, but I lost your phone number."

After settling with Todd Josh had calmed down a little but when he heard that crap he went ballistic and belted him straight off the hood of the car; Mike landed upside down in a snowbank.

Josh: "Don't ever say something that stupid to me again."

He walked around the front of Mike's car to punch him again and as he did he watched Sammy break an Olympic track record for the hundred-yard dash on packed snow. Todd was totally out of working order and Sammy was running for parts unknown. Josh grabbed Mike by his ripped collar and pulled him up and sat him back on the hood of his car hard enough to dent it. Fortunately, it did prove to be Mike's car.

Mike: "Please don't call me stupid; Mom does that, and it really hurts". "Fuck with my friends or my aircraft again and you won't live to see Spring Breakup; you have been warned." Mike tried to speak again but his voice was strained, and he had tears in his eyes; he was whimpering. His voice was high in pitch and Mike now had a bit of a lisp. He tried to speak, spit out a tooth and a little blood and said, almost whispered: "Ok I got it, honest, I got it; but you've got to believe me, honest I didn't do it!"

Josh was going to hit him again but really had a problem finding an uninjured target area. Then, as if to break the stress of the moment, Josh heard a laugh, almost a cackle. He looked up to the porch to see a handsome yet older black lady standing there looking down on the parking lot. Short sleeves at 15 degrees below zero did not seem to affect her.

Ruthie: "You must be Skip's friend Josh. Come back when a better mood strikes you; not for my Ladies, just for a drink at my fine bar." Then she pointed down at Mike and Todd. "I never liked those guys anyway."

Chapter (15)

Angel's treasure or business unusual   Mar. 1985

Josh drove back to the Valley slowly; punching out folks was not his forte and he was wondering if he did the right thing. Even if it was the wrong thing he certainly felt better about it on a personal level. Josh wasn't worried but would not be surprised to get a visit from the Troopers later in the day. He had decided to be what Claire would describe as proactive, and what was done was done.

Ever since his unintended involvement in the diamond mining incident almost two years ago Josh had been less relaxed and sometimes wondered if he might be better off as an ordinary charter bush pilot rather than a flying store keeper. The offer from Carter to fly gold from the mining operations in the Forty-mile District to the vaults of the banks seemed innocent enough, but the trouble on his very first day of deliveries was giving him some after thoughts.

They did not need the money that badly because after five years of college, a Masters, and a couple of false starts, Claire was finally happily pursuing her Geology career and doing well income wise. They also had sixty percent of the income from the store, and all the income from their ivory and craft business on the side. Even without his flying business Claire is doing well enough to support the both of them if necessary. Josh decided to have a conversation with his better half to discuss their future. He wonders if maybe the gold transport airplane business is too much too soon.

It would be turning cold later in the day, but it seemed that it might be winter's last gasp. The days were getting longer, much longer, and very soon winter's ice will be totally gone. And after that; Green-Out.

Usually in early May, the Aspen trees that grow on the hillsides of the Goldstream Valley turn from the dingy grey-brown of winter to the vibrant green of Spring and Summer. This event usually happens in just one day: "Green-Out". This is the day of almost universal optimism; maybe the best day of the year.

Breakup is always a time of dirty water and lots of mud. The store has to be mopped almost daily during breakup even though a lot of the regular customers leave their breakup boots at the door before entering the store. Some of the local folks are really nice that way: most are.

Angel sometimes guards the boots on the front porch and once when a bespectacled farsighted customer tried to take someone else's boots by mistake Angel let him know about it. She insisted he not leave with the wrong boots by keeping him on the porch and quietly barking; something she seldom did. Casey had sorted out the problem and Angel got a head pat from the almost thief and a jerky from Casey for her diligence.

Angel's family has grown again and now it also includes Matt. Her family is big, almost too big for her to handle by herself; her friend Spider was either no help or less help than needed, depending on the day. According to Angel, Spider is a nice dog and a good friend, but dumber than soup. Plainly, she just felt like a poor totally overworked guard dog.

A few days earlier in the week the water softener at Soapies did not back flush properly; it kind of worked half time but was wasting hundreds of gallons of water. Gary, the repairman, got busy repairing it and Angel spent most of the afternoon watching the repairs. The water softener is in the back room of the laundromat very close to Angel's well-hidden satchel of diamonds. Gary had been there before and had given Angel some great ear-rubs. Angel remembered Gary and knew him to be a good guy but when he was moving around some bags of water softener salt he was getting dangerously close to her small satchel of diamonds; at one time she thought she might have to chase him away. Angel didn't but she decided that maybe soon she would have to give up her treasure whether Josh asked for it or not.

It was getting too complicated for Angel to handle everything that needed guarding. Life had been a lot less complicated when her family was only Claire and Josh, and although she loved her large family she wished for that simpler time in her life to return.

When Josh arrived back at the store from his visit to Ruthie's Angel finally made her decision. So, a few days later when Claire and Josh were both at the store and after more thought she trotted over to Soapies and retrieved her treasure. She struggled thru the Doggie door and went behind the stacked bags of salt, rooted around with her nose, and uncovered the treasure that was hidden down and under an old green tarp way back in the corner. Angel grabbed the satchel that still had the scent of Pete on it and carried it across the parking lot and back inside the store. She just dropped the satchel on the floor between Josh and Claire and stood up putting her paws up on her master's shoulders giving him one nose lick, just like she always did. The nose lick usually made Josh very happy but today he smiled even wider. Angel got down on all fours, she wagged and strutted and knew she would soon get a treat; maybe a jerky she hoped.

Claire picked up the satchel and said: "Isn't this the bag Angel took from David Littlejohn when he and that fool Bob Adams stole the paperwork for the lease options?"

Josh looked and said: "I think so, let's have a look see"

The zipper was salt corroded and would not slide open. Josh took out his new skinning knife compliments of a not too skilled street fighter named Todd, but instead of cutting open the satchel Claire stopped him and produced a spray can of WD40 from under the store's checkout counter; she sprayed a little on the zipper. A customer came in and paid for a tank of gas and then another one picked up a 12 pack of Budweiser. The zipper soaked and in just a few minutes and with only a little massaging, Claire was able to unzip it.

Claire: "Nice knife, where did you get it?" "A guy named Todd reluctantly gave it to me a few days ago. He might someday get it back pointy end first, but probably not today." "Do you have any other confessions to make or do I have to find out what happened by way of the Skip Davis grapevine?" "Ya, well Ok, I ripped the knuckle of one; check that, on both of the driving gloves you gave me for Christmas. One was ripped on a guy named Sammy with badly bruised and damaged rather high cheek bones and the other on a couple of teeth from his friend Todd, the blood is also Todd's. Mike was there also but I took it a little easier, just a little easier on him. It turns out he was not all that much involved with Skip's plane though he did apparently know about the sand and grit ahead of time?" Josh continued:" Poor Mike; Mike wants badly to be a bad guy, but he just doesn't seem to have it in him." "Sorry I asked and let's just drop the poor Mike laments. He isn't worth it and I'm getting damn sick and tired of even thinking about that mental giant. Let's just see what's in the bag, let's see what the big fuss was all about; my God, they are beautiful; Josh, just look at these!"

Josh: "These don't look like the few stones Carter showed to me and Skip, something's funny here, these are not the same stones; I wonder where they are and why these are so smooth and shiny?" "Sometimes the diamonds that come from way down deep, I mean miles deep, get steam polished from the super-heated acidic gases in the depths. About one in twenty comes out of the ground looking this way, I think; look at the color depth in this one." Josh: "These are going in the safe and nobody is to know about them for now, right? Nobody, besides the two of us and our head of security; Angel." She heard her name and wagged and then after a few struts she just laid down next to the wood stove. Josh: "Are we here alone today, where is our afternoon help?" "Tony comes in at one, ten minutes ago, why?" And just then Tony came in thru the door, wet and cold. Tony: "I slid off the road and had to dig a small trench to get back on. So sorry to be late Claire." "It's Ok, don't sweat it. Just handle the register for a few minutes and I'll be in the office for ten minutes or so. When I get back you can restock the Pepsi and Coke coolers, Ok?"

With no customers left in the store Tony went to face the beer six packs in the cooler and then to the shelves displaying the whiskeys and other brown liquors. He found the broom and swept the dried mud from the entrance and then from the porch. There usually was not much going on at the store in the early afternoon. Casey was at the University and scheduled to show up at 5:00 to work with Tony until closing at 9:00.

After Claire was finally able to see the diamonds her attitude had done did a 180 degree turn. She quickly changed from a reluctantly involved distant player in the diamond scam to a "Holy cow! Look at those stones"; an enthusiastic partner. There were 29 stones nearly a half inch in diameter and 3 more, slightly larger and better polished. Neither of the Dynamic Duo had a clue what to do next. Angel understood only that they were very happy when she gave them her treasure and she was proud of the part she played by taking and hiding the treasure when she did. The excitement had not faded, and Angel got back up and walked around in circles with her hackles up strutting her stuff; she had her tail straight up, was really in charge and let everyone know it. Claire gave her some nice ear-rubs and said, "Good girl". Angel laid back down and quickly went to sleep.

Claire decided to have dinner at the Exchange next door so there was no need to plan the menu. She had a little paperwork to do at the store and to write the checks for the Friday payday. She said she would be done with the paper work around five. Josh would take her car home and park it in the garage next to the van when taking the diamonds to the big safe in the bedroom.

Sir Josh said: "I will accommodate your chariot posthaste with only the finest resting area and will be back at six to dine with thee; we shall have a fine dining experience." "What is this posthaste crap; are you a Bush pilot or a writer of poorly concocted prose?" "I am an Airship Pilot with a poetic flair and an amorous heart; beware and be prepared fair maiden." Claire: "I will hold you to that."

Angel woke up when Claire started to sound harsh; *"There they go again."*

Josh took the stones and drove the jeep down the road to their house; before locking the diamonds in the larger bedroom safe he counted them again and found one more, a cut and polished stone that was stuck in the lining of the satchel. There was now a total of thirty-three diamonds.

He needed to burn off some nervous energy and went out into the hangar and was cleaning the windshield on the Maule again when he got a call from Kevin at his hangar at FAI.

Josh had asked Kevin to install Car Alarms on both of his planes and they just arrived via the trusty US Mail Service. Kevin said he will install them whenever Josh gets the planes to his hangar and Josh said how about now? There is a payroll to be delivered on Thursday and a gold pickup to be made at a mining operation just a few miles from the delivery. The Maule is the plane of choice for the pickup and that is the plane he wants the alarm to be put in first. Josh said he will fly over right now, fuel the plane, and hang around while the alarm is installed.

Josh called the store and told Claire he was going to the airport to have an alarm installed.

Josh: "The "Stuff" is in the safe and I will be back before six; early dinner time."

The diamonds were locked up in the very well hidden safe and he needed some time to think about the situation. A trip to the airport was welcome to clear the gray matter and let his brain slow down to normal.

He started to call Claire to say he would be gone for an hour or so; that he is going to fuel the plane and then remembered that he just did call her. He had to slow down, relax and think a little.

After a very complete preflight from a checklist Josh took off for the short trip to FAI. He landed on 1 Right, departed the active runway at mid field and taxied the Maule over to the Northwinds. While Kevin installed the alarm, Josh borrowed the golf cart and drove it wide around the north end of the runways to the west ramp and found Matt in his hangar changing the oil yet again on his now repaired 185 getting ready for another pipeline surveillance flight.

Back at Northwinds after fueling the plane Kevin had strapped the alarm under the front seat of the Maule in less than ten minutes. The alarm is a simple device. It is twin "D" cell battery powered and reacts to movement of the plane. Wind will probably also activate the alarm, but Josh says he is willing to react to some false alarms in order to insure a bit more safety. It is self-contained and is activated by a single toggle switch. It is simple; after parking the plane the pilot only needs to release a lever to level the device and then retighten it. Then simply flip the toggle switch to ON and the alarm is set.

Josh: "That's the third oil change, what's going on?" "It's only the second; I flew it for three hours and Kevin said to change it and save the filter for him to look at. You do know that Kevin just disassembled my engine and while it was down I had him put in new rings and rod and cam bearings, and I also had him clean up the valve seats. "How the hell did he do all that in just three days?" "I pay him by the job, not by the hour." "I'll remember that in the future."

Matt: "To what do I owe this visitory honor?" "Is visitory even a word? I'm having Kevin install a motion alarm in the Maule. I think we should put them in all our planes. "How much will they cost me?" "Nothing, I bought four of them. They are battery powered and not attached to the planes electrical system. It doesn't even require a Log Book entry. "How much noise do they make?" "I'm not sure of the decibels but it's advertised to be heard at five hundred yards: enough so it will be annoying." "Sold!"

Chapter (16)

Whose diamonds are they anyway?   Mar. 1985

When Josh flew back and returned to his hangar he closed the Bi-fold door and again cleaned the Maule's windshield. He was still going in all directions doing about anything to burn off his pent up nervous energy. He set the new alarm and gently closed the pilot's door. Just to check it once more he rocked the plane just a little and quickly wished for ear muffs. The hangar was filled with an ear-splitting squeal that left no doubt he would hear the alarm from inside the house; he might even hear it from inside the store up the road a hundred or so yards.

It was just about dinnertime and he remembered Claire wanted dinner at the Exchange but as he walked into the house the smell of roast chicken was in the air; neither his nor Angel's favorite. Someone had put a chicken in the oven and it didn't take Sherlock Browning Holmes to guess who. Claire would be walking into the house in twenty minutes. Josh let out a sigh of submission and went to his liquor cabinet for three fingers of Black Label Jack Daniel's Bourbon and two ice cubes: five is his lucky number. Black Jack over ice is his favorite sipping drink and after turning the TV and finding the channel most likely to have the day's news he sat back in his recliner and smiled because he now knew where the diamonds, Angel's Diamonds, had come from.

It was no big revelation and just obvious as hell, after Skip speculated that the gold came from the Brink's Mat Gold robbery at Heathrow, England. This robbery dominated the news in November of 1983; it was the biggest gold heist in the history of London, maybe the entire world. If the ingot that Skip photographed was indeed from the Bank of England's inventory it would be nearly certain that the diamonds also came from the heist. Josh considered the timeline and it matched what he knew about the robbery in London; which was little more than what he remembered reading in the paper. There were around seventy cases of one kilo bars stolen; less than half of the two and a half tons of ingots were recovered. Only a few of the robbers were ever arrested, two had been murdered by their fellow bandits, and none of the diamonds were ever found; as he remembered it.

The Adams Crime Family, big time players in London organized crime, were the suspected perpetrators of the robbery and eventually two of them were convicted of the crime. The diamonds were worth wholesale only a few hundred thousand dollars, nothing compared to the value of the gold and so it seemed that little effort was ever made to find the stones. Someone should have considered that the diamonds might well be a road map to the stolen gold bars and maybe that part of the investigation should have been pursued a little more. Josh had the diamonds and the question was where and how did they get separated from the main body of the loot?

Carter Thomas had been in possession of the diamonds; how did he get them? Also, he seemed to care less if they ever surfaced after Angel took them from David Littlejohn and Bob Adams during the robbery of the mineral rights and lease options. Josh always thought that part was strange; he wondered at the time if the stones had any value, maybe they were only quartz or some other worthless mineral.

Then a new thought struck a note; Adams, Bob Adams; is he involved in the London Crime family or is the name just coincidence? Adams is a fairly common name but just the same maybe Bob Adams is a player and not just a hired goon.

Then the later incident with David's father, another thing that stuck in his mind that never made sense was that strange comment by Jim Littlejohn. "Give me my diamonds." That seemed to indicate the diamonds were really his. If he was just stealing them he might well have said "Give me the diamonds", but he didn't. What Jim Littlejohn plainly said was: "My investors want the diamonds, Give me my diamonds."

Strange how just a twist of two words could stick in his mind. Josh usually thought things out and considered most everything and this was one of the things that stuck in his mind as a mystery; Josh thought this part of the puzzle may now be pretty much solved.

He heard the kitchen door open and Claire walked inside and went straight to the liquor cabinet for a drink. Claire picked an 18-year-old scotch, poured it on some ice made by the only new appliance they had ever owned, and sat down on the arm of the recliner next to Josh. "What the hell do we do now?" Angel half sat down next to the recliner and also waited for the answer. Josh: "I'm working on it Watson, really working it."

The day came and went with zero good ideas emerging about the diamond situation. There was no news from Skip about the mold number from the gold bar that they had photographed. Josh thought that the mangled taped up duffle was now at the mining operation on the Coleville and he was pretty sure the ingots were either now being melted down and made into nuggets for the jewelry trade or soon would be.

It would not be a stretch to assume that whatever was left of the Fargo Group was aware that either Skip or his friends had possession of the diamonds. But a year had gone by and besides the attempted robbery at the Salcha Park Roadhouse by Mike Thompson and his friends, nothing seemed to indicate that anyone cared what the folks from Goldstream Valley were doing; which was very curious. And there was no reason to believe the roadhouse incident was in any way connected to the Coleville River operation. The only thing that Josh could do was to wait and see if Skip could verify that the gold bar was one of the ingots stolen in the Brinks Mat robbery and there was really no way of ever knowing for sure. All they had was a mold number and there might well be hundreds of them with the same number. And if it was proved to be one of the missing bars what then? And if it wasn't, what then?

Thursday morning Josh flew to FAI and borrowed the Crew-car from Kevin for the run to the Bank of the North to pick up the payroll for delivery to the Birch Creek Mine. He locked it in the safe in the hangar and as he did almost every time he locked the safe he pressed a large grain of black pepper in between the dial and the body of the lock on the safe. The pepper was not obvious to anyone besides Josh. He had yet to find the lock disturbed but intended to keep doing this just as a precaution.

145

Later in the afternoon tomorrow he was supposed to deliver the payroll to Birch Creek and still later pick up a shipment of gold at the North Palmer Mine and transport it back to the bank; kind of a round trip, double pay for that day. A few more trips like this and he would have the Aviation overhead pre-paid for the rest of the year; cool!

Matt came back from his latest pipeline surveillance photo trip in the early afternoon and after delivering the films to MJA studios and changing his oil yet again, he was free for the next four days. Matt planned on going with Josh on the payroll delivery and gold pickup job; he said he wanted to earn enough to treat Casey to a nice dinner at the Exchange and maybe, just maybe, he would propose to Casey, to give her the ring that he has been carrying around for the last two weeks. He mentioned this to Josh and asked what he thought about a proposal.

Josh thought about it and reluctantly said: "I got in the middle of Skip's proposal to Jean Lathrop a while back and was yelled at by two of my three favorite ladies, and now you want me to give advice about the other one. Not going to do it; besides that, I'm not Ann Landers you know and I sure as hell am not qualified to give council or any other sage advice about something this important; Just the same, go for it".

They left the 185 parked in the west ramp hangar where it belonged and only one electric heater that might, just might, keep the hangar around 15 degrees. They flew back to Goldstream Valley in the Maule. They would leave from FAI after picking up the payroll in the morning and fly to the Birch Creek strip. Matt asked why not bring the payroll to the valley and leave from there in the morning like the first time they made a pickup?

Josh: "That might be easier, but the west ramp hangar is our headquarters for the secured transport business and I think we should operate from there. I've kind of decided to keep any possible major conflicts away from the store and our employees."

That made sense to Matt especially since he had an interest in keeping Casey safe. The incident they had last year was exciting and it worked out well for the folks at the store, but someone could have gotten badly hurt, in fact someone did, but luckily it was not store personnel. Claire was the first of the Dynamic Duo to speak up, but Josh agreed it was not fair to put good employees in harm's way; Matt understood and agreed with the choice, it made sense.

Casey had a special request and wanted to treat everyone at the store to a nice dinner. She arranged for one of the larger tables to be reserved at the Exchange and picked out the wine for the table. Tommy was thrilled to have the crew from the store on a Thursday night and offered Casey a discount as long as she didn't tell Don about it. That bit of information was not news to Don, he had the discount deal figured out long before it was even offered; he passively agreed with the offer. The store closed early at seven o'clock with the "Gone Moose Hunting," sign taped on the front door. That was very unusual for the few customers who showed up to shop and found a locked door instead. Jean said, "They'll get over it."

Skip and Jean were at the Exchange and sitting at the bar by six thirty, Tony and his girlfriend showed up around seven, Rita came alone but claimed to have two appetites. Josh, Claire, and Matt were on time at seven and Angel was slow arriving because she was doing the last of her rounds. Casey was just a little late though it was excusable because she had been in the kitchen supervising Don's work. Not necessary according to Don but he knew what was going to happen and approved. The menu had already been chosen; this was not everyone order for themselves. Casey planned the food with Don and he said she had a good palate and put together a rather fine combination of standard menu items that were highly complementary to one another. Don had no special prep work to do for a customized dinner and was impressed that Casey even knew about prep work. Casey offered that she was 22, not 12, and as she gave Don a peck on his cheek he thought: "not too bad for a girl."

Between the soup and salad and entrée Casey said she had a little special something to say and when it was time she simply approached Matt, got down on one knee and proposed marriage to the man of her dreams.

147

Chapter (17)

So where is the booty and who owns it?   Mar. 1985

Matt and Casey set their wedding day to be in early June. They would honeymoon in February in Hawaii, 1986. They already live together but it will be their first real vacation, their first time to get away from the real world just lay back, relax, and smooth it. The plan to marry was not a surprise but the way it came about was equally not expected and the group of friends was very pleasantly surprised.

Casey has a PHD in Physics and is a nonemployee, an intern, at the Mapco Refinery south of Fairbanks in North Pole. Matt does not have a degree and barely made it through high school. He is a good, very good natural athlete and had his grades been better he might well have gone to one of several colleges on a football scholarship. But because of bad study habits or whatever, he chose instead to enter the aviation profession, as a pilot operator. While his dad helped him with the purchase of his first plane, Matt has done the rest by himself; and has performed fairly well, actually very well.

Matt earned his Commercial Flying License in the absolute minimum number of hours necessary to satisfy the FAA. He worked as an assistant guide for Bud Hastings, a Master Guide, for a while before accepting a contract, to do pipeline surveillance flying, from Carter Thomas, whose company is in charge of pipeline surveillance north of the pump station just a few miles south of Fairbanks. Matt is also a free-lance pilot and picks up a flying job here and there; he sometimes works for the store, or rather Goldstream Aviation Services, on necessary trips that Josh can't make because of other commitments. He has also promised to fly a few flights for Skip until he finds a pilot. He just fired the old one and needs some help. Skip promised no permanent work but so far Matt has flown more than he really wants.

Josh must keep reminding himself that Matt is not dumb; he is just young and has never spent much time planning and looking ahead. It's not possible to be a good long-time pilot without thinking ahead. It may be weather, it may be choosing a route or just plain lining up with the runway for landing; but a pilot must think ahead or quit flying; or flying will pop up and quit him. Planning rather than reflexes will keep a pilot alive and well; that was a quote from Horace Black. It is almost impossible to achieve success in most flying situations without planning: period! It's like skydiving and parachutes: "you don't need a parachute to skydive, you only need one if you plan to do it twice," that quote came from Casey.

After dinner Skip found himself having drinks with Josh while Tommy was busy giving a pool lesson to Tony and Matt. The ladies were busy getting into planning everything including the wedding reception and were already deciding where the happy couple would live, how many children they would have, and many other important things they could almost agree on.

Skip was frustrated waiting for information about the ingot mold numbers promised from a friend he has had in the Treasury Department from so long ago he hardly remembers the man's face. Robert Ross was the man and ever since Skip guided him on a successful Grizzly Bear hunt twenty-five years ago Skip has received a hand-written note with a Christmas card; every single year. Skip always responded, and the notes usually ended with a promise that Ross would revisit Alaska in the next year or so and they would get together for drinks. So, on a hunch that he might know or know how to find the information, Skip wrote to Ross asking if he had any information about the mold numbers of the London gold ingots. Skip said he was writing a murder mystery book and needed the information for accuracy of the writings. That was a bit of a stretch.

The discussion between Josh and Skip was, of course, about the diamonds, and the possible location of the missing two thousand pounds of gold bullion that both of our heroes were sure came from the Bank of London. Skip ventured that two thousand pounds of gold would be well beyond his ability to stay honest and should they ever find the booty, it would be up to Josh to keep them on the straight and narrow. Josh said he would pass that job over to Claire.

Skip had been involved in the attempted robbery at the Salcha Park Road House and at the time wondered what Mike Thompson had meant when he said the owners of the gold would not even allow or admit the robbery had taken place, had it been successfully pulled off. It was a curious thing to say at the time and the words still remain a mystery.

Skip: "Mike had been a low level working member in the Fargo Group for Jim Littlejohn and I just assumed he now was in the employ of the Cartel from Reno. But maybe he isn't, maybe he went rogue and now works for himself. Maybe he was just trying to steal a little from his old bosses knowing they would never report the theft or pursue the thieves. Mike's not all that bright but maybe when he realized that they killed his buddy David in the Super Cub wreck in Bettles, maybe he is just very pissed off, maybe." "Or maybe he's thinking he's next, who knows? He might be just trying to accumulate some money to buy a few more drugs for resale and with David gone he can probably partner up with Justin who most likely owns the drug business by now." "Maybe yes, maybe no; but I still want to know where and how Carter came to get the diamonds. Nothing makes sense there and it's driving me up the wall." Josh agreed: "I have had similar questions about Mike but every time I try to put the story together there seems to be no good explanation for his actions. Also, I don't think Carter had Littlejohn on the hook for the diamond scam before the London gold robbery at Heathrow. If you think about the timeline, Littlejohn was sniffing around selling drugs but that phony diamond deal was a while after the London robbery. As far as laundering the bullion, it's not such a far stretch to imagine the manufacture of nuggets on the Coleville or in the Forty-mile district, or maybe both. That might work long term to get top prices for the bullion and avoid the markdown they would have to take if they turned to the Asian or Russian black-market operations."

Skip was less than convinced: "It might also limit the number of folks that know the real source of the gold. That's about the only thing that makes anything logical in this Clusterfuck."

Josh still had questions: "Ok, but how about Carter; what the hell is his involvement in all of this? Carter has a business that is successful and ongoing. He is super profitable and has a loyal set of clients and almost no competition. My guess is that Carter doesn't give a rat's ass for either the diamonds or the gold. I think he's out to get Jim Littlejohn and he doesn't want him just dead; I think he wants him humiliated, broken, and dead broke. At least that's my guess. Carter could have killed him many times over; I don't think he wants him dead, I think he wants him miserable."

Skip nearly agreed but questioned: "Wonder what Jim Littlejohn did to Mr. Carter Thomas?" "We may never know but it's my guess that it's personal, not business. Maybe its family related, and it might not be just Littlejohn, it may be the folks he works for. My guess is it won't end up pretty. I think we should give it some space and if we do we might not get hit with the shrapnel." "Well this is pretty much just speculation for now. Figure out how you can build a fire under your friend Ross to investigate the gold bar casting mold numbers, I think we need that information, that's the next step."

Skip was a bit annoyed by the question: "I'm working on it. Other than Jean and Claire, who knows what we know?" Josh answered almost automatically: "No one as far as I know; let's keep it this way till we at least resolve the serial numbers. It's Wednesday again so Matt and I are flying to the Birch Creek Mine tomorrow with another Friday payroll and we are to pick up a gold shipment at the North Palmer operation for transport back to Bank of the North. I don't expect any trouble but--."

Just then the alarm went off in the hangar down the way. Josh was right, he could hear it clearly even from inside the Exchange.

Skip was nearly out the double front doors before Josh ever left the table. Of the folks playing pool only Matt knew it was the alarm from the Maule in the hangar and by the time Matt made it to the booth where Skip and Josh had been talking it was empty. Both men were at a dead run down the road toward the house and hangar. Josh was impressed that a mid-50s man with the beginnings of a gut could move that fast. Just the same he passed Skip just as they approached the hangar and when they did enter the hangar they found Mike Thompson trying to hide in a corner behind a roll-away tool box. Mike was not doing well, he was cornered by a very threatening certain shepherd, "Michael's Angel of Jordon." Josh reached into the plane and switched off the alarm.

Mike: "Call that damn dog off, she scares the crap out of me." "She is Just doing her job Mike. Angel: cut." Angel backed off about a foot but kept her teeth bared. "She remembers you Mike. Not good to be remembered that way by Angel." "She bit all the way through my hand last time; twice. I should sue you for damages or disability or something. She's a menace." "As I recall Mike, you were in her house as you are again. When you find Angel snooping around in your home please let me know and I'll have a talk with her."

Skip was a little puzzled: "To what do we owe this visit Mike; just what the devil do you want? I'm not fucking around this time Mike. I let you go free at the Roadhouse when you should have been arrested. That was a once-in-a-life time goodwill gesture. Let's hear it; you have about thirty seconds before you're turned into dog food, got it?" "Mr. Littlejohn wants to know how many you have and where they are." "How many of what?" "The gold bars." Josh pretending outrage: "What gold bars, what the hell are you talking about?"

"The gold bars from England. He wants to know where the gold bars are, the ones that were supposed to be delivered to the mine up on the Coleville." Mike was nearly crying and was really worried about Angel; and did she ever know it. Angel was growling again and was puffed up half again her normal size."

Mike continued:" Skip Davis was chauffeuring that mule Kelly up to Umiat in your old 185 when it crashed in Bettles. He was supposed to deliver the bars to the mine the next day, but he never arrived. I don't really care about the guy, but my boss needs the bars. I'm just trying to see if they are here. I told Mr. Littlejohn they weren't in your hangar, he made me come and look anyway." Skip answered: "The man's name is Ralph Kelly and I personally put him on the ground in Umiat. The Cessna with the unfortunate engine was my 180, not Matt's 185. It was my God-damn plane you fucking jerk! Ralph arrived in Umiat with his entire luggage; I shook his hand, wished him well, and left. He was planning on lunch and a flight to who knows where. Maybe a twenty-mile flight back to the mine in the afternoon or maybe not. He didn't say though I did ask, and he wouldn't say. I don't really give a damn about it now, I don't care! I have his 'John Henry' on a signed invoice.

Mike asked: "So, where is he?" "I was his God-damn pilot, not his fucking sitter you jerk! How the hell would I know where he is? You say he was carrying some gold bars that belonged to Littlejohn; what the hell is this about gold?" "Forget I said that, you say you left him in Umiat, where?"

"I left him at the fucking airport stupid, right next to Bud Hastings's hangar." "Don't call me stupid, I hate it when people call me stupid, you sound like my mother." Josh entered the debate: "Mike, I really think you're in the wrong business, I really do."

The hangar door opened again, and Matt came in with a Glock in one hand and in the other jackets for Josh and Skip. The hangar was just above freezing but it was ten below outside, too cold for short sleeves. He had been listening to the conversation outside that now seemed to be going nowhere. He looked at Josh, then at Skip. "So, Skip, who screwed up your 180?" Skip and Josh together: "Justin Littlejohn."

Josh: "Mike, how did you get here?" "My truck is just down Goldstream road about a quarter of a mile." "Then I suggest you find it and leave right now. Don't come back Mike, got it?" "That dog is vicious, you should have her trained." "She's trained Mike, she's trained very well. Get lost now."

He was gone quickly. For the second time in a week he had given away information and had his ass bailed out because of his own pure stupidity. "Poor Mike; you are right Josh, he really needs to find a better profession." After a few good words to Angel and an ear-rub Josh finally said: "I don't like any of this and I'm not sure what to do next, but I don't think we need the information from your treasury friend anymore; I think we know where the bars came from." Matt: "What bars?"

Skip ignored the question and continued his thoughts: "So, it looks as though the Reno Cartel does have at least some of the booty from the robbery at Heathrow in London and are busy laundering the gold bars into nuggets at two mines widely separated in distance; but why two mines?"

Josh:" They also seem to be hooked up, at least loosely, with Bob Adams, who may or may not be a member of an organized Adams Crime Family from the U.K. And it's a guess that Jim Littlejohn, his oldest son Justin, now his only son, and Mike, poor unfortunate Mike, are trying to take a little of it for themselves." Skip was almost laughing: "This is funny as hell. Carter's security firm is the fox guarding the hen house. How the hell does he do it? Somehow, he manages to stay not only alive, but also employed and apparently well-liked by the Cartel that he is in the process of stealing from and given the chance, will probably fuck up beyond all reality."

Josh: "And somehow with all this going on he managed to not only pull off a great con job on Jim Littlejohn and the Fargoettes, and sell them a worthless diamond mine, but he also managed to steal a couple hundred thousand bucks worth of diamonds." Matt was feeling a little miffed because he was being left out of the conversation; just the same he had to ask: "What's a Fargoette?"

They both turned and stared at Matt seeming to finally understand he was there; and then they giggled. Josh talking to Matt: "It's a very long story but here goes. Jim Littlejohn at the time was a lieutenant in the Fargo Group; a loose bunch of not so bright drug selling hoods from Fargo, ND. You remember the high heel boots that Jean usually wears? Well, Jean nailed him with a pointy-toed cowboy boot nut job after he punched her out and broke her nose. Jean has called Littlejohn a Fargoette ever since that incident because, according to her, he possesses the strength to beat up an almost 5'3" tall 122-pound girl. The name just kind of stuck and he hates it. Don't ever piss off Jean, man, did she ever mess him up; I'm not sure but I think he still walks a little funny."

Matt "So the gold we are transporting from the Forty-mile to the bank is stolen?" "Maybe some, we aren't sure yet, but not all or even most. Most of it is probably hard-earned gold mined by hard-rock miners from the Forty-mile District. I think that they are only making the smaller pieces into nuggets to increase their value; Likely it's legitimate. My guess is that only a little of it is from the London robbery. Probably from one single mine. I think the Birch Creek Mine, but I'm not sure. I'm not sure I even care." Matt asked again: "What about the Coleville River operation, what are they doing there?" Skip answered: "That one for sure is melting bullion, for God-damn sure."

Matt:" I still don't get it. Is it the Fargo Group or the Reno Cartel? What's the difference?

Josh: "This is just an educated guess but here goes. The Fargo Group were a small-time bunch of wanna-be Wise-Guys; they were drug sellers that had a pretty good deal going for them. They bought a franchise for the Deadhorse drug and liquor business from the Reno Cartel who are the remnants of an old Chicago crime family that moved to Nevada in the 1960s. Someone even made a movie about them. Anyway, Jim Littlejohn convinced someone in the Cartel that there were diamonds to be found on the Coleville River and they loaned the Fargo group nearly three quarters of a million to buy the leases and mineral rights on the property. When Littlejohn didn't find diamonds and couldn't make the payments they basically took everything the Fargo Group had but it was nothing compared to what they owed. There was a little real estate in Grand Forks, some cat houses, a few poker rooms, and that was about it."

Josh continued: "They were going to kill him but by that time they were also trying to launder some of the seven hundred pounds of gold they bought from the Adams crime family at a pretty huge discount. Gold was starting to go up in price and mixing some base metal increased the profit even further. Littlejohn somehow convinced them he could launder the gold bars into nuggets for them to pay back at least part of the loan. There was less than total trust there and the would only give him fifteen or eighteen pounds at a time. Still apparently the deal was going along Ok but David continued with his drug selling and it's my guess that the franchise had been re-sold by then to someone else: it was no big deal, so the Cartel just took him out."

Skip joined the explanation: "That is about all we know or at least think we know. The Reno Cartel are the Wise Guys it would be best to stay very far away from; they are big-time scary. Grizzly Air is no longer flying to Umiat; I am not going to get involved with these guys at all: period!"

Josh: "Goldstream Air isn't doing any business with the Coleville operation now or ever; I have been asked to haul a few pallets of freight from time to time, but as of about two months ago I begged out of most any business on the Slope. I think Bud Hastings is maybe hauling some freight out of Anchorage and I'm guessing he is now doing the charter work; flying the mules to and from Umiat and also toting them back to Anchorage. I wonder if he knows any of this crap is going on?"

Skip:" He will figure it out; I can't imagine him being involved with anything illegal that is this big. He might shoot a cow moose to feed a hungry villager but beyond that Bud has always been a straight arrow. Matt: "So where is the gold and who owns it?" "Whoever has it now? My guess is that it's mostly stashed in Reno under the thumb of the Cartel. Those well-dressed guys you saw traveling thru Umiat from time to time during the summer with the mini-duffels and attaché cases? They were probably bringing it north, fifteen pounds at a time. I guess the Grizzly Air Service which I bought four months ago was a major mover of stolen London gold; I sure hope I don't need a lawyer". Josh reasoned: "Not much to be proud of in that résumé." "Screw you very much Josh."

Chapter (18)

What goes North might not come South   Mar. 1985

The next day around lunch time Skip was again at the store arranging Via the Satellite phone, to transport one of the radios from his wrecked 180 to replace one that was needed in his 206. Skip had to buy back one of the two radios that were in the plane that he had just sold to the guys in Bettles. He was angry at himself for selling the plane so quickly, but why should he have kept it? Just the same, they almost gave it to him; charged him two bills for a nine hundred buck radio. What he was really concerned about was now he owed them one and it was yet another obligation that he might have to make good on some time or another. He hated owing others. To him owing was something you only did for friends and everyone else paid cash: everyone else. The plane he hoped to have transport the radio back to Fairbanks had already left Bettles and he would have to find other transport; he would work on that later.

Besides the radio, Skip's other more pressing problem was that Grizzly Air had been hauling around illegally gotten gold bars most of the previous year and he now owned the business. it's just a matter of good business not to do dumb things now that will jump up and bite your ass later. There are other air taxis in the area and if the customer wants contraband moved then the customer can find another taxi; it's that simple.

The customer however, has other ideas and the customer wants to know what happened to their latest mule, and in particular, what happened to the mule's golden cargo? So, when the phone rang, Josh answered it and after some confusion handed it off to Skip. It was a satellite call from Mr. Kelly's employer that wants to know about the last charter trip to Umiat.

Skip: "I guess you know that my Cessna 180 was destroyed and that we were barely able to make it to Bettles alive, and at that only after surviving a crash." Caller: "That is not my problem Mr. Davis, I just want to know the whereabouts of Mr. Kelly and his luggage?"

Skip: "I don't know and that is not my problem, or my concern sir. Mr. Kelly was delivered to Umiat around 11:00 am on Wednesday morning. He deplaned in front of the Hastings hangar, the white and brown one, and he signed a transportation billing invoice that I have already submitted to your business office with hopes to get paid before the end of the month. I can tell you that he was suffering from motion sickness and was in a very sour mood." "So, where is he? He was not there for the pickup at the proper time."

Skip: "To whom am I speaking sir?" "I am Mr. Kelly's employer, Mr. Farmer." "Mr. Farmer, have you ever been to Umiat?" Farmer: "Yes I have." "So, you know there are damn few places to hide. Umiat is little more than a crossroads with a place to get a burger and coffee and a pilot's lounge that is mainly supported by three oil companies; there is almost no resident population. Two hangars, a couple of cabins and a few prefab buildings and a cookshack manned by two cooks and a handyman that have been used by the oil exploration companies for the last ten or fifteen years; that's it. If there were an open bar in Umiat I suppose he may be there but Umiat is a dry town and there are no bars; beyond that I have no clue where he may be. He said he was waiting for someone and when I asked who: "he said none of your business". Mr. Kelly obviously had a life-threatening experience the day before and I understand that but he might have been just a little civil just the same. I left shortly after that and really have no idea about where he is or what his business was; it all seemed very mysterious. He might have said he was waiting for a Super Cub or something like that. He did have the satellite phone and I know the batteries were up because he made a call just before I departed Umiat. I just pointed him in the direction of the heated prefab where he could get lunch. God, he was in a foul mood and I had just about enough of his whining. That guy was a cry baby. If you suspect foul play I suggest you contact Mr. Littlejohn." "Jim or Justin?"

That's interesting Skip thought, whoever the caller is he knows the Littlejohns with instant recall. "It could be either one of those jerks. Jim Littlejohn and the Fargoettes have been a problem for me in the past. I think or rather suspect he or maybe one of his crew, was responsible for my airplane's engine being destroyed. That's why your associate Mr. Kelly, was delivered one day late to Umiat and by the way, we paid for Mr. Kelly's lodging Tuesday night together with his meals and drinks; Grizzly Air is a full-service operation." The caller then asked: "What the hell is a Fargoette?" "Long answer sir and trivial; do you have any other questions Mr. Farmer?" "Yes, I do; where the hell is Ralph Kelly?" "I don't know sir and it's not my problem." And Skip hung up the phone before the caller could respond.

Josh asked: "What was that about?" "A very dissatisfied ex-customer, I think. It seems Ralph Kelly may be missing along with his burden of 15 or so pounds of gold ingots. When I delivered him to Umiat he was looking for a bar, a drinking bar not a gold one, and he was very disappointed when I told him the place was again voted dry by its 13 residents in the November elections nearly two months ago. Kelly asked me how can it be an election year, it's 1985? I said I know that but apparently the North Slope Borough has elections on their own time table. But anyway, there were only one or two other planes that I noticed and maybe one in the open hangars. I don't know for sure, but the place looked unused and nearly empty, it is March you know; hardly balmy tourist season, I was halfway surprised there was anyone there at all, but I did see chimney smoke coming out of two of the cabins and also out of the cook house and the pilot's warm up lounge: It's the wind-sock for the airstrip."

Josh: "I can't keep accepting your collect phone calls; you seem to be a very costly friend all of a sudden." "Don't give me that crap, you have a Satellite phone line now, it was installed last week; Jean told me." "Is there anything you don't know?" "I would like to know where the fuck Ralph Kelly is, what do you think?" "I think you could clean up your verbiage. I have feelings you know, and gutter language is just plain hurtful. I am beginning to think you might be a bad influence on me." "So, what's next?" "The back room for a beer or the Exchange for a game of pool: your choice." Skip headed for the front door.

Chapter (19)

So where is Ralph?   Apr. 985

The pool table was as cold to Skip as the ice cubes in his Black Jack and it was not yet noon. After Skip beat Josh in a game of Eight-Ball it was Tommy's turn to play. Tommy ran the table on Skip twice, collecting his tariff both times before missing a rather easy shot. This ruse should have been obvious to Skip but instead it just baited him. If he played just once more he was sure he could win back his losses, so he did play, this time for five instead of just a buck, and he did not win, yet again.

Josh sat back watching the drama while sipping a Coke and rolling his eyes. He smiled and was not the least bit surprised that Skip could be so easily fooled, conned, stung, or whatever you care to call it. Almost everyone has at least one blind spot in their reality that may not be visible to them but stands tall, bright, and shiny, for others to observe. Skip's blind spot is his pool table skills. If asked, he would rank himself as an eight or nine on a scale of ten. Tommy Wilson who is a real 10 would judge Skip's skills at around four, or on a good sober day, not today, maybe five.

Other than his blind spot concerning his pool table skills, Skip has extraordinary understanding of the way the world operates around him, usually called street smarts. He can see things that are sometimes totally hidden to even the most perceptive and he has built his success on knowing the needs of people and selling into those needs to skim the small difference between the buying cost and the selling price, as profit.

Skip has suspicions that the association, the FMA, may have been created just so the output of many mines in the area could be put into combined shipments and the unusual profits from one of the mines, and origin of that particular bunch of nuggets and gold dust, could be hidden from scrutiny. After all, a needle placed among a bunch of needles is far better hidden than it would be in a haystack.

Wanting to know more, Skip decided to look into what the driving force was to create the FMA in the first place. He knows that miners are not usually joiners of anything but usually making an exception for a Saturday night beer bash or an early Sunday morning hanging. He wondered how the miners decided on Carter's security service; maybe it was just the name recognition of his consulting company. He wondered if any other security firms bid on the contract and who wrote the contract? Maybe Carter's was the only security service that would take a job in the Forty-mile District. These were questions he would find answers to and the answers might just satisfy some of his other concerns.

So where is Ralph Kelly and his cargo of 16 odd pounds of gold bars? One hundred eighty troy ounces at around three hundred fifty odd bucks is around sixty-seven thousand dollars and that's enough to be concerned about. Josh decided to take a little trip to Bettles to pick up the radio for Skip and he also decided he would fly a little further, a lot further in fact and make a visit to Umiat to hunt for clues regarding the elusive Mr. Ralph Kelly.

Skip had some pending business to attend to that involved renewing his Air Taxi license and buying some extra insurance riders from Jack Randolph at the State Farm Insurance Agency. He had contacted Harry Strubee in Spokane and retained his services; Skip wondered if he might be looked at closely regarding the crash on Airport Road in Bettles and he wanted no problems with the FAA or his "friend" Maury at the NTSB. The engine and Airframe logs on the 180 were not in perfect condition regarding some Airworthiness Directives, though they had been done according to Jonny Beard, the ex-owner of Northwinds Aviation at FAI.

Josh decided he would fly the payroll gig and gold pick up with Matt in the morning. Then on Friday he would fly up to Bettles for Skip's radio, and then further on to Umiat for a personal look-see. He could at least ask around at the cook shack.

The trip on Thursday with the payroll went without incident and when Matt made the deposit of gold at Bank of the North Josh was pretty sure he had a good system that was both safe and doable. Matt was finally vetted and could now carry his Glock legally. After a short swearing-in ceremony, he even had a new bright shiny Deputy Trooper Badge, though it said "Reserve" in fairly small lettering.

161

Claire had the billings under control and the flight hours were working out at just a little less than anticipated. Another dollar or two for the coffers was a good thing and after a rough start Goldstream Air was operating according to its business plan; thank you Claire.

As Josh planned his Friday trip to Bettles and beyond he decided to take Angel; it would be her first trip in the Maule. Angel was familiar with the new plane, she had even claimed it once or twice when no one was looking but she was still a little neutral about flying in it. Just the same, when she saw Josh with her new red flying harness, she started jumping around and was very eager to go. Very early Friday morning, the twelfth of April, Josh kissed his wife so-long and departed the Goldstream Valley in his Maule 235, with his faithful guard dog Angel.

The first stop on the trip would be the Bettles Aviation Services at the Evansville field. As usual they departed Goldstream Valley to the south-east, turned a lazy left, and were climbing slowly as they crossed the intersection of Ballaine Road and Goldstream road. Still climbing slowly when crossing over Clary Summit, they followed a course of 308 magnetic that should take about an hour and five minutes of flight time to their destination; The Bettles airport in Evansville. The highest peak along the way is about three thousand feet and the air on this day was stable, chilly and without wind.

As it turns out, Angel does not like the Maule as much as the 206 but at least it's better than the one they crash landed in two years ago, she wished for a ride in the 206 which is much quieter and does not bop around as much. The 206 does not have a great side window like the Maule has but it feels much more stable; important for a now ten-year-old loyal Canine: she just had a birthday.

Bettles airport is unpaved and nearly a mile long, it is a big airfield with traffic handled by Fairbanks Flight Service. Josh called on 122.2 to get a traffic check.

Josh: "Bettles radio, this is Maule 4430 Sierra Whiskey."

Bettles Radio: "4430 Sierra Whiskey, go ahead."

Josh: "4430 Sierra Whiskey is 10-miles southeast inbound landing runway 1."

Bettles Radio: "30 Sierra Whiskey, make a straight-in for runway 1, call in on 2-mile final."

Josh: "2-mile final, 30 Sierra Whiskey."

With no reported traffic in the area, Josh still checked on 122.9: "Bettles traffic, blue Maule 8 miles southeast inbound full stop landing runway 1, Bettles traffic."

Three miles out Josh changed frequency again to 122.2 and pushed the transmit button on the yoke: "Bettles Radio, Maule 30 Sierra Whiskey is on 2-mile final inbound landing for 1."

Bettles Radio: "30 Sierra Whiskey is cleared to land."

Josh: "Cleared to land, 30 Sierra Whiskey."

The gravel runway was not cleared of all snow but what was there was hard packed, so Josh did not have his skis down. The run-out was long, and Angel whimpered just a little on touchdown, remembering her last landing in Bettles in the 185 when they lost a tire and almost dipped a wing. Josh wondered how she ever remembered all that stuff. Dogs are not supposed to have long-term recall but somehow Angel did.

Josh: "30 Sierra Whiskey is off the active runway, taxiing to the Bettles Aviation hangar."

Bettles Radio: "30 Sierra Whiskey, taxi at will, Bettles Radio."

Josh taxied over to the hangar and pulled the mixture knob all the way out; the engine obediently sputtered and stopped. The hangar door was closed because it was about 10 degrees below zero, or maybe no one was there yet, or maybe it was too cold to get the hangar warm enough to work in today. Whatever the reason, Josh just wanted a radio for Skip and he would be on his way. As he got out of the Maule the man-door on the side of the hangar opened and Chuck Mason peered out and waved. Josh disconnected Angel's harness from the seat belt and they both walked across the entrance pad and into the hangar where it was not the least bit chilly. The partners had force-fed a large barrel stove and somehow cranked up the inside temperature to nearly 50 degrees; it was downright balmy. The 180, or at least the largest part of it, was back in one corner of the hangar with the wings off and the tail section was missing altogether. They had absolutely stripped it of everything that had value and the stack of undamaged parts and instruments was impressively tagged and cataloged.

Josh could plainly see that the value of the parts salvaged far exceeded the price they paid for the broken hull and he was glad to see that someone would benefit from the incident.

The radio was already boxed, and Josh was offered a cup of coffee and a semi frozen donut. Angel was given a donut also and she immediately warmed up to the brothers and decided to sit quietly and wait for maybe another: didn't happen.

Small talk, the weather, the forecast, the time until breakup, and how is Kevin adapting to the big city was the talk of the day. The brothers are planning to build another house as soon as breakup; their two families now shared the home they bought from Kevin and Molly and it was just a bit small for four adults and three kids though it seemed not to bother the kids, they were cousins after all.

As Josh was getting ready to leave on the last leg of his journey north, the Unicom radio that is always on in the hangar, started squawking. "Bettles traffic, this is red and white Cessna 3 miles north, in bound landing 19, Bettles traffic." Followed a minute or two later: "Bettles traffic, red and white Cessna on right base in-bound landing 19, Bettles traffic."

A red and white Cessna 182 on wheels came in from the northeast, entered the pattern on a right base leg and landed. The 182 taxied up near the Sourdough Lodge and parked. As the passengers left the plane Josh spotted Ralph Kelly walking, almost running, toward the restaurant. Justin Littlejohn was on his left carrying a leather satchel much like the one with the diamonds that Angel took and had remained hidden for nearly two years' time. A third person Josh did not recognize followed along.

Angel, watching Josh, remembered the day that David Littlejohn and Bob Adams stole the oil leases and options from Josh and Pete behind the store. That was the day Angel took the satchel of diamonds; she caught that same excitement in Josh now as he watched the three of them walking toward the Lodge. Angel was no

164

longer looking for a free donut; she was in her guard dog role, just waiting for a command. With a low growl she was now outside the hangar watching, hidden behind the Maule's tail, ready and waiting.

Josh asked Paul, who seemed to be the leader of the partners, if he would do him a favor and see what they were doing at the lodge.

Paul: "Yes, I will, but I am curious and wonder why you can't do that yourself, why do you want second hand information?" Paul recognized Ralph as Skip's passenger when Skip crashed on the road very near the airport and destroyed his 180 nearly two weeks ago. He remembered him as being a pretty loud, pretty mean drunk. During that visit Ralph had pissed off the bartender and most of the wait staff in the lodge, and also the housekeeping girl when he barfed all over the bedding. He also stole a roll of duct tape from the maintenance guy who is the housekeeper's husband.

Paul: "He is pretty much not welcome here, but I guess they will probably serve him. FYI, you and Skip are on probation whether you know it or not, you were the guys that got him blitzed to begin with."

Chuck: "I probably wouldn't want to eat what the cooks will put on his plate." "The guy on the left is Justin Littlejohn. I had a run in with his brother David awhile back. David is the one who died in the Super Cub crash just off the north end of this runway a year or so ago. These folks are up to no good. I don't want to be identified or involved in any way; I just want to know what they are doing here, that's all." Paul ventured: "A man by the name of Adams was here last week looking for Ralph Kelly, I have his business card. This Adams guy claimed he was looking for Ralph and would pay for information to find him. He said Adams had been in a fairly old Cessna 210 and that was strange because not many retractable gear aircraft were flying around in the very cold weather; you can't put skis on them and wheels this far north in the winter is just like an accident waiting to happen."

The description that he gave matched Bob Adams. Paul was pretty sure the 210 was from Anchorage; he said he had seen it both at Merrill Field and also in Talkeetna a few, maybe 6 months ago. It had Canadian registration letters and that was why it was distinctive to him. Paul offered that he had no intention of calling Adams to claim the finder's fee. He said both he and his brother Chuck, had decided not to become involved in whatever was going on. Chuck said he thought that this Adams guy was a bit spooky and he would not miss him if he never showed up again.

Paul agreed to visit the lodge and order four hamburgers to go even though it was still a bit early for lunch. He would try to see if they were staying overnight or just here for the bathroom and an early lunch.

Chuck: "Does Angel like onions?" "She would probably rather have another donut."

Chapter (20)

Angel's Treasure

Ten miles north of Bettles at 5,000 feet, and with a newly acquired sidekick, Bob Adams, was quiet and seemed depressed. He had been looking for Ralph Kelly and his satchel of ingots for more than a week. He had flown into the Umiat strip twice and was sure that Ralph Kelly never caught the short ride from there to the mining site up the Coleville. There had been about a dozen planes into the Umiat strip in the previous week according to the log kept by the three-man crew in the cook shack. Most of the planes were of no interest to the Reno Cartel because they were oil-related flights concerned with a small construction project at the airstrip that would start as soon as the snow melted. Pilots working for Bud Hastings had flown all but four of the charters.

One of the planes into the airstrip near the end of the previous week seemed to have no good reason to be there. The flight was not really related to oil exploration, and the pilot had been a cash customer at the cook shack. The pilot of that plane had paid for a twenty-four-dollar hamburger and other than complaining about the cost, said very little else about his reason for being there. The cooks thought his business was probably tourist related; maybe a new guiding service for lower 48 fishermen or he might even have been a travel agent. It was a little too early in the year for that, though it was really not the concern of the three-man resident crew of two cooks and one maintenance technician.

The plane was a red and white Cessna 182 on wheels, not skis, which was strange. Because anyone operating north of the Brooks Range in winter should have had skis. That alone seemed to be a mystery. It was no mystery to Bob Adams because he was pretty sure the red and white Cessna was involved with the disappearance of Ralph Kelly and his golden cargo.

During the past week or so Adams had been to most of the near villages including Allakaket, Hughes, Wiseman, Anaktuvuk Pass, as well as most every other place with an air strip. He had been to the Deadhorse Airport in Prudhoe Bay twice and because of some strong political links involving presidential portraits on high linen content green paper, Adams had been able to scan the FAA log book entries and see nearly all the flights in and out of the area commonly referred to as the North Slope. He also picked up a passenger, another enforcer from the Reno Cartel that had flown in commercially just one day earlier. After better than eight days' time Bob Adams was tired and weary of searching. He was fairly sure that Kelly and his cargo of gold bars were long gone from the interior of Alaska.

About ready to abandon the search he fueled his Cessna 210 in Allakaket and planned his last stop at Bettles for lunch and a bathroom break before giving up and ending his failed search for Kelly. Adams planned to overnight in Fairbanks to look at the FAA tower logs there and introduce his young sidekick to a warm welcome at Ruthie's House of Pleasure down off south Cushman, on 23rd Avenue. If the Tower Logs at FAI gave no hints, he would fly back to Anchorage the next day and admit defeat though he would promise to keep up the search if that was what his bosses wanted. He would also turn in his highly-padded expense receipts and, if lucky, he might get a few days off.

Adams was on short final over Evansville for Bettles airport runway 19 before he spotted the red and white 182 parked in front of the Sourdough lodge. He could not believe his good luck and told his young friend that he should make sure he was ready for most anything. "Check your weapon. Look over there: he as pointing. If that's the plane we're looking for this operation could get very damn interesting."

He sounded like an experienced wise guy, a real slick operator, and how he loved to play the role of a big shot. In fact, he was a lieutenant but still a bit of a working grunt for the Cartel out of Reno, not quite yet into the management spot he craved. Big Bob was considered a little bit special because he is a pilot but mainly because he's the nephew of the ruling brothers of the semi-notorious Adams Crime Family operating out of London, England. To Bob's credit, he had been involved in one successful takeaway theft two years ago. Although successful, the theft had not been profitable for the family. To his discredit, he had been arrested for assault a month or so later involving the same people entangled in the previous robbery. He had been jailed for a short period and after that had been on court-supervised probation for six months. Because of that incident and a now broken allegiance to Jim Littlejohn, who had gone rogue, Bob Adams now gets a little more respect from the Cartel and is considered a semi-trusted member of the group. He is no longer on probation with them and he wants badly to find Kelly. If he doesn't find Kelly, or at least find out where he is he might soon be shipped back to London. He badly needs a victory because there is much more to do regarding the business plan between the two crime families and he wants to be an important player. He also has a few plans of his own, big time plans.

Chuck Mason had walked over to the lodge to see what Kelly was up to. When Adams pulled up near the lodge he parked the 210 in close behind the 182 in a way that would make it hard for the 182 to leave without first moving the 210. Josh and Paul saw the parking maneuver and thought it was a strange way to park a plane. Then Josh recognized the plane as an older Cessna 210 that had wing struts; the first 210s had struts and are often mistaken for a182.

Josh: "Paul is that the 210 you saw Bob Adams in last week?" "I think so; it's the right color and has Canadian tail fin numbers, or should I say letters? Yes, that's him getting out of it now. Looks like he picked up a passenger somewhere because last week he was alone. If he is still looking for Kelly, I guess he might have found him. This could get spooky."

Josh: "Wish I was a fly on the wall; I would really like to know what's going on." Paul offered: "I can walk over to the lodge and see what is going on. I want to make sure Chuck is away from the trouble. My guess is that there will at least be a fistfight, this should be interesting. "Ya Ok. If you need help yell out." "Just stay put inside the hangar and I'll be back in ten minutes, and don't worry, as long as there are no fireworks Chuck can take care of himself. He's damn tough for a little guy, he used to box in the Golden Gloves tournaments back home."

Josh: "That's fine with me and I will sit tight here; I want nothing to do with Adams and I would just as soon not let him know I am even around." "What about your plane, won't they spot it?" "It's fairly new to me, Adams has no reason to know it's mine. I don't think he knows or cares what I have in my flying machine inventory and I guess I'm about the last thing on his mind right now."

Angel was still on her feet watching the goings on. She was puffed out and her hackles were up. Angel looked funny and her red flying harness made her look like she had crimson tape tightly wrapped around her body, just about ready for a Christmas bow. She was now silent but totally aware that something was going on that made Josh uneasy. They waited for what seemed like half an hour but in reality, was just a few, maybe five minutes, before there was the first indication of trouble.

Ralph Kelly was the first to come out of the lodge a few seconds after what sounded like a shotgun blast. He was holding the small duffle that Josh recognized as the container for the eight gold ingots he had before he went missing. Ralph was running and making a bee line for his plane. The parking area was hard packed snow and very slick. When Skip left him out in Umiat two weeks ago he took back both his parka and over boots that Ralph had worn when flying. Kelly was now in leather-soled hiking shoes and traction on hard packed snow had obviously not been an overriding design goal when the shoes were manufactured. His jacket was open and flying in the wind as he ran; he had no hat and was hardly dressed for subzero temperatures. Bob Adams and his sidekick were next off the porch but were being slowed down some by Justin Littlejohn; the third guy was nowhere to be seen. Bob Adams pulled out a handgun and made a threatening sweep pointing at the nearest of his desired targets: Ralph. The gun went off once but was not even close to where he thought he was aiming. Kelly was still running but his feet went into overdrive when he heard the gunshot. Whether because of either poor planning or over estimating his athletic abilities, Kelly was unable to stop as he approached his plane and he fumbled the package when raising his hands to protect himself from the eminent collision with the propeller. The satchel tumbled and skidded under

170

the plane's body, caromed off one of the main gear's tires, and burrowed into some soft snow next to the berms on the far side of the plane that defined the parking area and runway boundary. Despite using his hands to catch himself Kelly kind of skidded forward barely avoiding a crash into the propeller by grabbing the propeller tip and swinging around and under it. He then gracefully collided with the wing strut, kind of looped around it and crashed into the airplane's pilot door. His upper body stopped but his legs kept going and he found himself flat on his back about to be run over by Bob Adams who, despite having better boots to run in, had no better luck getting stopped. Adams also ran into the propeller, hitting it so hard it partially turned the plane back toward the runway; it was undamaged, propellers are tough, but so was Bob. But even being pretty tough, Bob nearly knocked himself silly when his head hit the prop and as it did his gun went off again. Damage to onlookers was nil because the slug just hit the ground nearly between his feet and must have ricocheted because a small portion of the bullet, or something, went into his ankle and a little blood spurted out and stained both his boot and the snow pack. He screamed like he had been hit with a howitzer round as he dropped his gun and then grabbed his ankle.

Meanwhile Bob's accomplice had been chased and tackled hard by Justin and his pistol was also lost from his hand. It disappeared as it skidded into yet another snow bank. Though Bob's pursuit had been somewhat moderated and slowed by his running smack into the Cessna's propeller and shooting himself in the foot, still he regrouped and caught up to Ralph as he was attempting to enter the 182 thru the passenger door on the far side of the plane. Ralph had the airplane's door open and Bob slammed Ralph's hand in it so hard Josh thought he could hear bones breaking from fifty yards away inside the hangar. Ralph was now really hurting, but was still somehow undeterred. He turned and kicked Bob in the gut. He wasn't aiming for the gut but with very slippery street shoes it was the best he could do and as he kicked, he slipped and lost his footing again. He pulled himself back up by grabbing onto the wing strut with his one still-working hand and steadied himself. Before he could kick

Adams again he was knocked off balance by the third person in his group. The somewhat late to arrive Mr. X seemed to have no malice but, like the other folks, had also been unable to stop on the hard snow packed parking area. He helped Ralph to his feet and seemed to be apologizing.

Justin was about the only one firmly standing without the use of supports. After his flying tackle he seemed to be quite proud of his demonstrated athletic skills. He had his pistol in hand; he was the only one who had not lost his weapon and was swinging it around when Bob's sidekick, who Justin had just tackled, stood back up and lunged at him and yet another shot was fired, still in vain.

One of the two cooks from the lodge, came out of the side door to see who was doing all the shooting in the parking lot. This wasn't the first time it's happened but usually the shooting is much later in the day and generally after a little, or maybe a lot of booze has been consumed. The cook was yelling half in Spanish and half in English. It turns out he had been pretty heavily into the Cooking Sherry but just the same got everyone's attention; he was yelling that he had just called the cops.

The Evansville/Bettles law enforcement response time is usually measured in days, not minutes, but since a couple of the bar patrons were now on the front porch of the lodge gaping at the fight and cheering for one side or another, Bob Adams and his less embarrassed sidekick, decided to leave while they still could. Bob's sidekick had lost his Glock in the snowbank when Justin tackled him and neither felt as though they had the upper hand in the scuffle. Leaving seemed to be one of their options, and possibly the best option. Adams, now unarmed, retreated to cover on the far side of the 210 and hunkered down in relative safety.

But the choice was not theirs to make. With the odds in their favor but not really wanting to fight Justin Littlejohn, Ralph Kelly, and Mr. Unknown were very intent on leaving. Justin turned and gave Bob Adams the finger as the three of them jumped into their 182, which had been conveniently turned back toward the runway by the odd bodies that had been slamming into it. They fired it up and didn't even try to find the runway. Whoever was the pilot de jour just put

172

the balls to the wall and took off nearly 75 degrees to the centerline of the strip.

Somewhere there must have been a violation of FAA regulations regarding Departure Protocol as applied to General Aviation Aircraft but, in spite of taking off nearly perpendicular to the runway, they did get into the air successfully.

Bob Adams was actively rooting around in the snow berms and finally found his pistol. His sidekick also found his lost Glock and now rearmed, they apparently felt the chase was still worthwhile. Adam's foot was bleeding a little, but he looked and seemed not critically hurt. So, with his foot still attached and seemingly able to function he found new energy and the chase was on. Bob jumped into the 210 and as his sidekick got the tail pulled around they were ready to give chase. The 210 had nearly full tanks and far greater range than the runaway 182. Adams fired the engine and headed toward the airstrip for a record breaking but saner southern departure; if there had been a record it was now broken. He followed the southern direction of the 182 and was sure he could outclimb it and when he did he would spot that damned red and white 182 against the white background. He would find it, and he would follow it until its fuel tanks ran dry, and he would catch those bandits and get back his package when they landed. His plan had only one very small flaw. The one Kilo gold bars were not in the southbound red and white Cessna 182, they were in a snowbank at the Bettles Airport hidden from view by all but one.

And then there was quiet. Josh had not left the hangar during the display of manly intrigue that had just happened out on the aircraft parking area. He had not wanted to be involved in any way and was content to remain well-hidden yet entertained inside the hangar. After the 210 was airborne he looked around and found that he was now quite alone and wondered where Angel had ended up. Angel sometimes gets weird when gunshots are fired. But soon, in less than a minute or maybe two, Angel came back into the hangar. She came in backwards dragging and tugging the taped-up duffle that had skidded away when Ralph fumbled it trying to avoid the propeller just before denting the side of his plane. Angel pulled the

173

duffle right up to his feet, looked up almost like asking for instructions, and wagged. Josh saw the duffle and just said "Good Girl". Angel sat right next to him kind of at attention. Josh picked it up, hefted it, and guessed it was fifteen maybe eighteen pounds. Without a second thought he carried it outside the hangar and put the package in the back seat of the Maule, tucking it under his winter survival suit. Walking back into the hangar he gave Angel an extended ear-rub and she wagged again, sighed, and then walked over and laid down near the wood stove. The stove was burning down and needed tending with a bit more fuel, so Josh added a few branches and two hefty birch logs. He then sat back in a chair to read the latest issue of the AOPA monthly magazine. Angel seemed relaxed, but her ears remained up and her eyes were wide open.

Chuck and Paul returned after about fifteen minutes with three hamburgers and a bag of soggy fries that cost roughly fifty dollars; residents do get a hefty discount. Both plainly had enjoyed a few celebratory tots of whisky or whatever the booze of the day was. The clue leading to that discovery was heavily on his breath and the fact that Chuck was already walking a little funny. The brothers claimed to have stood for a round of drinks to commemorate the departure of Bob Adams, et al. Josh thought maybe he had a few more than just one.

Paul "Bettles is a strange place!" "And it's not yet noon." Said Josh. Paul had three cans of Coke, and there was already a bottle of water for Angel in the hangar in addition to a couple of now thawed doughnuts. He got busy telling the story of the clash inside the lodge when Adams first spotted Ralph Kelly.

Adams had quietly walked up behind him at the bar, but Kelly must have seen him coming in the mirror because when Adams spun him around he was met with a horse killing punch squarely between his eyes. There had been a pretty good fist fight at first, but it degraded quickly into some hair pulling, ear biting, and floor time. A little blood was spilled and there was a broken chair and a table with a new and slight downhill bias on one side of the top.

The brothers along with the other bar patrons had stayed totally out of the fracas. Paul and Chuck just stood off to the side as

Ralph Kelly kind of got the best of the slightly younger and larger Bob Adams. Adams might well have shot him if he hadn't dropped his weapon during the wrestling match on the floor of the bar-room. Justin Littlejohn is no fighter, and according to Paul, he received a sound pounding by Bob Adam's sidekick who was also kind of small but still seemed very tough. Kelly was besting Adams in his contest of mayhem and only decided to leave the lodge after the bartender pulled a pump shotgun from under the bar. It was meant to scare the crap out of him and to stop Adam's sidekick from shooting Kelly after finishing with Justin Littlejohn. Unnoticed, he had been about to gun down Kelly who was successfully punching-up Adams after the hair pulling and obligatory verbal threats. The bartender finally gave the order to stop which everyone ignored. Then finally, the fighting did stop when the bartender accidently fired his shotgun, blowing a real nice framed picture of an Episcopal Priest and his Gull-wing Stinson off the wall and damaging the door into the kitchen area. It was loud, and the message was pretty damn clear: leave or get shot.

According to Paul, the bartender is not generally that assertive but because he knew Kelly as a loudmouth drunk from two weeks previous he was probably pissed enough to shoot him given any reason, even a weak one. That's when Kelly ran for the door with that little duffle bag, or whatever it was. Adams followed and so did Littlejohn, but the bartender insisted on someone paying the cost of a chair and table. He said he would shoot the two that were left inside unless they paid up for the furniture. They both argued it was the other guy's fault, but the bartender said he cared less which side they were on; he wanted three hundred bucks or else. They settled-up for one hundred each and the Bartender pointed to the door and said he would follow in two minutes and by then they damn well better have their business settled or be gone.

Paul: "For some crazy reason he gave Bob's sidekick back his pistol. Maybe he wanted a shootout or something. So, Bob's sidekick went running out of the bar, but the last guy stayed for a minute or so. Then he said: "what the hell" and went running out the door trying to catch the others. I don't understand the logic in giving back the handgun but maybe he just wanted to be done with it and not have someone come back looking for it at a later time."

Both Paul and Chuck were pretty damn proud of themselves for not getting shot or something. They were also fairly well looped. After eating his hamburger Josh wandered out of the hangar and retrieved the Glock that Bob's sidekick had lost for the second time today in yet another snowbank. He handed it to Chuck, Chuck gave it to Paul, and Paul said he didn't want it. The Glock came back to Josh and he put it in the Maule in the pilot's side pocket next to his sun glasses and a very well used sectional chart of the great state of Alaska.

Chapter (21)

The problem with Angel's treasure   Apr. 1985

Bettles to Goldstream Valley is a short trip of just over an hour in a Maule M-5. Angel was asleep soon after they left the airport and only woke up as the plane touched down on their home airstrip behind the Golden Valley Store. April brings longer days and warmer temperatures though the nights are still subfreezing most of the time. The Fairbanks area is fully a month ahead of Bettles in regard to the arrival of warmer weather. When Josh and Angel left Bettles it was 10 below zero and winter but as they arrived in the Valley about an hour later it was the beginnings of spring. A bit of an icy slushy puddle formed in front of the bi-fold hangar door and Angel jumped over it when she left the building running for the store. She could still jump and run almost as well as when she was young and on the Seattle Police Department, but now she was older, and her hips hurt a little when she jumped, so she wisely just took it a little easy. Angel saw Casey on the upstairs porch above the rear loading dock and wagged. Casey waved and yelled out: "Angel: jerky time". Angel hurried because it was not just the wood stove anymore, it was now treats and then the warming wood stove. So, with typical canine logic She took first things first.

Angel had not forgotten her latest adventure about her grabbing that little duffle bag. The duffle was what those bad guys had been arguing about and it was no longer theirs. It was a pretty clever shepherd that took the duffle satchel, and no one even noticed; Angel knew it and was proud, she was strutting and didn't even stop to claim a bush as she hurried to see Casey. But unlike two years ago when she had taken the diamonds, this time Angel gave the booty to Josh right away. Josh had the duffle bag now and it was no longer her problem and she could do her job guarding the store and their new house without the worry of other things; she was again just the store's security manager and unconcerned about Angel's Diamonds or any other treasure.

Josh now had the problem, but he was good with problems. As Angel ran to see Casey for treats Josh stayed behind in the hangar for a few minutes thinking about what to do next. This last incident in Bettles was not of his making, he had not been involved in any way, yet he was the one who ended up with the treasure, Angel's Treasure. Mainly he was unsure what to do with the newfound gold ingots. They weren't his and he likely wouldn't keep them, but he knew of no way of returning the gold bars to the rightful owners, whoever they may be.

Angel's diamonds had been locked away in the big wall safe for some time now; no one seemed to be looking for them and Josh had little concern about them. He wasn't sure what to do with the diamonds but somehow, he felt it would work out.

Now this new problem, the gold bars, presented him with a morally different conundrum involving ownership. Someone would be looking for the gold bars that he was almost positive had been stolen in London England, some two years ago. Whoever would come looking for them was most likely not the real owner and they would probably use whatever was necessary to secure them. This was a problem that, among other things, needed input from a good attorney. Josh thought he would talk to Claire and see if she had any ideas. Josh needed someone to share his anxiety with and Claire was good council and usually better with abstract problems; but he was pretty sure they needed a lawyer.

Then he looked around, came back to reality, and remembered it was Friday; Claire would be working at her office at the Geophysical Institute today. She was there about half time now and working on yet another proposal for funding involving satellite imaging and how she may be able to determine the slowly changing permafrost boundaries using returns from the Synthetic Aperture Radar (SAR). Josh was thinking that Global Warming is what the folks in Bettles could use a little of, maybe what they needed. It had been damn cold in Bettles.

Josh pulled the small duffle out of the rear seat of the Maule and carried it into the house. He turned the dial to the proper four coded numbers and opened the big bedroom safe. After weighing each bar to the gram on his electronic ivory scale he neatly stacked the bars in the safe, closed the door, and spun the dial to relock the safe. Each bar had measured just 2 grams shy of one Kilogram. Josh thought his scale might just be two tenths of a percentage point off; he was pretty sure, or maybe gravity was just a little different in Switzerland. Josh smiled and decided he would have to ask Claire about gravity because she was the scientist in the family. Whether or not gravity was in question he was now the official babysitter of eight one Kilo bars of 99.99 pure gold ingots, of unknown ownership.

The S&W 44 revolver he carried when flying went into his lock box under the bed. Then walking back thru the hangar, he pulled the Maule in backwards next to his 206 so he could lock up the place before walking up to the Exchange for a beer. Josh remembered the Glock in the side pocket of pilot's door and just shoved it back behind his belt thinking he might show it to Skip at dinner, maybe like a trophy.

Claire and Josh planned to eat dinner at the Exchange when she got off work. Skip and Jean were supposed to join them since Jean was working early today and would already have the Friday pay-checks written and passed out. Maybe Casey and Matt would join them too. Josh hoped to eat around six o'clock; it was a Friday and the restaurant would be really busy at dinnertime. Josh wondered how Don kept the kitchen going on Friday without the extra cooks, waiters, and the bus-boy that worked the weekends. It seemed Friday night was a big one for the Bar but not nearly as much restaurant business as Saturday night. Don kept it going with just the help of one cook, a bus-boy, one waiter and the dishwasher. When questioned by Josh, Don responded: "I know as much about Bush Flying as you know about running a restaurant: which is next to nothing." "Ouch" Josh pretended to have hurt feelings and Don simply said: "Get over it Fly-Boy." "Now where the hell did you learn that?" as he glanced over at Skip; Skip just smiled; Don one, Josh nothing.

Don said the big question they had was about closing the restaurant part of the business on Mondays. Tommy wanted to close it, to give Don some well-deserved time off but Don said if it were closed he might well kill the Monday night bar trade. It turns out that the bar was pretty active because of the Monday night football game and their Satellite dish and big-screen TV, or maybe it was practice for the Tuesday night Dart League that dragged in the bar trade, or maybe the pool tables. Whatever it is, it works.

Josh had Skip's radio and his extra spare pair of glasses that he had forgotten in the plane. Skip was the only person that Josh knew who kept a spare pair of glasses in case his spare glasses went missing. Chuck Mason had found and retrieved them; Skip would be pleased.

The gold bars or ingots, whichever they were called, occupied his mind. The phone rang back at the store and Jean answered it; it was Carter wanting a payroll delivery and to complain about some photos that were not up to snuff. Casey retrieved Josh from the Exchange; running back he was sort of out of breath as he promised to deliver the less than complimentary message to Matt. Matt would not be pleased.

Josh hung up and sat for a while thinking about the shooting episode at Bettles before going back to the Exchange. It made him chuckle and he wished Angel was around so he could rub her ears and tell her she did well.

For Angel it wasn't a problem, she already knew it and was strutting her stuff all over the place. Sadly, no one noticed except Casey. Angel was proud of her actions in Bettles. She didn't know gold from lead, but she did know she was pretty hot stuff about now and was very proud. After eating her treats and an early dinner that Casey had prepared for her Angel continued to strut around for a while before laying down to rest. She laid next to the wood stove in the store and quickly fell asleep. She was tired, but content and she dreamed of her younger days and her life on the Police Force in Seattle. She very much missed her litter of five little pups and wondered where they were, wondered if she would ever see any of them again. Angel had been a very good mother; she kept her pups clean and well-fed but was unable to keep strangers from taking

180

them from her. She bit one of those strangers really bad when they took her last pup and was really in hot water for a while. After that she was no longer a Police Dog. After that she was only an unloved canine and might still be living in that stinky prison cage if Claire hadn't rescued her. First Claire and then two seasons later, Josh became her new family and now it was fun again. She was so much more than just a pet doggie now and even in her dreams she strutted her stuff and protected Josh and Claire. They were now her new pups, her new family and no one was going to take them away from her, she would see to that.

Arriving home from the Institute Claire drove her Jeep into the garage and walked back up the road to the Exchange for dinner with the group. Skip was there already drinking Black Jack on the rocks and Josh, after having his ruffled feathers stroked by Don, was enjoying his second Becks in the bottle. Sometime after 5:00 when Tony was to take the late shift, Jean arrived and shortly after that, Casey and Matt arrived. Casey again had messed up hair and with that smug look on Matt's face Josh could only wish to visit his youth again. He wondered why youth is wasted just on young folks: It seems unfair.

Josh didn't speak about the gold bars, but he did tell everyone the story of the fight between the Adams two-some and Justin Littlejohn, Ralph Kelly, and the still unknown accomplice. The Keystone Cops might have been better fighters but probably not better pilots. Josh had been impressed by the performance of the 182 and its 75-degree to the runway slightly downwind takeoff. Whoever was flying it nearly put a wingtip in the snow as it left the ground and made a left-hand panic turn over the frozen float pond at nearly zero altitude to miss the row of trees on the northwest side of the pond. Spectacular as it was, it might have been a bad day for those involved had the pilot snagged that wing tip and cart wheeled. He thought that pilot might make a damn good Crop-Duster.

Skip lamented: "Foolish flyers seem to enjoy the grace and good fortune of the gods of flight, or maybe the pilot was just very lucky." "Whoever was flying that 182 is a damn good pilot. He must be very familiar with the plane or be a really good, no, a really spectacularly good pilot. I wonder who it was and why he was involved with that motley crew? Kelly doesn't fly, and I've seen Justin's skills, so it must have been that third guy, I wonder who he is?"

Skip: "Let's get back to the important stuff, have you heard from Carter lately?" "Yes, of course, how could a week go by without hearing his charming voice? He called a while ago and wants another payroll delivered on Thursday to his security guys on the Birch Creek airstrip. He also has a small pouch of nuggets for the bank vault to be picked up at the North Palmer Mine. Oh, and he has a few problems with some pipeline photos that Matt took on his last trip north. Either the camera has moved in its mount or Matt was flying well off to the right of the pipeline. My guess is the mount moved. Do you remember who installed the camera mount to begin with? Was it MJA?" "Don't ask me, I got my first and last camera when Brownie was the camera du jour. All this new 35 mm motorized crap is just too complicated for me. There are too many knobs to turn and levers to push and fiddle with. I like things simple and easy.

Jean: "No you don't, you like it when other folks turn the knobs and push the levers for you. You're quite capable of turning the knobs but you're just too damn busy with other crap to do it yourself." Skip asked: "Who the hell put a bee in your bonnet?" Jean countered: "You've been moping around for a week trying to figure out how to get involved with this gold mining crap. For Christ's sake Skip, do it or not. There, I give you permission, just stop this moping around; it really gets on my nerves." Skip turned to Josh and then to Claire, and then back to Josh. He winked at the both of them and simply said: "What can I do to help out?" Claire looked at him and then to Josh. She stopped to consider Skip's comment and seemingly accepted it.

Claire: "I was involved with paying for the annual inspection and getting your business discount for Matt on the 185 before his business license was approved by the Borough. I think Jonny Beard or one of his mechanics did the mount. That was when he still owned Northwinds before selling it to Kevin. You should know that, where the hell has your head been?" "Somewhere else I guess. I wasn't going to tell you of the entire adventure, but I guess I better let you detectives in on the rest of the story."

Skip: "Brace yourself Jean; here comes the smut!" Jean: "What the hell are you talking about you poor demented older person? How about a bit of silence so our Knight in shining airplane can speak? Come on Mr. Fly by Knight, in your best Paul Harvey style, tell us the rest of the story." Jean then ordered a round of drinks for the table, on Skip's bar tab of course, and when they were delivered Josh told the story; this time the full story, of the Bettles adventure.

Josh: "Angel did it again; she snatched a duffle from Ralph Kelly that was loaded with eight gold ingots. I'm pretty sure the same ones that Skip and I saw when he crashed his 180 in Bettles. It was Angel's Diamonds last time; this time it's Angel's Treasure. She took it right out from under their noses and they never knew it. Those idiots were so busy fighting each other they never even saw her when she grabbed it, neither did I. She took eight one-kilogram gold bars worth about seventy thousand bucks and I'm pretty sure they will never ever figure out who has them. I can see some real big problems in the near future for a couple of rival gangs.

Claire looked skeptical and questioned: "Is that really enough money to start a gang war?" Josh said: "I know it's not a lot compared to the millions in gold bars that they supposedly have, but they will not tolerate being ripped off. If the Cartel lets a theft like this slide and word gets out, they will be a target for every lowlife with a gun."

Skip: "So Kelly was a courier, a mule for the Reno Cartel. The Cartel likely bought a portion of the gold from the robbery in London in 1983. I guess Kelly got tired of being a mule and decided to steal it himself. Somehow, he got mixed up with Jim and Justin Littlejohn, and I guess, the third guy; the pilot. As I see it, Adams and his sidekick are Enforcers working for the Reno Cartel and are involved with, or maybe even running the operation that makes the nuggets at the phony diamond-mine; now a phony gold-mine; how quickly things change. He probably took over the operation when Jim Littlejohn went rogue after they killed his kid.

Jean: "Who does the marketing of the nuggets and how does the Birch Creek Mine at the Forty-mile fit into this overall plot? Ok, I see that some of the players seem to be changing teams, but to me, the whole idea of making nuggets in Alaska with stolen gold is beginning to sound a little farfetched. There must be more to this than stolen gold. "Josh: "What I think I know is that Jim Littlejohn and what's left of old Fargo Group are still big into the drug importation and sales business. Most of their product goes to the pipeline workers now because that's where the big money is. Skip: "The construction of the line is complete, has been for a while, but in Prudhoe Bay some infrastructure is still being built out. The payrolls, although smaller, are still here but the drug business is shrinking. When the big bosses in the drug business leave there will be a scramble to fill their places. I bet that's why the Cartel just sold the drug franchise instead of getting in the business to begin with. Many of the newly established hoods will die in fights to establish themselves as the new kingpins; it will be a mess for a while. I guess that's what we are seeing now.

Casey: "The construction phase of the pipeline was completed years ago and not much negative has happened since then. I don't think it will be as bad as you say." Casey was a recent graduate of the University and because there is quite a lot of happy weed, and even a little cocaine on campus, she has had some experience with the drugs and the drug users. In her view, the drugs seem to cause very few problems and she is not sure that they are all that important in the overall character of life in Fairbanks. Skip, sounding like someone's father, or at least a know-it-all uncle: "It's like that story about the guy that fell off the rooftop of a ten-story building. When passing the fourth floor on the way down he was asked how he was doing and he said, "so far it's not a problem."

Casey: "That's pretty silly Skip, It's a seventh-grade analogy." It was difficult for Skip to let such a comment slide. But this time he held back his anger, not because he was getting softer and mellowing in his old age, but because Casey might, just might be right, maybe. Still, a very cold quiet hit the get-together; Josh cut the tension as best he could. "How did Littlejohn ever get into the gold business at all? And the biggest mystery to me is what does Carter Thomas have to do with the stolen gold? Does he have any involvement beyond contracting for security services? Skip: "Littlejohn isn't in the gold business; he's just trying to steal a little from the guys that rubbed out his kid; There is no way in hell that he can go up against the Cartel. Tell you what: he's going to wake-up dead one of these days and we best steer clear. As far as Carter goes whatever he's doing is his business; not ours."

Silence replaced the drug and gold discussion and then Claire said: "I think Carter should get his diamonds back. In fact, I'm pretty positive he should. I don't want the damn things, not at all. We should talk to Harry Strubee and see what he has to say about it, and what our liability is concerning both the diamonds and the gold." "Ok, I agree about Angel's Diamonds but let's keep the gold out of the discussion for a while." said Josh. "I agree about the diamonds because we got them from Carter and he likely should get them back." But let's see how the Forty-mile business goes before talking too much about the gold. I don't like keeping the stuff but if the Cartel thought we had it, thought we took it from them we might be in deep-shit.

Chapter (22)

Carter's diamonds   end of Apr. 1985

Another Thursday delivery was scheduled but this time Skip was not involved. Josh and Matt picked up the payroll at the bank going thru the normal paperwork and then driving back to the store before taking off for the Birch Creek Airstrip. The safe at the hangar at FAI was not used this time. They did this because Claire did not want to establish a routine pattern for the pickups and deliveries, so far so good.

This time it was a payroll delivery at the Birch Creek mine that would be distributed to several mines in the area. After that they would pick up gold from the North Palmer Mine and deliver it to the Bank of the North. Josh left Claire a map of the proposed trip that he promised he would follow exactly. There would be no radio transmissions though he would leave his transponder on to satisfy the FAA regulations for flying thru "Charlie" airspace. One other change of plans was that he planned to stop for one full hour at North Palmer mine before flying back to FAI. Claire would drive to the Security Office at FAI and chauffer them to the bank after he overflew the store on the return trip. The plan like several others seemed to be foolproof.

The skies were really clear, and the longer days were starting to bring warmer temperatures throughout the region. As with the other trips they followed the Richardson Highway east to Delta Junction and then further east past Tanacross and Tok and on to Tetlin Junction before turning left to follow the Taylor Highway north to Chicken. It was reported that the airstrip at Birch Creek was beginning to thaw so the skis on the Maule were pumped half down which meant the wheels protruded just a little beyond the ski bottoms. The runway had a southwest exposure and it turned out it could have been used without skis. It was a pretty good gravel runway, fairly hard and dry in spite of breakup. The payroll delivery went well but the money had to be counted twice because of some sticky new bills.

The landing at the North Palmer strip was a bit more difficult because the strip has less of a southern exposure and was glassy smooth hard-packed snow. There was also a little cross drift and Josh did a "go around" on the first attempt but then smoothed the second landing. The elevation was just a bit over four thousand feet and the temperature considered shirt-sleeve if you were from the Interior of the state. The thermometer indicated It was 35 degrees and the smoke stack on the cabin showed about a 5-knot cross breeze. Hector met them at the office cabin door with his second in command Charlie, a very handsome Border collie mix. Charlie had been friendly when they last met but was a bit tense now. Maybe he was concerned about Matt who was a stranger to him.

They did the usual how-dos and Hector poured two more cups of coffee. Josh asked Hector if he might have one maybe two jewelry quality nuggets that he could buy for Claire. If not, could he hold one or two back for his next trip? Hector said he had a couple of nearly one-ounce nuggets that he could sell for melt value. He opened a lower desk drawer and brought out an ancient glass-covered gold balance and then looked around and spotted two small nuggets in an unused ashtray next to the typewriter on the other side of the room. Josh thought: "Hell of a way to run local security."

Hector reckoned $330 per ounce and his scale indicated just a few penny-weight over two ounces. Hector said:" $675 for the pair if you want them both." "I have about four hundred dollars. Matt, do you have enough to cover the difference?" " Just take them if you agree with the price of $675. We can settle up later or you can pay Carter when you see him tomorrow and he can settle up with me. We were on a handshake for thousands last year, so I think I can trust you for six bills today."

Matt: "You say Carter will be around the store tomorrow? What's the problem, or is this going to be just a friendly visit?" Looking harshly at Matt, Hector said, "Carter will be looking for you. That's all he told me, but I think he needs to chew your ass for some bad pipeline surveillance photography."

He said that more as a joke than any serious comment, and also with a twinkle in his eye. But just the same Matt felt unsure of

187

the comment. Josh and Hector shook hands on the nugget deal and Josh noticed that at the handshake Charlie became relaxed and nuzzled his knee a little; he now wanted an ear-rub. Seems Charlie, like Angel, is also in the security business. Next trip he will bring Angel for sure. Matt was also involved with Charlie's ear-rub and drinking some pretty bad coffee while Josh was asking about anything that Hector knew about the Coleville River Mine.

Hector had some ideas about the gold that they were supposedly finding there. He said he knew that Jim and Justin Littlejohn were involved in the distribution and sales of most of the illegal drugs finding their way to the North Slope. He just wasn't sure how high up in the drug network they were, and he claimed he didn't really care. Hector guessed the nuggets that were supposedly coming from the mine were just payments for the drugs and the gold from the producing mine was a convenient way of laundering the drug payments.

Josh: "Do you think the gold from some legitimate mining operations is just being recycled and taken to the Coleville mine, so it appears the mine is really producing?" "Maybe, maybe not. I think that may be true for at least part of it. In fact, I wouldn't be surprised if the gold you are transporting for us today will somehow be carried by someone like you once more, but next time coming south from the Coleville mine, or maybe not. They seem to be producing more than we are right now, so they must have either a big bank of nuggets or another source of gold. Like I said, I just don't care. I don't like the drug business but trying to stop the flow of drugs is like trying to keep the sun from rising tomorrow morning. My personal goal is to just keep the flow of drugs out of the Villages. There isn't a lot of money in the villages so I'm having some success, I think."

Matt: "Wow, if this was Alice in Wonderland, it couldn't be any more curious." "Who the heck is Alice"? said Hector:" And how does she fit into the mining business?" Josh said: "Your childhood is incomplete without 'Alice in Wonderland' but more on that later." He continued: "The drug business is far bigger than the gold business right now. and don't look so surprised Matt, I think you know that the markups and profit margins are far higher on drugs than on gold.

188

Look around you; do you see any miners driving fancy cars? Hell, it's the druggies that are buying gold, not the miners that are buying drugs. About the only thing the miners can usually afford on a Friday night is a half rack of Budweiser."

The conversation wandered until it included salmon fishing on the upper Gulkana River and ivory trading in Nome and on St Laurence Island. Hector was familiar with several of the ivory carvers that Claire frequently bought from but was also able to offer the names of other carvers that had not made the store's list of suppliers. Josh thought it strange since Hector was an Indian and the carvers were almost all Eskimos and the two groups generally did not get along. Hector explained that since the passage of the Native Claims Settlement Act, the two groups had both set up management teams to protect the lands and newly acquired capital and had come to realize they were much better off together than apart and constantly bickering about what were usually trivial matters. He acknowledged there were large cultural differences between Indians and Eskimos, but there were also huge similarities that should not be overlooked.

Matt was listening to the conversation and was pretty sure no major changes in the Natives' welfare or well-being would happen because of the present discussion. Frankly, he was pretty bored. At nearly fifty-five minutes into the conversation, Josh said they had to leave. He again thanked Hector for the two nuggets for Claire and signed his name for the small cloth and leather satchel with about sixteen pounds of gold in it. As usual, the pouch was locked with a crimped lead pellet on the security wire. When delivered to the bank, if the wire was unbroken and the crimped lead pellet intact the pouch would be taken at face value and the transport considered secure. Then Goldstream Air would have yet another invoice for its month-end billings, life was good!

The takeoff was less than perfect because of a stronger cross wind and a runway that was glassy with a few little moguls at just the wrong places. Once in the air with Matt flying, they headed south down the Taylor Highway and, as usual, did not cut the corner at Tetlin junction. The ceiling was unlimited and the flight back to the

Fairbanks area was uneventful and very smooth. Matt flew low over the Tanana Flats to stay below any air traffic in the pattern for FAI and after crossing the Tanana, headed straight for the Goldstream Valley. Flying over the store and the next door Ivory Exchange, Matt exercised the prop and was surprised to hear a radio call to them. It was a male voice and the message suggested that they land or there would be trouble. This was not supposed to happen.

Before Matt could respond Josh switched off the radio and navigation master and grabbed the yoke to keep the plane on course.

Matt said: "We better get down there and find out what the heck is going on. They want us to land: didn't you hear?" "They don't know if we heard the transmission or not. For all they know we had the radio off and will be waiting for Claire at the Security office at FAI, let's just let them wonder for a little while." They continued flying south back toward FAI and Josh flew very low till they were well out of sight. Then he turned a little west and lined up for a landing at the small potato patch strip at Ann's Green-House where the Railroad tracks cross the Murphy Dome Road. Josh landed with the skis full down and taxied as far from the road as he could before parking. Josh and Matt both had their sidearms and Josh also had his .222 20-Ga. over and under survival gun. Josh grabbed the little satchel with the gold and stuffed it into the berms fifty yards or so away from the Maule. The little airstrip had probably been plowed once, maybe twice this winter but there were still enough of the berms left to hide a small package. They put on their jackets and walked toward the road. Matt wondered who would pick up anyone carrying a gun, but Josh said he personally knew 99% of the Murphy Dome traffic and the very first vehicle that came by would pick them up and be happy to drive them to the store.

The first vehicle to cross the tracks was a Ford pickup driven by a long-time customer of the store, a frequent laundromat user and a very friendly beer drinker. James was just driving home after work, spotted Josh and Matt next to the road and stopped even before Josh got a chance to flag him down. He asked if he could help with whatever the problem was and offered to drive the pair to the store. Josh asked if James would take them past the store to the Grizzly Air hangar as quietly as possible. James assumed they were surprising Claire or something and asked if it was her birthday. Josh said it was an "or something" and James grinned from ear-to-ear. Not a clue but James smiled just the same thinking he was likely going to be part of the surprise.

Josh didn't know if what was going on was being directed from his hangar or maybe from the store. There was a radio transceiver in both places. After James dropped them off, Josh asked him to drive back out to the road and not to stop at the store today. He said Ok but was kind of unhappy not to be able to be in on the surprise, whatever it was. Just to get rid of James and ensure he would not be involved in what was going on Josh offered to buy James and his wife a beer and some finger food if they would join them later at 8:00 pm at the Exchange. James was pleased and said he would be there at 8:00 pm with his wife.

James left looking forward to a small party. He was happy to be invited and he thought, he hoped, that he and his wife were finally being accepted into the upper crust of Goldstream Valley Society. Seems James was a bit of a climber.

Josh entered his home from the kitchen door while Matt, pistol in hand, came in through the man-door and into the hangar. The place was deserted and normal in every way. They met in the front room without shooting one another and thought the problem must now be in the store. Josh left his 44 and picked up a Glock pistol and a double-barreled shotgun made in Belgium that had been designed by a shirttail relative of his: John Browning. Matt was so uptight he was overheated even though he was now out of his very thin jacket and the temperature was around 35 degrees. They decided that Josh would enter the store from the rear loading dock and Matt would stay on the front porch and enter only when it seemed safe or if he thought there was trouble. If so, he would burst in and surprise whoever was there causing the problem and save the day: what could go wrong with that plan?

Josh: "Give me a few minutes and listen before you do dumb. This could really be serious; I don't want folks getting hurt, got it?"

"Ya, but what if Casey is in there? Casey is supposed to be working later today. What if she came in early? She might be there right now. I'll kill the S-O-Bs that give her any shit, I'll kill them dead." "Let's find out who the bad guys are before we go killing anyone; first we just rescue the innocents and then we apply our special brand of justice." *What the hell did that mean?*

That brought Matt back to reality enough that Josh thought he could probably trust him. Josh tried the lock on the back door and found it open. He entered quietly and walked thru the store room and into the very back of the store next to the big Coke cooler. He saw Jean clearly and just a little of Claire who was talking to someone he could not see. Josh kept in the shadows and advanced toward the front of the store with his Glock in front of him at eye level. His finger was not on the trigger, but it was on the guard and ready for action. He had been in situations like this in Vietnam and had even gotten shot at several times, though never successfully. He was just about to step into the main checkout area and confront whoever was causing the trouble when Matt came charging into the store knocking the front door half off its hinges. Matt half broke down the door, caromed and bounced off the wall, then back into the door, and then back hitting the wall again. Then while obviously hurting, he wanted to yell but instead squeaked: "Police, drop your weapons. Do it right now!"

Jean and Claire turned and looked in disbelief as Carter, who had been in mid-sentence, backed up into the potato chip display. The upgraded display stand stood the test and was not knocked down. Carter had a look of surprise but seemed to grasp the situation quickly. He smiled, raised his hands and said: "Please don't shoot me, I am young, relatively, and have so much to live for."

Josh, in his frustration, stepped back into the storeroom and tried to find somewhere to hide. Failing that he started unpacking some cans of Ivar's Clam Chowder. This was embarrassing, and he wanted badly to find an excuse for his and Matt's actions. He realized a little too late that he had overreacted to a simple radio call to land and talk out a problem about marginally bad pipeline photography. He tried to figure a way to blame the invasion on Matt but thought better of it since he was the senior responsible member of the team. Finally, he walked out to the front of the store with his tool box and said: "Where is the door that needs some repair?"

Angel was standing at attention and had no idea what was going on. She wagged and went over to Claire and sat down as if joining the group for some gossip. Josh asked if someone would drive him back to Ann's Green House to get the plane and a few thousand bucks worth of gold that he had hidden in the snow bank. Immediately he had three volunteers. Matt agreed to stay behind and fix the door.

Before he left for the plane, he explained there would be an 8:00 pm gathering at the Ivory Exchange for all of those who could leave the store and were not too embarrassed to be seen with him. He said the gathering would include James and his wife. Josh just then realized he did not know the last name of James and felt badly about that.

Chapter (23)

Carter gets the booty   Apr. 1985

Josh had no problem finding the satchel in the snow berms, but he did have trouble turning the Maule to point east and had to pull the tail around by hand. The short flight back home was uneventful, and it gave him a chance to calm down a little. After locking up the gold in his big bedroom safe and picking up the diamonds that he intended to give to Carter, he was back to the store in less than an hour. The whole group was in the store front sitting on lawn chairs drinking coffee. Angel was sleeping next to the woodstove and Matt had been trying to spin a story to justify knocking the front door off its hinges. It was fixed well enough to last until a real carpenter could be employed: he hoped.

Matt finally admitted, at least to himself, that he might have been shot several times had there been some real hoods in the store. Carter wondered out loud why Matt hadn't just opened the door like any rational person might have. Matt had no good answer for that other than at the time it seemed like the thing to do. He wanted to surprise whoever was in the store because he thought there was a tactical advantage to surprise; and he certainly did surprise them.

After explaining his actions, if it were possible to feel any worse about the situation, he now did feel worse. Matt knew very well that Jean was already scheming some new jokes. That she would probably remind him of the door busting incident in the days, weeks, months and probably even the years to come. He decided he would try to be very nice to her but knew in his heart that Jean would be relentless; it would be a first-hand critique that would be long-lived and he would be the brunt end of many jokes in the future. Matt's only hope was that Jean would do something equally dumb. *Poor Matt!*

At nearly 8:00 the Super Six plus Carter met at the Exchange and talked of the warming weather, high gas prices, and any and every bit of local valley gossip there was. The talk continued with the arrival of James Wyden and his wife Jodie; Josh finally knew their last name. Tommy had no pool challengers for the evening and with the Friday-Saturday Bartender making the drinks, he had two days off from his bartending duties. He was thrilled to mix with the group and not feel as though he was ignoring his mixology duties.

James said for a gay guy he thought Tommy was not all that bad. It took him a full three minutes to pry his foot back out of his mouth but Jodie, his wife, was even more embarrassed than he was. Skip could only say "The times they are changing." Nothing else seemed to fit.

It seemed that silence reigned and they all got wet. To break the quiet and change the subject; Carter asked if Matt would take a look-see at the camera mount in his 185 to find and then fix the problem. He said it would probably not involve carpentry work, so he was sure Matt could handle it. Surprisingly, Jean said nothing about wood working and Both Matt and Josh wondered if she even heard the remark; maybe she was slipping. Matt simply said he would fix whatever was necessary and then he would fly the pipeline again at his own expense. Carter thought the pictures were somewhat off center, but they were still within limits and the pipeline would not have to be photographed again to satisfy the contract.

Matt said the pipeline security flights were very important to him and he needed the work badly to get his dad paid back. Matt said his dad had been very sick but was just now starting to respond to the Chemotherapy treatments. He said the treatments were very expensive and his dad needs the payments to keep up with the medical expenses. Carter thought for a while and then asked if Matt would consider working directly for his security firm rather than sub-contracting the work as he does now. Alyeska would not care just as long as they continued to get the photos. The work would be the same and the pay might be just a few dollars less, just a few, maybe thirty bucks a week less. But any extra flying he would do could be billed out by the mile and after paying the operating expenses of his plane he probably could net around $50.00 an hour after expenses. Matt looked puzzled and started to speak but jean elbowed Skip and cut him off in mid-sentence. After a quick conference with Jean, Skip said he needed a moment with Matt and they got up and walked into the pool room to talk. Skip told him that Carter was offering him a job with benefits that would probably include medical insurance for his immediate family and that under the right circumstances it might, just might, include his dad. Matt didn't understand the job offer at first but now he did. They walked back to the table where the group was having yet another round of drinks with still more appetizers: compliments of Don Peters, the head chef and both life and business partner of Tommy Wilson.

Matt said he wanted to hear more about working for Carter. He was touched by what seemed like a very generous and kind offer. Matt had a tear in his eye and Angel nuzzled up close to him and licked his hand wondering what the problem was. Angel had a really big family to care for and protect.

James and Jodie left soon afterwards, and the conversation changed. Tommy and Matt decided to play a game of pool and Claire and Casey wanted to watch so each guy would have a one woman cheering section. Jean arrived after closing up the store at 9:00 and joined Carter, Skip and Josh; she wanted to hear the story concerning the diamonds.

Josh told the story about Angel hiding the diamonds and how recently she brought them back. Carter was not surprised to hear about the diamonds; he knew Angel had taken them but didn't know she had kept them for nearly two years. Josh wanted to give the stones back to him and although Carter would be happy to get them back he would say nothing about their origin. Skip kept pressing him about the real ownership and Carter finally realized that he was not getting the diamonds back until he told the whole story. This was difficult for him; it was something he seldom did on any subject. Still Carter figured he was likely to need Josh and Skip, mainly Skip he thought, for this next scam and so reluctantly, he agreed to spill the details of the diamonds.

Carter's security firm was just one of several freelance companies actively looking for the gold that had been stolen from the Brink's airport vault in London a couple of years ago. A little less than half of the gold has so far been recovered, and none of the diamonds.

At the time Carter's wife was working for one of the underwriters in the pool of insurers involved with the transfer of over two metric tons of bullion. She heard a rumor from a seedy, but generally reliable informant that about four hundred or so ingots of gold bullion were for sale on the "down-low". She thought it might be some of the booty from the Brinks London robbery.

About half of the stolen ingots had been recovered in Europe, two people had been arrested and several others were being closely watched. Whatever had not made it to the Swiss Gold Market was thought to have made it to America where it was discounted and quickly portioned to several American crime families.

The portion going to the Fargo Group was Carter's target and he put together a small platoon of retired military people he had used before and trusted. They were to quietly invade a small warehouse and office complex in the town of Grand Forks North Dakota that was supposed to contain a meeting of the gang: the Fargo Group. Carter was not there but he had put together the plan. His security platoon found and disarmed the gang and opened a safe containing fifty-five of the stolen ingots from the London robbery; the information Carter's wife had gotten proved to be true though the amount of gold had been exaggerated. Much later it was confirmed that the majority of the gold bars had been portioned to the Reno Cartel with only a small ration given to the Fargo Group.

Still It proved to be a good plan and the raid was successful and not one person got hurt. After the gold bars were taken the bad guys were just disarmed and released. That practice is quite common with private security company operations; if no one gets hurt, no one gets arrested.

While the rumored numbers of ingots were not exactly correct Carter's firm did recover nearly four hundred thousand dollars' worth of the gold bars. But the word got out that Carter's wife was involved with the tipoff because the snitch took his reward for the information, got drunk, and bragged about the easy money. Two days later the informant accidently fell into the Red River and was drowned; further, Carter's wife was run over by a hit and run pickup truck a few weeks later in a shopping mall parking lot in Houston.

Jeanette, Carter's wife, is still on crutches; it has been nearly two years now, but she is still making progress with her recovery, slow but steady progress.

Carter's firm was paid expenses and a ten-percent finder's fee by the underwriters. He was of course pissed off; usually when you let the perpetrators go it is sort of unwritten there will be no retaliation; maybe the Fargo Group failed to read the unwritten book. To make matters even worse, Jim Littlejohn had the balls to send a message with condolences regarding the "most unfortunate accident" that Carter's wife had suffered. The crowning touch was when he proved stupid enough to sign the note of sympathy and have it delivered to the hospital where Jeanette was recovering with a small vase filled with a handful, about a dozen for-get-me-nots.

It turns out that Carter had managed his security consulting business so far removed from his personal life that Littlejohn never connected Carter to the raid at the warehouse. Littlejohn only knew of Jeanette as the snitch and since she had always used her maiden name for any of her business purposes Littlejohn knew very little about her.

Carter has always been a believer in first things first, so he decided he and his family would get lost. He first moved his family, his wife and daughter, out of the Houston area. They moved northwest to the Olympic Peninsula, on Washington's north coast. There they put down new roots and settled under new names that were actually; their old names. They bought a newer home in an upper middle-class neighborhood on Bell Hill; just outside the small town of Sequim. Carter established himself as a retired engineer and struggling writer. His cover persona also included part time work as an Environmental Consultant for anyone, usually non-profits, which were willing to contract his services and pay his rather high hourly rate. He also took up golf.

One month later, after he had moved to the Pacific Northwest and hidden his identity, Carter went after Jim Littlejohn, and, in fact, the whole Fargo operation, with a vengeance. With just a week of limited reconnaissance Carter broke into the Fargo Group's business offices in Grand Forks, North Dakota early one Friday afternoon. He was armed with a mostly illegal automatic weapon and fully prepared and capable of blowing every one of the bastards away; that had been the plan. But the whole Fargo Group operation, including Littlejohn, had taken the afternoon off to start a long weekend and no one was there.

So being unable to find Littlejohn, he snooped around a little and discovered a pretty stout combination safe in the basement of the building. Searching further, he was able to find the combination for the safe hidden on a sheet of paper under the desk calendar in the largest office in the building; it must have belonged to the boss. When he opened the safe he found no gold bars. What he found and kept was a small box containing what turned out to be the missing stolen diamonds from the London robbery and about forty thousand dollars in cash which he pocketed: that was for expenses, he claimed.

He planned to come back to finish his work but soon developed what was proved to be a better plan that he was much less likely to go to jail for.

Carter: "It was almost five months later when I was under contract with the Seven Sisters to investigate the drug trafficking into Deadhorse that I found out about Littlejohn's involvement with the drug trade. The Reno Cartel apparently sold the Fargo Group the drug franchise for Deadhorse, only Deadhorse, for some cash and continued percentage of the gross sales. The drugs going into Ugnu-Kuparyk are another franchise altogether that was likely sold by the Cartel for, I would guess, for a similar cost and percentage. I'm not positive of this but I think that's about how it was. "

Littlejohn was just a minor player. He was doing the scheduling and collections and managing the drug toting mules into Umiat, which was a hub of sorts, and from there into Deadhorse. But he was a pilot; he could fly. I guess they thought he was trustworthy and since flying seemed to be important to the main players in the Cartel they must have shown him some deference and promoted him. Along with his responsibility for managing the Deadhorse drug distribution, they sold his son David, the liquor franchise for the whole Deadhorse area. It was not all that big a deal, but it was there for them if they would fly around a few drug shipments when needed in other places. The Fargo Group had few friends in Alaska. The closest friends they had were Teamsters and the Teamsters were not all that happy about the drugs either."

The story was starting to make some sense to Josh and he was getting a new appreciation for Carter as a manager. Putting together that sting was classic, and Josh now pretty much understood the vendetta.

Carter: "I really dislike the guy. I now know he didn't order the hit on my wife, but I still hold him and his crew responsible. I intend to destroy that little prick one way or another. I got him once and I fully expect to get him again, but as for right now I would rather see him squirm than get killed. I didn't sabotage their Super Cub in Bettles if you were wondering. My best guess is that the remnants of the Fargo Group that merged into the Cartel from Reno were the ones who sabotaged the Cub, I think."

Skip: "So Littlejohn is the now the drug pushing King Pin? "Well at least he thinks he is. The rumor was that David and Justin Littlejohn had kept the drug distribution going after the Reno Cartel pulled back the drug franchise and kicked them out of the phony diamond mine on the Coleville. Jim, the father, went rogue and joined Justin after David got killed. He joined up what was left of the Fargo Group and they are back in the drug business much like they were before the guys from Reno took over."

Josh: "I don't understand, why were they pushed out in the first place?"

Carter: "They borrowed a bunch of money and sold the Cartel a partnership in a diamond mine that has no diamonds: or so they think. The Reno Cartel is what's left of an old Chicago crime family that just plain does not do drugs. That crime family is fairly famous: someone did a movie about them some years ago. But with that said they seem to have no problem selling the drug franchise to the highest bidder; don't look at me that way, it doesn't make sense to me either." Josh said:" So are they in the drug network or not?"

"They seem to act more like drug brokers or managers of the traffic and are interested in keeping the peace and collecting a percentage of the sales without getting their hands dirty."

Carter: "And now they have new problems; they are reported to have about nine hundred pounds of gold bars and want them turned into nuggets so they can launder the skimmed Casino revenue from Reno and Las Vegas and then retail the nuggets for cash. I'm not positive but I think that's all they want"

Josh "So what's the war about?" "Its drugs, the Cartel does not want drug sales to corrupt their nugget manufacturing and sales business. The Cartel keeps their varied enterprises separated, nearly totally compartmented and they want what's left of the old Fargo Group who did not merge into their Cartel gone: they want them gone. They're at war now because they're being robbed right and left and they want to make their bucks and be left alone. I think they may have gone to the Teamsters for some muscle, and maybe some capitol to buy the ingots at a pretty steep discount. I guess they damn well better be paying that loan back."

Carter continued: "Littlejohn is ripping off the Reno guys every chance he gets. Likely it's personal because of David's crash; causing that crash was a very stupid thing to do." Josh: "What about Bob Adams, what's his play in this?" Carter was on a roll and continued his story which was very unlike him. Usually he's tight lipped and says only what is necessary. But today it seems different, it's like he's reading a book or something."

Carter continued with the story: "Bob, or Big Bob as he likes to be called, is a nephew of one of the Adam's Crime Family bosses out of London. The family is somehow hooked up with the folks from Nevada. I'm not sure what he is really up to but he is pretending to work for the Cartel as far as I know."

Skip: "So Grizzly Air is the air taxi of choice for the guys from Reno? I knew about the flights to Umiat when I bought Grizzly but there was no indication of any funny stuff going on. I just had a pilot that I was trying to keep busy during a very slow time of year. I wonder what else I bought that I don't know about."

Carter: "Every four or five weeks Adams has fifteen, maybe eighteen, pounds of gold carried in from Reno or Sparks, or maybe even Tahoe. I'm not sure where the gold is being warehoused but I am going to find out and, by the way, I am damn well going to take it from them. It comes into Fairbanks by whatever is available that overflies Canada from the Reno-Tahoe area. Until recently they weren't using mules as such. Charter pilots from private transportation companies were doing the transport and, in most cases, didn't even know what they are carrying. Grizzly Air had been doing the charter flights up to Umiat. In Umiat they have a Super Cub on wheel skis to haul the bars to the mine. Another charter operator from Merrill Field picks up the courier, usually on the same day, and they fly him back to Anchorage, and from there back to Reno. The courier sees the mine but none of the operation; the air taxis only see the couriers one way; and the courier is supposed to keep his mouth shut." *Good luck there.*

Jean: "So all this crap is just to turn bars of gold into nuggets? I don't see why they don't just do it in Nevada at one of their burnt-out mines, there must be a thousand of them."

Carter: "That's a good question. If one of the burnt-out mines in Nevada started producing gold, there would be a modern gold rush and it would soon be seen as a scam. The way it sits now is Bob Adams has a foreman and small crew at the old "diamond mine site" that pretend to be miners but are really there to melt bullion and make nuggets. These are the same folks who had been working for Littlejohn two years ago when he got burned badly in the diamond sting. They were minor players then and still are now, but Adams pays them fairly well and they get two weeks on and one week off, usually in the thriving metropolis of Anchorage, sometimes in Fairbanks. Bob Adams has been totally forgiven for the money lost in that diamond sting. Everybody blames Littlejohn anyway. Adams did his jail time quietly and seems to be well thought of in the Reno Cartel. He was the lowest level grunt two years ago but is now at least a Lieutenant in the operation."

Josh: "So Littlejohn looks like he is squeezing the Reno Cartel a little by trying to hijack some of the shipments. Mike tried but failed with us but with others he had some limited success earlier before Goldstream Air got involved. He must have bribed Ralph Kelly. I wonder if Adams or one of his assistants will ever catch him. They damn near did a few days ago in Bettles. It was pretty close and there was a pretty big fight with even a few gunshots, or so I'm told."

Josh realized he almost spilled the beans that he was there that day, almost.

Carter: "If they do catch him, poor Ralph." "So, the Reno Cartel turns the stolen bullion into nuggets and Littlejohn and his crew sells what they can steal. But they continue with their real work, which is to bring drugs into their Deadhorse distribution network. So, what is Hector doing?"

Carter: "Let's' not worry about Hector right now; he isn't involved with the London gold."

Josh: "Bullshit! What do you mean not involved? We know very well that a least a portion of the gold from the Fortymile district are manufactured nuggets. Get it? Manufactured! And I know for a fact that at least some of the nuggets are exactly the same alloy and that doesn't happen when Mother Nature is in charge. And I know damn well that most of them likely started out as bullion. What do you mean not involved, you think we are stupid? News flash for Carter; I am quite recovered from my fall off the turnip truck, Get it?"

That part of the conversation was a bit of a stretch. Josh was fairly sure that at least some of the gold from the North Palmer operation was manufactured, but he was not positive. They had not yet been scanned, so that part was speculation though it seems to be correct. He would know for sure as soon as Claire could scan the two nuggets he bought from Hector.

Carter: "How do you know the alloys are the same?" "I have the use of a spectrum scanning microprobe, the business end of a Scanning Electron Microscope and I can read the alloy mix down to the one tenth of one percent, that's how I know!"

Carter: "Oh."

Skip: "So what's really going on at the North Palmer and the Birch Creek Mines and just which one do you control, or is it both of them?"

Carter: "If what I am about to say goes any further, I will come down on you with both feet and I really mean it, Ok?" "The only reason I'm telling you this is because I may need your help in the future and I think you don't back down from trouble." "I'm a little old to be chasing bad guys." "I'm telling you I may need help and if you don't help me this drug distribution crap will take this state right into the toilet. Are you in or out?"

Josh and Skip looked at one another and after a few seconds looked at Jean, she nodded and then they nodded together.

Skip: "Ya, Ok, we are big boys and can keep confidential stuff confidential."

Carter: "We might have borrowed a hundred fifty ounces of nuggets that came from the phony Coleville Mine from the bank, we just might have. We might also have you fly some of those nuggets from the mines in The Forty-mile to the Bank of the North almost every week. The part you don't know is we may just pay one of your competitors, Tamarac Air, to fly the gold back to our two mines on the Birch Creek drainage. Then later, we let you take them back to the bank again. At first we went through the melting process to change the alloy a little and recast the nuggets but now we just add or subtract twenty or thirty ounces and do a round robin to and from the bank."

Skip: "So how much do you pretend to produce in a week's time?"

Carter: "Eight or nine pounds some weeks, ten or eleven other weeks. Want to buy a few nuggets?" "You're just plain nuts. What can you do with one hundred troy ounces? Hell, I have half that much in my five-drawer bedroom dresser?" "Don't be so damn smug, I know it doesn't sound like a lot, but remember that the gold gets recycled almost every week." "So, you really are in the recycle business, first with the diamonds and now with gold?"

Carter: "What diamonds? I know nothing about any diamonds."

Jean was intent and about to punch him: "Cut the crap Skip, and pay attention." Skip." Ok, I am listening, and learning but you have to agree this is so neat the story line could turn into a book." Jean: " And then after a month on the best sellers list, into a movie; but for now, shut the hell up and pay attention."

Carter continued: "According to the receipt books at Bank of the North, my mining operations produce right around ninety, maybe as much as one hundred thirty, troy ounces most every week. That is in addition to the gold we really do produce which is around ten, and on a really great week maybe fourteen ounces. Littlejohn has a mole at the bank with a really bad drug habit that he has been supplying in return for some of our internal information. Allen Balla, the manager at the bank, put this guy in charge of logging the deposits of all the mines in the Forty-mile. He has been recording the shipments and feeding Littlejohn the raw numbers about the gold we are producing. I wonder how long it will take Jim Littlejohn to try to take it from me; what do you think?

Skip: "I think its fraud; you maybe not, but Balla, the manager at the bank? You bet its fraud." Carter:" Ok, it might be fraudulent if the gold wasn't really being delivered to the bank, if they were just phony numbers. But remember we do make the deliveries; we have made every single one. And the bank has been weighing and reporting these deposits to the IRS in the normal way, just as they do for every other mining venture. The only difference here is we are shipping the gold to a refiner who may not be melting it; but there is no requirement that they have to melt. We just pick it up from them and send it back to the two mines on the Birch Creek drainage. That whole drainage looks like it is just one big Glory Hole; you do know what a glory hole is right? Well, Jim Littlejohn knows what a glory hole is: in spades!"

Josh: "You don't have a hope in hell of scamming him again; no one is that dumb." "Everyone has a blind spot and there's a big race going on right now. It's running around and round the track, right between Jim Littlejohn's ears; it's a race between Greed and Caution. Littlejohn will lose that race riding Greed every time, every time for sure. Don't forget, I run a very legitimate security business that provides a necessary service. I just have a little gold mining business running on the side. As soon as I sell those very productive mines to Littlejohn, complete with the very long pointy shafts, I will be out of your hair, at least for a while."

Skip: "No way Jose, he isn't that greedy or dumb." "He is so damn dumb he's been trying to get Hector to skim a little and offering him some pretty big bucks to just get a look at the books; to see if they match the figures he gets from his informant at the bank. He figures he can leverage Hector after he gets the information on the mine and Hector gets used to the big paychecks. I think he is pretty close to dropping the hammer." "Who does he think owns the operations? Certainly not you." "No, certainly not me. I haven't even been to the Forty-mile mines though I have been to Chicken Creek once or twice on security matters; that is my business you know. But I have never even been to the mining operations and my profile has been so low as to be invisible. He doesn't even know I exist. Littlejohn thinks a few local politicians from town own the two mines. As far as he knows it's a local group headed by Bill Wally, the Mayor, and some of his family. He thinks Hector is just a greedy Indian willing to do most anything for a buck." "That's quite a story. Is Bill really involved?" "No, hell no! He's a radio announcer not a crook. Do you know him? Heck, he's a good guy."

Josh: "I want to go back two years or so and just fly booze north to the river bar on the Coleville; that was fun. Remember when the bees were after me and I had to dive into the river?" "I remember it. That was a bad day for Sam, but he did finally get a new twenty-foot-wide bottom out of it. Hector saw to that; don't mess with Hector or his friends." "That was only two years ago; seems like half a lifetime."

Chapter (24)

Diamonds are not forever   Apr. 1985

Josh didn't really know whether to believe Carter or not. He really wanted to believe him and whether or not he was being told the truth, he would at least no longer be in possession of stolen property. Josh handed the satchel with the raw diamonds over to Carter. He actually felt some relief to not have to worry about them any further. Unknown to anyone but himself, he kept the one cut and polished stone he had found the last time he looked in the satchel. That one was to be Angel's Diamond, she had earned it.

Skip thought he should have gone to New York and sold them under an assumed name and invested the returns in oil stocks, something that pays a dividend; maybe Chevron or Exxon. Jean thought Skip should mind his own business and butt out of other folk's problems. Claire thought the diamonds were an anchor and was really happy to rid their lives of them. *So at least everyone was now in agreement.*

Carter: "Now that I have these diamonds back I intend to return them to their real owners which are the insurance companies that covered the original theft. If there's a finder fee and I think there will be, I intend to turn it over to either the store or your aviation business; which would you prefer?"

Claire: "That is a generous offer but why give us all the money? If there's a reward you should get at least some to cover expenses." "I get my expenses and my monthly retainer, and this is not charity, its business. So where should I send the check?"

He directed the question to Claire who had just wandered back to the table from the pool lounge. She was not sure and just looked at Josh. He said they should pay any money they got to Skip to help with the replacement of his 180 that was destroyed on his trip to Bettles with Ralph Kelly.

Skip: "Don't worry about the Cessna. That little beauty is being taken care of by my underwriters. I'll come out of that little incident just fine; I might even get a little newer plane out of it." Josh said: "If a finder's fee happens just write the check to the store and we'll hash it out; maybe Angel can have a new collar or something." Josh didn't mention that it may have a cut and polished stone on it. In fact, he has full intentions of giving any finder's fee it to charity, and the charity of choice will be Matt's father's medical expenses, but he didn't want to say so until the fee materialized, if it ever did. He gave a sigh of relief, shook hands with Carter, and walked to the bar for a beer and a glass of wine for Claire. Carter left the Exchange quietly and Jean, Skip, and Claire found they were alone in the lounge. Matt was still in a pool game with Tommy and Casey was his cheerleading section. Tommy won the contest: of course.

After the pool lesson ended and part of the story about Carter was told, as much as could be told, the six friends settled down to a light dinner and a few after dinner drinks. Claire felt like a weight had been lifted from her shoulders and the subject of Angel's newest treasure did not come up again.

Mid May is a muddy transition time for the Goldstream Valley. Breakup is either over or most folks are pretending it is. The skis are off the planes by now, but the mornings are still below freezing a lot of the time.

It's strange but if there is little wind, the smell of defrosting dog poop permeates the air in the Valley for a few weeks during the big thaw; there is a never-ending supply of jokes about it that survives from year to year. The long list of jokes still seems funny though everyone has heard them many, many times.

Most of the kennels will be in a holding mode for the summer and pretty much idle. Newly whelped pups will be looked at closely and evaluated for the next racing season. Pity the poor pup that doesn't run, won't pull and can't learn the difference between "Gee" from "Haw".

It takes just a few short months before the newly modeled gene pools, that each kennel tries to upgrade will be proven or not. Just like the racers at the Indianapolis 500, every year during the off-season preparations are made, plans are implemented, and hopes are high. But when the starting pistol fires there will be no excuses and folks are going to just run what they "Brung", and win or lose, plan for still one more year of racing. Next year is next year, but this year the first dog teams that cross the finish line will win; along with the guy or gal on the back of the sled. The breeding and the training is proven or not; each and every year.

The team leaders, the lead dogs, must not only run faster and pull harder; they must also have the respect of each and every member of the team. Life can be pretty tough for a new lead dog, but there are also benefits. Most of the leaders don't live in the kennels with the rest of the racers. They live in the home of the mushers much like pets. This better treatment seems to ensure their leadership position with the teams and strengthens the bond with the team owners. The lead dogs, the team leaders, strut their stuff when mixing with the racers and great deference is usually shown to the leader.

Salmon are taken from the Tanana River in the fall by the Tanana river fish wheels that operate all day and all night long without need of human assistance. The fish wheels trap the migrating salmon swimming up river and hold them for transport to "Fish Camp" where the trapped fish are gutted, halved, and smoke dried on racks, right on the river banks as they are caught. The fish that make it to the Tanana River near Fairbanks are mainly Chum and King salmon. These fish have had a very long trip and are not in the best of shape. Some of the local people in Fairbanks sport-fish and eat them but most of these fish while still fairly heavy in oils are thought to be pretty ripe and will mostly become just dog food. The salmon sustain the kennels very well for the winter and long into the summer months.

Training for the chosen racing pups will start as soon as the first snows in the fall. One or two of the new pups will be put in harness and run with the veterans during the training runs. They will be watched for speed and endurance and also how well they are accepted into the pack. The culling process is rapid, and pups not chosen for the teams will be traded to other kennels, sold as pets, or otherwise disposed of. Unneeded dogs are expensive to feed and care for and are eliminated quickly, such is life and death in the sport of sled-dog racing.

Angel has no love of sled-dog racing and won't even allow racing dogs into the store, not even the team leaders. No one is allowed to strut in the Golden Valley Store except Angel. Several team leaders have tried to push their way in and Angel pushed back real hard when they did. She has other canine friends that are allowed into the store; Spider from the Exchange comes to the store nearly every day and many of the store's customers have pets that come in with them when they are shopping. The one rule they must all follow is nobody marks any territory inside the store or for that matter, anywhere on the building. Angel holds her tail high when the canine visitors are on the property but never does that when she is visiting the Exchange or other places in the neighborhood, even if no other pets live there. There is a social order for canines in the Valley that must be followed by all.

One day, usually around mid-May, the trees, the Aspens on the hill sides of the Goldstream Valley go green, all of them usually on the same day. The residents call it Green-Out and usually celebrate the annual event with either Happy Weed or vast amounts of iced Budweiser, normally both. This year Green-Out was on Thursday and a few of the Smith Road residents celebrated by bicycling up and down Goldstream Road stark naked while smoking weed and singing Bob Dylan musical superlatives. As bad as singing was without instrumental backup there still was a fairly attentive audience.

Skip and Jean were two of the most appreciative in the audience but failed to join in when asked. Skip claimed it was still a little cold while Jean said Skip was just an "Old Fart". Just the same, she respected his temperature sensitivity but insisted she would have joined in if he had. Tommy was so embarrassed by the public nudity he refused to even watch the event. Don was less sensitive about the public display of nudity but claimed Tommy probably couldn't ride a bike anyway. Summer in the Goldstream Valley is never dull or boring, just usually a bit smoky.

Chapter (25)

Jim's folly   May 1985

United States Smelting, Refining & Mining Company (USSR&M) is the parent company of Fairbanks Exploration Co. (FE). The FE at one time managed nearly all of the major gold mining operations in and around the greater Fairbanks area.

The FE built the dredge now floating on a pond near the town of Chatanika a short twenty-five miles or so north of Fairbanks on the Steese Highway. It's over Clarey Summit, very close to the Poker Flat Rocket Range where the tailing piles from the dredge seem to extend for miles. The FE built several other dredges in gold-bearing areas in and around Fairbanks and they also built the Pedro Dredge that now sits rusting away near the town of Chicken on the Taylor Highway, in the Forty-mile Mining District. The FE owns a large portion of the patented land and many mineral claims, of which some are leased back to the mine operators.

The FE controls the land and the operational Federal and EPA permits for the lease on the land that the North Palmer Mine operates on. The Birch Creek Mine is miles away but on the same drainage and is also on this leased land. The mining or sub-surface mineral rights are owned by the FE, but the Birch Creek miners have 65 years to go on a 99-year lease to operate independently, just as long as USSR&M is paid ten percent of the gross revenues from any of the minerals taken from it.

Jim Littlejohn first became aware of this while reading thru some land leasing information he received nearly two years ago. This paperwork was included in some stolen documents his son, now deceased, and Bob Adams took from a security consultant and the owners of the Golden Valley General Store who were major sellers of the R&R Canadian Whiskey being run into Deadhorse. It had taken nearly eight months to chase the Golden Valley Store out of the liquor business; but finally, Littlejohn had prevailed.

He had been aware of that information but never really had an interest in it until finding out what a real moneymaker the mines on the Birch Creek Drainage were. There were two mines on this drainage: North Palmer Mine and the Birch Creek Mine; both were limited partnerships owned by local businessmen from Fairbanks. The Birch Creek operation was doing extremely well unbeknown to the owners, because of heavy skimming by the mine manager; the manager was stealing nearly 90% of the find and getting rich on the skim.

Littlejohn decided he would find a way to take that skim. While investigating the take from the Birch Creek mine he found that the North Palmer Mine manager was also under-reporting its results by about the same amount. Then when he discovered that both mining operations were managed by the same person, Littlejohn thought he had hit the motherlode.

He was able to find this information because he had access to the raw gold deposit receipts at the Bank of the North; there was a clerk working there that would have had a real drug problem had Littlejohn not been supplying his habit. The gold deposit receipts recorded proved to be far greater than the reported output from the mines as described in their annual reports. The manager of the operations was taking the skimmed findings from both mines on the Birch Creek Drainage and recording these deposits as coming from three fictitious mines on a totally fictitious drainage that didn't even exist in the Forty-mile District. The skimming was profound and showed positively that Hector Redhorse was a crooked, albeit a wealthy mine manager.

Jim Littlejohn had Hector Redhorse, who was the operations manager of these mines, by the short and curlies and he intended to take control of the mining operations from Redhorse. He would leave him with what he had stolen and just a few bucks, just enough to ensure he would remain quiet about the squeeze.

Littlejohn had some history with Hector Redhorse. He was still pissed off at Hector for screwing him out of the price of a riverboat that his son David and a helper had shot up on the Coleville River two years ago. If Hector wanted to stay out of jail for embezzlement, he would lobby and convince the mine owners to sell out, he would somehow get them to sign over their ownership of the leases and sub-surface mineral rights for the two Forty-mile mining properties; or else Hector Redhorse would be exposed.

Littlejohn offered a pittance, less than twenty percent of what he thought was the true value for the claims. The existing owners were a consortium of rich folks just wanting to be a little richer, or so Littlejohn thought. He knew none of them were miners, none knew or cared anything about mining. The group had been put together by the Mayor of Fairbanks who was no longer an investor. The shares had been resold. It was little more than just a shell LLC with most of the shares owned by a Houston Texas, investor. The offer was eight-hundred thirty-five thousand dollars for a complete transfer of land lease and all the sub-surface mineral rights for the remaining years of the leases, to the brand new "J&J Mineral Exploration LLC." The consortium took the offer saying publicly they had made very little money lately and was happy to be getting just some of their investment back. Privately the minority owners of the shares not owned by the Texas investor, wondered who the lunatic was who wanted their leases so badly.

The money to purchase the leases came from Littlejohn's drug distribution network. He put up nearly one third of the cash himself, that was all he had. The rest of it was not his, but it was borrowed from the cash flow that he owed his drug suppliers. When they wanted to be paid he knew he could put them off long enough to get the cash flow from the mines to pay them. It would be kind of like a zero-interest loan.

Littlejohn told Hector that he was to support the deal or he would most likely go to jail for embezzlement. He might just have taken strong-arm control of the property, but he needed to show a legitimate lease transfer of the claim, and a reasonable price for it or the FE and their parent company, USSR&M, might look too closely at the transfer and not allow the deal to go through. They had rights of first refusal but allowed the transfer because they would now be getting their 10% of the gross from both mines; not just the Birch Creek operation.

When Littlejohn confronted Hector Redhorse with the evidence against him, Hector caved and said he would recommend the investors sell out. But he said he knew the business very well and offered to continue to manage the work done at the mines for a small percentage. Littlejohn told him to "Go to hell." Hector was given five thousand-dollars in hundred-dollar bills and told he would have until one day after the deal closed to leave the properties and "take that damn dog with you."

The transfer and closing of the deal was handled thru a bonded security consulting business that had handled other legal business for the FMA; Carter Security Inc, Houston, Texas. The deal closed on a Thursday in late May and given the one-day notice, Justin Littlejohn personally flew Hector, complete with two suit cases and his dog Charlie, from the Forty-mile Mining District to the Chena Marina airstrip. They arrived in a red and white Cessna 182; it was a clear Saturday morning.

Justin left Hector with a bottle of R&R whiskey to heal his ego and drown his sorrows; he thought he was damn clever; Hector thought Justin was a damn fool. Justin advised Hector to stay out of the mining business and to just do what Indians are supposed to do. He said: "Mining is no place for an uneducated crooked Indian." After carrying his luggage away from the plane Hector walked around to the pilot's side of the plane where Justin was sitting just about ready to depart. Hector put his hand up on the wing strut where it attached to the underwing and with one arm lifted the plane up and onto just the other main gear tire and the nose wheel. he said: "Justin: I think maybe it's about time for you to leave; daddy is waiting." And with that said he dropped the plane nearly three feet.

Justin turned white as a ghost realizing he had just deeply insulted a man that could hurt him badly if he was so inclined. Justin just squeaked "Clear", started the engine and without so much as a magneto or carburetor heat check made a down-wind departure. Justin badly needed a bathroom but spent no more time at the Chena Marina Airstrip that day.

It might seem to be less than the best day in his life, but Hector didn't appear to be deflated or even a little defeated; he promised Carter he would not hurt Justin and he had kept his word.

Hector and Charlie seemed stranded as they stood off the side of the runway by the complex of Tee Hangars that stood next to an older culvert style hangar. These were once owned by an A&P friend of his, Kevin Hayton. Hector and Charlie just stood around for a few minutes and took in and enjoyed the Fairbanks sunshine. Hector heard that Kevin had sold out and moved south; he wondered how he was doing. With the economy winding down and jobs disappearing, many of his friends had left Alaska; maybe he would also: maybe not.

After a few minutes to reflect on the fact that he was no longer a miner he left his luggage and walked about a quarter of a mile to the huge log home on the far side of the airstrip belonging to a shirt tail cousin of his: Don Wright. He asked to use the phone.

Hector: "Hello, this is Hector Redhorse, is Josh Browning there?" "This is Josh. Hello Hector, what can I do for you, are you at the North Palmer Mine?" "I'm at Don Wright's house by the float-pond at Chena Marina. Is my invitation to visit still open? I need a place to crash till I can get to the bank on Monday and then arrange for a ride to Allakaket." "I will either take you to Allakaket on Monday or arrange your transportation, and you should stay with us until then. My wife, Claire, has wanted to meet you for a long time. I will be there in fifteen minutes: look for me in a silver jeep CJ. What do you have going on in Allakaket?" "That's where I live. I will be waiting over by Hayton's old tee hangars; by the way, I have Charlie with me, will that be a problem?" "Not a problem at all, Angel will love the company."

The drive to Chena Marina took less than fifteen minutes and within the hour Josh, Claire and Hector were in the Browning's kitchen drinking coffee. Josh was listening to the story of how Jim Littlejohn had outsmarted himself yet again. Claire was more entertained than Josh had seen her in a long time and she was darn near bubbly. Most anything that that was bad news for Jim Littlejohn was happy news for Claire. Since the day that Littlejohn punched Jean, and then Jean got in her licks, Claire became one of his fiercest enemies.

215

Hector: "Carter and I bought the mineral rights to the North Palmer mine from USSR&M nearly two years ago, with some of the money we got from the Coleville property. I heard that some of the fireworks, at least an almost robbery happened right here. Anyway, when they got control of the mineral leases and options on the Coleville River diamond mining property; we ended up with enough cash to buy the mineral rights at the North Palmer in the Forty-mile; what an adventure this has been. We already had a 99-year land-lease with 65 years still left on it. I have personally owned the sub-surface mineral rights on the Birch Creek property since the Claims Settlement Act. It had been part of the deal worked out between USSR&M and the tribes and this part was done without government help. Carter helped me set up the LLC for insurance and Liability concerns but mostly he and I owned both the Palmer and Birch land leases and all the sub-surface rights.

A lot of the tribal members got both individual holdings and shares in the new Native corporations that were formed. All I had to show was a continuing interest in operations involving the land use. My continuing interest involved gold mining that I had been doing in the summer since I was seventeen. Lately I have been managing both local mining operations ever since we finally acquired the mineral rights on the North Palmer."

Josh: "I wondered what happened to you. So, you were actually running both mines for that time?" "Yes, but like I said, even before that when not in school I had been managing the Birch Creek mine. For longer than I care to remember it has been a real drag. First you buy fuel, and then you hire a mechanic, babysit a dozen cases of TNT, buy more fuel, fire the mechanic, what a rat race. It gets a person in a bit of a rut and I don't like ruts. I have a girl in Allakaket that I intend to marry, and I have enough money to start up most any business I care to. Don't know what it will be, but it sure as heck won't be involved with mining! That's for pretty positive."

Josh: "I wonder if there will still be payrolls and gold transport business for my transportation security operations?" "I would guess yes, there are now eighteen and soon to be twenty-one working mines that are paying for your services. A few more, maybe a half dozen, are also getting interested as the word gets out. The miners have been happy to get their findings safely to the bank without the constant fear of being ripped off. Just yesterday I contacted better than half of the mine managers in the area, all I could contact, and recommended they change the staging place for the payroll deliveries and gold pickups. They more or less decided that for the summer they would stage out of Chicken; out of the "Back of the Bar" at Smithies. It's a neat place, have you ever had a beer at Smithies?" "Yes, Claire and I flew into the Chicken Creek airstrip a year ago for lunch when she was trying to do some photography of the Forty-mile Caribou herd."

Hector: "Carter will still be providing security and policing of the Forty-mile District. I'm not sure anyone in the Forty-mile even knows I have a relationship with him because after the Coleville diamond mining adventure we have tried keeping a very low profile to hide any association we have. I am halfway surprised he even told you. Was it that obvious?"

Claire: "Yes it was pretty obvious to us. Aside from the change of management, how profitable do you suppose the North Palmer mine will be for the new owners?" "It makes a few dollars. If they watch their spending and manage it well, it might make a good living for someone. With the price of gold going up it could be a winner but not at the price Littlejohn just paid. I think he's screwed if he borrowed the money. The interest on a note that size would be a sponge on his profits; he paid nearly half a million too much. If Littlejohn wants to survive, he might actually have to get his hands dirty. I wonder if he knows how to run a dozer, a loader, a crusher, and a sluice, and if he can handle hard-rock blasting? Hell, he might just have a lifetime of hard, but honest work ahead of him; what are the chances of that?"

Claire: "I don't think that jerk has an honest bone in his body and I would bet he never did a day's work in his life. Did you know I shot him once a couple of years ago?" "I kind of heard the story from Carter." "You should have seen it; it happened at our store just up the road from here. Carter was there but not involved in the fracas of course; he is never involved". "Carter is the guy that somehow manages to be seen but not recognized. Littlejohn was screwed totally two years ago, and he still thinks that he and Carter were just both trying to get the options and leases for the diamond property and that he won the contest. Littlejohn hasn't a clue that Carter was the guy who screwed him. How the heck does he do it? He sets it up, he causes the trouble, most of the time he's even there but somehow, he's never held responsible for the results. Not in the least is he ever held responsible for anything! He is my uncle and I love him dearly, but I repeat, how does he do it?"

Josh said: "I think it has something to do with how well he dresses. He just looks so good he must not be involved when the bad stuff happens. You should have seen him working the Troopers at this last attempted robbery, they were calling him Sir and calling me: "Hey you." I swear the Troopers did everything but ask for his autograph."

Claire: "And Carter speaks so well with such perfect tempo! Maybe we should take speech lessons and learn to smile a little more. I swear, I would buy a used car from him at list price."

Josh: "He's a bullshit artist with a personality and presents twice his physical size. I don't have a clue how he does it, but if he starts teaching classes, I will sign up for a few semesters."

Angel and Charlie were romping around and then Spider showed up. Charlie was friendly enough with Spider, but Angel was very protective just the same. Angel showed Charlie how fast she could run but Charlie was not impressed. Spider took the two back to the restaurant thru the doggie door for a treat but when Don saw three dogs in his kitchen that was past his limit. He not so quietly escorted them out the same door they came in through and then latched it. Spider bumped his nose and whimpered a little when he tried going back through it and found he was locked out. That was sad for him and he tried to get some sympathy from his new friend. Charlie was less than caring and just wanted to know about the treat that he had been promised. Failing that, all he wanted to do was run around with Angel. Spider felt like a fifth wheel until Angel brought him some year-old bones she had been saving and then he was happy again.

It was still early in the day; Casey was supposed to work the shift from noon till closing with Rita. Jean was invited to lunch with Josh and Claire and to meet Hector. Jean showed up just after twelve noon and helped Claire make some ham and cheese sandwiches. Coke, chips, and sandwiches were the bill of fare. Hector seemed to be very content after making a few phone calls to his girlfriend, and to Carter, who was back in Washington State tending to some family matters.

Carter kept his personal life completely separated from his consulting business and even Hector did not know his Washington identity, nor did he want to know. Carter meant to keep it that way, but no plan is perfect; once, his wife answered the business phone by mistake with: "Hello, this is Jeanette." Luckily the call had been from Carter, so no damage was done, but after that Carter had the business phone relocated only to his office, so it would be obvious which phone was ringing.

Claire asked: "Hector, do you know the manager of the Native-owned store in Allakaket. We do a bunch of business with that store, Josh will fly there at least once a month with groceries and we buy most of the Native art and crafts he manages to trade for." "Yes, I do, the manager is Sterling Redhorse; he is both a cousin and a friend of mine. Sterling is smart and hardworking, and I want to hire him if and when I ever get a business plan together and need extra help."

Hector said he did not like all his relatives and they for sure did not all like him. He didn't appear to have the alcohol-addictive gene in his makeup and has no love for the folks that can't handle booze but still use it. Hector considers it a personal weakness and will not tolerate continued excessive drinking. It's particularly hurtful to him when it happens to folks close to him, both friends and especially family.

Jean: "But you had no problem selling pallet after pallet of R&R into Deadhorse." "Not a problem, not the same problem at all. Whiskey has some very positive uses and if used in moderation it's almost medicinal, and boy, was it really needed there in Deadhorse. But even if it wasn't needed I wouldn't try to stop it because it's not

219

my calling to babysit the world, or even a little bit of Alaska. I drink a few beers on occasion, even to excess once in a while. Usually it's just once a year at the Fur Rendezvous in Anchorage. Everyone has their own set of standards and as long as these standards don't hurt others I have no business trying to direct the lives of others. Besides, even if we tried, it wouldn't work.

Jean thought: "Another damn Republican."

Josh: "Ok now, with that part of the world's problems solved and no new ones on the horizon we can have a few beers and I will introduce you to some of the most interesting people in the area. We should also have a bubbly with Skip; you remember Skip, right? No, I guess that's not right, I bet you have never met him. Jean, do you know if Skip is going to be around a little later?"

Jean: "He had a charter scheduled to Wiseman today; he flew it himself. I expect him in less than an hour, around 3:00, but you know him. Maybe he'll be here and maybe not. If there was one thing I could change about him it would be his inability to keep a schedule. He just plain drives me nuts because he never seems to keep a schedule but whenever he's needed he just seems to show up."

A voice came from just outside the kitchen door: "You rang?"

Jean: "How the hell did you make that trip so quickly and when did you land? I didn't hear you, what's up?" "I own a Cessna 206 with a new engine, so I am speedy. Also, Horace has been after me to practice how to land with a dead engine from anywhere in the pattern and I've been doing just that. I am turning into a real ace doing dead-stick landing, that's how I did it without you hearing me."

Josh: "This handsome young fellow here is Hector Redhorse. Hector, this is my friend Skip Davis, Jean's husband." "Your legend precedes you Skip, my pleasure."

They shook hands and in spite of the early hour, Skip found a lonesome quart bottle of Jack Daniel's finest, in a familiar cupboard. There was a full ice tray in the freezer and after some small amount of cursing about ice cubes, albeit softly cursing, he was more than content to be sipping some of Tennessee's nectar of the gods with his three-favorite people, and a new acquaintance. "God, that Hector guy is big!"

Jean: "Did you get the invoice signed?" "Of course, what do you think I am?" "I know what you are, just give me the damn invoice and I'll quit bugging you." "Is that all it takes? How about I give you two invoices and you promise to not bug me until tomorrow?"

He handed her a second invoice. It turned out he had picked up two passengers for the return trip and made money both ways, he even got a fifty-dollar tip for delivering the two oil company executives right to the Alaska Airlines passenger gate at FAI, a full five minutes before the flight to Seattle was scheduled to leave. When leaving Wiseman, Skip went to eleven thousand feet and put the ball to the wall to make FAI before the Alaska flight departed. They just made it. He couldn't wait to tell the story and was a bit deflated when Jean said it was about as interesting and exciting as winning a two-dollar pot in a card game. She was not impressed so Skip felt no need to share his fifty-dollar tip.

Chapter (26)

Hector and Sally   May 1985

Hector borrowed Claire's jeep and visited some friends out on Chena Hot Springs Road Sunday morning. Cook Bittner, the Veterinarian out there looked Charlie over end to end and said he was as fit as could be. Charlie didn't really like having his ends checked but tolerated it because he was pretty sure it was going to happen one way or another.

Hector and Cook had been friends since high school and had been referred to back then as Mutt and Jeff. Even in high school Hector had been well over 6' 2" while Cook was less than 5' 6" standing on a chair, or so the story goes. After high school he claims to have grown some but no one trustworthy has shown up with a tape measure yet. Hector had kept tract of Cook, he had a special fondness for him because Cook always treated him like a friend when some of the others treated him as just another dumb Indian.

Driving a little farther out the road into Pleasant Valley, around milepost 23, he visited Tacks General Store and bought one of their semi-famous pies to take back to Claire. She had mentioned how she really liked the blueberry pies for sale there but didn't get out to Pleasant Valley as often as she wanted.

Hector just wanted to drive a little, be by himself, and clear his mind of the happenings of the last few weeks, months, or maybe even years. He had financial independence now and after many fairly tough years he was happy to be out of the mining business; finally, he could put it in the rear-view mirror and become a normal person again. He is concerned that when Jim Littlejohn finally finds out he has swindled himself again he is really going to be pissed. And If it turns out he bought the mineral rights with half a million dollars of other people's money he will not only be pissed, he will be livid, and probably want to kill someone. Jim Littlejohn will most likely become very dangerous when he finds himself between a rock and a hard place. He has the type of personality to blame anyone, maybe everyone, but surely never himself.

Hector wanted nothing to do with a mad-and-not very smart crook from Fargo North Dakota. He has pretty much decided to get far away from the shrapnel that will most likely fly when Littlejohn's latest mining scheme explodes. He is not going to Allakaket to stay on Monday. That is just going to be his first stop, weather permitting. Hector is just going to pick up his Cessna 170 and his girlfriend, Sally, and from there they are going on a trip thru Southeast Alaska and will end up in Sitka, out on the Pacific side of Baranof Island.

Sitka in the springtime is not a bad place to be; Hector and Sally are anxious to see the cabin that Carter leased for them. Carter promised Hector a disappearance if that's what he wants, and that will be one of the options he and Sally will consider. Once they get there, they will spend a month, maybe two, getting reacquainted, and getting used to each other again while making plans for the future. It will be the honeymoon before the honeymoon. Hector plans to get a haircut and buy some contemporary clothes. Like Sally, his girlfriend, he is half white and half Indian. His father was an Episcopal priest that took a Native Alaskan wife, a good man that died in a plane crash when Hector was six. Because of his mother's wishes, he was raised Indian and made to adopt his mother's maiden name. His birth certificate name is Smithson, Hector James Smithson. Hector plans to adopt his real name if he and Sally decide to change their identity. Hector will join modern society as a semi successful businessman, which he is.

Sally said once she might like to live in Hawaii; considering Hector Redhorse is a manager, and a damn fine one, he can live and work wherever he wants, maybe even Hawaii. Hector Smithson has a good ring to it, but then again so does Hector Redhorse.

Charlie whined and put his paw on Hector's knee. The driver might be deep in thought but not his loyal sidekick and friend Charlie. They were on the Hot Springs Road, halfway back to the Steese highway before Hector realized he had been daydreaming, the car must have an auto pilot or something, or so he thought. Hector wondered if Charlie would like Hawaii; or maybe they would just stay in Sitka.

Chapter (27)

So where is Kelly, again   mid May 1985

Back at the hangar in Goldstream, Josh had just gotten another request for a Thursday payroll delivery and a serious gold pick up. This time the transfer would happen at Smithies Café and Bar, very near the Chicken Creek Airport. Josh had been into the airstrip several times and it was within walking distance, very close to Smithies. Because of the amount of gold there would be less second-guessing and a bunch more planning. Josh decided to hire Skip for the day and fly the 206 into Chicken Creek. Matt would ride shotgun, with a real shotgun; Skip and Josh would be carrying only side-arms. At nearly four hundred per ounce there would be around one hundred eighty thousand in melt value; 35 pounds of gold is not trivial. Skip agreed to go along if he could log the flight as "Pilot in Command"(PIC). He finally admitted to Josh, and only to Josh, that he was working to get his Instrument rating current again, and that he needed to increase his recent logbook hours. Josh pointed out that he claimed to have an instrument rating all along, but Skip just ignored the comment. Skip thought most of this FAA crap was just that: "Crap." You could either fly in the clouds with a compass and artificial horizon or not. Either way, he claimed it was a self-correcting situation.

His last flight north to Umiat ended with a crash landing just a little short of the airstrip in Bettles and Skip was a firm believer, almost religiously, in "getting back on the horse" after being thrown. Skip has no intention of repeating that trip in any way, shape, or form, though it had been a real adventure. He was determined to make this trip without incident and felt as though if he completed the trek past Bettles and on to Umiat, he would be kind of giving the finger to the sometimes-evil Gods of flight, which struck down his last effort.

Grizzly Air Taxi has a charter for an oil company worker who was going to Umiat for some unknown reason. The amount of traffic going to Umiat instead of Deadhorse was a puzzle to Skip: he had a suspicion that there was more going on there than anyone would admit and wondered if the Prudhoe oil fields might be expanding toward the south west sooner than later. Whatever was going on the passengers were not talking about it: they just never said a word about their business which was strange because most passengers would talk your leg off and normally it was pretty difficult to just get them to shut up.

At Umiat Grizzly was to pick up another passenger and then fly that one on to Deadhorse. This was for tomorrow, Monday. Skip offered to have the flight take Hector and Charlie to Allakaket on the way if they needed the transport.

Skip had fired the last of his contract pilots because he failed to show up for work and likely lost customers and a lot of future business. He would not tolerate that bullshit from anyone in his crew and started to see that contract pilots didn't really consider themselves to be in his crew. They were independent; too damn independent for him. He decided to talk to Jean and see what she thought about hiring a full-time pilot instead of just contracting a trip at a time. The fired pilot got his last check and nearly a fat lip for complaining to Jean about what a jerk Skip was. He had no idea she and Skip were married and thought Jean was just an older broad that worked in the office and might like a roll in the hay: not today asshole! Jean just might forget to send in his 1099s next tax year.

Skip's newest prospective pilot was a younger guy that Josh had talked to only once and said he was wanting to fly the Alaskan bush; he indicated he had heard good things about Grizzly Air. That was a little strange because Grizzly's reputation with its pilots was not all that good. Josh said he thought the guy was probably an Ok pilot but knew nothing about his work habits; he was from the mid-west and had done some oil business air taxi flying out of Moorhead Municipal, near Fargo North Dakota. Josh had seen his log book to check his hours and type rating and saw his home airport was not Moorhead or Fargo but was indeed Devil's Lake Regional, that is north-west of Fargo.

"You are on your own regarding the guy's ability to show up when promised." Said Josh. Skip just said he would see and called the airport manager at Devil's Lake Regional. The manager told Skip the guy was poison; it seems this new prospect had been under scrutiny by the local sheriff for drug trafficking, among other things, and one day about two weeks ago the guy had just left the jurisdiction. Skip realized he would most likely be a drug mule for the Littlejohn's and was trying to join-up with Grizzly to get a paycheck while ferrying more drugs to Umiat; Skip was pissed but instead of flying off the handle he just told the guy he had already filled the position. He wanted to tell him to piss up a rope; but didn't.

Skip wondered if Littlejohn could possibly be that stupid; did he not know that Grizzly Air was just a few yards down the runway from Goldstream Air and that he and Josh were friends? Or maybe Littlejohn was crazy enough to get close and try to take him out again.

Then finally, after talking to Jean about tempting fate with another trip to Umiat, Skip decided to pay Matt to fly his passenger to Umiat after dropping off Hector and Charlie in Allakaket, and then on to Deadhorse. Matt took the 206, and with Hector flying from the right-hand seat and his passenger and Charlie in the back, he slept most of the way and the flight went without difficulty. Matt was happy for the work especially since Hector was doing it, at least as far as Allakaket. The flight continued to Umiat and then on to Deadhorse, still without a problem. After leaving Deadhorse, and because there were no return passengers, he was able to stop in Bettles for a twenty-dollar burger and soggy fries on the return trip.

In Bettles he caught some local gossip from Paul Mason about the red and white Cessna 182 that Ralph Kelly, Justin Littlejohn, and Mr. Unknown got away in the day of the fight in the bar. It turned out Bob Adams had been unable to find and follow that plane. He had been back to Bettles once, Adams was still looking for Kelly and the stolen cargo. The red and white Cessna seems to be Justin's newest plane; he was in it when it was last in Bettles and has been seen in it in other places. Most recently, when flying Hector from the Forty-mile to Chena Marina airstrip near Fairbanks.

When Adams was last at the lodge, one of the cooks there asked a few questions about the parking lot shooting incident; Adams told him to: "Shut the hell up and make my damn lunch." That's not a good thing to say to someone who is preparing your food, but it is a good time for the cooks to use the stale buns and out-of-date ground-beef.

Adams knew the Deadhorse drug trade and he knew that Umiat was the main hub for drug transport into the Deadhorse and Prudhoe Bay area. Umiat is also the drop off place for gold going to the Coleville river mine that is laundering the ingots from the Brinks London gold robbery. He knew that the people transporting both the gold and the drugs were kept in the dark as much as possible about the business. For the last several months he had been toting a duffle or a satchel or two, of gold himself. If arrested, it is good if the mules know little about the business, and if grabbed by aspiring competition, it is also good if they know nothing.

Justin Littlejohn has a very small network of people because just a few people are needed to handle twenty or so pounds of drugs a couple of times a month. The fewer the people the fewer possibilities of leaking information to either the Law or the almost-nonexistent competition and it also keeps payrolls down and profits up.

But Justin Littlejohn is making a mistake by spending too little on his own security. Other than just one senior level Trooper that is on his payroll, he has almost no local street enforcement in Deadhorse because there is no real competition there. Occasionally a trucker will bring a few pounds of funny weed or even some cocaine into Deadhorse. But that only really seems to stimulate the market some and it is no big deal to him. Bob Adams; however, saw this situation and realized that Justin's grip on the Deadhorse drug market was weak. He had once been an employee and knew the business and most of the contacts fairly well. Adams was thinking he might take a try at moving up in the world.

Adams had also worked the diamond mine for Justin's father but became disillusioned when the Reno Cartel took over the diamond deal. There, despite his London contacts, his influence and importance diminished. Jim Littlejohn stayed with the Reno folks and managed the mining effort. David and Justin broke away and continued with the drug trade. Although Bob was still working, actually managing the mine nearly half time, he also worked when he could with David and Justin. He was never very well liked, they employed him, only as a grunt. At the time he got little respect and that bothered him a lot. He almost quit a couple of times to go back to England, but when David was killed, his situation changed, and Justin started to rely on him more and more to help manage the drug business.

Adams ended up knowing as much about his drug distribution and sales network as Justin. But Bob could not totally leave the mining operation that had, by now, turned into a laundering process for the stolen gold ingots. Now, though knee-deep into the drug trade, he still had to act as a mule for the Reno folks hauling twelve or fifteen pounds of gold once a month.

But Adams has plans of his own. He knows that when the gold from the London robbery is finally all processed, and the family is done with Alaska, he might be free to compete in the drug business on his own. Bob had been planning to set up his own operation and he made Ralph Kelly an interesting offer. Adams would make him a player in the new drug business if he would agree to steal the gold shipment he would be carrying to Umiat and, most importantly, make it look like Justin Littlejohn did the deed.

Adams would be stealing from himself, but with the stolen booty, he could finance his first drug buy, and Littlejohn would not only get the blame, he will finally have some competition. But Adams has more than just a little larceny in his blood. After the theft he planned to kill Ralph Kelly. Justin Littlejohn would be blamed, and Bob Adams would be set with bucks for his first buy when the London gold had finally all been melted and resold.

Finally, the plan was coming together and all he has to do now is just find Kelly and grab the gold. Adams now wonders if Kelly has maybe figured out his plan and is lying low or maybe Kelly is just running with Justin Littlejohn to make the theft look real. Either way, Ralph Kelly was a walking dead-man.

A wide variety of illegal drugs are available from the one Detroit crime family that Justin deals with. They have direct access to drugs coming into North America from Asia; they come into Canada thru the Vancouver Island trade in Victoria. The main Asian crime family involved is well-respected, if there is such a thing as respect in the drug business. They only deal in cash and they seem to buy and sell fairly; they say what they will do and then do what they say. Chasing down folks who owe money has been a needless exercise in the past and has added a lot of unnecessary overhead. Doing business for cash brings out the very best in the very worst people and enforcement problems are either nonexistent or very seldom and finally, no one owes anything to anyone. "You pay your money and you gets your stuff". It works most every time and keeps out the folks who dream big, talk loud and fast, but somehow can't produce.

Adams is tired of being treated like someone's little nephew, which he is. He wants most of all his own operation, or at least wants control of it if his uncles agree to expand their business into drugs. Bob's plan is to have the operation set up and already financed before proposing the business venture to his uncles.

By now about a third of the gold that the Reno Cartel controls has been melted down. In another six months or so, the remainder will probably be taken care of. It's just a matter of time and Bob can sit back and wait but first he must find Ralph Kelly. Bob Adams thinks Kelly has the fifteen odd pounds of gold and Kelly thinks Adams has it. Both are wrong, Josh Browning has the gold bars compliments of Angel, and she isn't saying.

Chapter (28)

The forty-mile mines   May 1985

The round robin to Umiat via Allakaket and back via Bettles went without any problem for Matt. Fortunately he got some unreported sleep because Hector can not only navigate but is also a pretty good pilot. Hector even did a pretty good job landing the 206 though Matt was close on the controls with him.

His girlfriend Sally is a fairly lucky person because Hector seems totally devoted to her and he is not all that unlucky himself; she is a looker with a nice smile. Matt wished them well; not knowing any of Hector's plans he just said good luck. Matt gave Charlie ear-rubs and said maybe they might meet again. Anyway, he hoped they would.

Planning for the payroll trip to the Forty-mile on Thursday was pretty much a rehash of the other trips. Matt and Josh will pick up the payroll at around ten in the morning just after the bank opens. They will take Cushman Street south to Airport Way and straight to the Airport Security office. They will be driving Skip's Travel-All and Matt will ride shotgun with a real shotgun. For a very small fee the Troopers will provide an escort if arranged in advance, but Josh thinks it will attract more attention with a police escort then without one. Nobody is going to hijack a Travel-All in day-light hours on Airport Way, or so he says.

Skip flew the 206 in from Goldstream and fueled it up at Northwinds. He gave it a very complete preflight and it was good to go. The three of them took off north from FAI and took a right turn after reaching pattern altitude, flying right down the Richardson Highway.

Then, four minutes into the flight, Josh took a hard-right turn and backtracked to the south part of town. Josh kept low and landed quickly, a straight in approach and final into Metro field. He taxied up next to Skip's new 180 that had been patiently waiting through the night. Skip, Matt, and the payroll money pouch, were transferred into the 180. The plan was for Skip and Matt to wait on the ground for a full fifteen minutes before departing to the Forty-mile. The arrival time was the important number and even if they had to fly in circles the flight was to land at the proper time, Skip would see to that. Josh had a pouch similar to the one with the payroll, but it was loaded with cut up bond typing-paper. He said his good-byes and quickly departed in the 206 for the Forty-mile mining district.

The flight south was smooth and like the previous flights, after passing over Delta Junction he continued east. But unlike previous flights, Josh then cut the corner with a hard-left turn at Tok and headed straight for the Chicken Creek Airport. It was a very quick flight and Josh saw and heard no other air traffic in the area. Before landing he radioed on 122.8 announcing his intentions to land northwest on runway 31: he heard nothing. On landing he rolled up and parked in the tie-down area at nearly mid field. There were several aircraft tied down but one that he looked at the closest was a white Cessna 180 that was parked and chocked, but not tied down.

Josh set the parking brake on the 206 and stepped out onto the pad. He grabbed the payroll pouch and started to walk toward the one single hangar at the field. There was a footpath from the hangar leading east toward Smithies Café and Bar. It was a shortcut. The roadway took a much longer route, so Josh planned on using the footpath. He had walked less than fifty yards past the hangar when two figures dressed in camouflaged clothing appeared. They had been lying down in the tundra and he just walked right past them. Almost invisible, they just stood up and approached him from behind with handguns drawn. Before Josh was aware of them and could grab his weapon, he was told by his old friend Mike Thompson to stop, to give up, to drop the pouch and his Glock, and step back a few yards.

Mike: "Lift your pistol from its holster with just two fingers and drop it in the tundra next to the payroll. Then just keep walking toward the café and don't even think about whatever you are thinking about." "What the hell does that mean?" "Just shut up and do it. I got you fair and square this time Josh, just get it done. Dammit, do it."

Rather than taking the chance of getting shot, he did as ordered. He was told to keep walking and he did. When he was another hundred yards or so along the path, he heard another voice, a command to stop. He stopped and slowly turned, but the order to stop had not been directed at him.

The order had come from two people who had been inside the hangar. It came from the immaculately dressed and spotlessly clean, Carter Thomas. Carter was there in the company of one of his security men. Mike Thompson and his associate were busy getting fitted with handcuffs. Josh walked back toward the hangar, picking up his Glock and inspecting it for dirt and grit. As he holstered it he recognized Marvin, Mike's friend from the Salcha Park Roadhouse.

Carter and his security agent had been in the hangar when the three bandits had arrived in the white Cessna but thought they were just customers of Smithies and had not watched them beyond taking the path to the bar.

Josh: "Marvin, how's it going? I see you finally have that ketchup stain out of your shirt, looking pretty spiffy you are." "Go to hell Josh." "Bad attitude Marvin, how did you get mixed up with Mike again? You don't learn very quickly do you? Where's Todd, the third member of your team?"

Mike was saying nothing. Carter was threatening both of the bandits with years in jail and worse. He was really pissed and wanted to know "who set it up?" Who leaked the information of when and where the payroll was to be delivered. Carter was getting nowhere, and it was clear, while he was a great security manager, he was obviously a very poor inquisitor. Carter was frustrated, and he grabbed Mike by the collar and said: "Yes Mike, where is the third guy?" About then he saw that Mike and Marvin were two of the three guys from the white Cessna and realized: he had just 'Done Dumb'.

As he asked the question he had it figured out, because just that quickly he heard: "Let him go and get your hands where I can see them."

It was Todd, the third bandit from the Salcha Park Road House incident. He walked into the hangar with a pistol in his hand

and a smile from ear to ear. Todd: "Get those handcuffs off of my friends and be quick."

After being released, Mike handcuffed the three of them together in a daisy-chain, and then around the leg of a work bench next to a wall on the side of the hangar. Todd then took a roundhouse swing and hit Josh square in the face. He knocked him and the others to the hangar floor. Josh tried to stand, and he was hit again. He now had an open bleeding cut on both cheeks. Todd kicked him in the chest, ripped his shirt and sent his sunglasses flying. Josh was handcuffed to the other two around the workbench and was totally unable to either fight back or even dodge the beating. Todd continued to punch and kick at him letting him know it was pay backs for the punch out at Ruthie's. Todd took his Glock and also his holster, thanking him sarcastically for the weapon and said the next time they met it would be worse. Todd thought of himself as one mean S-O-B, Josh thought he was walking dead.

Mike had been yelling that they had the payroll and they should get going but Todd kept cursing, kicking and punching, he seem to be really enjoying the moment. Finally, when he stepped back to catch his breath they heard some yelling and noise from the direction of the café. Mike said he heard a couple of four wheelers start up and they should get lost before they had to fight the whole town. Mike: "Let's get the hell out of here, or we'll soon have more targets than bullets. Let's go, we have about two minutes to get into the air."

Todd: "Just a little more: this is fun." "Dammit Todd! Do you think you're a big man by kicking a guy in handcuffs? We leave right now Dammit, right now!"

Mike had the payroll in his hands and wanted no other trouble. Then he did a strange thing as he looked at Josh with real sadness in his eyes, as if to say he was sorry about Todd. And Josh, though pretty bloody and hurting, seemed to understand; he nodded back.

Mike and his two-man crew ran for the white 180 and it was just off the airstrip when two of the locals on a four-wheeler from Smithies Café drove right thru the doorway and into the hangar. A second four-wheeler arrived with one of Carter's security man on board, He had a handcuff key and they got quickly released. When he walked out of the hangar and into the sunlight, Carter saw the dirt and other stains on his suit. As he was brushing it off he looked around and found his hat and the sunglasses that Josh had lost. He returned them. He also tried to help the guard that had been involved in the handcuff daisy-chain. But this guy seemed to be in shock. He had taken the job for the weekly pay, which was not all that great, but mainly so he could wear a uniform and be respected by his girlfriend, he had most definitely not taken the job to be involved in this sort of crap. The guy quit the job on the spot, handed Carter the phony badge, and started walking back to the café where his car was most likely parked. Carter told him his health care benefits would last through the end of the month and, if he reconsidered, he could be rehired on Monday providing he passed the phycological evaluation.

A few more would-be rescuers arrived, but they seemed to be half drunk and mostly stood around patting each other on the back and talking about how they would have handled it if they had arrived two minutes sooner. Josh walked back toward his plane and found his first aid kit. Carter got most of the bleeding stopped with a few butterfly band-aids but the bruising would take some time to heal. Josh was pretty cut up and his face was starting to swell and puff up. Josh was more pissed off than hurt; he was already planning his next meeting with Todd. Mike didn't seem to take any pleasure when Todd was beating on Josh in fact Josh saw that Mike had tried to stop it from getting any worse. Josh had no idea what Mike was all about; he was truly a mystery.

Carter and the guys from the bar walked back toward the café. Josh said he wanted to think a little and would join them in a few minutes. He sat in the right front seat of the plane reading an article in the AOPA monthly about turbulence and laminar flow wings. After reading it twice he almost convinced himself he understood what he was reading. It was the second time this year he had wanted a cigarette. Josh was looking at his watch when Skip's 180 did a low pass over the runway. He pushed the master switch on, toggled the radio to 122.8 and announced that the field was clear of trouble. On the next pass the green and white 180 landed and turned off at the ramp near mid-field. Skip was the PIC and quite proud of his nine-hundred-foot short field landing. Matt was not impressed. Skip parked his new plane smartly right next to the 206 and was first out of the plane.

Skip: "Just what the hell happened to you? It looks like your face was on fire and someone put it out with a rake." "Nothing to worry about, just small problem that won't be solved today, but someday it will." "I hope it isn't catching." Josh said: "Let's get this money to the guy paying the bills and we can sweat these details a little later." Matt stepped out of the plane with an Ithaca pump shotgun in hand and looked around. He particularly eyed the only building, the single hangar that stood between the tie down ramp and the foot path leading up the hill to Smithies. Skip had the payroll pouch in his grip and carried Claire's Ruger Mini-14 cradled in his arm. He gave Josh his own personal handgun, his Glock and holster. The three of them walked the foot path to Smithies and five minutes later entered the Café building from a side door into "The Back of the Bar." There were five miners at a poker table: they had been playing a game of seven card stud and were barely aware of the robbery at the airport. It wasn't the first robbery that had happened in Chicken. Carter's security patrol man changed his mind about employment opportunities and reenlisted. Carter let it slide. He was embarrassed and already making excuses about the stolen payroll saying it would be a few days until they would be paid, but they would be paid. It was obvious that some of the miners had been sampling, in a big way, the main product of the saloon. It was not yet noon but already several were half in the bag and a couple of others were totally looped and most likely seeing double. Only one of the miners seemed really upset while the others were just trying to arrange for an extension of their bar tabs.

Matt put the payroll pouch in the middle of the poker table and asked "Which of you is an officer of the FMA? And who can sign for this delivery, who wants to count the cash?"

Josh: "Step up gentlemen, its payday!" Carter had been standing off to the side trying to take up as little space as he could and not wanting to be the center of attention. It was bad for his business and very bad for his ego to have been responsible for the loss of the payroll. He was still trying to brush the dirt stains off of his sport coat, but he had somehow cleaned his hat and shoes.

Carter was totally surprised, and it was the very first time Josh had ever seen him speechless. He thought they had lost the payroll and had been getting the story together in his mind for the insurance company; the paperwork would have been endless.

Carter: " So what did they steal?" "A real nice money pouch from the Bank of the North and about six pounds of cut up bond paper. I had also included a Bret Harte short story about the 'Outcasts of Poker Flat.' You should read it sometime."

Matt: "We had a run-in at the Salcha Park Road House awhile back, and though we didn't plan on this today, it's not surprising it should happen. These guys see a pretty big prize and they're not all that bright.

Carter: "What the hell made you think there would be a problem here? This is the last place I would have thought there would be trouble." Skip said: "And so it was here but I tell you what; there will never be a next time. There were five of them at the road house and they got a "get out of jail free card". This time they thought they got away with it. Next time they'll be damn lucky to see the inside of a jail cell. And as for that Todd character? That son of a bitch will be drinking tea with Noel Simpson." That comment was taken as pure bluster and made no sense to anyone except maybe Josh. Josh turned toward Skip and paused before asking: "What does Noel have to do with anything? " Skip went dead silent; He knew he said too much, but finally he said to the folks at the poker table: "Does anyone care if I join the game? What's the game, draw poker? Is there anything wild?"

Josh did a double take on that comment about Noel, the phony FBI Agent that turned out to be really a P.I. who was somehow worked for or was at one time employed by the Fargo Group. Josh had not seen or heard about Noel Simpson since a disagreement he had with him several years ago that ended with Noel flat on his back on the floor at the Exchange bar and Josh with a bruised knuckle. He decided to get the full story later.

Josh: "Sure, go ahead, but I want to get lunch and then pick up the gold for our return trip before the weather gets funky. I think we can leave these fine semi-sober gentlemen here to pursue Lady Luck while we fill our gullets in the café. Any arguments?" "I'm not hungry right now so I'll play for a bit. I have my own plane you know." "You can play for the time it takes us to eat but you are flying back with us or you won't get paid." "Fine, Ok, and fuck you very much." Then he turned back to the card table and said: "Now let's get the cards in the air; what's the limit gentlemen?"

The poker game continued with the new player. Skip said he would play only until he was kidnapped by his associates. One of the more intoxicated players asked what associates were? Skip looked at his cards and raised the bet two bucks.

The man who finally signed for the payroll turned out to be the treasurer of the FMA. He said the gold shipment would be arriving soon, escorted by mainly sober miners. And lunch for the non-card playing pilots would be compliments of the FMA; this time only, he said with a smile.

Chapter (29)

A bit of a mystery   May 1985

Flying the gold shipment back to Fairbanks was straight forward and not a problem. Matt flew Skip's 180 back to the Valley while Josh and Skip hauled the gold satchel to FAI and then to the Bank of the North. Josh pushed Skip on the question of Noel Simpson and though Skip tried to evade the interrogation he was unable to hide the facts any longer and finally broke his silence on the demise of Noel.

Almost three years ago Noel and Josh had an incident at the Exchange that ended with Noel flat on his back on the floor nearly unconscious after a one punch fist fight. Then an hour or so later while walking on his way back home Josh had slipped on some ice and got a concussion when he hit his head on the frozen roadway next to a power pole. When he woke-up he was home on his sofa with Claire and she told him what had happened. But what was told to him was not what really happened.

What really happened was Noel was hidden, lying in wait for Josh behind the power pole and when Josh walked by Noel Black-Jacked him. Noel was a cold-blooded killer and had no compunctions about killing Josh; he was about to finish the job when Angel, who had been following Josh home, must have jumped Noel from the side. She must have hit him hard and with such force, that he fell toward the pole and his head was impaled on a climbing spike on the side of the power pole. Skip was driving in a few minutes later and found Angel standing over Josh and still growling at Noel's body that was hanging, still twitching, from the climbing spike. Skip dragged Josh into the front seat of the Travel-All, and after unhooking his head from the pole, put Noel's body on the tail-gate. He then drove down the road to find Claire and get Josh some help; for all he knew Josh was critical. After finding Josh was just out of it for awhile Skip decided, over the objections of Claire, to make Noel bear bait. Skip put Noel's body in the 206's cargo door and in-spite of it being at night in an unfamiliar airplane and flying at less than 200 feet of altitude, he flew out over the Tanana Flats, and while the plane was on auto-pilot, he managed to dump the body somewhere near the Bonnifield Trail. He said later that finding the airport in the darkness on the way back was about the hardest part of the adventure; he nearly stubbed the nose wheel on landing but made the trip nearly unhurt.

Claire was really upset and threatened to end their friendship but Skip insisted that in this case Frontier Justice was appropriate. If not, and the whole story came out, Angel would most likely be put down and any of Noel's friends, if he had any, would have Josh, and probably everyone else attached to the store in their sites. Probably the best thing to do was just "Shut the fuck up".

Putting down Angel was the final argument that made Claire reconsider, so after four ounces of Tennessee whiskey and some time to think the problem through Claire agreed to not speak about the subject, ever again. They also agreed that Josh would not be told unless it became necessary and that was maybe the hardest part because Claire didn't like secrets from Josh. The very last thing Skip did was to drive Noel's Chevy into town and leave it parked on two-street with the keys in the ignition.

After hearing the full story Josh went silent for most of the trip. After they landed at FAI Josh asked if Skip thought he should tell Claire that he now knew and Skip admitted he did not know the answer to that question. Josh decided he would wait until the next time Claire has too much to drink to broach the subject of Mr. Noel Simpson.

Paperwork at the Bank of the North went quickly and when he finally landed back at the store, Josh explained to Claire about his newly acquired bruises and cuts and the butterfly bandages on his face. She seemed to be more upset than he was, or at least it looked that way. After considering the confrontation at Chicken Creek Airport and his injuries, Claire was wondering if Josh thought a small but reasonable charge could be attached and added to the invoice billings to FMA for his pain and suffering. She was known to sometimes squeeze blood from a turnip, but this question was so off the wall that it took him by surprise and he had to listen to the question twice. After thinking about it and the rest of the revelations of the day he just said: "Whatever."

She insisted that Josh take the question about his injuries seriously. "And, I want a description of this Todd Character. He could come into the store tomorrow and I wouldn't know it; what the hell does he look like? Does he have a tail and maybe green scales, how about horns? Seriously, I want to know who these jerks are. I know what Mike looks like. Does he still walk with a limp? They seem to be doing their best to fuck up a pretty nice system that we have worked pretty damn hard to develop. These guys are going against the both of us, not just you, and Matt. If I have to go on the next payroll delivery I will! Do you get it? This crap is going to stop, or someone is going to get dead, and it won't be one of our team."

Josh: "Bad language is hurtful and unnecessary." He said that with a wink trying to defuse and lessen her anger, but God only knows why. He was also pissed off and very frustrated. Josh spoke again: "Ok, I get it; if I had even a clue how to handle these guys I would do it in spades. Other than getting a bigger crew and more firepower, I am pretty much clueless."

Claire: "So, as I see it, someone is getting the delivery and pickup information. They are somehow finding out about your schedule; let's start by finding out how the hell they get this information?

He has always been surprised by how quickly Claire could get to the center of a problem. Josh has total trust in the folks around him but now he is wondering about the friends of his friends. Mike's bandits, Josh decided to call them "Mike's bandits", knew when he was to arrive at Chicken, but they didn't seem to know he was using two planes, and they didn't know about the phony money pouch. Also, they seemed to either not care or not know about the gold pickup. What is that all about? They should have known there was a lot more value in the gold shipments than in the payroll deliveries; puzzling. So, they knew his route but not all his business; or so it seemed.

Jean got involved and decided to make a chart that listed the previous payroll shipments and the gold pickups. Then she listed the

240

folks who had knowledge of the transportation schedules; anyone who was involved, in any way who might know where and when. It was a pretty big list of folks but by the time it was complete and rewritten a few times, the big list became a rather small one. The most common names were always Carter and Josh, usually Matt, hence Casey, and of course, Claire. Skip knew the schedule as did Jean, most of the time, but not all the time. And there was also airport security at FAI and the FAA. Josh always checked the weather at his destination and along the route before any of his flights. That meant Flight Services people knew he was looking at the route and destination; FAA even knew approximately the when: the time.

Anyone at the bank knew within a day of a delivery and maybe a gold pick-up, but that was too vague, so Jean took the bank off the list. Josh was thinking about two years back when he was first flying liquor to the Coleville. Carter always seemed to know where he had been. On one particular trip he had gone to Ambler to deliver a few groceries before picking up a package on the Coleville River. Somehow Carter had known about it although Josh had never told anyone about the trip except Claire. That had puzzled Josh, but he blew it off as unimportant at the time. Now it was no longer unimportant, and he wanted to know how Carter knew about his route. If Carter somehow knew his route and schedule from any outside information, then others might also know. Josh decided to have a few words with Carter.

As hard as they tried, it seemed impossible for anyone that they were aware of, to know the timing, route, and destination for the payroll deliveries and gold pickups. How about just the payroll? Again, Carter would know most of the information but not the probable times. He might know the days, whether or not in the morning or evening, but not the time. How does one keep track of an airplane hauling a payroll to obscure places at random times? A lot of his trips, by far, most of his trips, are not hauling payroll, but are hauling cargo to strange places: mines, villages, even a random air drop where no landing area is available. How would anyone know which flights were worth hijacking?

241

Jean said: So, there must be a trigger at the bank; the Cashier would know. The Cashier would have to order in a larger amount of cash than normal the day of a payroll flight or the day before.

Claire: "Are the payrolls really enough to make a change in operating cash?

Jean: "For sure, banks sometimes go for weeks without a cash shipment. Usually money out is about the same as money in, usually. I think maybe part of the information the bandits need comes from insider information at the bank. Someone, probably a lot of folks, have the information that a payroll pouch is being stuffed and sealed. I think we should try to figure a way to make that information unimportant."

Claire: "Ok, let's just pick up the payroll at random times; maybe several days ahead of time. We have a safe at FAI and one here. They are both secure. Hell, sometimes I can't even get them open, and I know the combinations." Skip said: "I want to know who! I want to know who the stool pigeon is at the bank. I'm sure it's the bank that's the tip off." Claire added: "What about the weather information you get before your trips Josh, what can you do to hide your destinations?" "I can get information over the phone as usual, but I can also go in person and talk to people I trust. Let's try to hide the dates of the payroll trips. We can't change the destination. The payroll deliveries pretty much always go to the same destination. But we can hide the delivery time and even the date, fairly easily. I think we will do that. I probably don't even need weather briefings most of the time: usually I can see the weather east into Canada from the upper porch behind the store.

So, the deliveries won't always be on a Thursday in the morning or early afternoon. Carter can do whatever he needs to improve the security on his end of the line. I am not going to worry about his problems.

Yes, that's a good idea: we will not always make the delivery on Thursday anymore. And one other thing; I think I might get weather information for days that I have no intent to fly. Maybe what these bandits need is a little too much and maybe bad information.

Angel felt left out of the conversation and was just a little sad. She knew Josh had a problem with his last trip but was not sure what it was, Angel did know if she had been there she could have helped. She stayed very close to Josh and nuzzled his knee a few times while the group was talking about whatever the problem was. Angel decided to go on the next trip. She knew where her harness was, she would get it and keep it hidden near the plane for the next time. If she had her harness ready to go, Josh would have to let her go next time, for sure.

Now that there was a plan she thought the swing on the front porch of the store needed policing and more important, Casey would probably give her a jerky if she asked. Angel left the house and trotted up the road to the store for a jerky and a nap under the swing; it was part of her job you know.

Instead of increasing output, the gold shipments from the Forty-mile District slowed down during the summer. Output from the North Palmer slowed to the point that miners in the area thought maybe the new owners had another outlet for the gold, or maybe they were just holding back the mine's output. The gold prices were spiking, changing twenty to thirty dollars, sometimes fifty dollars from day to day, and rumors were that gold would go to three thousand bucks an ounce. Gold miners, even very experienced miners, are subject to these rumors that always circulate but are seldom true; it's a symptom of Gold Fever for which there is no known cure.

The Birch Creek mining operation continued, but the output from the mine has now also decreased to where it is no longer the star performer in the area. The Littlejohns' were managing both of the mines and the son Justin, was learning to operate some of the more complicated equipment. At the Birch Creek mining operation, he was putting in twelve to fourteen hours a day and some folks said he was turning into a savvy miner.

Mike Thompson didn't seem to work for Justin Littlejohn anymore. He would probably make his presence known again, but for some reason Josh was not concerned about Mike. Mike was inept and had no real experience in thievery or robbery, or larceny, or whatever it was that he considered his occupation. Mike was not able to think very far beyond right now. Josh had been referring to him as The Polaroid Bandit. "Right here, right now." That was Mike through and through.

Mike's friend, Marvin, also seemed like just a young guy, fairly confused and plainly in the wrong business. Josh could see a future for Marvin selling tacos from a truck or maybe hawking hot dogs from a steamer on a street corner in Seattle. He probably would have flunked out of Bandit School the first week.

But as for Todd, that was a problem just waiting to materialize. Josh was pretty sure he knew what would happen if they met again, when they met again. Josh had given it some thought; only a true sociopathic coward abuses someone unable to defend themselves just for the fun of control and inflicting pain. A real sociopath is seldom encountered but when they are Josh knew they were to be dealt with according to a very different set of rules. He was prepared to throw out his moral compass to make this loser go away but he wasn't spending his time planning for the next meeting; he pretty much had that problem mapped out.

Skip had not been at the airport in Chicken for the robbery, but just the same agrees that more determined action should take place if there was yet another robbery attempt. Other than that, he seems to be in a world all by himself and feeling pretty good about it. After taking delivery of his newer green and white Cessna 180, he had been flying many of his charters himself. Matt was still his only pilot and was happy and willing to fly on contract rather than be on the payroll. Matt is always telling him how much better it would be if he had just put a few extra bucks into his budget and upgraded his buy to a 185. Skip thought the only reason for the extra horse power would be for a float plane. He insists if he wants a real performer he would buy a Maule.

Grizzly is an air taxi service and has little need for the extra load-carrying ability of the 185. Skip said he hauls mostly people to mostly bush airports. For obvious reasons he has no love for river bars or other off-airport landings. He argues that a 180 is a pretty perfect airplane for him. When he got his new plane, it had less than one hundred hours on it and was one of the very last ones built before Cessna discontinued production of the plane in 1981. The previous owner had an auto pilot installed and he really loves that feature. His only problem with the plane is the paint job; he does not like green and white on an airplane.

When Jean looked at the color she thought it was a little drab but Ok. There was no color not Ok except maybe black. Since her time in the Air Force she had always had an aversion to the color black on aircraft. Her husband had flown black planes and had been killed in a black plane and she never really forgave the CIA for letting him fly into what they had known was a semi-suicide mission. Jean and her husband had been very young and felt they would live forever. Because of his death, and short of any retirement or other benefits, she mustered out without even a Medal for her husband's death, or even her time in the Air Force. They would not even acknowledge his service, not the CIA. Jean really hates the Black Birds, as they were called.

Fifteen-odd years later and after a few false starts and another failed marriage, she was finally starting to get her life back together. It had taken that long for fate to find her another good man, though not without some major social warts. Thirty-seven years old, manager of a successful General Store, and married to one of the most dynamic and determined, but foul-mouthed businessman she had ever met, Jean thought life was starting to get a little better. It might be perfect if she could just get Skip slowed down to half the speed of sound, just half.

Chapter (30)

Who goes where and when

Since accepting the job as manager, on Fridays Jean usually works the early shift at the store from 8:30 in the morning till 2:00. After that she works the books, writes the end of the week payroll checks and usually finds someone to make a bank run before the 4:30 closing time, or she will make the run herself.

Similar to that, at the Gold Bar lounge, Skip also writes the checks on Friday afternoon and usually does the check register if there is time and if he feels like it. Skip says: "He runs the business; the business does not run him." And that seems to be a quote to hang on the refrigerator and save for posterity.

He usually has a weekend bartender for Friday, Saturday, and sometimes Sunday nights though Sundays are marginal in the winter. Skip has a new partner who is supposed to be the managing partner, but so far that has not worked out and besides that, Skip is not all that happy with his work ethic. Ambition and desire does not always equal performance, though it does help. Skip thinks his new partner will shape up in time, how much time is the question, and his patience is running thin.

So, with Friday nights off for everyone, it gave the four friends a chance to have a quiet dinner, usually at the Ivory Exchange out in the Goldstream Valley. It normally is a good way to end the week, but this time it was a little different.

On Friday morning Josh told Claire he had some business to take care of and took the short hop over to FAI to visit a friend. He taxied right up next to the control tower and parked the Maule there rather than going to transient parking. Angel had jumped into the back seat when he was preflighting the plane and Josh pretended to not notice her hiding in the back during the flight over to FAI. Angel thought she was clever; Josh was happy for the company of a good friend.

He let Angel walk with him up the steps to the tower after getting permission to come up and observe operations. They buzzed

246

him in and on entering he immediately noticed Maury Fitzgerald going over some flight-logs with Ray Ballantyne at a desk away from the operations area and in a corner of the room; not quite a corner because it is a round tower. Ray begged off the conversation with Maury and walked over to the counter to see Josh. He bent down and gave Angel an ear-rub: Angel wagged.

Ray: "Angel and Josh, there's a hand to draw to, what's up bud?" "I need some information and wondered if you had a little time?" "I assume this is related to FAA business?"

Josh: "I am pretty sure it is."

Maury got up from the chair and walked over to the counter and said, "I have been planning to come out to Goldstream to see you, do you have a minute?"

Ray: "let me have a few minutes to handle some things and I'll pick this up when you're finished with Maury. As the shift supervisor I have a bunch of paperwork you know". "When did you get promoted to a position of importance?" "I'm the Shift Supervisor, who said anything about importance?" And he turned away and walked toward his desk.

Josh: "Maury, so what's going on now, more crap about the Super Cub?" "Yes and no. We now know who did the cable sabotage on the Super Cub at Bettles and we know it wasn't you. You are clear in the investigation." "Well congratulations on your Dick Tracy-like discovery. How long was it going to take you to tell me that? Do you know I have been paying an attorney? Do you even care? No, I guess you don't." He turned to walk away a few feet and then turned back. "Dammit Maury, do they really pay you for this? For Christ sake, Claire has been sweating bullets! Were you ever going to let me know?" Maury was not the least bit apologetic nor did he seem to really give a damn one way or another. "This is no apology and don't take it that way. You are just no longer a person of interest." "Well screw you very much for that information! Don't get in my face again."

He turned away again and started to walk over to an area to watch the controllers work the radios. Maury followed and pressed on over to Josh and got in very close; he seemed to be about to say

247

something, probably not all that complimentary, when Angel pushed in between them and growled. Angel had her hackles up; she was just waiting for the word. "It's Ok Angel, good girl." Angel backed off just a little; she retreated a few feet and then stood there firm and she was paying very close attention and was very ready. Ray noticed the dispute, dropped what he was doing and quickly walked over toward Maury. "Are we about done with our business Maury? Is there any more tracking information I can get for you?" "No, I think not, that's about it for today. See you next week about this same time."

He looked at Josh and if looks could kill Josh would certainly at least have the flu. Maury picked up the log sheets, and was about to say something, but instead turned and walked toward the door and then down the tower stairs.

Ray: "I won't miss that guy one little bit. Besides just being a cockroach with the NTSB he's a hard one to work with." "What's he doing here anyway?" "The NTSB and the FAA are both looking at some new Air Traffic Control techniques, but since both the agencies kind of hate one another it's not an easy task. I've been instructed to help out if I can but it's a tough place to be because that guy is a first-class jerk." Ray continued: "I'm sure you've heard of GPS? Well, they are considering building some GPS-based systems to track and then control all the air traffic in the US. It's a long time away, but the powers that be are looking at some of the problems and some of the possibilities of such a system. It's no big secret, but few people know how closely we keep track of most all air traffic. I can tell you where the planes are, how many there are, also the probable destinations of every single plane in the air in a thousand-mile radius; nearly from the Pacific Northwest to the Pole. We can get this information now in less than five minutes and they are working now on a system to do that in real time. Are you excited about that? Don't you just want to celebrate?"

Josh: "It's too early in the day to drink, but: "La-de-da". "You don't seem that impressed. What does it take to excite the "Sir Josh", the Great White Knight of Goldstream?" "A hell of lot more than that." Ray thought for a few seconds and smiled: "Well Ok then, how about this?"

He had a small computer going on a near desk. Ray typed in a few commands, cursed softly, and made a few corrections to his typing, cursed and tried again; then finally a sheet of paper came out of a printer.

Josh: "What about your typing abilities? Will the system improve them?" Ray just rolled his eyes a little: "This printout is your recent aviation history, Josh. This is your life according to the great FAA network in the sky. Take a look, at where you have been, or at least where your planes have been, for the last thirty days: read it and weep." Josh looked at the spreadsheet and saw they had indeed recorded his flights, they had somehow known where he had been and when he had been there.

Josh: "Why are you keeping track of me, what did I do?" "You did nothing; I have this information on all flights in the area and any other place where this system has been installed and is being evaluated. It's just a very small part of the proposed much larger system. It's the program that Maury has been working on. They want to see if it would really work on a larger, much larger scale. I've been told they are trying it in Portland, Salt Lake City, and here. Just for one year or so, just to see how well it might work and what the problems might be." "Why is Maury working on it, what is he doing anyway? I thought he was an investigator." "He was until last year but now he's involved with what they call 'IT Traffic' or something. Though I work here I don't know all of what's going on."

Josh: "I've been saying that for years." "It's a big organization Josh, be nice and don't piss off the FAA or maybe your next Medical Certificate will get lost in the mail." "Like that's never happened." "So, what can I do to help my very favorite "Fly by Knight" Bush Pilot today?" "I hadn't talked to you since Skip put his 180 into the graveyard at Bettles and I wanted to know exactly what happened as you saw it and also, to say deep thanks for helping. Ray sat down at the desk and opened a drawer and pulled out a book. He opened the book and started flipping through a few pages until he found the proper place.

Ray started reading: "Skip was out of engine and didn't think he would make the airstrip. He apparently hadn't been into Bettles since the Airport Road realignment and was gliding, sans motor, in and out of the clouds, low scud, and ice fog. I guess he either could not or did not see the road, and he seemed ready to put the plane down in the stunted spruce forest just south of the strip. I had him on radar and just pointed out that there was a road three hundred yards to his right. He was pretty low, but still managed to slip it right a few hundred yards and, according to this, he came out of the ice fog right over the road. He was doing seventy instead of fifty and was way too hot to make the right turn at the corner. You should see that plane, what a mess."

Josh: "I did see the plane or really what's left of it and you are right, it is a mess. So, he told me that you knew it was him driving the 180. Did you recognize his voice over the radio? How did you know that it was Skip?" "It's this new system I have been telling you about that we are trying out for the NTSB. It keeps track of the planes with only intermittent radar information." "But, with Skip going into Bettles it was a real-time situation and not a database search, or whatever you call it?" "Yes, real time, that's what I just said, look at the sheet I just printed out for you. Look at the last entry, take a close look." "Wow, you have me here, at the tower." "When you call in for weather info, or file a flight plan, which you never do, or contact us for any reason; the time, location, direction, altitude, or anything else, it is recorded. And your request to enter the tower and observe operations was recorded. The system tries to match up the returns with planes probably in the area according to other inputs: requests for weather, departure vectors, and the like. Hell, we were keeping track of you once last month when you mistakenly used an incorrect tail number. That number was for one of Kevin's planes. What a coincidence, you and Kevin." They made a little eye contact and Josh lost that one. He was beginning to understand more about how folks were keeping track of him but wondered how the information was getting out of the new system and into the hands of the unwashed.

Josh: "Who can access this information? Can Claire keep track of where I fly and if I get there, and when?" "It's not public information but if you guys were underhanded and clever you could do it." Josh asked: "How so?" "Can't really say Josh, it's not public information."

Walking back to the plane Josh was talking to Angel and he wished she understood more. He saw that she had brought her harness and wondered if she could take an IQ test what she might score. Bet it would be really high for a canine, and probably even higher than Mike Thompson might score.

Chapter (31)

The internet and other magic

Casey and Matt were having dinner at the Exchange celebrating some anniversary or another. According to Jean, if it involved food, drink, and romantic moments, they would celebrate the incoming of the tide, given the chance. When Skip saw them at another table they were invited to join the Friday group and the six of them had dinner together.

Small talk went from: "I saw the first barn swallow today" to: "I think we need to have the drain field for Soapies expanded again." On the far end of the table Claire and Casey were hard into some remote sensing problems with the Synthetic Aperture Radar (SAR). On the near side Skip was just plain covering Matt with some bullshit about how a plane's glide ratio, or the distance it can cover horizontal without power for a given altitude, is the same regardless of the load. Then when Matt started agreeing Skip changed his mind and insisted a loaded plane would glide even further if it were loaded aft because it would change the angle of the wing slightly and increase the cord, but it would still have to be within the weight and balance envelope. Matt was having none of that crap and informed "His Majesty of the Sky" that he was at least as educated as Skip was and besides that, Skip was no astronaut.

They decided to settle the argument in the usual way with a game of pool. Somehow or other it was assumed that the Gods of Pool would award the more favorable shots to the most intellectually pure competitor: at least it seemed that way.

As that was going on Casey and Claire were done with the discussion of the SAR question and were now telling Josh about how the Terabytes of data from the SAR Satellite were transferred to digital tapes via the Ethernet cables or something, and the TCP/IP protocol connects many computers together in a network. His eyes were trying to spin, to rotate like the wheels on a slot machine might, and he claimed it hurt. So instead of listening to further digital crap he asked: "What the heck exactly is the Internet?" Claire gave him

252

one of those looks and spoke like she might to a seventh Grader: "Where have you been lately, are you really that ignorant?" And Josh, pointing to the north in a grand sweeping gesture said: "Out there in the backwoods and wilds of Alaska trying to scrape together enough business to make a living for the two of us."

Claire: "Maybe you should try to learn just a little about technology you know, for the two of us."

Josh turned toward Casey: "Casey, can you tell me more about computers on a network? How do you know where the stuff goes, who gets it? If it's on one computer how do I get it on another computer?"

Claire: "Why are you asking Casey? What the hell is wrong with my brain?" "She has a PhD and you only have a Masters, why would I believe you?" "Because I wash your socks, that's why!" "The Maytag washing machines at Soapies wash my socks, you only supply the coins."

Casey: "Ok children, let's stop fighting. Concerning data transfer, it's not just that easy, it might be in the future but right now it's not that easy."

The Dynamic Duo were holding hands under the table, it seems that sometimes even their closest friends don't know when they are clowning around and when they are really having words, sometimes Josh doesn't know either, but he usually finds out at bed-time.

Josh: "Ok, but consider this; so, it turns out all my travel information, route and destination, has been being recorded by the FAA and someone else, someone outside the FAA has been somehow getting this information. How would that happen? I just talked to Ray in the tower at FAI about a new system the FAA is testing and I'm pretty sure that's how Mike and his crew found out when and where we would be making the payroll deliveries. I just don't know how they got the information. Could it be this network stuff; can they just steal it from the FAA with another computer or something?"

Claire: "If you're pretty sure that's really how Mike and crew got the information then it's easy. Either you don't let the FAA know what and when your deliveries will be made, or you give the FAA the wrong what and when. I think we can figure out how to do it either way. Which way shall we do it Sherlock, or shall I say Dr. Fly by Knight Holmes?"

Josh: "That's not totally a bad idea, don't know; let's think on it for a bit."

Matt and Skip wandered back to the table kind of slowly and nearly despondent. It seems Matt won the game of eight ball against Skip but then Tommy challenged Matt and took five bucks from him. It was not much of a contest and after that he played Skip for five bucks more. Tommy of course won, and then played the both of them giving the twosome twice as many shots as he took, he won again. Skip: "I really don't know what the moral to the story is, how about you Matt, any ideas?" Matt: "Not a clue."

Claire: "How about just not playing pool against Tommy Wilson? Do you ever see Don playing pool against Tommy? My father always told me not to get into a contest unless I had at least a fifty percent chance of winning. Does that mean anything to either of you? For the last two years or more, I have watched you guys play against Tommy and, between the two of you, I can only remember one win, and it was by Skip. When the hell are the two of you going to figure out that Tommy is using you as an annuity. Do you care? And if you do, when will you learn?"

Skip: "That's cruel and hurtful Claire. I nearly win quite often. He isn't that good, he's just very lucky." "Yes, and if you practiced more you might get luckier but you would still lose. Tommy is a pool-playing Savant, get it? A Savant that won't be bettered when playing his game on his table. What's the point of even talking to you guys, when it comes to pool, the both of you are as dumb as soup!"

Claire picked up her wine glass and swirled it a little before taking a sip. The dinner had been perfect, the wine great, and the company friendly despite Claire's disparaging comments concerning the pool playing skills of the gruesome twosome.

Carter's secretary Ginny called the store from their offices in Texas at around seven thirty. Tony took the call and sent Angel over to the exchange to get either Claire or Josh. Josh ran back to the store and listened and took notes as Ginny gave him a list of the next few payrolls and the proposed gold pickup and transport times, weather permitting of course. The payroll deliveries were easy; every Thursday thru May, June, and July except on the fourth. Since the fourth was on a Thursday that payroll delivery should be on Wednesday. The amount of cash would be increasing because of the added personnel at the mines. The deliveries would be pretty big; some as large as one hundred thousand bucks. The deliveries would be to Carter's security men at Smithies, the Chicken Creek Café. The deliveries were to be made to the "back of the bar," the card room. That would be a worthy target for most any group of bandits but might also be a little dangerous for them.

The gold pickups could be mostly at the option of the courier, and Josh could put those trips together whenever, but they should be at least once every eight working days, once a week was favored. Despite the FMA, some of the mines wanted to plan their own pickups and would be choosing other air delivery companies. Josh planned to make a gold transport pickup on most every payroll delivery day. He still planned to have at least two people make each of the flights and to have no added stops along the way.

Josh walked back to the Exchange but kept the phone conversation to himself. He was very interested in the Internet or whatever it was called. Was it the World Wide Web (WWW) or the Internet? Why does everyone seem to talk in code about computers? They are as bad as the FAA when it comes to initials or acronyms.

When he returned to the Exchange, Casey and Claire were back to the SAR returns, and Skip was lecturing Jean and Matt on the plight of the small businessman. Jean asked if that was about businesses managed by very short people or businesses that had limited revenues, hence small profits. He was on this kick because he usually talks around the perimeter of a problem before deciding. The problem was that Skip was considering hiring a pilot. He had gotten an inquiry from a young guy who just got laid off recently in Galena. The pilot is nearly dead broke, really needs the log book time, and badly wants to stay in Alaska.

Skip: "He has all the right ratings: IFR and Commercial for any planes that Grizzly Air will ever own. He says he will be around for a week or so and really wants the work. Oh, he also has an A&P ticket and will do small repairs and some maintenance if I want, though I really want Kevin to keep doing the maintenance on my plane. But he would be handy for any repairs needed in the bush. Anyway, I told him to come back in a day or so and we would talk. I want to see if he can fly into the short tight stuff. Can I borrow your Maule for an hour or so to see what he can do?" "I guess so. But talk to him first and try to make sure he's no bullshit artist. If the Maule got dented I would have to fly your Super Cub into the tight stuff and I have a problem with the slow speed and the noise. Also, I couldn't take Angel along, she only likes modern aircraft." "Be assured I will take special care and screw you very much. My Cub is a great plane and you have no cause to disparage it." "Yes, I totally agree, it is a really great plane if fact it's just about "State-of-the-Art if you like 1937 technology." "I hope Angel bites you."

Chapter (32)

The plan man   June 1985

Ralph Kelly was enjoying his down time in Kenai. Since turning the gold bars over to Justin Littlejohn in Umiat and then seeing Justin lose them to Bob Adams a week later in Bettles, he had been on his own. The excitement at the lodge at the Bettles airstrip was more than he cared to repeat. Ralph never thought of himself as a fighter. He was an independent businessman who had always skirted the fringes of the law. Whether as a drug or gold toting mule, or maybe even a getaway driver, he was never one of the main actors. Typically, he was just one of the hired help who did the job and tried to keep from getting dead.

Ralph felt sorry for Justin losing the gold package. He never had any intentions of stealing the package for Bob Adams, but since it did work out that way he was probably due a payday. He wondered if it would be a bonus or a bullet, either was a strong possibility.

It had been Justin's idea to stop for lunch, not his. He told Justin to get that package as far away from the North Slope as he could. It was Justin who had screwed up. He thought Justin was a bit of a dork and should have stuck with his drug sales. But Justin did pay him thirty-five hundred bucks and while that was less than he was promised it probably was more than he had earned.

So, Ralph finally had a few bucks and in spite of losing the satchel, he was very happy to no longer be considered a mule which was mostly thought to be the lowest of the lowest positions. He was finally out of the transport business.

With his final thirty-five-hundred-dollar payment and other money he had saved, Ralph thought about a vacation trip to Hawaii but then decided it would wait till fall. Right now, he had a few weeks before going south and was going to enjoy a little bit of Alaska and relax. He would taste the goodies his share of this operation would buy. As hired help he had gotten paid even though the loot had been lost. Ralph planned on relocating but decided to see the Kenai

Peninsula first. Soon he would be leaving Alaska for better opportunities, probably something with his brother in Portland.

He closed his checking account at Bank of the North and after getting a fifty percent refund on his prepaid monthly rent, he was feeling pretty good. The landlord might have told Ralph to take a hike but instead had been fair and Ralph thought, maybe even generous. In Anchorage, Ralph rented a car from Hertz at the airport, and drove down the Sterling Highway toward the town of Soldotna. From there he turned a little north and ended up in the oil producing town of Kenai. Ralph spent most of his time touring the many local bars and most every strip club that he could find along the way.

The Cook Inlet oil fields were first developed in 1965 and are very close to the town where the Kenai River runs into Cook Inlet. These oil fields developed slowly by today's standards and the town of Kenai grew as the oil fields expanded. In spite of the growth, the town had been fairly stable for a period of over fifteen years, a long time of stability for a boom town, a very long time. Kenai has a small oil refinery that supplies maybe half of the oil products used in the state. The refinery is a supplier of fuel to the military and for the international air traffic that passes through both Anchorage and Fairbanks over the polar routes, the top of the world flights. The Alaska Railroad hauls oil tanker cars to Fairbanks nearly every week and this is strange because Fairbanks also has a small refinery; they must use a lot of fuel in Fairbanks.

The Kenai River is a huge attraction for tourists, fishermen in particular. It's a glacier fed river that has a strong run of Pink, Silver, and King Salmon. At times the river banks around Soldotna are so crowded it is difficult to find an unoccupied place to stand and fish. Extremely large King Salmon are taken every year near the mouth of the Russian River where it flows into the Kenai above the town of Soldotna just off the Sterling Highway. Already the river guides are preparing for the summer run of salmon and then shortly thereafter, the summer run of tourists. Motels and campgrounds are mostly reserved by now and are just waiting for the rush of visitors. Tourism is good business, but the tourists really know how to screw up a pretty nice place. Thank God they bring money, lots of money.

Ralph is not a fisherman; he is more a hustler who could make a buck maybe fishing for fishermen but probably not fish. He found himself sitting at a small side table at Eddie's bar and strip club near the town of Kenai. He was eating a plate of fish and chips with a side of coleslaw when a little mousey kind of bald headed guy walked in the door of the lounge, crossed the floor over to his table, pulled up a chair, and introduced himself.

Pete; "Hi Ralph, my name is Pete and I think I can help you. I hear that some of the Adams crime family from London, England, and some of their American associates are looking for you. I don't think they will find you here but without my help they most likely will eventually find you."

Ralph jumped up looking for somewhere to run. He had no idea how he had been found and was fairly sure he was in mortal danger. He was going to run but had no idea where to. Ralph knew the guys looking for him usually traveled in pairs. The other guy was for sure armed and probably out in the parking lot right now. He took a couple of deep breaths and after looking a little closer at Pete he thought maybe there was no immediate danger, so he sat back down; but his desire for food had disappeared. Just who was this little guy that seemed to know about him?

Ralph: "Ok Pete, its Pete isn't it, that is what you said?" "Yes, I said my name is Pete, and I may end up being a good friend of yours." "How's that?"

Pete:" You have some pretty high-powered hoods looking for you in Fairbanks, Anchorage, and I understand, also in Honolulu. They're striking out because you aren't there, but they don't know it. The folks directing this Clusterfuck are clueless and are getting more pissed off by the day. You and Justin ripped them off and they want the gold back, even if it's not really theirs. If they find you, they might just rip your head off. Can you imagine what their spending rate is? The tote of gold you took, it wasn't that much in the overall scheme of things, but if they let you get away with it then any of the other mules will think they can do the same. They want to get you and make an example of you, and they won't stop until they do."

Ralph: "Who are you and how do you know so much about me and my problems?"

Pete: "You know me, I'm Pete and I work for a security consultant that's a friend of yours whether you know it or not. His name is Carter Thomas and he's from Houston, Texas. He runs a security consulting service there."

Ralph: "So how is this security consultant a friend of mine?"

Pete: "He is looking for the gold, the big pile of gold that you have been so busy carrying just a small part of every couple of weeks. You help him find the source and he will help you go stealth and never be bothered by these guys again, ever. He isn't interested in putting these players in the slammer, he just wants the ingots, the gold bars, and for sure the finder's fee. The right information will get you a substantial payday and probably freedom from the hunt. But be warned, the wrong information will most likely get you found by Big Bob Adams."

Ralph: "I know they are still looking for me, but I don't know why. I don't have that small duffle and Justin doesn't have it either. They took it back from us in Bettles two weeks ago. Look, I quit the system. I am done with this carrying around fifteen pounds of stolen shit or hauling drugs for a lousy seven hundred a week. I have been doing this for entirely too long. I hate small planes; they are too noisy, too cold, and too bumpy and I get air-sick, I'm done with that crap. I don't know why I'm so popular anyway, I don't know why they are after me, but I just know they are."

Pete: "They want their gold back, they want the gold and think you have it." "I don't have the gold, either does Justin; they took it from us in Bettles." "They think you have it, if you don't have the satchel who does?" "Holy crap, am I ever screwed!"

Pete: "Not so Ralph. Right now, you are golden, just don't muck it up and you will remain golden."

Thomas Security had found Ralph without working up a sweat, or rather, Pete had. Ralph had used his own name when renting the Anchorage apartment six months ago: big mistake. Then when he closed out his bank account it was obvious that he was leaving Anchorage. But the mystery began when he rented a car from Hertz. A simple check on his credit card caught that one. They wouldn't take cash, no car rental outfit will. He sure as hell wasn't driving to America so he must have been going on a walkabout before leaving the state. If he was going to Fairbanks he would have just flown Alaska Air. Besides, what would he do in Fairbanks? That was one of the places that Adams was sure to be searching for him. No, if he rented a car he was either going toward Valdez or Homer. Pete guessed probably Homer, and a guy with Ralph's mentality would no sooner pass up a strip club than Billy Graham would pass up a tithe. So just before leaving Anchorage Pete visited "The Great Alaska Bush Company" and talked to a couple of his friends who danced there. According to one of his friends, two of the girls there had been offered an expense paid summer trip to Homer if they could get the time off. The invitee fit Ralph's description. Neither accepted the offer, one of the girls said he seemed nice enough but she was a dancer, not an escort. But now at least Pete knew which direction to search.

After that revelation Pete had just driven south on the Seward Highway, around the Turnagain Arm and at Moose Pass, he took a right on the Sterling Highway and headed toward Homer. He stopped at most every roadhouse and bar and talked to the bartenders, and there were a bunch. Staying sober was a small but manageable problem because Pete never drank more than a few sips from each draft beer he ordered; he is a well-disciplined person and not easily distracted. Pete's cover was that he was a PI, which he is, and was trying to find Ralph because his mother is sick, and his father needed him in Seattle. Pete is a little guy who can turn sincerity on and off not unlike a light switch on the wall. Carter had taught him to dress well and to talk quietly and make a person lean into him just a little to hear what is being said. It's almost like an instant friendship that is created, it seems personal and most of all, harmless. Pete uses his people skills and appearance well.

It took Pete less than three days to find Ralph and less than fifteen minutes to turn him into an informant.

Chapter (33)

Finding the runaway Ralph   June 1985

Even the smallest amount of information can have consequences when put together with other small bits and pieces of seemingly unimportant data. Finding the answer to a complex problem is sometimes just adding these bits and pieces to a matrix and watching the obvious appear. Carter was building up this matrix slow and sure and the location of the hoard of gold bars was getting close to discovery.

Pete had Ralph return the car to Hertz at the Kenai Airport and then go to the ERA counter and buy a one-way ticket to Anchorage, and then book thru to San Francisco. ERA is a feeder to Alaska Air, so he was able to connect thru Portland and then all the way to San Francisco. Ralph used his credit card and Pete gave him the fare back in cash. ERA issued the tickets; he would have only a one hour stop in Anchorage. It would be a good trip if he was in fact really going on it.

After that part was completed, they sat in the bar at the Kenai airport and looked for a guy about the same size and age as Ralph who also had dark hair. It took less than five minutes before Pete spotted what was most likely an oil field worker. He was alone at a single table next to the wall and he was probably going south for R&R.

As Pete and Ralph approached the table from opposite directions Pete stumbled and ran into Ralph as he was going by his table. Pete dropped the ticket on the floor and continued; Ralph went back to the seat at the bar. The guy at the table picked up the ticket folder and called to Pete.

He said: "Hey man, you in the blue jacket: you dropped this," and he handed Pete the ticket folder. Pete thanked him and offered to buy him a drink as a thank you. The guy's name was Robin and he quickly accepted the offer of the drink and some company.

Pete and Robin had a drink together and Pete explained that he was a timekeeper on one of the oil rigs in the inlet and this was a ticket set for one of his men who decided at the last minute to stay on the rig for another two weeks. The man needed the money and at time and a half, rather than travel to San Francisco for his R&R, he could stick it out on the rig for a while longer. Pete explained that he tried but couldn't get a refund on the tickets since they had been purchased in a block. So, the tickets were going to waste and though it was no big deal, but he thanked Robin anyway for his integrity. Robin thought about it a little and said: "I'm going south, I'll give you half the price of the tickets, what do you say? We can both make a little."

If Pete would sell him the set of tickets he could get a refund on his existing tickets and they both would make a little walking around money. Pete said Ok, and for one hundred eighty dollars Pete gave Robin the ticket that was good all the way to San Francisco.

Pete: "Please just use the name Ralph Kelly if you are asked. That's the name on the tickets at Alaska Air and I don't want my company to find out I sold them instead of just giving them back. They can't get a refund anyway so it's not like stealing. He winked and said: "Want another one for the road?"

By the time Pete got back to the bar Ralph had another two or three drinks and Pete nearly had to carry him to the car. When Ralph was 'three sheets to the wind' he was suddenly in a very good mood and talked about nearly everything Pete wanted to hear.

Ralph had worked as an enforcer and a part-time mule for one of the middle managers of the Fargo Group before the Reno Cartel took them over. Despite his just average size he was a fierce fighter. But his boss never seemed to appreciate his manual skills and soon recognized he was far from being the brightest bulb on the Christmas tree. After the takeover he had not been treated like a trusted member in the new group, never got a bonus, never got much praise, and was given no benefits. Any time he would complain about his plight his boss would just point to the door and tell him to make a choice.

It turns out that the further up the food chain, the sharper the teeth, and Ralph had no teeth at all. He was given no health insurance, or a company car, never even an invite to the weekly

263

dinner meetings, nothing. Ralph had been loyal to the Fargo Group but quickly developed a ration of bitterness for the Cartel from Reno because of this poor treatment. Bob Adams recognized this and decided to take advantage of the situation.

Adams had a plan; He said if Ralph pretended to get hijacked in Umiat, it could buy him a big payday. Ralph said he would think about it, he wasn't sure if he could trust Adams. A couple days later while In Fairbanks, he chanced to meet Justin at Ruthie's and he asked Justin what he thought about the proposed deal. Justin said he was probably being set up and if it were him he would get lost quickly. Ralph understood that Justin had no ax to grind, after all he was in the drug business and not involved with the Reno Cartel or the gold. Ralph had not worked with Justin for some time and while they had never been good friends Justin had at least been civil to him and Ralph thought he could trust his advice. Ralph listened to what he had to say and believed it.

That was when Justin suggested to Ralph that he go ahead and hijack the gold, but instead of giving it to Adams he should give it to him instead. Justin said he would split the booty 30-70. Justin would pay him thirty percent at melt value when Ralph delivered the loot. That sounded good and it seemed like the thing to do. Ralph had already decided to leave the Cartel and get lost so the deal was struck but it didn't work out nearly as planned. Justin picked up Ralph in Umiat a day late because of Skip's wreck in Bettles the day before. After Ralph was missing for the second day the Cartel got word to Bob Adams and he was told to find Kelly, get the gold, and "Don't be all that nice about it."

Although being a day late if things had gone as planned Kelly would still have been in Portland by the time anyone noticed the theft. But this did not work out because on their way to Anchorage the engine on Justin's Cessna swallowed a valve and they barely made it to the Pitka Airstrip in the thriving town of Galena: population 482. There was a mechanic there, but it was nearly a week before a cylinder and piston could be found and the engine repaired. It took almost all of Justin's money just to eat and sleep while the repairs were being made. But Justin still intended to pay

Ralph as he said he would. All he had to do was fly to Fairbanks and withdraw the cash money from the bank that Ralph was promised. For some dumb reason Justin decided to pick up a passenger in Galena. It really wasn't all that dumb a reason; Justin needed the gas money and he was getting sick and tired of listening to Ralph complain about everything and anything.

The passenger, Tyler Clarke, seemed innocent enough, he was a contract civilian Air Force mechanic going south to Fairbanks. Tyler gave Justin one hundred bucks and loaned him money to fill the tanks for the ride to Fairbanks. That's when Justin made the mistake of flying into Bettles for a bathroom break and a doughnut; he couldn't afford lunch and that's where Bob Adams spotted them. Adams took the gold from them and the only thing Justin got out of the deal was one hundred bucks and some gas.

Ralph: "Boy was that guy Tyler ever a great pilot and did he ever hate guns. He was piloting the plane when we left Bettles. He promised or threatened, depending on how you look at it, that he would fight the both of us if we argued with him; he was very persuasive. Justin not only wouldn't argue with him he was afraid to even look him in the eye."

Pete: "So?"

Ralph: "So we flew into Fairbanks, took a taxi to the bank, and Justin paid me thirty-five hundred dollars plus the cost of a plane ticket to Anchorage if I promised to get lost. I did promise to leave, and I will, but I decided to take a little down time on the Kenai Peninsula before going home to Portland to visit my brothers. I have a little over seven thousand bucks and I'm thinking of buying a gas station: what do you think of that idea?" "Depends on how you look in bib overalls." "Don't be mean Pete, I just want to get away from this gangster crap and a gas station is a good honest business. Oregon has no sales taxes and it's a hell of a lot warmer there than it is here most of the time."

Pete: "Ya, but it rains a lot, so much in fact that you grow moss on your balls." "Really, Are you sure about that?" "That's what I've been told, rains every day except Sunday and sometimes even then."

Ralph: "Must be about the wettest place in the US." "Probably is; do you want another beer?"

They spent the night in Ralph's motel room and the next morning, after gaining his confidence, Pete made Ralph the proposal: if he would come back to Fairbanks with him and talk to Carter, and really tell him what he knew about the folks toting the gold bars to Umiat, Carter would get him safe passage to Portland and two grand to boot.

Ralph: "I guess I could do that and I could really use the money."

It was agreed and after a haircut and bleach job on what was left, they were ready to go travel north. Ralph's haircut made him look ten years younger and maybe like a poorly done up Punk Rocker, but certainly not a thief in hiding. He also shaved his mustache and after looking at himself in the mirror for a few minutes, maybe more than just a few, he wondered what Pete thought.

Ralph: "How about the new look Pete?" "Looks good Ralph; I guess your own dear mother wouldn't recognize you in one of her photo albums." He was very pleased, and Pete acknowledged that he not only looked quite different but probably a lot better. Pete also thought to himself; there really was nothing he could do to help him wise up.

Ralph: "I think I look great, I definitely like the new look. If we fly back, can I have the window seat?" "We will fly to Fairbanks and you may have the window."

Back in the Goldstream Valley it was half past spring and a quarter till summer. Business was picking up a little for the store and Jean and Claire were busy putting together the formal bid for the firefighter's food box contract with the State, and also building up the bid sheet for the BLM.

On the aviation side of the business, Josh and Matt were to fly to the Forty-mile with a payroll delivery for the FMA on Thursday. But that would be after a short hop to Bettles in the 206 to deliver some aircraft instruments needed by Paul and Chuck Mason that

Josh had picked up at Bachner's over on Philip's Field. Andy Bachner had purchased the altimeter and artificial horizon and one of the Narco radios from the Masons in Bettles less than a month ago and now the instruments were making the trip back.

Earlier in the day Skip and Matt drove over to the Bank of the North and picked up the payroll pouch for delivery to the Forty-mile and brought it back to the Valley. Matt carried both a sidearm and an Ithaca shotgun, he also wore a security guard uniform. Skip was having a problem driving and staying in his proper lane because he was laughing so hard. Because of this Matt was really irritated with Skip and said he should take the job just a little more seriously.

Skip: "I am very serious about security but it's not easy driving the clown car." "What the hell does that mean?"

The trip back from Bettles with the instruments went smooth and Josh refueled at Northwinds Aviation at FAI before bouncing back to the valley to pick up Matt and the payroll. When Josh landed and pulled up to the hangar to pick up Matt and the payroll pouch, Skip was pulling the Maule out of the hangar and caught a glimpse of the pilot that Skip was interviewing for the new position. Josh had to look twice, but he was pretty sure that it was the third man who had been with Justin Littlejohn and Ralph Kelly in Bettles.

Josh killed the engine on the 206 and just positively had to hear what was going on, but first he needed a private word with Skip. He walked up to the two of them for an introduction.

Skip: "Tyler, this is Josh, he runs Goldstream Air, he is not my competitor in the Air Taxi business because he does cargo and I only do people.

Josh: "Tyler, I'm pleased to meet you; can you just give us a minute?"

Tyler: "Absolutely."

Josh: "May I have a word with you Skip?"

Skip to Tyler: "Please do a preflight on the Maule and don't bother with the lights and crap like that, just do the stuff that matters. By the way, this is his plane so make it look like you care. Check the oil and gas and the tire pressure while I have a word with him."

Tyler: "Sure, I'll just take a few minutes to look this plane over. I have never flown a Maule. It will be a fun plane if it flies like it looks."

Josh: "Skip, what's the scoop on this guy? I am pretty sure I saw him in Battles last week working for Justin Littlejohn. Try to find out what you can."

Skip; "You saw him in Bettles doing what?" "I'm pretty sure this is the guy that I told you about that was there with Justin and Ralph. This guy didn't seem to be involved with that big fight, but I think he flew the plane when they took off from Bettles. If so he's a hell of a pilot. Anyway, find out what you can about the Bettles incident." "Ok, I guess I'll just ask him how he got here from Galena. That should answer the question but hell, stick around for a few minutes and help with the interview. You can ask a few questions too. I will tell him you might also be interested in using him; Ok?" "Sounds right, let's do it."

Matt walked out of the hangar with a payroll pouch in one hand and an Ithaca pump shotgun in the other. Josh asked him to put the payroll in the 206 and to sit for five. He would be ready after asking Tyler a few questions.

When Tyler saw the gun, he backed up a few feet and looked a little nervous. Josh explained to Tyler about the payroll delivery and that seemed to lessen his anxiety a little.

Skip: "Tyler; go ahead and tell us about your flying experience and start from the beginning."

Tyler: "I'm twenty-six years old and I just finished up an Air Force contract in Galena as a civilian mechanic and observation plane pilot with Uncle Sam. I learned to fly in a 115 hp Citabria in northern California, in Marin County. My parents enjoy operating a small vineyard. Though they are mainly retired, they bottle eight to nine hundred cases each year. I worked the vineyard during high school and bought flight lessons with my pay. I did a bunch of crop-dusting in the San Joaquin Valley, also in California, and I did a little work spraying orchards in Washington. Then four years ago I came north to Alaska as a contract mechanic for the Air Force and when not turning wrenches for them, I have been flying for a few other operators on and off. My log book totals around 2800 hours, mostly single engine land, some float time and about 120 hours of twin time in a Cessna 310 and about 50 in a Piper Seneca. I've kicked around working for a few outfits, never been fired, most recently Jimmies Air Taxi out of Galena. The owner has a nephew that he promised to employ so I was laid off about a week ago. He said he would give me a good recommendation: Jimmy said that."

Skip: "Where are you staying in Fairbanks?" "At the Red Barn apartments on University Avenue." "I didn't see a car; how did you get here?" "I bought a bicycle with my last ten bucks, it's quite a little trek out here." "You don't manage your finances very well, do you?"

Tyler: "I manage my money just fine though I may be just a little too trustworthy. "Skip: "How's that?" "I caught a ride from Galena a few days ago. I paid one hundred for the ride and loaned the pilot enough to fill the tanks. He promised to pay me back when we got here but stiffed me for the gas bucks when I asked. Not much I could do about it. I just trusted the wrong people. Besides that, I damn near got shot by a couple of jerks in Bettles.

Skip: " That's quite a story, tell us about it, how does it end?" "We landed there for the bathroom and coffee and the two guys I was with got in a fight. They were fighting two other guys that flew in a few minutes behind us. They showed up just as we were ordering coffee and a doughnut. It was a real fuckup, pardon the French, but it was near deadly. They were arguing over a little duffle of I don't know what, maybe guns or something, don't really care. Anyway, I got the hell out of there but not before the damn bartender got my last hundred bucks for some busted up furniture that I had nothing to do with breaking."

Skip: "So what finally happened, how did you finally get away from whatever the fight was about?" "When the jerks I was with got tired of fighting and saw we could make a break for it I didn't wait to use the runway. I took off from the tie down area across and over the frozen float pond and went south and stayed low until we were out of sight. Then I doubled back and landed on a roadway close to the strip just a few minutes after the guys that were chasing us took off looking for us. We had a 182 and they had a 210. In a straight-out flight they could have had us but Einstein's they weren't."

Skip "So then what?" "This Justin character wanted to leave me on the road up there in Bettles and I told him we were going to Fairbanks and I was flying. If he didn't like it, he would have another fistfight on his hands. He got pretty beat up in the bar at Bettles and wasn't ready for another match. I flew the plane and we landed at Phillips Field. That's where he stiffed me. What a prick!"

Skip: "Get your bike and put it in the back of the Maule, it will fit without taking it apart. We can go for a putt and I'll drop you at Phillips. You can ride back to your apartment from there." Tyler turned and walked over to where his bike was. Skip told Josh he planned to hire him if he could fly. Josh said he could fly in spades!

The flight to the Forty-mile went like clockwork and it was complete and over with in less than three and a half hours. Claire had two more billings to add to the books and was able to give Matt a small advance to make the last payment to his dad and finally pay off the note to the bank on the 206 that had turned into a 185. It was complicated, but it was over and finally paid for.

Matt decided to work for Carter because of the health insurance coverage for his dad if Carter agreed to let Josh have priority on his time for the payroll flights: except of course for the pipeline photography flights which were still to be #1. Carter quickly agreed to this. It turns out for just a few bucks less, that's like twenty bucks a week less, Carter has the same pipeline surveillance flights as before and will now also have a personal pilot whenever he wants or needs one. Josh wondered just how the hell he manages to get away with it; every single time Carter comes out on top and always ahead.

The only times Josh had ever seen him without a spotless, and what appears to be a, custom tailored three-piece suit was when they would meet on the Coleville River sand bar, but even then, he was primped, clean, and without a blemish. And here he is again without a speck of dust or even a wrinkle, and now he also has his own personal pilot: and a smile ear to ear. Josh decided to observe and copy him when possible; to study and learn, and then follow the Carter technique of success.

Chapter (34)

Carter and Ralph get together

Pete and Ralph arrived in the late afternoon on Friday under phony names via Alaska Air. Pete usually carried at least three sets of ID and all Ralph had to do was remember the name Mike Tullis. He managed to do that with a minimum of stuttering but with a very red face. Pete wondered how he ever learned to flush a toilet.

They had burned thru the last of Pete's cash in Anchorage and arrived broke but undiscovered. Ralph had a goodly amount of cash, actually a lot of cash, but he refused to spend any of it and Pete thought: *"what the hell, he probably had been burned once or twice before."* And Pete understood that maybe more than most other folks would have, so he let it slide.

Carter's security company had a long-term rental suite at the Captain Bartlett and he let Ralph have a bedroom for one night only. Carter intended to grease him up with a bottle or two of scotch, keeping him on the fine line between blabber mouth and sleep, not too close to sleep. Carter just wanted to know everything that Ralph knew about the Reno Cartel and what was left of the old Fargo Group. Then he would pay him as Pete promised he would, and buy him an airline ticket to Portland, or where ever he wanted to go, coach class. Pete joined Ralph and Carter for dinner because Ralph had learned to trust Pete and he seemed very comfortable around him. As the conversation progressed Ralph asked: "I'm wondering if you have any open positions for a savvy investigator? "Carter responded and said: "I am getting out of the investigation business altogether but if you have an interest in investigating, why don't you consider setting up a PI agency on your own when he you get to Portland? All you really need is an office, a desk, an ad in the Portland Times, and a phone." "I would also need some business cards." "Yes, good idea; Kelly Investigations sounds like a good name, how does that sound to you?" "I was thinking about keeping my name out of it so when I sell the company there won't be any strings left between it and myself."

Carter: "That's what I did and never regretted it." "Ok then, that's settled."

The dinner went well and back in Carter's suite the scotch was by the bottle. Carter was heavy into the conversation while Pete played solitaire and listened closely. Pete was to raise a single index finger if he caught Ralph in any sort of a lie, but during the entire conversation Pete kept his hand closed.

Carter was learning more and more about the Reno Cartel and was getting a history lesson on the Fargo Group before they were taken over. With the travel information he was getting from Ralph, he was pretty sure the gold bars were not in Reno or even in Salt Lake City as he had been told by others. He was thinking the gold stash was maybe in Grand Forks, North Dakota. That was where the Fargo Group was from and had their business headquarters. He had a suspicion, but it was just one of many, that the gold had been there all along. Carter had investigated and knew the old Fargo Group had set up a legitimate mini storage business. They had built two storage facilities in the town and were making a few bucks with legitimate rentals but mostly they had laundered skimmed casino cash into the cost of the real estate and construction costs of the storage facilities. And they also had a great place to hide anything that needed to be hidden away, very securely. He wondered if any of them had hurt their shoulders patting themselves on the back with that business decision.

Carter needed some help and thought about an old friend working for Michael Baker International, a civil engineering firm doing some design work on the North Slope. He happened to have his satellite number and thought, what the hell, it's only seven thirty, go for it. Carter gave Pete the high sign and Pete asked: "Ralph, how about a few hands of Rummy, five bucks for the win and five cents a point cumulative."

Ralph hadn't a clue what cumulative meant but was ready for any card game that Pete wanted to play. They sat at the table and played as Carter dialed his satellite phone from the balcony of their second-floor suite. The phone rang three times and was answered with a firm "Hello".

Carter said: "Oscar, this is Carter Thomas; how are you and what's going on?"

Oscar: "Doing just fine Carter, what can I do for you." "Whenever I call you always think I need something; that is just plain hurtful." "Just the same, what do you need?"

Carter: "Who do you know that builds or better than that, designs mini storage, in the Midwest; Grand Forks, North Dakota, to be exact?" "It would probably be a local contractor doing the work but most likely an Engineering firm like ourselves that would be drawing up the plans. What do you need exactly?" "There are two mini storage facilities owned by Fargo Storage, in Grand Forks, North Dakota. One of them is on Stewart Avenue near 17th in Grand Forks and I need a copy of the plans." "Let me look into it. I'll get back with you tomorrow, Ok?" "You bet, my best to Julie."

Oscar; "Ya, but that ended last year. Just the same, shall I send your best to Julie with the next alimony check?" "Don't bother, I never really liked her anyway, I thought she was a climber." "You were right!"

With the conversation over and the investigation getting closer, Carter felt he could let down just a little and have real scotch with his ice, instead of the iced tea he had been sipping. Slowly but surely, life was getting a little better. He picked up the land line and dialed his home number.

Carter: "Hi Jeanette, sorry to miss you but now that I think it of it you must be over next door playing your Friday night poker game. Hope you win, love you, kiss Carrie for me, bye!"

Skip hired Tyler on the spot after just a short flight in the Maule. To say the very least, he was impressed because Tyler didn't just fly the plane, he put it on like he might a tailored sport coat and it did just about what he was thinking. Skip wished in his fondest dreams that he could fly a plane like that. He also did something that was totally out of character. He gave Tyler the use of Jean's Ford pickup, with Jean's Okay of course, and two hundred walking-around bucks. It was very strange for Skip to be generous with strangers, in fact he is generally downright stingy with anyone not in his inner circle and profanely loud when he is doing it. Skip just said he was mellowing out in his old age while Jean wondered if it might be early signs of Alzheimer's.

Neither Josh nor Skip planned to fly over the weekend, Josh was free until next Tuesday. Then Skip remembered he had promised to take his bartender on a fishing trip on Monday to Minto Flats to catch a few Northern Pike. He made a quick phone call to confirm the outing. The plan was to launch Skip's flat bottom river boat in the Chatanika River at a small ramp off the back of the Murphy Dome Road and then motor down to the larger of the two lakes in the Minto Flats. Josh decided to join them, it was a trip that had been planned several times before but just never happened. Also, they had not informed their respective "war departments", hence had not received the necessary "kitchen passes."

With the "flying for bucks" done, at least until Tuesday, Josh had the planes secured and he was looking forward to a few days off. As he left the Grizzly Air hangar and walked next door, he was trying to figure out how he would convince Claire he needed some fly rod time. He decided to take the cagey avenue of approach and simply confess his stealthy fishing plans. Josh received a "kitchen pass" because Claire thought he deserved a fishing trip and more than that she thought he needed some male bonding.

Skip walked into the kitchen a few minutes later and invited them for a few drinks at the Exchange, maybe more than a few. The plan was to have a few drinks and then when Jean showed up after closing the store, they would come back to Josh's hangar and grill a few hamburgers. Well, that was the plan but after sampling a couple of Tommy's barroom artistic concoctions it seemed that cooking was out of the picture. Josh had a couple too many and ended up singing Red River Valley, in a high falsetto voice with Don, while Skip was trying to play the piano. Despite the hundreds of hours of training for a career as a concert musician, sadly, he wasn't much of an artist with the ivories after all. Tommy was doing his best trying to sing harmony and while not perfect it was probably better than the Red River Valley presentation without it. The only one not having fun seemed to be Jean. She had been trying to run the Golden Valley

Store like a German staff sergeant might and a few of her very best customers, rather than being impressed, thought it was humorous. None of them would believe she was truly that ruthless. When Jean would ring out the register she even counted the pennies. On this night at closing she had spilled the change and started cursing. The two customers in the store at the time thought she was just trying to imitate Skip and laughed even harder. She needed a victory and was thinking about making another try at installing a time clock' Maybe this time Josh wouldn't notice. But Jean knew that Claire would probably snitch on her anyway, so she gave up with the time clock effort once again.

When Angel saw the local folks being a little nasty by laughing at Jean she came over to console her, Angel nuzzled her knee. Jean saw that she had at least one supporter and handed out some jerky. Angel wagged and decided to stick around until closing. When Nine o'clock came, the store closed on time as usual, and after ringing out the register she said her goodnight to Rita, locked the doors, and headed to the exchange. Jean had expected a simple hamburger from Claire's grill in the hangar down the road and she was totally surprised when she saw that Skip had ordered her one of Don's work of art. The burger was rare and ready for her when she arrived. She gave Skip a kiss on the forehead and got busy destroying the results of Don's culinary artistry; there seemed to be very little stress late into the evening in the Goldstream Valley.

Saturday morning broke warm and breezy. The forecast was for rain in the afternoon, but it was clear and bright now. Josh and Claire decided to take a ride out to Chatanika and if the light was right, Claire would grab a few photos of the old dredge that still floats in the pond across the highway from the Chatanika Lodge. This dredge is larger than the one at Chicken Creek but with no more character. Claire got a few fine shots of the dredge, it was front-lighted and had billowing clouds over the White Mountains in the background. She recently got her creative photo juices flowing again and after being turned down several times by Alaska Magazine, she planned to submit these dredge photos and thought, "this time maybe," at least she hoped.

Angel was not sure what was going on with the camera and tripod stuff but felt she should protect it from all threats. Whenever a tourist would get too close to the camera she would step between the person and the camera and whine a little and wag her tail. She got a lot of great ear-rubs and decided these were the same tourists that showed up at the store. Funny though since there was nothing to buy around the dredge. Josh asked if Claire could get any photos from the air that might appeal to the buyers of fine photo art. She recognized the sarcasm in the question and asked if he really wanted to go to Minto on Monday, and if so, maybe she would go along and act as their guide and chief camera person.

Claire: "You don't care if I come along, do you?" "Someone has to watch the store." "Angel can do that from under the front porch swing: she can do that." "Do you want a new lens or something?" "Just a little respect now and then." "I'm sorry, what can I do to be forgiven?" "Just be nice and keep your socks on." Josh smiled and nodded and Angel thought: *"here they go again"*.

Saturday evening Tyler was supposed to show up at 7:00 at Skip's house and meet the entire group. Claire decided to put out salami and cheese, chips, pretzels, and little weenies on toothpicks. Instead of at Skip's house, Claire set up the goodies, medium priced wine, and iced Budweiser, in their hangar. Everyone was told to "please remove the toothpicks if Angel was the intended recipient of the weenie; and please put all your empties in the recycle trash can marked "Recycle" and garbage in the other marked "Garbage." This seemed a simple request, but she knew it would never happen. Casey was responsible for the recycling effort and promised to spread the gospel of St. "whoever is the patron saint in charge of garbage", to the other less dedicated folks in the group. If Casey wasn't a Physicist she most likely would have been an Environmentalist; Skip commented she would have a lot fewer friends.

At 7:00 Tyler was a no-show: by 7:30 he had still not appeared. By 7:45 Jean was pretty sure Skip had been conned out of two bills and that she may have lost her truck. Then just as the group had formed a general and complete dislike for Tyler and were promising to never help a stranger again, he came walking down the road, kind of limping. He was banged up some and didn't look all that well. Jean described his appearance as "Beat to Shit."

Tyler: "Sorry I'm late but I got held up." "What happened?" "I got held up, really, held up, but I know who did it." "How's that?" "I was in Bettles two days ago getting a ride from Galena from two guys who were bound for Anchorage. I told you the story about the fight and how we finally got away. Anyway, at around quarter till I was on my way out here and I was cut off by these same two guys in a blue Dodge pickup near that greenhouse, out that way. He pointed around left on Goldstream Road. "

Josh: "You probably mean Ann's Greenhouse where the railroad tracks cross Murphy Dome Road." "Yes, there were railroad tracks." "Where is my truck?" "What's left of it is in the ditch where I ended up when they cut me off." "Son of a Bitch! So, what the hell happened?"

Tyler: "So this big guy says where the hell is Ralph and Justin? And then: where is my gold?" And I tell him I don't have a clue what he's asking about, and he lets me have it right here." He points to his face on the left. Claire comes out of the house back into the hangar with a first aid kit and a wash rag and starts to clean up Tyler's face. She puts two bandages on over some antiseptic cream. Tyler thanks her and continues the story. His face was truly messed up. Tyler continues the story: "Bob, the big guy, was holding me and firing questions about some gold, and the little guy was hitting me in the gut; fortunately, he wasn't much of a puncher. Finally, I wrestled loose from that big clown and then I started swinging. I got a couple of good shots at him and I hit him so hard in the beak I felt it break; he bled like a stuck pig. The big guy was down, after that his little friend wasn't so brave when it was one on one. He started running back to his truck for something, maybe a gun; I don't like guns, so I took to my heels and started running. I used to run track and there was no way that little jerk was going to catch me. I think I ran for several miles before I heard their pickup coming just as I was coming

278

up the hill back there." He pointed toward the left out on Goldstream Road again.

Skip: "So how did you run with a gimpy leg?" "I ducked off the road but got caught on a tree root and fell. That was when I twisted my ankle a little." "You stay here with the three girls while Josh and I go have a look at Jean's truck." Matt: "what am I, chopped liver? I'm coming too."

Jean: "The hell with that, I'm going! If Bob Adams bashed up my truck I am personally going to bash him. I'll dent his God damned head like a well-used garbage can!"

Claire: "How are you feeling right now Tyler?" "I guess Ok; sorry to be so late, do you have any food left; how about a Budweiser?" Casey: "Hi, my name is Casey; I work at the store and Matt is my boy-friend." She brought him a beer and a dozen or so weenies on tooth-picks and a plate of cheese and crackers along with a filet of smoked salmon. Tyler forgot about his bruises and ankle and applied his effort to the salmon and crackers.

Skip and Jean left by the side door and then Jean poked her head back into the hangar and said, " Angel come." Angel trotted out, and soon they heard Skip's Travel-All leaving up the road. Josh and Matt sort of looked at one another and then, as Matt flipped the switch to open the bi-fold door, Josh fired up Claire's Jeep and they also went to see the damage; to see if they could help pull the truck out of the ditch or whatever.

Chapter (35)

The plans arrive   June 1985

When Carter got a copy of the construction plans from his friend Oscar, he found that the architect had designed a very secure 12 by 12 room right in the middle of the mini storage complex. The building contractors had constructed the storage facility with only two minor changes as shown on the "as built" plans; none involved the room in the center of the complex. The steel reinforced concrete room had eight-inch-thick walls and ceiling and the room was labeled as a "bomb shelter" on the plans. There were only three duplex electrical outlets and only one single light fixture in the ceiling of the room. There was also no plumbing, no ventilation, and no other creature comforts or utilities. As Carter viewed the plan set he was positive that it sure as hell was no bomb shelter. Looking further at the design plans Carter observed there was only one hallway in or out of that part of the building, and the entrance to that hallway could easily be seen from a warehouse and office complex that was conveniently right across the two-lane street from the mini storage. Then when looking at the elevation view of the plans and some accompanying photos, he realized that he had been to that office complex once before.

He had been there a while ago; it was after his wife Jeanette, had been run down at the mall, after they had gone dark and relocated to Washington State. Carter had been so totally absorbed with Jeanette's assault and so totally pissed off he decided he would just gun down, he would simply kill the whole God-damn gang. He would have too but on the Friday afternoon of this ill-planned massacre Carter entered the office complex carrying a highly modified Ruger Mini 14, with two twenty round clips, and a Glock 9mm hand gun. After defeating the alarm system, he found the warehouse and office deserted: the entire staff was gone, apparently, they went home early for a long weekend. He was disappointed but did not leave empty handed because that was the day he found and opened a safe and picked up almost forty thousand cash dollars and a small bag of diamonds, mostly uncut.

At first, he planned to go back on a later day to complete the job, but after slowly being overcome by common sense, he developed a better and safer plan: he decided to let them kill themselves.

The diamond mining scam was a classic sting. It took Carter more than three months' time and over sixty thousand dollars to set it up. Early on he found he needed major help with the logistics.

Carter had a brother who had been an Episcopal Priest with a small church in Allakaket and who was also flying a circuit to other villages to spread the gospel. His brother died in a plane crash in the Alaska bush many years ago. He had a Native American wife and one son, Hector Redhorse, who by coincidence was an assistant manager of a small gold mining operation in the Forty-mile Mining District East of Fairbanks.

Carter's sister-in-law wanted to raise Hector according to the Indian culture and changed his name from Smithson back to her maiden name, Redhorse. Carter was no stranger to name changes because he had also changed his name from Smithson to the very generic name: Thomas. This was to protect his family when he went into the security consulting business. Carter and Hector kept in touch over the years and Carter even paid for Hector's college tuition thru Graduate School. When Carter's wife was hurt, Hector wanted to help in any way he could and when he found out his uncle was after the same people that were trying to distribute drugs into Deadhorse, and moreover the rural Native villages, he was willing and very able to help. Hector was a miner and had the experience that Carter needed. He became more and more involved and though grateful that Carter was trying to keep him from getting too involved in the sting, there was no way that Carter could keep him out of it, though he tried; good luck with that one because Hector would not back down.

Hector was a great asset who made the plan possible and although the sting worked out, it did not have the desired ending. Jim Littlejohn, who Carter had suspected of driving the truck that ran down his wife, was still alive. The Fargo Group would have eliminated him for sure, but the Reno Cartel had taken over the North Slope operations by then and though they didn't much like the loss due to the diamond sting, they absorbed it just the same. The Cartel let Jim Littlejohn continue to work for them providing he would manage the melting of the gold ingots from the London robbery and produce gold dust and nuggets that would seem legitimately taken from Mother Earth. He was to manage the shadow mining operation and make it look like it was a real producing mine. He was to and keep his crew in check and that meant sober and out of trouble with the law.

The Reno Cartel had acquired the gold bars at a steep discount. Together with the markup on the melt value of the gold plus adding up to fifteen percent base metals, and the fact they could launder skimmed casino earnings, they had both a "Gold Mine" and a real gold mine. But the part of the agreement that Littlejohn did not follow was that he was to get out of the drug trade. After the substantial losses on the diamond mining scam Littlejohn was to surrender his Deadhorse drug franchise; he was to have no further involvement with the distribution and sale of drugs on the slope. That franchise had already been sold off to others to recoup at least some of their money Littlejohn had lost. Most Cartel members thought he should be eliminated instead of just losing his drug business but none had the balls to question the Cartel's boss.

David and Justin Littlejohn didn't follow those orders and David died. Jim Littlejohn should have controlled his sons a little better, but he did not and between David's greed and Justin's inability to follow the rules the Cartel had little choice but to end the competition in drug distribution business. They did however, make a critical mistake by sabotaging his plane and getting the NTSB involved in the investigation. By now Maury Fitzgerald, the NTSB investigator, had determined that Josh Browning was not involved in the Bettles Crash. Maury was pretty sure there was a common antagonist between the Bettles crash and the sabotage of Goldstream Air's 185 that happened near Fairbanks and probably also the crash of a Cessna 182 in Fargo, North Dakota, several years earlier. In all three cases the sabotage was done in the very same way. The control cables were mostly cut and with the help of an acid bath made to fail when the plane was being flown. Maury discovered the 182 and the Super Cub from the crash in Bettles had been registered to the same corporation in the past and he felt he might have found the link he was looking for. He did not understand what the manager of a mini storage facility in Grand Forks had in common with a placer mining operation on the Coleville River, but he was determined to find out.

Working thru the FBI, and with help from the IRS, Maury found a common shell corporation employer in years past. Their 401K retirement accounts had been set up by a common employer and that was too big a coincidence for him not to see. Maury not only smelled a rat he could almost hear it running around and nibbling at the cheese.

Summer was threatening and with the weather slowly turning warmer a little fun was needed. Jeans pickup had been fixed, more or less: it only needed a tire and a tie-rod, and life at the store became close to normal; as normal as the Valley ever gets.

A fishing trip had been planned for the up-teenth time with all necessary Kitchen Passes requested and cleared. Finally, after seemingly endless delays the Minto Flats fishing trip was to commence and Josh and Skip were busy loading Skip's flat-bottom with the last of the fishing and camping gear. As they completed the packing Josh was unhappy to see Maury Fitzgerald arrive. Maury wanted to confer with Josh about the sabotage of his 185 two years ago. As before, Josh told him to leave the premises and to "go pound sand." Maury ignored the order to leave and continued his spiel of what seemed like genuine apologies and assurances that Josh was not a person of interest in anything regarding the NTSB. Josh was happy to hear that but was surprised, totally surprised, when he was asked to help in the investigation. He finally shook hands with Maury and while not gleeful about it, he accepted his apology. But Josh said he would not help: that he did not want to get involved. Josh said it was not his job, that he was a store keeper that flew a few groceries to the bush and that was all he intended to do.

Skip was not all that impressed either and walked away telling Josh to pick him up at the store; he would get a few beers for the cooler. With Skip gone, Maury was still trying to get Josh involved and told him something was going on with the folks who owned the Cub that crashed in Bettles. "I heard the FBI had a really big operation going in the mid-west involving the same folks who were the registered owners of the Cub: I don't know what but it's something pretty big. Since it might have something to do with the damage to your 185 I will let you know if it turns out to be public information." Josh did not take the bait and just said: "Whatever."

Up the road at the store, as if on command, Carter Thomas arrived. Claire was working the counter and Carter was talking to her about the events on Friday. He was very outgoing, and this was quite unusual to say the least. Mr. Secret was suddenly Mr. Blabber; and now what is this all about?

But the real reason for Carter being there was to tell Claire that there was a finder's fee for recovering Angel's Diamonds and she would be getting it very soon. It would be around twenty-five thousand dollars. The money would come from an insurance company though he was not sure which one and the fee might not even be taxable. Carter said she should see a tax accountant on that question for sure.

He asked if Skip was around? Because he had checked at the Gold Bar in Fairbanks and they said he and Josh were going fishing with the bartender, and that they would be leaving from here.

Carter: "That doesn't really sound like Skip. Were they really on a fishing trip or was this just a story?" Just then Skip walked in the front door, past the counter, and toward the beer cooler. He noticed Carter and came back to join the conversation. "Carter how goes it? I don't think I have ever seen you in less than a three-piece suit so what's going on with that? Are your dry cleaners closed or out of business?"

284

Claire: "Carter, you are admonished to ignore him. He's in a bad mood because his truck got banged up on Friday and he's looking to hurt someone."

Monday mornings were generally worked only by Jean and Rita, but Claire wanted to help with the books to end the quarter. Jean came walking in and caught just the last part of the conversation and said: "It's not his truck, it's mine and we both want and damn well will inflict a little pain."

Carter, turning just toward Claire: "Maybe the check should go just to the Browning's?" "No, make it to the store please. Guess what Jean? We just got a bonus." "Hot damn, will it be enough to put a down payment on a pickup?"

Carter "Probably, maybe two." That was enough to catch the attention of Skip and he looked at Claire with a puzzled look. "Later with the story I guess."

Just then Josh and Maury came walking in and Claire instantly got uptight. That was enough to disturb Angel who had been guarding the floor next to the wood stove. She came walking over and stood between her and Maury. She did not growl but her tail was down, and she stood fast between them and was not going to move.

Josh: "Maury tells me we are no longer persons of interest in the Super Cub crash that took out David Littlejohn. He says the culprits were probably from the mid-west and might be being corralled as we speak. Carter opened his mouth to say something and then closed it just that fast. He walked over to Angel and stooped down, rubbed her ears and said she was a good friend. Angel gave him a nose lick but still stood firmly where she was and watched Maury. Carter didn't even wipe his nose lick off. Claire thought he must be sick, Jean wondered if he might be a Carter impersonator. Without his three-piece suit and now an unhealthy lick from a canine; what the hell just happened?

Maury: "Well I just wanted to tell you what I knew and to say I'm sorry if I caused you grief. I am an air crash investigator, not a people person; I'm not even sure why I was told to investigate this case at all. It's not really my job but it was neat to be a deputized FBI agent for a while." Skip: "You were deputized?" "Special Agent Assistant; that was the moniker."

Skip: "Neat." What he didn't say was "big fucking deal!" It just proved something that Skip had said many times in the past; the bigger the badge the bigger the prick.

He shook hands with everyone including, but reluctantly, with Skip, and said he would be leaving the Fairbanks area in a day or two. He had one more trip to Bettles and then he would head home to DC. Josh didn't bother to tell him the folks who had information about the Bettles crash were now at FAI. Whether or not he was a person of interest, he still thought Maury was a bit of a cockroach and felt no compunction to offer the information. As far as Josh was concerned Maury could go piss up a rope.

After Maury left, Carter invited everyone who could come, to join him at the Exchange for some drinks compliments of "Thomas Security Services" but paid for by his expense account with the FMA. Josh thought something was different and Claire just knew something substantial had happened. She had never seen Carter so serene and so calm; his façade had evaporated, it was gone.

Over at the Exchange after the drinks had loosened everyone up, Carter told Skip he was pretty sure there would be no more charters to Umiat from those duffle-carrying couriers. That was such a small part of Skip's air taxi business he said he would hardly miss it. What he did miss was the fishing trip that he promised his bartender. Skip just said he would give him the day off with pay and they would for sure do it sometime soon: "I promise!"

Carter "The placer mining operation on the Colville will close soon. I guess it will be in receivership and If I can get control of the property again I might try to donate the surface rights to the 'Sportsmen of Alaska,' a group I founded and became the president of just about an hour ago. I'll add into the donation a bunch of conditions that can never be enforced or even agreed to. This will tie it up in court for years and ensure I can control it for a very long time, if not forever. You never know, if diamonds might really be found there." As he said that he turned toward Claire and winked. Claire was speechless.

Tommy walked over to the table with a phone call for Carter; how would anyone know he was there? Carter answered and after a very short trite conversation he hung up the phone and announced there had been a major FBI raid and some arrests in Grand Forks regarding the Brinks Gold robbery in London, England several years ago. Hundreds of pounds of gold were seized as evidence and it was reported that a mid-west crime family had mostly been shut down and the principles arrested.

Carter: "There were warrants out for some people reportedly now in Alaska. Some of the names are not familiar to me but one of the names on one of the warrants is Bob Adams and he is known to be either in the Fairbanks area or on the North Slope. That's not our problem but I think its newsworthy of distribution.

Our security services and other work in the Forty-mile will continue and don't expect it to get any easier. when some of the bad guys go away others replace them at light speed so don't let down your guard."

Josh: "I'll drink to that and Carter, I have a favor to ask. Will you please give this envelope to Hector: Its contact information he requested about some of Angel's pups. "Josh handed Carter an envelope. Carter said: "If it involves Angel certainly I will, and very soon."

Angel heard her name and walked over to Josh and nuzzled his knee. She sat next to him and looked toward Claire, but she was just about not there. Claire was, at least in her mind, hundreds of miles north on the Arctic plain a little north of the Brooks Mountain Range on the Coleville River. Claire could see the remnants of a Kimberlite caldera in her mind's eye. She visualized the now nearly flat Coleville Caldera; the very old, very ancient Coleville Caldera that surrounds a very old and very ancient kimberlite pipe.

Chapter (36)

Guess what, its Todd again

About a week after what was left of the Fargo Group were arrested in Grand Forks, North Dakota, there had been an exodus from the placer mining area on the Coleville just a little south of Umiat. One of the miners took a D4 Cat when leaving. He claimed it as his own and said it was because of back pay owed that was never paid. His back pay is now about twelve miles East by South east of Umiat sinking into a slowly thawing ice road. He was on the way to the Dalton Highway about eighty-five miles farther to the East. The D4 Cat didn't make it.

Skip's air taxi service, Grizzly Air, was contacted several times for charter flights from Umiat to Anchorage. Tyler took two of the flights which turned into a round robin but then Skip said he was unable to fly any of the other requests because of previous commitments. The truth is he just didn't want to get close to anyone involved with the Reno Cartel in any way. Skip thought they must be livid losing the amount of gold that Carter figured they had in Grand Forks and it might just have bankrupted them, he hoped. Even if not going bankrupt they had lost almost the entire Grand Forks operation, all the gold bars and other cash, and a big holding of real estate.

The next request that Josh received for a payroll delivery came directly from Carter. He had not one word to say about the Cartel or the Coleville River operation and talked about the schedule only. He needed a payroll delivery and a small gold transport for pickup at a rather isolated tunnel mining operation. That might seem to be double billing but the way the contract was written it Goldstream Air would be allowed to bill twice, if two landings were made: even if it were on the same trip on the same day. One trip and two billable invoices made Claire almost giddy.

Through the end of April and into May the payroll and gold transport business had gone pretty much as planned. One week there were two deliveries, but mostly the payrolls were delivered on

Thursday to the "back of the bar" at Smithies, the café in Chicken. Small amounts of gold were usually picked up at one of three mining airstrips all within a thirty-mile radius of the Chicken Creek Airstrip. Josh and Matt usually made the flights in the 206 but if they had to go into a very short strip they would take the Maule. When Matt was flying the pipeline, Skip filled in but insisted he log the flight as PIC.

Tyler wanted to make some of the trips, but he was not vetted, insured, or deputized: too bad for Tyler. But he was getting in many flying hours hauling folks around the state for Skip. Grizzly Air Taxi was keeping him busy and he was a regular at both the store and the Exchange. When Jean bought her new pickup, she sold the old Ford to him after the insurance paid to fix the front end and radiator. By now he felt like family and Angel reluctantly accepted yet another member.

On the Fairbanks end of the deliveries they sometimes flew into FAI and sometimes flew into the Valley with the gold shipments. Once Josh and Matt flew into Metro field and Skip met them for a run to the bank. It was working out well and Goldstream Air was making a pretty good buck. They sometimes did not make the bank run till the next day and Claire who did the planning, was pretty sure no one would ever know the plan because it was made up in real time at random. Someone wanting to steal the gold shipments would have one out of in three chances of picking the correct landing spot and would have no idea of the timing; other than it usually was on a Thursday.

Then on June 13th, a Thursday, a large gold shipment was to be picked up at the Black Rock Mine that was bound for the vaults at the First National Bank on Noble Street in Fairbanks. Josh and Skip were to pick up the shipment on a less-than-500-foot hilltop runway, little more than the aircraft wheelbase-wide. Despite Skip's whining about logging the PIC time in his log book, Josh was piloting the plane and the landing was typical of short field landings. It was to be quite slow with a very steep descent and, of course, 40 degrees of flaps. The Maule was so far behind the power curve they might not have been able to make a 'go around' if necessary, even considering the 235 hp engine and the fact that it was a Maule. The cross-wind component was severe and constantly changing first blowing up the hill, gusting across the strip, and then a downdraft on the other side. The rather tight landing was assisted by a short-silent but very sincere prayer just before the landing; a tail-wheel-first touchdown. This was to protect both the plane and the occupants; God must have been listening.

The shipment which weighed almost thirty pounds was in two parcels. Carter's security guards, were there along with one of the miners and a smiling cat skinner named Jose who either could not or would not, speak English. The mine was down in a small canyon and the airstrip had been carved out on the ridge top. Whoever did the carving was obviously not a pilot and it seemed probably, not much of a Cat Skinner either. The strip plunged off steeply in both directions and had been a real bitch to land on because of side drafts. Josh carried both the parcels and Skip carried only the shotgun which seemed fair to Skip.

Carters security guards did not want to walk up the hill with them. In fact, they only seemed to care about the proper paperwork and they appeared to have no interest in the gold. The short field takeoff was Maule normal. Prop, mixture, and throttle to the wall; when the tail comes up, release the brakes, count five rotations of the tires, and push-pull the yoke. When the tail hits the ground, the main gear jumps skyward; then you push the yoke a little forward, not too much, and you are flying at ~30 knots, with any luck. A Maule 235 is a cool airplane!

After the sphincter, tightening, short field, cross wind takeoff, they had a totally uneventful and relaxing flight back to Fairbanks. They were following the Richardson Highway and when flying past the Salcha Park Road House Josh did a flashback. Josh remembered when Mike Thompson and his band of irregulars attempted the robbery of their first gold shipment from Chicken Creek, the day when he and Skip let the perps go to avoid a ton of paperwork and maybe more important: publicity about the flights. The question was still out as to whether, they did the right thing by not arresting the would-be thieves. It had been their first payroll delivery and the first gold transport to the vault at Bank of the North.

Josh questioned at the time if he would see Mike and his crew of wannabe bandits again. He wondered if maybe Mike would leave the business of robbery to professionals and take up a business vocation more to his aptitude and abilities.

That was not to be because Mike had been involved in yet another attempt to rob. This time it was a payroll delivery at Chicken Creek Cafe. That robbery nearly worked, in fact it did work, but Mike's crew only got a decoy package filled with bond paper instead of green backs. The real payroll arrived shortly after the thieves had left the area. Josh had been beat up badly during the robbery, but it wasn't Mike who did it, and in fact, Mike had tried to put an end to it, and finally he did stop the beating.

So, despite the problems caused by Mike Thompson and his crew of screw-up's, Josh had developed a bit of affection for him, not his crew, just Mike. He did not seem to be vicious or cruel or even very nasty. Instead he seemed to almost be good natured when attempting some of the weakest and poorest planned robberies. While Mike was trying to accomplish villainous acts his eyes and body language seemed to be apologizing for his actions and Josh saw him to be a real enigma.

They landed at FAI and taxied up to the Airport Security Post. Immediately the guards were giving them a hard time again and it seemed if there was anything to comment on in a negative way, they did. Skip was nursing some bruised feelings because Josh did not let him land the plane at the Black Rock Mine and was not in a mood to take shit from anyone else. After some verbal antisocial intercourse, the guards remained physically unhurt. The only thing bleeding were their egos and they were bruised only on the inside. Gladly for them, they had not been receptive of Skip's offer to step outside and discuss their problems like men. The guards had heard enough of Skip's contempt to greatly increase their vocabulary concerning negative personality traits and, while only an opinion, the marital status of their mothers. They were still unsure how much they could push Skip. He was a Reserve Deputy Trooper, but they didn't know for sure what 'Reserve' meant. Skip only knew if these fuckups mouthed-off to him much more he was going to kick some ass.

They left agreeing to disagree. The guards said they could leave the plane next to the Security Post for one hour only. Other than that, they said very little but instantly relaxed when Josh and Skip, particularly Skip, left the building. As the Travel-All drove away from the Security Post the guards were agreeing that if Skip had said much more they would have had to accept his invite to settle the disagreement in a manly fashion, after all they were Airport Security Guards and should not be trifled with.

From FAI Josh and Skip were to make the bank run. Then they would drive back to the airport. Josh would fly the plane back to the Valley while Skip would drive back and the four of them would have dinner at the Exchange. It seemed easy enough. Then, just as they passed through the Airport Security Exit Gate, a blue Dodge pickup drove up and halfway blocked their way, as they approached Airport Way. A stranger that Skip thought he had seen before, but could not identify, was driving the truck and he got out and walked up to Skip who was in the Travel-All driver's seat. Skip got out of the Travel-All, leaving it running, wondering what the fuss was about. Josh stayed in the car and took his Glock out of the holster and held it under the transport paperwork he had been preparing in his lap. The stranger seemed to be no threat and handed Skip a cell phone that was muted. Skip had used a Satellite phone before but never a cell phone with a mute function. He was a little confused at first, but he finally pushed the right buttons and heard Claire's voice on the other end.

Claire: "Please just let JJ know that I need to see him before you guys make the bank delivery. Carter is here and there might be a problem. He wants to meet you out here at the store and he will handle the deposit from here. Not to worry, just tell JJ it's Ok."

Skip asked Claire to hold and handed the phone to Josh through the window of the car. Josh listened as Claire repeated the message.

Josh: "Ya fine, if he wants to do it that way it saves us a bank run. See you in about half an hour at the store. I'm leaving the plane here in Matt's hangar, so Kevin can look at a problem tomorrow. The two of us will drive back in the Travel-All. Take care CJ; love you."

292

To anyone else the conversation might seem aboveboard but both Skip and Josh knew that when either Josh or Claire started referring to each other by their initials, there is definite trouble brewing. Josh pushed the call End button and turned his head toward the guy who had just given Skip the phone. It looked like he wanted to give him back the phone and he held out his arm through the car's window. The stranger wanted to walk away but was also waiting for his phone. He obviously wanted nothing to do with either Josh or Skip. He had done his job and now only wanted to leave. As he turned and extended his hand for the phone Skip recognized him from the robbery attempt at the Roadhouse. This was one of the guys that had been in a tug-of-war with Matt for the gold pouch at the roadhouse. Skip remembered this guy had also been sort of nasty to Ted's wife when she dropped the tray of hamburgers and fries in the restaurant. At the time Skip thought he was a bully and a bit of a prick, and now, right now, that little bit of recall hit a unique and sour chord in Skip's melody of life concerning the treatment of women.

Skip gave a reassuring smile and asked: "Have we met before?" "I am not sure, I don't think --" and the stranger's life turned hurtful and ugly. His lights nearly went out as Skip got to him before Josh could even open the car door. When the stranger totally woke up he was less three teeth, had a very puffy bleeding cheek and one eye was nearly swollen closed. There might also be a question of cracked or maybe two-piece ribs: X- rays would tell. That's the problem with a combination punch delivered by a trained, though ageing Boxer; a "Combo" is mostly muscle memory and once a Combo gets started it's just all one move and very hard to stop; and Skip doesn't even recognize the word stop, to be a part of the English language.

Josh drove the Travel-All back to the Security Post to get the plane and as they arrived the guards were quickly leaving for a very early lunch. The plan was for Josh to fly to Goldstream and Skip would drive there, arriving after Josh had hopefully scoped out the problem. Skip would go into the store as if there was no suspected problem. He would have only an ankle holster with his 'Belly Gun' as he called it, a 9-mm Llama. Josh would take the gold satchels and stash them, so Skip would not be concerned about them.

The Stranger was tied up with interlaced bungee cords on his ankles and wrists. He was bent over backwards like a prawn and in the rear of the Travel-All. While going over Murphy Dome Road on the way to the Valley, Skip was gathering what he thought might be necessary information; the stranger was in fear of his life and telling pretty much all there was to tell. After hearing what he needed, Skip pulled over to the side of the road and after parking, he walked around to the rear and opened the tailgate of the van. Skip cut the boot laces from Stranger's left boot and pulled it off. He stripped off his sock and stuffed it completely in stranger's mouth. Skip smiled a bit; the sock must have been nasty. "Good reason to do your laundry a little more often" was Skip's only comment.

Josh was already in the air on his way to the Valley and planned to dead stick a stealthy landing into the airstrip behind the store. He was staying very low over the few trees and would land in the first few hundred feet of the airstrip. There was an unoccupied house on the far southwest end of the runway and he would park the Maule behind it and then first find out whether the problem was in the hangar or the Store. Josh was pretty sure it would be the store since Claire had been scheduled to work early at the store and she had been the one on the phone. Angel would probably hear him land regardless: she had the ears of a Shepherd. He hoped she would be a help if she could find him before they, whoever they were, knew he was there. Whatever the problem, Josh was sure they would be looking for the Travel-All and probably thought they were clever and had not yet been discovered. If Josh got set before Skip arrived they should be in good shape to handle the problem.

The Maule landed silently on the far end of the runway and glided to a stop on the right-hand side of the runway very near the unoccupied home. He got out and walked around behind the plane and picked up the tail. He pushed it much like he would a wheelbarrow; he pushed it off the runway and behind the empty home to conceal it. Josh carried the two pouches of gold up the right side of the runway and after seeing that it was empty, used his keys

294

and entered his house from the side door. He was in the kitchen and finding no better place, he put the pouches in the kitchen stove's oven. Josh had his Glock in a shoulder holster and he went into the bedroom and opened his gun safe. Rather than a two-shot Browning, Josh picked up a 12-gauge Ithaca pump shotgun and pushed four 3-inch magnum shells of buckshot into the tubular magazine. He put four more in his back pocket. Josh thought he had enough fire power to go to war. He removed his boots and changed into his running shoes that he last wore just one year ago. He remembered the old days when he had time to exercise; time to run with Claire and enjoy the sights and sounds of the Goldstream Valley. Those were good days, and he wondered if they might ever return.

After the short walk to the store he quietly climbed the outside stairs to the upper floor and entered Casey's apartment as quickly as he could. He remained quiet, and soon maybe after about five minutes, Josh heard the Travel-All arrive and park off to the side of the lot. He listened closely and found there was some conversation in the store but even with his ear to the heater vent he could not make out what was said. Maybe he thought he could hear Carter and Jean arguing about something, but it was unintelligible. He strained to hear and identify any other voices.

Skip just boldly walked up the front porch steps into the store as though nothing was suspected, and Josh listened when Carter greeted them. Then Josh heard a voice that he recognized as belonging to Todd. Josh wondered if Mike was also there and if he was at it again. He wondered where and just how many. His mind, his reflexes, his whole being was back to his military training days and he was pretty much on auto pilot. Where were they and how many were there? That was question number one: where and how many?

Josh felt a friendly nudge on his knee. He was back to reality quickly when welcomed by Angel. She had come up behind him quietly, and there was no jumping around and wanting an ear-rub, Angel knew this was business. Angel had been in the store with Claire when Mike arrived and was a little confused because Claire never told her to "mark", her command to stand fast. Not sure what to do she just quietly backed away and waited in the storeroom for some direction. Then when Josh arrived she went upstairs to find him and tell him there might be trouble. He somehow already knew, she was surprised.

Angel went down the inside stairwell into the main stockroom first and was followed by Josh a short time later. Then they quietly slipped into the darkened liquor, wine, and tobacco stockroom. Minutes later someone ran up these stairs and locked the apartment's outside door. Someone else closed the door by the loading dock and he heard that lock snap closed. He now knew there were at least three. With the doors closed and locked there was now only one way in or out of the store. Josh thought whoever they were now knew he had not been a passenger in the Travel-All and surely, they wondered where he was. He thought they expected him to arrive soon; that he was not yet in the store and that he would probably have to come in the front door; surprise!

Josh continued to listen. He was nearly positive that he could hear the voice of Mike Thompson and his cohort Todd but there was at least one other voice he had not heard before or at least did not recognize. Carter and Claire were there for sure and since it was later in the day he thought probably Jean would be tending the register. The talk was getting louder, and Skip was starting to sound off. Josh could hear Jean trying to calm him down and Claire was even getting loud; which was totally unlike her. Still, there was little question about what was going on and it was un-good!

Angel walked out into the front of the store and proceeded to lie down next to the cold woodstove. Nobody seems to even notice a dog and she kept quiet keeping her eyes on Claire. From his vantage point in the semi darkness of the liquor stockroom, Josh could just see her back foot and tail. He waited just a few more seconds and then walked around the corner into the front of the store and as he did he heard footsteps of what he assumed were customers coming up the front steps of the store.

He said very loudly: "The store is closed for inventory and some needed repairs, please come back tomorrow, sorry!"

Josh had not loaded the chamber of the shotgun. This was so he could rack in a shell as he came around the corner. It was a sound meant to intimidate and it mostly did. Mike and Todd were there, Todd had a pistol in his hand, but it was pointed in the wrong direction.

Josh: "If either of you move I will shoot Todd, put it down Todd. Don't get me any more excited than I am right now." Todd had his Glock pointed at Skip and only said: "I'm not dropping anything; I will shoot this old fat S-O-B as sure as the sun comes up tomorrow if you don't back down."

Claire and Jean were both tied into chairs and they had Carter tied up but standing next to a support column in the middle of the store next to the potato chip display, he was facing away from the counter. It looked like Skip had been disarmed and was about to be tied up, Josh could see his handgun on the counter top.

Mike spoke-up: "Josh, I said drop it or I will shoot you dead where you stand. Don't get tense; all we want is the gold and we'll be gone." Skip "Not a chance in hell of that, the gold is already in the bank." "It is like hell, you give it to me right now or he will start shooting." Josh caught the movement of the third member of the robbery team as he came around the wall that separates the liquor store from the grocery sales area. It was Marvin and he had a handgun, a Glock probably. He was pointing it out in front of him and he began firing in Josh's direction almost without aiming. It was kind of like the "A Team" movies with many rounds being fired but no blood, except this time there was a hit. Skip had tried to duck for protection behind the checkout counter and was shot or grazed by either a bullet or a ricochet.

When Josh saw Skip get hit he turned his aim away from Todd; he swung the Ithaca to his right; aimed and shot Marvin squarely in the chest killing him instantly. Josh tried to jack another shell into the shotgun, but the gun would not eject the empty shot shell casing, it seemed to jam halfway through the reload sequence. In that split-second Josh realized what he had done. He had put 3-inch magnum roll crimp buckshot shells in a gun with a 2-3/4-inch chamber and the empty expended shell casing was too long and would not eject out the bottom, as Ithaca pump shotguns do. Todd had already turned his pistol that had been aimed at Skip toward Josh and started to squeeze the trigger.

Todd: "This one is for my broken nose at Ruthie's you prick."

Claire screamed: "Stop, Angel: Mark"; giving Angel the signal to attack, to protect her. Angel was on her feet and charging at Todd, but she was older now, older and slower than in her younger days. In canine years she was well past her prime: nearly old age, and now a little too late to help. Todd turned away from Josh and fired at Angel twice hitting her once; and Angel went down and stayed down. Claire yanked at her restraints. She scraped the skin from her forearms as she ripped the arms off and mostly demolished the chair she was tied into. As Claire rose up she turned and further crashed it into the checkout counter, mostly freeing herself. Her forearms were still loosely tied to the support arms of what had been a chair and she was able to use the loosely tied ropes, and arm of the chair, as a kind of a sling.

Claire whipped the sling, the left-hand chair arm around at Todd and hit his head and shoulder squarely. Though bleeding Claire was not only free, but also a major threat. When the chair had first cracked Todd had flinched and was distracted momentarily. Angel almost had him: almost. Todd then turned back and fired at Josh hitting him in the upper right arm and shoulder. Josh dropped the jammed shotgun and was trying to grab his Glock with his other arm while Skip who had regained his pistol, was now trying to aim and shoot at Todd. Mike tackled Skip and he was smashed head first into the counter and was temporarily stunned. Mike stood back up with Skip's pistol and had the drop on Skip and pretty much everyone. Todd turned back and steadied his aim at Claire. He was unsure who to shoot first but decided to take out Claire since she had the sling and he had been hit twice by it badly. He fired his pistol once and missed and was about to shoot again when his head exploded with blood, brains, and pieces of skull flying and covering the floor. Everyone in the store except Carter, who couldn't move, turned toward the hand that was holding the weapon responsible for the killing shot: it was Mike's hand, it was Mike.

Mike: "I really hate that Son-of-a-Bitch. He had no reason to hurt anyone, no reason at all. All we had to do was pick up the gold, maybe clean out the register, and then leave. But no, he had to try to shoot someone: I wish I had never met that prick."

Josh: "What the hell Mike?" Josh had been hit in the right shoulder, but the bullet seemed to have missed the bone. He was bleeding but able to stand. Josh had been unable to grab his holstered Glock on his right with his left hand. Mike stood there for a second or two collecting his limited thoughts.

Mike: "Where's my brother?" "Who?" "He was at the airport; he gave you the phone." Skip: "Oh him, he's tied up in my Travel-All, a little under the weather, it's locked." Mike: "Gimme the keys." Skip threw him the keys and untied Jean and showed no concern about getting shot. He wanted to help Josh but thought Jean would be better help. He then untied Carter who had been bound tightly and had been facing away from the shooting. His suit had been protected by the post from the blow-back of Todd's blood and brains and he was, as usual, spotless. Carter totally ignored Mike and tried to help Claire who was attending to Angel. He took off his sport coat and helped Claire put Angel on top of it as a way of carrying Angel away from Todd's body. But besides that, and a few kind words there was little he could do. There were two dead people in the store, Josh had been shot in the shoulder, and Angel was down and seemed maybe critical. Claire was trying to comfort her but she either could not or would not move; she was whining softly.

Skip quickly regained his "Cool" and realized even though the shooting had stopped there was indeed a very small problem with Mike Thompson; he was still loaded for bear. Skip's next line was sarcastic but made a point. "Don't try to go too far Mike, it's low on gas." "Great, really fucking great, low on gas and no loot; just fucking great!" Mike stepped over to the register and punched-up no sale. The register opened and he took the twenties and tens. "Not much of a sales day was it?

He was swinging Skip's pistol around, walking almost in a bit of a daze and was tracking blood all over the front of the store. Josh was shot but it seemed to be a through-and-through bullet hole in his outer upper shoulder and arm. Jean was tending to it, ignoring the rest of the hassle and for some reason like Carter, she seemed totally unafraid of Mike. After several pads and a yard of gauze, the bleeding was mostly stopped. Still he was hurting and insisted that he needed a smoke

Skip: "Mike; listen to me. You have my car, a hand full of bucks, and your brother; that's as good as it's going to get. Now get the fuck out of here!"

Jean: "For Christ-sake Skip! do you even listen to the words you say?" "What, you want him to stay? He's the one with the God-damn gun, or didn't you notice?" They looked at each other again and finally Carter spoke up: "Good point Skip! Mike, you just got the best deal that will ever happen, I suggest you take it. The best you can do is get a head start and get lost now."

Mike dropped the clip out of Skip's Llama and put it and the clip on the checkout counter. He headed for the door without saying a word. He was scared, he had no clue where he was going but he knew any place was better than here in Goldstream Valley. Maybe his brother could help him because, God knows, he was in too damn far to help himself.

Chapter (37)

Angel lives

June 1985

Angel didn't seem to be in any pain and was not bleeding but neither was she able to walk or even move very much. Her front legs could move but she had no movement toward the rear. There was a bullet hole in her front shoulder, it had almost missed her but didn't. The bullet seemed to have traveled almost her full length under her skin and there was an exit hole high on her rear haunch. Long before the Troopers arrived Claire was driving Angel out to Chena Valley to see Cook Bittner, their Veterinarian. An hour later while Cook was patching her up, her rear feet started to twitch a little. Inside another ten minutes Angel tried to sit up, she struggled and then did manage to sit. Within a half hour Angel was upright and was able, barely able, to drunkenly walk over to a bowl of water for a drink.

Claire was wiping tears from her eyes and was hugging Angel so hard she whined a little. Cook said he now thought he had seen about everything. Cook surmised the bullet traveled just under her skin on her left side all the way from stem to stern and the shock wave might have given Angel such a spasm that her spinal cord had a short-term trauma, paralyzing her for a short time but after a while, the stress and then the paralysis just faded away. Cook didn't know and surmised she maybe would, maybe not, have long term problems with coordination. Angel was in pain and she was whining a little when she walked so Cook gave her some pain meds and was ready to send them on their way after showing Claire how to change Angel's bandages.

After hearing the story about the robbery and shooting at the store Cook said he might stay away for good or at least call to see if the coast was clear before visiting. Claire told Cook to get stuffed but then gave him a kiss on the forehead, she said besides the bill she and Josh owed him big.

Back at the store, Trooper Detective Curwen, who had been there before, wondered why the Golden Valley Store had been the target for robberies as often as they were. Carter assumed the role of spokesperson again and was burying the detective with useless information while failing to mention anything about either the payroll or gold shipments from the Forty-mile. Skip explained that he was just a friend, and of course Jean's husband. He said he was not involved other than just being at the wrong place at the wrong time.

Josh freely admitted to shooting Marvin after Marvin shot Skip, who it turned out was only grazed with a ricochet. He claimed self-defense of a friend and the detective agreed. Skip said his Travel-All had been stolen by Mike but failed to mention his reluctant passenger or the punch out at the airport.

After several weeks of investigation, Detective Curwen wrote it up as a failed robbery. Since the day of the attempted robbery there had been a bulletin making Mike Thompson a person of interest in the robbery. Skip said he thought the head shot to Todd, whatever his last name, was a mistake and Mike drove away in panic after the accidental shot. It kind of seemed reasonable and since both Josh and Skip were Reserve Deputy Troopers, their testimony was taken with a greater weight than others would have been who weren't deputized.

Carter was a very good witness for the store, and he said that like Skip, just a random customer at the store that day though he did know both Claire and Josh and claimed them as friends. He was believed and even quoted in the Daily News Miner, but under a different name.

Jean summed up her thoughts: "He could walk through a stockyard and come out with clean shoes that smelled like roses. I don't know how he does it, but crap just plain doesn't stick to Mr. Carter Thomas."

The End.

302

86079104R00185

Made in the USA
San Bernardino, CA
25 August 2018